"We all have the power to become Wisdom Runners...to be so connected and in tune with the life forces on this earth that other dimensions in time and space open to allow for true healing and emotional evolution to occur. This book is about being a victorious survivor, the power of inter-species love and our ability to work together with the rest of the animal kingdom to conquer our fears. Like all competitive sports involving animals, the world of dog sledding has its share of secrets. It warms my heart this book highlights how we can successfully participate in this sport while never compromising the promise of a full, content and joy filled life for every dog on the team."

Karen Becker DVM – Wellness Veterinarian Expert – Healthy Pets at Mercola.com

"I finished the Luna Tales last night...I thoroughly enjoyed it and feel it's such a great, important tale for adults and young ones alike. It definitely feels like Narnia and has elements of the Wizard of Oz... yet all with the awakening elements and teachings of intuition, psychic communication, the power of love and light...I mean, wow, I think the scene when all the doggies are doing the MC Hammer dance and the jig to the "Devil went down to Georgia' song and the Ice Beings imploding...well, that was one of the most powerful and fun ways to deliver some huge Truths...one of the best scenes I've ever read in any book!!! Overall, this Book One of the Luna Tales is a compelling adventure story in a magical world with fun, sympathetic characters, who transform themselves and their world in powerful ways via ancient wisdom and Truths...I recommend it highly to anyone!"

Mikaela Jones, Author, Screenwriter, A Little Book of Light

"A beautifully woven epic tale of the age old battle between Good and Evil. A brilliant tale of high ideals and adventure - Of friendships forged across the species barrier, life and death struggles, love, loyalty and duty. A great adventure story where birds, horses and dogs talk, and sing… Where joy and laughter overcomes evil, and all commit to making a stand on the side of good, and seeing it through, no matter what . . An empowering and uplifting read."

Sandie Hartley, Hartley Associates, Pretoria, South Africa

"Luna Tales- The Wisdom Runners is a well-written adventure story that is full of valuable life lessons. It is a tale of the power of love and courage that bring about healing. Jennifer learns she has strength she never imagined she possessed through her relationship with the sled dog pack. It teaches the power of teamwork in finding our path in life. The Wisdom Runners opens the reader up to the possibility of a higher level of awareness and strength available to us all. It is full of humor and suspenseful, thrilling action which brings the story to life."

Liz Maudlin – Photographer- with corgis Lily, Gus and Bruiser

"As an animal lover—especially huskies…I was totally engaged in The Luna Tales from the first Chapter!! My heart felt for Jennifer as she started down a new life. But knowing the quirky ways of huskies and sled dogs/-I just knew she would find adventures with Luna–and boy did she!!! As they all slipped under the bridge and into the magical world of the wisdom Runners.. And ALL their friends… The adventure never lets up!!! I could see my JJ laughing and dancing with the dogs…. Being just as silly as they are!!! But the book kept me on the edge of my seat—many times/-wondering who would survive and make it back to Earth!!! After awhile/-the magical world—seems so real!!! The writing was so vivid—I saw it all!!!! You will laugh—cry–and be involved in the adventure from the very first chapter!! So many characters—so many adventures….You won't put the book down!!! I'm waiting on the sequel!!!!!

Donna Midge Adams
Volunteer for Mission K9 Rescue Helping Paws that Serve.
Hiker of the Appalachian Trail to raise awareness and
money for canine non-profits

"An epic North American fantasy complete with breathtaking imagery, and an unforgettable collection of characters and magic, The Luna Tales is an enchanting read. Enter a portal in Vermont, and join Luna and her "unchained gang" of sled dogs and friends, as they race across time to save a young girl, and overcome the darkness and division that threatens to change their world forever.....A creative depiction of the insidious negativity we face in our world today, reading this story inspires hope, and puts the magic back in the lives of children and adults of all ages. The Luna Tales lends insight into the special connection between humans and animals, and gifts us with a new appreciation for the gallant warrior souls we call "pets". This first of an up-coming series is destined to become a classic right alongside C.S. Lewis's Chronicles of Narnia - and a North American challenge to Harry Potter. I can't wait to read what happens next."

Angela Robey, Angela Robey Fine Art,
http://angelarrobey.wix.com/robey-artworks
Silver Moon Ranch
https://www.facebook.com/WitchWellsAZ/

"Dr Blair has written what I fervently hope will become a classic for children, teens and adult survivors of neglect and abuse. Drawing on her many years as a Jungian therapist, as well as her own life experience, Dr. Blair has created a beautiful, healing world around her young female protagonist; a world that seamlessly blends reality and magic, as well as incorporating sound therapeutic principals. The result is an engrossing story that can be read on many levels by the young reader. Animal and nature lovers will find much to delight them. Fantasy fans will enter a wondrous world in which they will want to dwell forever. Most importantly of all, children, teens and adults searching to find their way out of trauma, abuse and neglect will be inspired, healed and empowered by the loving message conveyed by The Luna Tales. A beautiful book by a beautiful soul."

Valerie Thomas, Voice Artist, Animal Advocate

"I loved Book One of The Luna Tales. I work with clients who are challenged, often emotionally challenged, and this book offers wonderful insights and supports. Deborah Blair and I share the understanding that simple, sustainable food and exercise is not only healthy but also healing. The Luna Tales gives many guides for positive living and positive action and good change for quality of life. But best of all are the teams that include dogs and people working together in all kinds of ways. As a proud member of Corgi Nation, I look forward to The Luna Tales - Book Two – Journey to the East!"

Barb Meyer, CPC, CES, Life Coach, Focus on Ability, Inc.

"A tale that encourages us to nourish ourselves in body and soul and does so with emotion and truth. If you have felt our world keeps inching or sometimes racing to a dark place, you'll recognize what the main characters are fighting. You will also feel the important ray of hope that...we will be able to light the world (and any worlds connected with us!) with truth and kindness. There is a call within these pages for us to each change – a call to rebalance the equation."

Tanya Sousa – Author – The Starling God

"I was VERY excited to read about my friends the UN-Chain Gang- and The Wisdom Runners! You will laugh and cry—and WOOOOO at the top of your voice while reading about Luna and all the adventures. Being a Siberian Husky-I felt myself joining in with the pack as they headed to the other side of the portal!!! You will learn all about the magical world of the wisdom runners—and will be at the edge of your seat—waiting to see who makes it out—and back to Earth!!! So for now—I'll just give this book 4 paws up—and a high fluffy tail!!! It's a magical world—full of good and evil...But as you know—GOOD—always prevails!!!"

JJ B Pumpernickle, III - Husky and Facebook Lawyer to Corgi Nation!!

This book is dedicated to my brother, Jim Blair, Luna, Peaberry, Lioness, Buttercup, Bear, Buster, Amos, Lucky, Gretel, Llewellyn, Aslan, Blueberry, Simba, Mufasa, Leonard, Abbie, Songan, Hanobi, Charlie, Melvin, Annie, Waffle, Barney, Pancake, Fusulli, Rose, Rainbow, Rambow, Polly,Lily, Stormina, Fuchsia, Bandit, Maple, Wes, Phyllis, Ben, Jerry and the rest of the UN-Chained Gang; his team of incredible Alaskan huskies. Winning international, national and regional sprint dog sled championship race titles, they have proven that dogs can go fast AND be wonderful, loving friends who deserve to live free and unchained. Generations of pack/human-raised dogs, they introduce children and adults to the wonders of Canine Consciousness, ethical dog sledding, concerns for animal welfare, and how to care for our wonderful planet. They are true Wisdom Runners.

And to my sister, Hilary Blair. May all children, teens and adults find the healing support and inspiration that their bodies, hearts, souls, and spirits need to heal and continue to thrive, despite the odds and challenges that life throws their way!

And to good friends, too soon in the light:

Deb Brandenburg and her corgi, Barney Boots

North American Champion Musher – Keith Bryar

Katie Moore

The Luna Tales

Book One

The Wisdom Runners

DEBORAH E. BLAIR

Deborah E. Blair, M.S., Ph.D.
Eden ETHICAL Dog Sledding
Healing Into Authenticity

Healing Into Authenticity Press
Vermont

Edited October 2017

Contents

A human being is part of the whole called the "universe," a part limited in time and space. However, with most humans, he/she experiences themselves, their thoughts and feelings, as something separated from the rest, a kind of optical illusion - delusion of... consciousness. This delusion is a kind of prison for us, restricting us to our personal desires and to feeling affection for a few persons nearest to us. Our task must be to free ourselves from this prison by widening our circle of compassion to embrace all living creatures and the whole of nature to all its beauty. Nobody is able to achieve this completely but the striving for such achievement is in itself part of the liberation and a foundation for inner security.

Earth Scientist and Philosopher – Albert Einstein
As paraphrased in The Book of Wisdom Runners

Prologue

Screaming, threats and shouting. Shattering sounds as tossed vases and lamps hit walls in the room beyond the door where Jennifer lay in bed trying to have sleep find her. It was the nightly lullaby that she could not ever remember not remembering. Burying her head deep into two pillows, twelve-year-old Jennifer clamped one hand over her exposed ear as she hugged Grace, her corgi, tight to her.

Curling her toes as hard as she could to try to ease the tension, feeling Grace alert close to her, breathing softly, Jennifer tried to find a calm, safe center within. She recalled the pictures of galaxies and nebulas from the Hubbell telescope, trying to remember all of the wondrous feelings she had whenever she looked longingly at the pictures, imagining what it might be to visit each of them one day. This was the way she had learned to fall asleep; to escape the mayhem of her father and stepmother's fighting.

Suddenly a boom crashed through the house, shaking the bed. Then silence. Then continual screaming. It was Toni, her stepmother. But there were no answering bellows from her father. Terrified, Jennifer rose from the bed and Grace followed her. Dressed in a t-shirt and sweatpants that she always wore to sleep in as she often had to get up at all hours of the night, Grace and she moved silently to the door, their footfalls masked by Toni's endless screams.

Opening the door of her bedroom to the all-white den that lay beyond, her brain tried to make sense of what was before her. Her father lay on the floor amid broken objects, the arms and legs of his athletic body akimbo. The jaw of his handsome, tanned face was open, slack; his brown eyes staring blankly at the ceiling. From his chest, a dark red stain oozed over his silver turtleneck, down his left side onto the white carpet. One of her father's handguns, a Magnum, lay at the border of the spreading burgundy stain. Toni, dressed in tight jeans and a sequined top that barely covered her breasts, stood gripping the sides of the doorway, still screaming. Jennifer wanted her to stop, wanted Toni's grating, always hate-filled screams to stop so that she could make sense of the scene before her.

Grace growled. Jennifer looked down, her brave companion stood in rapt attention; Grace was all business as she placed her small, sturdy torso between Jennifer and danger. Grace pricked her ears forward, focusing upward towards the mirror on the left side of the room. In the large, ornate, silver-framed mirror that stood over the white couch, came a glimmer and reflection of what seemed to be large gold, hypnotic eyes. A hazy reflection of a large, cat-like face came into focus. Grace growled again in warning.

"Pick, it up… Jennifer… pick it up!" hissed the reflection from the mirror, cutting through her stepmother's screams.

Jennifer froze in place. She tried to will her feet to move but they were glued to the floor. Her breath would not come. Grace growled again. Jennifer knew Grace was holding back from barking, having been hit before by Toni when she tried to protect Jennifer.

"Move, Jennifer, NOW!," hissed the low growl of a voice. The cat face with the golden eyes was becoming clear in the mirror.

Toni's screams stopped suddenly as if a chord was invisibly snipped. Makeup smeared, her face lined and haggard from the decades of drinking, she looked towards the mirror. Blood shot eyes tried to focus. The cat opened its jaws, baring its fangs, then hissed. "Jennifer – move your feet, pick it up now!"

Grace continued to stand guard between the cat and Jennifer. A heavy force took hold of Jennifer's immobile legs and moved them toward where her father lay. Fright went to numbness as she felt her body being moved across the fifteen feet that separated them. The seeping blood surrounded the gun, the stain continuing to grow across the white carpet.

"That'ssss right little Jen, keep moving!" the hissing voice ordered.

Standing over her father's body she tried to close her eyes. She tried to speak, but her throat tightened and no sound came out. The numbness inside grew.

"Pick it UP!" hissed the voice from the gold cat eyes in the mirror.

A force pressed her upper body downward, and Jennifer found herself bending to pick up the heavy Magnum with both hands. Her father's blood wet her fingers as she grasped the gun. Rising to a standing position, her eyes focused on the red wetness of fresh blood on the gun and her hands. The inner numbness deepened as it spread through her chest and throat.

Suddenly a blur of blonde and white streak of a dog raced across the large room. Grace ran toward the cat image visible in the mirror, braced her front legs and barked as ferociously as her twenty-six pounds and generations of corgi herding, protection instinct could muster. Gold eyes flashing, the cat image bared its fangs, hissing at Grace. With a flash of light, it was gone. Grace continued to bark, then ran as Toni threw a crystal vase that shattered brilliantly into shards against the wall over her head.

Toni, weaving and unsteady on her feet, turned her gaze towards Jennifer and her husband's body. Her brown eyes started to turn reptilian black as the skin of her florid face became ashen grey. She burned with hatred.

"Jennifer!"

Jennifer felt as if her throat closed, wrapped in cold. She could not answer Toni. This was a nightmare. She willed herself to wake up to find her father hung over but ready to take her to school.

"Jennifer, I am speaking to you!" Toni shrieked.

No longer contending with the menacing, spectral cat, Grace turned and walked towards Toni. She planted herself between Jennifer and Toni. The corgi was fearless but knew that Toni could easily take her away from Jennifer should evil whim fill her selfish heart.

"Jennifer! Answer me right now!!!!" The chords on the sides of Toni's neck bulged and strained as her nostrils flared. The energy of hatred had an independent spirit of its own as it moved through Toni's body.

Jennifer was struck mute. An invisible force had a strangle hold on her throat. She could not find a way to make her voice answer Toni. She could only stare at her snarling stepmother and then down at her father's body. She felt Grace protecting her. This was so frightening; Jennifer wanted to grab Grace, hug her tightly, feel the safety Grace always gave her and make all of this go away. The room started to spin slowly as she stared into Toni's black eyes.

Toni smirked. She walked over to the phone and dialed 911. Smirking again, drawing herself into her best semblance of a hysterical victim pose, she shrieked, "Help! Help! I want to report a murder! My stepdaughter has just killed my husband! I am so frightened! She still has the gun and may kill me now! . . . Yes! Please, come quick!"

Toni hung up the phone, smiled silkily at Jennifer, then walked placidly out the side door to wait for the police. Clutching the gun, blackness swirled inside Jennifer's head as she dropped to the floor.

* * *

Above a hill, not distant from the home where Jennifer lay unconscious, a rent in the air spread vertically. Light poured through, and from the light emerged figures that arranged themselves on the hillside. Bright, shining, large, powerful dogs of light. Despite the Los Angeles warmth, snow fell around the light that revealed a tall, powerfully built, manlike-being dressed in what looked to be warm garments of white. The doglike creatures of light came to stand with him in the flying snow. They looked to be a dog-sled team of angelic dogs and their angel musher. A nearby coyote pack sat down and howled their joy at the peace coming from the beings of light; neighborhood dogs joined in.

The dogs of light and their musher watched as the police cars sped towards the modern house. They watched as the uniformed officers surrounded the home and listened to the shrieked lies pouring out of Toni's mouth as fake as the tears that streamed from her reddened, mascara-streaked eyes. They watched as the police entered the house to find Jennifer prone next to her father's body. They watched the arrival of the ambulances. And they watched as the lead detective entered the house with Toni one step behind him, wailing about Jennifer's murderous intent.

The dogs stood and focused intently on the house. The musher raised his right hand, a beam of light shot forth surrounding and entering Jennifer. A second beam flew to surround and enter the brave corgi, Grace. A third beam surrounded and entered the detective. No one at the crime scene could see but all three felt a kind of protection, peace.

As forensic photographers snapped pictures of the crime scene, paramedics helped Jennifer to a stand position and gently lead her to a waiting stretcher. She blinked hard. The many uniformed people moving about in her home, her father's body on the floor, and the blood-stained carpet made no sense to her. Gone was the memory of the night and the figure of the large, gold-eyed cat in the mirror. Gone was the memory of smirking Toni and the phone call to 911. She tried to speak. Gone was her voice; she could not remember how to make sounds and form them into words. Jennifer's head felt like it was filled with numbness and cotton with no thoughts able to form through the layers of padding. Nothing made sense.

Toni pushed passed the officers. "Murderer! Murderer! You always hated me! You always hated your father! You were so jealous of us you killed him!"

The lead detective, Marlowe Merlin, turned towards Toni. "You are contaminating the crime scene and threatening a possible witness. Officer Jennings, arrest this woman, now! Read her her rights."

"You son of a…" Toni caught her mouth up short. Then quickly arranged her face into her best seductress, yet innocent woman smile. "But Detective, surely you don't believe I had anything to do with this!"

"Ma'am, I don't know what went on here. However, despite how things look, I don't think that a small twelve-year-old girl could lift a Magnum, never mind have the strength to fire it and kill someone with one shot." He paused to return Toni's stare. "What I do know is this. You do have the strength and you have a number of prior convictions for assault. You and your husband have had a number of altercations and according to our records, he filed for divorce a week ago and took out a restraining order against you."

Toni looked shocked. She made her face innocent. "That was all a misunderstanding… we were in love! He was just being dramatic! He was an actor!"

"That's enough! Arrest her, read her rights and take her to headquarters. Book her and get her ready for questioning. Oh – make sure to test her for drugs and alcohol!" Detective Merlin turned as Toni was led away screaming.

He walked over to the stretcher where Jennifer lay strapped in. "Listen honey, I am sorry that your father is dead. I don't know what happened here tonight. I don't believe you were involved, but we'll have to look at this from all angles. The medics will take you to the hospital to have the doctors check you; I believe you are in shock. When you feel better in a few days, we will have you answer some questions."

Suddenly Grace, held by an officer near the front door, twisted free and ran to the stretcher with the officer in pursuit. Pushing between Detective Merlin and Jennifer, she raised up on her short corgi hind legs, resting her front white paws on the rail next to Jennifer's face. Concern showed in her brown eyes.

Tears started to stream from Jennifer's eyes. She reached for

Grace and stroked the soft fur of her forehead between the alert, stand-up ears.

"Is this your dog?"

Jennifer managed to nod her head. Still no words would come.

"I can tell. She loves you… and you love her. I love dogs, too. I promise to make sure she is taken care of while you are away."

He paused, brushing a lock of dark hair from Jennifer's face and then stroked the back of Grace's head. "Child Services are going to have to take charge here. We will try to locate family for you. Jennifer, I am sorry, but things will get a lot more complicated before they will get better."

Moving back the detective hooked his fingers through Grace's leather collar and nodded for the medics to carry Jennifer to the ambulance. The crime scene bustled with cops and forensic personnel around him.

Behind the house, on the hill, the musher again sent forth beams of protective light to the detective, Jennifer and Grace the corgi. Then he gave a nod to the giant white sled dogs. Stars seeming to bristle from their fur as the snow flew around them; together they passed back into the vertical rent of light. They left behind only a strange, huge, un-Los Angeles like patch of snow to whisper to those who had hearts open to know – mostly the pets, wild animals, and trees of the earth - that they had been there.

Chapter One

Once Upon A Time percolates in the heart, soul, and spirit. Our stories can heal us, help grow our gifts, and influence the choices that we make. What we choose has direct impact on the fabric of being in all realms and planes of existence. Thus we pray to the Divine for wisdom to learn the truth in the stories so that we may have the courage to make choices that contribute to peace and enlightenment of all.

Book of The Wisdom Runners

Jennifer woke slowly. Her arms and legs felt heavy and stiff as she lay in a cocoon of warmth. She wiggled her toes and rubbed her left foot over the right foot; feeling her feet this way each morning was somehow comforting. Opening her eyes she saw an unfamiliar wood ceiling slanting to a sharp peak directly above the bed. It took her a moment to realize she was not in Los Angeles. Big toe rubbing across big toe was at least familiar.

Something else was missing. Her breath drew in sharply, tears started rolling down her cheeks. Grace's warm, soft-furred body was not under the covers next to her, breathing steadily and helping her to feel safe. Since Jennifer was taken by the police from her home, she had only been able to visit with Grace twice before being put on the plane to Vermont to stay with an aunt and uncle she had never met before. Grace could not come with her because her stepmother, Toni, had insisted the dog belonged to her. Toni hated the dog but would do anything to be mean. Jennifer hoped Grace was safe and not as lonely as she was without her.

A chorus of many dogs barking brought her out of her nest of pillows and patchwork quilts to look through the window over the bed's headboard. Beyond the covered porch roof were twelve large dogs bounding this way and that. They were blond, white, grey, black and reddish. Some had white socks, some had dark masks on their faces, some had floppy ears, and others had ears standing up. Chasing wildly they jumped high over garden fences, knocking down brightly colored flowers, and flew over each other without breaking stride. They seemed to be smiling as they played. A lean man with grey, shoulder-length hair came into view. The dogs danced around him with delight and bounced after the toys he threw.

She drew in her breath and held it as she studied the man. He looked scruffily dressed in black jeans, and a torn blue sweatshirt, over a red shirt. This was her uncle whom she had not met until late last night.

A Family Relations Officer of the courts of California had put her on the plane at the Los Angeles airport. Jennifer had wanted to scream as the plane taxied to take off. As it rose into the air she wondered if she would ever see Grace again.

An airline agent kept her in a windowless office for the three-hour layover at Chicago's O'Hare airport. She had tried to placate Jennifer with a sour-smelling, boiled-forever hot dog and a cola drink that made her stomach nauseated just to look at it. Jennifer's father would never have allowed her to eat that.

After a very bumpy second plane flight, she landed in Burlington, Vermont. Dressed in jeans, friendly but soft-spoken, the Aunt Sarah she had never met, greeted her there with apologies that Uncle Jim had not been able to leave their farm to meet her, too. She also apologized for not having been able to get permission for Grace to come to Vermont with Jennifer.

"Jennifer... I cannot begin to understand all that you have been through. I am sorry that your father was not close with us. But please try to understand that your Uncle Jim and I are very sad, too; your dad was our younger brother. We love dogs. We know that you are very close to Grace and it is must be so hard for you to be separated, especially with what you are going through now. We are going to try to get her here for you."

Aunt Sarah had paused to give her a chance to answer. Jennifer tried to speak but nothing came. Her throat felt glued shut. She looked around the small, Vermont airport and wished she could wake up from this nightmare life had become.

Someone from social services in California must have filled Aunt Sarah in about Jennifer's shock reaction and the inability to speak. Called selective mutism, there is no actual physical impairment. A psychiatrist and social worker had explained to Jennifer that as the trauma and sadness of her father's death started to heal – they called it Post Traumatic Stress Disorder – PTSD - that Jennifer would probably regain her ability to speak naturally. They had encouraged her to be patient with herself, to try to speak, but not feel guilty and upset if she could not. They assured her that if her voice did not come back within a few months that speech therapy would help. In the meantime all adults who were responsible for her care would be informed so they could be supportive during this time of grieving for her father and during the investigation of his death.

It was dark as they left the airport in Aunt Sarah's pickup truck. She offered Jennifer fresh juice, fruit and sandwiches from a cooler that sat between them on the bench seat. Jennifer could not eat but tried to politely nod here and there to Sarah's explanations of the Vermont landmarks they passed. Playing soft classical music on the radio, they rode the hour and a half through the winding, Vermont mountain roads, trying to be courteous.

When they arrived at the farm, Uncle Jim came to the door of her aunt's cabin and nodded hello.

"Hey, Jennifer. I'm your Uncle Jim. Good to meet you." He

extended a hand, then withdrew it awkwardly when she did not reach out to take it.

"Did you have a nice plane ride?" He bit his lip and shifted his weight from one foot to the other. He seemed shy. Jennifer knew he was trying but she could not answer him. Truly, she did not want to and just wanted to be home. She wanted her father. Only that was never going to be possible again; she choked back her tears. She willed herself to be strong.

Now this morning she studied him and his dogs from her hidden perch at the second floor window. She had only heard about "Uncle Jim," usually with blatant disgust from her father or stepmother; now suddenly she was living on his Vermont farm where he ran a Canine Consciousness project studying dogs as caring, intuitive, sentient beings and ran an educational sled dog touring center. She did not want to be here. She had no choice.

Jennifer felt the dark, heavy feeling in her stomach get thicker, garnering knots. She curled back down into the warmth of the pillows and quilts. Closing her eyes she tried to will herself back to Los Angeles. Back with Grace. She wished that just wanting something to be true could make it so.

The smell of coffee and something baking mixed with the scent of the wood of the walls, floor and ceiling. The dogs continued to bark outside as they ran around the cabin in their play. A soft tapping came at the door to her room. "Jen, are you up?" her aunt asked from outside the door.

She lay still.

"Jen, if you are up I have pancakes and fresh fruit. Come down for breakfast when you are ready. Your uncle would love for you to meet the dogs and later, if you would like, we could go into town to shop for clothes." Jennifer heard her aunt's footsteps disappear, and she sighed with relief.

She finally pushed out from under the covers and slid from the bed. The bathroom was in the hall with a window that looked out over a side yard where a stone barbecue and wooden bench swing stood amongst white and rose colored peonies, spires of lupines, daisies and colorful lilies. She saw a large meadow beyond and further out a mountain ridge. She could smell pine trees that drifted through the window. Jennifer peered at herself in the mirror. At least her own face was the same - dark, thick hair, large, green eyes.

After washing up, she slipped into her jeans, sneakers, t-shirt and green sweater. Other than her pajamas they were all the clothes she had. Three weeks ago, released on bail, her stepmother had returned to their home and thrown out all of Jennifer's clothes. Toni told the police and the child protection agency that had temporary custody of Jennifer, that she would not have the clothes of a murderer in her home. Toni refused to pay to replace them. The lawyers said for now they could do nothing as her father's money and their home's ownership was in dispute until both Toni and Jennifer were cleared of suspicion of murder and/or one of them was tried and found guilty. Further, Toni was disputing the divorce filing and her father's new will that made Jennifer his sole heir.

Jennifer found herself feeling shaky and nervous as she descended the narrow wood staircase to the start of this new chapter of her life. "How am I going to live here?" she wondered. She could not speak to communicate.

At the foot of the stairs she paused. She took a deep, soft breath as the social worker assigned to support her after her father's death had taught her to do. After two more deep breaths she stepped forward into a large great room.

It looked like something in a fairy tale. In the center stood a massive fireplace built of rounded stones. Low wood rafters ran across the room, with a wood ceiling above them. Two walls were set with windows looking out on the fields, forest and mountains beyond. Another wall held the sink, kitchen counter and the front door leading to a covered porch. Two couches, tables and lamps of wood, with natural bark intact, furnished the room.

Although the smell of pancakes cooking was one she loved from her L.A. life, now she felt her stomach clench at the thought of eating. Under a row of windows she saw a table set with a platter of pancakes, bacon and ham, and a glass bowl holding a melody of blueberries, melon balls, bananas and strawberries. Aunt Sarah stood with her back leaning against the kitchen counter, a mug of coffee in her hand.

"Have a seat, honey. I didn't know if you eat meat so I made bacon. I'm a vegetarian but your uncle loves meat with his breakfast – as do the dogs!" Her aunt was small, petite, with long, graying blond hair; her faded jeans and a purple sweater softened the intensity of her presence. Her piercing blue eyes were softened by the crows-feet that crinkled when she smiled. She seemed to be taking all of Jennifer in at once, curious and yet reining herself in, trying not to be overwhelming to this niece she had never met.

Sarah crossed to the table, placing a few pancakes on Jennifer's plate and pushed the butter towards her. "I can make you an egg if you'd like."

Jennifer shook her head slightly. Biting her lip, she looked down at her feet. She wished her sneakers were not so worn and beaten up. She wanted to like this aunt she did not know, but was it ever going to be possible?

Sarah caught herself sighing. Had she already failed completely? She had no experience with kids or teens, especially not ones whose father had just been murdered, let alone a twelve-year old niece that she had never met. Trying to sound cheerful she asked, "You sure? Henriette, Lucy, Hawk and Eagle give us some delicious eggs. You don't know what real eggs are till you have them from happy hens and ducks!"

Jennifer shook her head again, harder this time. Sitting down at the table, trying to be polite, she took some butter for her pancakes, pouring maple syrup from a small pitcher. The pancakes were thick, dotted with blueberries; they smelled delicious but even so she was not hungry. She put the fork down. Her stomach squeezed tight – she felt dark inside.

Why couldn't she speak? Jennifer had always been shy with people she did not know – or did not like – but this was different. It was scary. What if she could never communicate again? She reached up and grabbed a lock of her dark hair and started to pull and wind it around her finger.

Just then the door opened and Uncle Jim came in; although fifty-nine, he moved like a much younger man. His shabby clothes gave him a ragged but timeless look. Her aunt was the same. They were not part of her stepmother's L.A. set, with the carefully coiffed hair, long, manicured nails and trendy, expensive clothes.

Jennifer didn't like her stepmother's friends, nor most of her father's friends. They spoke shrilly, forcing laughter and seemed not to care about the troubles of people or planet around them. Their life revolved around gossiping about the famous people they knew, having a meal at a good table where they would be seen by the paparazzi at the latest L.A. hotspot restaurant, concerns over who was getting what part in what newest "in" director's film, and who had the best cocaine. They loved to say horrible things about friends not present at whatever gathering they were at, gossiping endlessly about who had had what cosmetic procedure and how they were denying it and making excuses about having great genetics and flawless faces that needed no surgery to the press. Always concerned about appearances, her stepmother and her friends could blah blah blah about nothing all night long.

Her father had been caught up in this shallow merry-go-round of glamour and fast living. An actor and singer since childhood, on the fringe of the Hollywood elite in middle age, after early success in the rock era of the seventies, he made his money acting in science fiction and horror B movies. He always struggled to hang onto his tentative position as a working actor in Hollywood and its social scene. Sometimes it seemed that he took no notice that she existed.

But often, as if out of the blue, he would soften. He would become the buddy Jennifer loved. Whispering and sneaking to get around Toni, they would drive to a mountain location where they would spend the weekend talking about nature, the planet, looking through her telescope and dreaming about the life they could have if they lived on planets revolving around other stars. From the public and his social circles he hid that he had no formal education, but privately he encouraged her to read and dream. He had sent her to a top private school in Los Angeles that specialized in the sciences because he knew she loved learning and excelled in math and sciences.

Jennifer took a deep breath and tried to slow her good memories of her father. She looked from her aunt to her uncle and wondered what had caused her father to leave them behind. They seemed like good people. She wished she had met them before her father's death. But she hadn't. The lawyers had indicated that since she was twelve years old, if Uncle Jim and Aunt Sarah passed their evaluation to be her legal guardians, and if she was cleared of any suspicion of her father's murder, that she would have no choice. She would have to live with them.

Jim filled his mug with hot coffee from the pot on the old fashioned, wood cook stove. He looked over at Jennifer. "Sleep well?"

She nodded.

Suddenly there was a crash on the porch. Jim winked at Sarah and Jennifer, then moved to the door. "Hey! What did I tell you? Stay off the porch and stop causing trouble!" Seven dogs came to the door and peered at him intently through the screen. He chuckled.

"The dogs are trying to get at the squirrels on the bird feeder by jumping from the top of the porch railing. They are in constant motion and curious… and playful. It wouldn't be a problem if they were just crashing furniture and mowing down the flowerbeds because we can fix those things. But they can get hurt if they turn something heavy over on themselves – so we have to watch them." He shrugged and sat down opposite her.

She looked into his large brown eyes. They reminded her of her father's eyes. Both her aunt and uncle had faces that reminded her of her father, their younger brother, Saul. Somehow this felt comforting and yet upsetting at the same time. She wanted to be home with her father and Grace.

But her father had been focused on his appearance. Whereas her aunt and uncle had soft wrinkles on their faces and grey in their hair, he had been relentless in his constant visits to the dermatologist, plastic surgeon, gym, and hair salon. By age forty-five he had had his first facelift. She remembered bringing him tea to sip with a straw as he rested at home in bandages, with swelling and dark-purple bruising, before his face would heal to a smooth, taunt, chiseled look. Once famous and the darling of the tabloids as a child actor and singer, he had never been able to accept aging. Jennifer didn't think Aunt Sarah or Uncle Jim would ever have a facelift. She liked that about them.

"You don't seem hungry. You had a long trip from Los Angeles. I don't fly much, but when I do, I'm not very hungry either," Uncle Jim said.

A long pause ensued as he sat, trying not to fidget. Finally he jumped up, "I have a dog you might like to meet. I know she would love to help you with those pancakes."

Uncle Jim crossed the room to the door. "Hey Luna!" he called. "Luna, get in here!"

An all-white, medium size, longish furred dog rushed in the open door. Woofing in alto tones, she circled Jim. She had a tail that curled over her back, small white ears, pointed up, and a light, reddish, walnut brown nose. "Luna, look we have a new friend who is staying with us." Jim gestured towards Jennifer.

Luna looked over at her and then skidded across the wide-board floor. She came to rest in a sit next to Jennifer. Eyes warm brown and intent, Jennifer saw that Luna had black ringing her eyes as if someone had taken an eyeliner pencil and given her a thick line to set off her white eyelashes. Cautiously Jennifer reached out to touch the top of her head. Luna moved forward and woofed. Jennifer jumped, pulling her hand away. This was not Grace, her corgi. She bit her lip.

Jim chuckled. "Luna, calm down. Don't scare Jen!"

"She's just happy to meet you, Jen," said her aunt. "If you aren't eating your pancakes, break some pieces off and toss them to her."

Jennifer loved sharing all of her meals and snacks with Grace. Toni was disgusted with this behavior and depending on her mood would sulk when Saul defended Jennifer and Grace or start screaming and raging that he had better get that filthy dog out of their nice, white home. From the time her father had brought Grace home, as a pup from the breeder, cute as a bear cub with her stub of a tail and her short little legs, Grace had established that Jennifer and she would share everything. They had been pals, equal siblings for four years, doing everything together.

Looking at the white dog sitting before her, Jennifer broke off a piece of pancake with her hand and tossed it high. She was surprised as Luna rose up on her hind legs, snatching it from the air; it was gone in an instant and Luna was back sitting at attention as if she had never moved. Jennifer giggled. Grace could not have jumped that high!

Jennifer tossed another piece and Luna snatched it, returning to an immediate sit, staring eagerly. Jennifer laughed softly and threw another piece. This white dog was much more agile and athletic than her short-legged Grace.

"You can feed her all you want. With the dog sledding, swimming in the ponds and running around on adventures, it's all we can do to keep weight on these dogs. You might take a few pieces for yourself, too; pancakes are good to keep your energy up, especially for a growing, twelve-year old girl!" Jim said.

Jennifer tossed another piece to Luna.

Jim stretched and poured more hot coffee into his mug. Smiling, he watched Luna egging Jennifer on, encouraging her with her antics in the way that she had with most children she met. Luna was very good with children, especially those traumatized or ones who faced challenges of autism and other special needs. "She is the queen of this kennel. We have other males and females who are alpha, pack leaders to the others, but Luna is the top ruler. She is the mother, aunt and grandmother of a number of the dogs here. And believe it or not, she has many fans, all over the world, including Korea! They write to her and she writes back..."

Jennifer eyes opened wide. She looked at her Uncle. Was he teasing her?

Jim chuckled. "I am not kidding you! Ask her, she is a very wise and incredible doggie! When I'm not looking she might just start talking to you!"

Jennifer reached out and stroked Luna's white head. Then she scratched behind her ear. Grace liked this…

"So what are your plans for the day, Sarah?" Jim asked.

Her aunt was cleaning the counter from breakfast. Above her hung an array of pans, spoons and ladles from hooks in the low overhead beams. Over the old-fashioned, wood-burning cook stove were bunches of plants drying, hung up side down by string and colored ribbons. Sarah grabbed a red-plaid towel to wipe her wet hands. Glancing up at the herbs and then to Jennifer, she laughed.

"I guess our life here must seem very different than what you are used to in L.A. These are herbs." She pointed up at the low ceiling.

Jennifer looked at Sarah and made a confused face.

"Well, this is how they look when they are drying. I grow them in one of our gardens. They are so much better when they are grown fresh, organically. Those herbs that people buy in bottles, even at the health food store, just can't compare to ones grown and used fresh or dried at home."

Jennifer nodded. She continued to stroke Luna's white head. She wondered if her aunt and uncle could get Grace, whether they would be friends.

Sarah nodded at Jim. "Well… Jen didn't bring many clothes and if she is up to it, I thought we could take a ride into Johnson and Morrisville this morning. Maybe we can find her some good sneakers, hiking boots, a few more pairs of jeans, and some long and short-sleeved t-shirts might be good for her around the farm. I promise you, Jen, you are going to get dirty playing with the dogs and going out exploring in the woods."

"Don't forget hats," Jim said. "Jen, you'll want a straw one with a big brim for sunny days, a good rain hat, and a parka." Jim looked at her thoughtfully. "Sarah, maybe see if you can find her a backpack for snacks and things when she goes out exploring the woods and trails with the dogs."

Jennifer looked from her uncle to her aunt and then back again. They were trying to be kind. She could hear Toni's voice, shrill hoarse from smoking for decades, mocking them, "Losers! Hats? Who are they kidding? They think they are something but they are peons! Don't get comfy, BABE! It won't be long before I make sure you are locked away for good!" Thinking about Toni's voice and face made her shiver.

Jim turned back to Jennifer, "Do you like to take photos?"

She shrugged. Her father had lots of cameras and she had liked taking pictures of stars through her telescope.

"Well, I do. There are lots of things around here to take pictures of – the dogs, flowers, wildlife, and the Vermont views. Someone sent a chunk of gift money along for the dogs and I think that we could get a nice, small digital camera for you," he said. "Hey, Luna, since you have a new friend, would you like to buy her a camera so that you and she can document your adventures?"

Luna woofed. Jennifer thought that Luna really understood Uncle Jim.

Jim got up and stretched. "I gotta get back to the dogs and chores. The work here never stops. Tomorrow I will show you the sled dog barn and educational center we have. You can meet the dogs and get to know them. They are the Un-Chained Gang – they stand for ethical treatment of all dogs – no chains here!"

Jennifer nodded and then studied her plate sadly, wishing her father and Grace were here to explore the woods of Vermont with her.

"I am not sure that Luna is going to be willing to share you with the other dogs, but we'll see," he laughed.

"Hey, Luna, you comin' with me or are you stickin' with Jen?" Luna looked at him but did not budge. "Jennifer, do you want Luna for a friend today?"

Jennifer looked at her uncle and then at Luna. She shrugged

noncommittally. If she could not have Grace for now, then it would be nice to have this dog for a while.

"Well, why don't you just see how you feel? If you find you don't want her along then have Sarah send her over to the barn." Jim tipped his fingers to the brim of his baseball cap and headed out the door whistling.

Luna looked at Jennifer and woofed.

"She wants the bacon on the platter," said Sarah. "Why don't you eat what you want and give the rest to her."

As Sarah washed the pans and dishes Jennifer fed Luna the bacon and managed to eat a few pieces. Sarah was definitely not mean to dogs like Toni was. When the platter was empty Luna put her paw on Jennifer's thigh, staring up at her intently. "Woo-woo!" Luna woofed.

"Luna, you are such a beggar!" Sarah laughed. "Why don't you take Jennifer out in the yard while I get ready for the drive to town? Jen, there is a pink leash by the door that you can use for her. Luna is three-quarters Siberian husky, which makes her more of a roamer than Jim's other dogs. Until she gets bonded to you, please use a leash so she doesn't go on an adventure."

Sarah finished washing a pot and hung it over the stove. "I'm going to change into clean jeans and get my wallet." Sarah left the dishes drying on the rack and ran upstairs.

Luna followed Jennifer to the door and sat. Her white legs were much longer than Grace's. After clipping the pink leash on Luna's collar, they went out onto the covered porch, down the wooden steps and into the yard. The cool morning Vermont air smelled of pine and the wild rose bush next to the porch. The sky was bright, clear blue, unmarked by a cloud; it was not smudged by the smog that marred the Los Angeles sky even on the most clear days.

Jennifer looked around the yard and to the mountains across the meadow. This was not Los Angeles. She felt lost but decided to sit on a glider out in the yard amidst flowers of a garden gone wild. She was surprised when Luna jumped up next to her, snuggling as near as she could get. It felt good to feel her body pressing close.

It wasn't Grace but it would do. Jennifer stroked Luna's head and then gave in and hugged her, burying her face into the fur on Luna's neck. Tears started to roll down her cheeks.

The phone rang in the house. Aunt Sarah answered it. Jennifer reached into her sweater pocket for a tissue. Aunt Sarah's voice got quiet but firm. The tears started to stream as Jennifer realized that it was Toni, her stepmother.

"We tried to reach you several times last night, both when Jen arrived at the Burlington airport, and again when we got home..." Sarah said.

"Toni, I told you to reverse the charges in our messages... I am sorry that you didn't get them..."

"Please stop threatening... Toni I won't listen to that language... the Family Court judge asked the state to place her with family. Our brother had filed to divorce you and you are under criminal investigation. We are trying to support Jennifer through this..."

"Toni I can't help it if the state and the police are investigating you. We had nothing to do with that. We literally have had no contact with you so how would we know about your activities, criminal or otherwise?" Aunt Sarah was trying to remain calm.

Jennifer knew her stepmother was vicious when she wanted something. She thought she could scare people by screaming, using nasty language and threats to get what she wanted. An aging actress, Toni could flash a camera-ready smile for photographers but behind closed doors was usually a twisted-faced, shrieking monster. As Jennifer listened, the darkness inside of her stomach was getting thicker, squeezing the breath out of her. She clung tighter to Luna.

"Toni, you have to speak to your lawyers about that. Your husband, my brother, took our mother's entire estate. Jim and I sent money to help with Jennifer's expenses after our brother's death but we feel no obligation to you..."

"I don't know what to tell you. I don't know where you get the idea that you deserve money from the books I have written or my brother's non-profit foundation. We are trying to help out with Jennifer so that she gets the care she needs. After the police and state investigation we will see what the judge recommends. We are NOT willing to buy Jennifer from you... "

"Look, I am going to hang up now. I am sorry you are hurting for money..."

"Okay, Toni, that's it... please think about it... if you cannot control yourself on the phone then I am going to ask the court to have all phone calls supervised by a Family Relations officer until the judge comes to some decision..."

". . . Toni... that's it... I am hanging up now."

The house was quiet. Toni was trying to ruin her stay with her aunt and uncle. At school when Jennifer would make a new friend and told her father over dinner or Saturday breakfast about her and how much she liked her, Toni would listen and ask questions about the new friend's parents. Later when Jen's father was out, or drunk, Toni would smirk at her and then call her friend's parents. If the friend's parents were in the film business she would shamelessly cajole or beg for a part in their new film. Or ask for money. When they would try to politely refuse she would start screaming at them. Jennifer's stomach would knot as her cheeks and neck burned with embarrassment listening to Toni. It inevitably ended with her new friend's parents telling him or her not to continue a friendship with Jennifer. And Toni mocking her with her sharp, nasty voice, "Your friends parents are nothings! Zeros!"

A few minutes later her aunt came out into the yard dressed in black jeans and a bright, turquoise pullover. Jennifer and Luna looked up at her over the back of the glider.

"Oh, honey, you have been crying! Did you hear me on the phone? I am so sorry!" Sarah said. She reached into her back pocket and offered a blue bandana. "It's a handkerchief. Take this one; I carry several." Jennifer took it and wiped her eyes.

Sarah squatted down next to her. "Look, I'm sorry. I know you don't really know us, and your father has only been gone for six weeks and your stepmother is carrying on. But even though Jim or I may have some heated conversations with Toni, we won't let that influence how we feel about you. Or about her, either, because

Toni is just not well," she paused, looking off towards the mountain ridge.

"Jennifer, this is a hard time for you. Your uncle and I will try to make it as easy as we can. We have never been parents so you will have to be patient and help us along. I know how hard it is to live with a very difficult mother... and stepmothers. What you have to know is that it is not your fault; you are not bad, no matter what your stepmother says to you or about you," Sarah said.

Jennifer felt a strong tug on her pant leg. Looking up at her was a white duck face with black eyes and an orange beak. Next to it was another. Both looked intently at her.

Sarah laughed. "Well, here is the egg-laying contingent! I think they must be checking up to see if you had your protein this morning! The ducks are Henriette and Lucy. If you look at the daisy patch, to the right there, you can see the hens, Hawk and Eagle, who are scratching for worms, bugs and table scraps."

Henriette grabbed Jennifer's pant leg again, shaking her head vigorously. "She wants you to pat her. They are quite friendly; we have raised them since they hatched. Just reach out your hand and rub gently on the back of her head under the feathers, using the tips of your fingers."

Jennifer was surprised at how soft Henriette's white feathers were. The duck closed her eyes and moved her head back and forth gently against Jennifer's fingers; she looked like she was in a state of bliss.

"She's nice, isn't she? Now maybe you will want some eggs!" Sarah stood up and motioned for the ducks to move off. They waddled away, white tail ends swaying widely back and forth as they walked on their stiff legs and webbed feet. Jennifer wondered if Grace would want to chase them or use her corgi herding instincts to keep them rounded up.

"Let's not dwell on the phone call. Why don't you go into the house and splash some cold water on your face. Meet me at the truck across the drive at the four-bay garage next to the big barn. Do you want Luna to come shopping with us?" Sarah asked.

Jennifer nodded. Luna watched her intently. Jennifer reached out and stroked her white head again. She felt tired. How was she going to face this new home?

"Okay, I'll bring her with me and we'll wait for you in the truck." Sarah got up, brushing off the knees of her jeans.

* * *

The four-wheel drive pickup truck was so high off the ground that Jennifer had to step onto a running board and then pull herself up onto the passenger seat, using the special handle over the door. Luna and three other dogs were in the back seat of the cab; they immediately began swarming her with kisses as she landed on the seat. They were licking her happily, tails waving, while growling at the same time. Jennifer cringed against the dashboard.

"Cut it out!" Uncle Jim said firmly as he came over to supervise. "Jen, they aren't growling at you. They are arguing over which one owns you. It's part of dog pack pecking order. Luna wants them to know that she has first dibs on you and the others are arguing with her because they want to claim you. It sounds worse than it is."

Jennifer nodded that she understood.

"You have already met Luna. Peaberry is the big, thin, freckled, blue-eyed, wacky looking dog next to her; he is friendly but quite silly. Don't let his appearance fool you, he is an award-winning sled dog leader; he is also the dad and granddad of many of the dogs here." Jim tossed Peaberry a treat, which he snapped out of the air. Jennifer had never seen such bright blue eyes.

"And this is one of my favorites, Stormina; sometimes I call her 'Big Ears!" Stormina was mostly black, long and thin, with large, soft-brown eyes, and very big, black ears. She looked both dignified and loving.

"And this one is Rose. 'Roly-Poly Rose!' Rosie is very sweet and a good sled dog. Aren't you Rose?" Rose blinked at him shyly. Jim threw treats rapidly to all four dogs; they caught them like frogs snapping flies out of the air.

"How did you four dogs get in here? Did you jump in through the open windows?" Aunt Sarah came up behind her brother. "Jen, these dogs have no idea that gravity is a major force of nature that most canines must contend with. They just lift off the ground whenever they feel like it and end up wherever they please."

Jim waved Sarah's words away. "Who would you ask to leave? They want to go for a ride with you. The other three snuck in when they saw Luna in the truck." He grinned at Sarah. "Here is a list of what we need while you are in town. I called ahead and they will have the cases of dog biscuits and farm supplies ready."

Smiling, Sarah jumped in behind the steering wheel. Soon the group of four canines and two humans were down the driveway and onto a dirt road leading away from the farm and cutting into a heavy forest area. "We built this two-mile road so trucks and cars can get to us from the main road. There is an old road beyond our driveway, but it is impassable most of the year except by ATVs - All Terrain Vehicles - during mud season, and snowmobiles in winter," Sarah said.

Jennifer looked out the window, studying the trees that grew so close to the road. They weren't like anything she had seen in California. She looked back at her aunt.

"Our road allows us to live in thousands of acres of wilderness – and to share it easily with guests who come to meet the dogs. Everything lives out here! You'll see moose, bear, deer, hawks and many other species of birds. We are safe to stargaze, read and sit out in the area that surrounds the barn and cabins because the more dangerous wildlife think that the dogs are a wolf pack; they don't come near the pack's territory. But when you go exploring beyond the barn and cabins, always have Luna or another dog with you for safety." Sarah reached out and turned on the radio to a classical station.

Jennifer found herself enjoying the ride and the music. She had always wanted to play the violin and liked to listen to Mozart while she read and studied. Toni had made fun of her and played loud rock and roll when her father was away working. She found herself relaxing as the road descended off Eden Mountain. Jennifer was caught by the long-range views of the mountains and Vermont's green farmlands that spread out, like a patchwork quilt, in front of them. Traveling down Route 100 the farms, white houses and red barns were enchanting to view as they listened to a symphony on Vermont Public Radio.

* * *

They didn't return until near dark. The back of the pickup truck was loaded with large cases of dog biscuits, wire for fences, blueberry bushes from the farm center, and sacs filled with pounds of rice, millet, grains, nuts, seeds and spices from the food co-op. But more surprising to Jennifer were the many bags filled with clothes and things just for her.

Aunt Sarah had taken her to a shop in Johnson. The inside was crammed with shelves and racks of colorful clothing. Soon Jennifer had eight pairs of pants, shorts, soft cotton t-shirts and sweatshirts in bright colors, a pair of green mud boots, hiking boots and sneakers. They also found a wide-brim straw hat, a good canvas hat for the rain and a yellow rain slicker that could fold easily into a backpack. When they drove to the sports store in Morrisville they bought a deep blue colored backpack, with endless pockets, and a waterproof digital camera.

It had been an easy day. Whenever her dad would take her clothes shopping he had been tolerant of her love of easy, casual, stretchy clothing. But once home her stepmother would examine each find and either smirk in disgust or roll her eyes and make fun of Jennifer's taste because it was non-trendy by L.A. and Hollywood standards. "Why can't you be more like our friends' children? They know how to dress!" she would demand. Often Jennifer would go to bed crying, hugging Grace tightly till she fell asleep.

Aunt Sarah was different. She let her choose several different styles of pants and tops in the soft green, black and blue colors that she liked and then try them on. She gave genuine approval when something fit. "That really looks great on you," or, "That's a nice color," and then would ask, "Just be honest, do you like it?" If Jennifer nodded, Sarah would say, "Well, let's get it!"

On the ride home to the farm, Jennifer felt the heavy feeling in her stomach battering at the sense of happiness trying to fill her heart. The happiness wasn't about the shopping; lunch at a country-store with a veranda overlooking a fast moving river; or individual ice cream cones at a Vermont homemade ice cream stand for Aunt Sarah and her, and each of the dogs. It was the sense that she could really like a life in the country with Sarah, Jim and the sled dogs. Of course Grace would have to be here, too. But she didn't want to allow herself to hope; she had a deep knowing feeling that she could not have happiness in life.

* * *

There was darkness all around. She was hiding. Shots rang out – then her stepmother was screaming. She tried to stay immobile, but her arms and legs crawled on their own, moved by a controlling force, pulling her from her hiding place. Grace was barking and barking her corgi protective warning. Her father was lying on the floor. The force brought her to a standing position; she saw nothing but blood flowing dark red over the white carpet. Her limbs now froze in place; her eyes refused to close. Deep inside she felt a wrench as a scream ripped up and out of her mouth…

She couldn't move. She needed to move. She screamed and screamed…

Suddenly there was light. Hands grabbed her, pulling her up. "Jen, what is it? Luna and I are right here! Wake up! Wake up, honey!"

Jennifer struggled to breathe. Her body shook and tears ran

down her face. She could feel her aunt's arms around her. Finally her breathing slowed. She pushed back away from her aunt's embrace.

"Luna is here. Let me go get you some water; I always find that helps when I wake from a hard dream." Luna moved close to her as Sarah slipped from the room.

She returned carrying a tray with a tall glass of water, a thermos, and some mugs. "Here, sip on the water. I heated up some milk with honey and some chamomile herb – it's sort of sweet tasting. The herb will relax your nerves and the calcium in the milk will help us both get back to sleep."

Sarah handed Jennifer the glass of water into her still shaking hands.

"Sip it slowly. Do you want to tell me about the dream?" Sarah asked.

Jennifer shook her head.

"That's okay. It helps to talk. Maybe you can tell Luna about it when you walk in the woods; she's a good listener." Sarah poured some of the hot milk mixture into a mug and exchanged it for the water glass.

Jennifer sipped it experimentally. It was sweet and good. She took a bigger swig.

"You like it?" Sarah asked.

Jennifer nodded. Even holding the mug felt soothing.

"You might like to learn about herbs. They can be helpful in our lives for relaxing, promoting good health and helping to heal illnesses that spring up," Sarah said.

Jennifer nodded. She had often wondered about the herbs and spices she had seen at the health food stores and farmers markets of L.A. The grip of fear that she had from her dream slowly faded as they sat in the bedroom under the eaves. Sarah rearranged the pillows and patchwork quilts, somehow putting order back into Jennifer's mind after the nightmare seemed to tear her apart. Jennifer had woken up screaming from nightmares since she could remember. Somehow, sitting in this small room with Luna and Sarah, she felt safe.

"Ready to try to sleep again?" Sarah asked.

Jennifer nodded and settled back into the pillows. Luna cuddled up close. Sarah carried the tray out and switched the light off at the door. "Sleep well, you two."

Jennifer reached out and hugged Luna close, just like she loved to hug Grace. She listened to Luna's soft breathing; she felt soothed. Sleep came soon after.

* * *

Dogs were barking outside; she could hear their footfalls as they raced and played. Slowly opening her eyes Jennifer found she was nose to nose with Luna. Luna's soft brown eyes, with their black rims, stayed focused as she gazed back into them. As she wondered what Luna was thinking - Luna's tail started to thump under the covers, causing the quilts to rise and fall. Jennifer giggled; Grace's nub of a tail never made a sound or moved the covers like this. Somehow it seemed so natural to be this close with Luna. She hoped Grace and Luna would be friends.

Stretching, Jennifer pushed out of the bed. From the piles of new clothes she selected a bright blue t-shirt, jeans and yellow cotton socks. When she went to wash up, Luna jumped off the bed and followed. Then they made their way downstairs.

"Good morning, gals!" Sarah called. "Did you sleep okay after I left?"

Jennifer nodded and slid shyly into place at the big table. There was a platter holding waffles and bacon, a big bowl of berries and melon, a glass bottle of milk and a pitcher of maple syrup. Sarah brought a skillet over from the old-fashioned stove and slid two sunny side-up eggs onto Jennifer's plate. "One is from Hawk, and one is from Eagle, the two chickens. They laid them this morning just for you!"

Jennifer was hungry. She took a waffle onto her plate and spread it with butter and syrup. She cut a piece and dipped it into the yolk of the egg. It was excellent. Luna pawed her thigh; she wanted some. Jennifer giggled and then shook her head no, playfully. Luna huffed at her.

"Luna, scoot yourself out the door for a pee; you haven't been out since last night." Luna did not budge for Sarah. Her aunt crossed her arms over her chest and made a mock stern face, "I am not kidding you, you get out that door right now."

Sarah closed the screen door behind Luna. "Normally we have to watch her because of her penchant for running off on adventures. But she really likes you and she knows that she can beg lots of waffles and bacon out of you. She will be back soon." Sarah's eyes sparkled.

A few moments later Luna was at the door scratching to come in. Sarah opened it. Luna rushed across the wide floorboards and jumped up on the bench next to Jennifer. She stared at Jennifer's plate.

"Luna, you ratfink! Get down right now. You are not funny!" Sarah stared at her.

Luna didn't budge. Stifling a laugh and trying to appear stern, Sarah crossed the floor and hauled Luna down by the collar. "Sit on the floor, right now."

Jennifer giggled, then looked at her aunt. She tossed Luna a piece of waffle and then took another piece for herself.

Sarah sat down across from Jennifer. "You have a whole summer to explore around here. Old logging roads, abandoned farms and a ghost town that one of the sled dog trails will take you near. Luna and some of the others will help you to find lots of great places."

"Before you get started you should meet the rest of the dogs and see what your uncle does over at the barn. People come from all over the world to meet his dogs. Right now this is the only tour center in North America where the sled dogs are kept free-range, unchained. Many sled dogs live their lives on chains from just a few months old until they can no longer pull." Sarah sipped her coffee and looked out the window, blinking back tears.

Jennifer looked down at her plate. When Luna woofed at her she tossed her a piece of bacon.

Sarah cleared her throat. "Don't mind me, Jen. I am not a very emotional type, but I love dogs and all animals. What happens to sled dogs upsets me. Unless they have caring owners, many are shy and aggressive because they have little interaction with humans. There are many good people with sled dogs, but just like with greyhounds and dog racing, there are many abuses."

Jennifer looked into her aunt's blue eyes. She wished she could say something. Let her know that she loved dogs. She wanted to tell her about Grace, how much she missed her, and what a good dog she was, too. But no words would come. Finally she nodded, hoping Sarah understood.

"It is very sad that many pet dogs, sled dogs, cats, and other pets do not have the life that all of Earth's creatures deserve. Isn't that right, Luna?" asked Sarah. Luna looked at her and woofed; she seemed to be following their conversation as if she understood it totally.

Jennifer and Sarah laughed. "She knows more than one might think. Dogs focus on sleeping, playing and eating for most of their day; but they also have a huge amount of wisdom to share with people if we can learn to tune into it."

After breakfast Luna and Jennifer walked across the drive to the barn. Dogs appeared behind the tall fences, peering out curiously. A few started to yip and then tone a long note, singing. More joined in until they all were singing together in a canine chorus. They grew louder and louder, like wolves in the wild. Ice blue and brown eyes studied her as they sang. Luna led her to a door in the side of the barn where they entered.

Luna trotted ahead into an entrance room with Jennifer right behind her. Uncle Jim entered from a door to the left. "I was 'told' that you were coming," he chuckled.

"Would you like to meet the dogs and learn about dog sledding?" he asked.

Jennifer nodded.

"Here we raise healthy, happy, loving, sled dogs. Most of them are Alaskan huskies – it is a sort of mutt that is used for racing, bred from northern breeds of dogs. They don't look like the pretty Siberians and Alaskan Malamutes that most people associate with dog sledding – they are faster. We don't chain them, but we have six large pens for them to play and rest in when we can't supervise them. We call them, "The UN-Chained Gang' . . . I think you are a little too young to get that joke," he chuckled.

Just then three dog heads and front paws appeared at the window of the door. They really wanted in! A tawny colored one with a darkened muzzle started knocking at the window with her paw. Jennifer laughed; they were so insistent!

Jim looked at her out of the corner of his eye and smiled. "They want to be in here with us. But first, how would you like to learn to harness Luna? Then we can bring some more in, you can harness them, and then we can hitch them to a sled and go for a ride. Would you like that?"

Jennifer's eyes were wide. She nodded.

"What's the matter? You're surprised? You thought you had to have snow for dog sledding, didn't you?" he laughed.

"I have some special carts with wheels that come from Germany. It's fun and fast, just like being on a snow sled, without the cold of winter," he said.

Jim grabbed a blue harness off the wall. "Here, let's get Luna to demonstrate for you."

"Now, Luna is different than the other dogs. She likes to harness herself, with just a bit of help from us." Jim pulled the harness over Luna's head. He held the right side loop out and Luna raised her paw herself and pushed it through. She did the same thing, with her opposite paw, when Jim pulled the left loop out. Jim then pulled the crossed strapping of the harness back towards her tail.

"Good Luna!" He tossed her a treat; she quickly snatched it and sat down to watch. It looked to Jennifer as if Luna was supervising.

"Okay, now we need a team of dogs." Uncle Jim let in a group of canines that crowded around them. Jennifer could not believe how eager they all were.

Taking the harness from Jim, Jennifer was able to get Flint harnessed with little guidance.

"Wow! You are a fast learner, huh?" She felt good that she could learn quickly and that her uncle noticed. Uncle Jim was easy to be around. She was starting to love the dogs already.

Soon they also had Stormina, Lioness, Rainbow, Blueberry, Lily, Bear, Lucky and Peaberry in their harnesses. Jim led the gang through a large door into a great room with big screens for videos to teach about dog sledding, a wood stove, kitchen, and couches. The dogs bounced everywhere, including onto the table, couches and chairs as they passed through. Peaberry landed upside down on one couch and lay there with his long legs in the air. Mostly black and white Lily and Rainbow jumped on another couch and commenced to sing, howling in complementary tones, their ice-blue eyes shining as if they were smiling. Jim shook his head, suppressing a smile, "Clowns."

Once outside the dogs cavorted on the lawn, teasing the unharnessed dogs on the other side of the eight-foot fence. Jim led her to a long, low metal cart that was chained under a tree. "I stand in back where I steer and drive; it is specifically designed to give you the same sense as riding in a snow sled."

He led her to the front of the cart where a large hook attached to a long, blue line with many lines running off of it. "This is our gang line. We are going to put the lead dogs on first and then work our way back till the last dogs, the wheel dogs, are attached here by the cart. They will make lots of noise while we are harnessing because they are excited; sled dogs love to pull and love to take people for rides."

Jennifer looked up into his eyes and tried to let him know that she understood. How to do that? Finally she nodded. He winked at her and nodded back. Then silently he motioned with his hand to follow him.

One by one they hooked the dogs up, starting with Peaberry and Lucky in the lead positions. Luna and Stormina were the second pair, then Lily and Rose, and Rainbow and Flint in what is called the point positions; and finally Bear and Lioness took up the end, wheel positions. The dogs were leaping against their harnesses, barking, howling and trying to pull. Jim handed her some goggles. "Put them on and then climb in!" he yelled over the din.

Jennifer seated herself and grabbed hard onto the bars of her seat. Uncle Jim got on the back of the cart, checking the brakes and steering. Finally he leaned down and snapped off the cable holding the cart to the tree, yelling "Hike!" The dogs launched themselves forward. With a whoosh the landscape became a blur. It seemed as if the dog team had leapt into another dimension: all barking and singing stopped as the dogs focused on pulling in unison. "Haw, Peaberry, Haw!" Jim yelled as he signaled which trail he wanted Peaberry to take ahead of them as they entered the woods. "Good doggies!"

The dogs' speed slowed to a pace that they could maintain over a distance. "That may have been a bit fast for you. You okay?" called Jim.

With the surprise of the fast and powerful dog team take off, Jennifer's head still felt pinned against the high back of the wheeled cart. She tried to nod.

"Jen, I can't see if you are nodding or not. Because dog teams are not steered with reins, but by my commands, I have to keep my eyes on each one of the dogs and the trail. But I have to know if you are okay. So when I ask you something, if the answer is yes, just raise your right arm straight up. Okay?" Jim paused.

Jennifer raised her right arm up and then lowered it.

"Okay! And if the answer is no, just wave your right arm back and forth from left to right. I'll be able to see that. Okay?" he asked.

Jennifer raised her right arm and waved it back and forth.

"Great! Okay. Now just sit back, hold on, and enjoy yourself," he said.

Jennifer raised her arm in the "yes" sign. She heard Jim laughing behind her. She smiled; she liked him.

From the woods the trail entered a large meadow. The ground fell away gently to the right. In the distance was a line of mountains that disappeared in the horizon to the west. Jennifer had never seen anything so beautiful. She raised her right arm in the signal, "Yes!" She knew he could not see her smiling. She wished she had known her uncle sooner. Why had her father so disliked him?

"Yes! Magical! That's what I say, too. I agree it is beautiful. No matter how long I live here, or go out on the trails with the dogs, I feel a state of constant wonder in this part of Vermont," Jim said loudly over the whoosh of the cart's wheels, the dogs' footfalls, and panting.

Jennifer pushed her right arm up in the air again. Her black hair was blowing behind her. She felt a great sigh release from deep in her chest; she felt free. Uncle Jim laughed again.

The trail bent to the left into a pine forest. The wheels of the cart were quiet as they rolled over the smooth trail, the surroundings cool and silent, like a natural cathedral. Then they descended into a huge meadow with a large pond near the forest edge. They circled the pond and came to a halt near a wooden post set in the ground.

Jim set the brakes and jumped off the cart. He put his hand out to help Jennifer pull herself out of the cart. "Hop out quick and help me unhitch the dogs."

The dogs were huffing and panting loudly. Jennifer helped detach them from the gang and necklines. Each freed dog made a beeline for the pond and jumped in. Soon all ten dogs were in the pond, still wearing their harnesses, reveling in the water. Some stood near the shore and others paddled around happily.

"Looks wonderful, doesn't it?" he asked. "Would you like to go in, too?"

Jennifer looked at him quizzically. She looked down at her jeans, and then pulled at her long sleeves as she looked back at him.

"Well, maybe another day when you bring some shorts to change into. They are fun to swim with. Some of them will actually pull you through the water with their tails," he said.

Jennifer laughed. That would be fun. Then she frowned. Grace should be here, too. Her little stub of a tail would not be good for pulling anyone in the water, though. Maybe she could hold onto one of their tails, too. The image of Grace being towed through the water by Peaberry made her laugh again.

"Here, watch this." Jim walked to the edge of the water and started tossing biscuits to the dogs. They swam here and there; snatching treats from the water, looking like a school of furry, playful dolphins. Finally they left the pond to gather around Uncle Jim, gazing up at him with rapt attention. Luna came over to sit near Jennifer.

"Okay, everybody. Listen to me! Who wants to race for a treat?" Uncle Jim cocked his head comically as the Un-Chained Gang's furry faces looked up at him. Some wagged their tails.

"Okay, everybody! Are you ready?" They continued to stare at him.

"Here is the treat." Jim held the biscuit over his head. "Ready, set, race! Ta-da-ta-da! - Charge!" The dogs took off to the left to go around the pond. Peaberry, Lioness and Lily were soon in the lead. Rose and Rainbow dropped out, plunging back into the water. Flint leaped at a frog at the edge of the pond. Lucky, Bear, Blueberry and Stormina continued to chase after the leaders. At the far side of the pond Peaberry, Lioness, Lily, Stormina, Bear and Lucky ran flat out; they seemed to float through the air. Coming around the outside edge they ran straight towards Luna and Jennifer; she could not believe how fast they were.

The racing group veered, running past Jennifer and Luna, and skidding to a halt in front of Jim. It looked as if black and white, blue-eyed Lily had won. "Oh, I think it was close but Lily won. Here's a treat, Lily. But all of you ran so you all get treats!" Jim was laughing as he tossed out biscuits to the eager dogs. Luna ran over to get in on the giveaway.

"Luna, you couch potato! You didn't even try to run. Okay, here you go." Jim tossed her one.

Suddenly the main group was off again around the pond, while others paddled in the water. Jim walked over to Jennifer. "They really love this. This racing game is one of many antics they made up on their own. I didn't teach them this. Many of the guests who come for the educational tours can't believe it. I just know that they love going fast, and seem to love making people laugh, so they keep it up."

After a few more races around the pond, another swim to cool off, lots of treats and silly frolicking, Jennifer helped Jim harness the dogs back to the wheeled sled. The ride through the beautiful woods, pastures and pines was beyond anything that she could have imagined.

Back at the barn she helped Jim water the dogs and take off the harnesses. As Jennifer helped distribute a bowl to each, Uncle Jim explained that constant watering for working dogs was very important so that they would not become dehydrated. After throwing more treats to the dancing, clowning dogs, they returned them to their large outside pens. She helped hang the harnesses and take care of the cart and equipment. Jim disappeared and returned with a large glass of lemonade for each of them.

They sat side-by-side on the bench just outside of the barn door. Luna and Stormina had remained with them.

The lemonade was sweet and good. Homemade. Jennifer wished her dad could have seen how fast she had learned and how she had helped. It would have been wonderful if they could have done fun things like this together.

"So, how did you like it?" Uncle Jim asked.

She looked at the ground considering. Suddenly she put her right hand straight up in the air and smiled at him, green eyes wide as she could make them. She laughed.

He nodded and stretched his legs. "I guess you liked it."

"Okay, we have had enough fun for one morning. It's almost noon and I suspect that Sarah will have something for you to eat over at her cabin, so why don't you and Luna head over. I have business calls to make and lots of chores, but maybe I will see you later or for dinner." He got up and stretched and started off with Stormina.

Jim turned back. "You did good today. I sense you have talent with communicating with dogs; they like you, which is the biggest hurdle. If you want, you can come and learn more about dog sledding and help me with some dog chores. No pressure. But if you want to do more with the dogs, I think they will like that." He turned and headed off with Stormina, whistling as he went.

* * *

Sarah was on the covered porch of the log cabin. She had set a table with a white lace cloth, dishes and food. "I thought we could have lunch out here if you are hungry."

Luna and Jennifer ascended to a feast: plates of green salad topped with cherry tomatoes, red and yellow peppers; homemade corn muffins; another bowl of mixed fresh fruit; a bowl of rice mixed with black and green olives, chives, and dill; and glasses of iced tea. After drinking from a bowl of water near the door, Luna took her place near Jennifer, staring at her plate.

Her aunt sat quietly, looking up occasionally, smiling at Jennifer as they ate. The corn muffins tasted wonderful, as did the salads and fruit. Luna caught bits of muffin and fruit that Jennifer and Sarah tossed to her.

"I am going to do some work this afternoon. Maybe you and Luna would like to take that new camera out to test it. We have an extra laptop that you can download your pictures onto when you come back. We can look at them over dinner and see if Uncle Jim has any suggestions to help you as you are learning. Sound good?" Sarah asked.

Jennifer nodded. She and Luna spent the afternoon exploring and taking pictures of wildflowers, bugs, frogs and lichen on trees and rocks – they even got one of a red-tail hawk. They fell asleep in the cozy, wood-lined room under the cabin eaves after stargazing with her Aunt Sarah.

Chapter Two

Adventures can come to us through the circumstances of our lives, cycles of our dreams, books that we read, and tales that we are told. One must be ready for an adventure – it makes the difference between a dull life and one that rises to the best of the gifts that we are born with. The difference between adventure and catastrophe is in the heart and mind: those with hearts that seek truth and love always go on adventures, turning the challenges and pain of their lives into passages of learning and value. Thus we pray that love and truth be the constant focus of our minds and hearts, and that we are always ready to go on an adventure.

Book of The Wisdom Runners

"Hello, Popsi! Is that you?" Toni crooned. Lit cigarette in her free hand, she paced the floor holding a cordless phone to her ear. She burst into a screeching cackle, "Of course it's me, Toni! You always know!"

Listening to the voice at the other end, she used one of her blood-red, lacquered nails to poke a blond woman sitting on a leather sofa, watching MTV on a muted, sixty inch, flat-screen monitor. Smirking and snarling silently Toni pointed at her empty glass and mouthed, "NOW!"

"Oh, you are such a kidder, Popsi! I don't know where you get your jokes!" she rolls her eyes. "Ahhhhhhhhhh!" she screech laughed.

"Popsi, I am just calling because I needed to hear your voice again. Really, if you weren't so handsome I would wish you were my real father," she said taking the margarita the blond woman handed her.

"Popsi, I just can't take all this investigation. I don't want to think that Jennifer had anything to do with her father's death because when I came into the room, the patio doors were open; I am sure that it was a robbery gone wrong. But she was standing there with the gun… but, then, all of my jewelry and Saul's diamonds were gone so I am sure it was a robbery." Toni listened while taking a sip of her drink and dragging on her cigarette.

"Well, we can't do much of anything right now, with the girl refusing to talk," said Toni. "I know, I know, Popsi. Jennifer was always a strange girl; she always had her nose in a book and we could never get her to take interest in fashion like most girls her age. It couldn't have come from your side of the family. It had to be that mother of hers… just like with Jim and Sarah…" Toni took another sip and dragged on her cigarette as she paced.

"Well, of course they must be like their mother, they certainly aren't like you and Saul…" She mimed gagging to her friend as she listened and rolled her eyes, impatiently.

"I am sure that my trouble with the police and the state is because Jim and Sarah have been making allegations that aren't true. I need to talk to you about getting your help in letting the state know what bad characters they are…" Toni said.

"Of course I would love to visit you in Phoenix. I keep telling you how much I miss you…" She listened, rolling her eyes. "Oh, Popsi, I would love to take you up on the free plane ticket and come Thursday if Grandma Dodi has to go to see her daughter… No, I don't mind at all taking care of you while she is gone. We have been such good friends for years, Popsi. We'll have lots of fun."

"Okay, I'll take that early flight in two days, and grab a cab to your place. I'll pick up the ticket at the counter; you'll have them put it in my name? . . . Mmmmm, kisses and love to you, too," she said.

Hanging up, she looked around the room. "Who do you think you are?" she shrieked.

The blond woman gulped, frozen.

"Sally, you just don't get it, do you! God I HATE you!" She finished her drink in one gulp. "Get me another one!" Toni stormed to the window and looked out of it.

Sally returned with the drink and handed it to Toni. She took her own drink to the couch and sat down.

"Stupid! You didn't put enough tequila in this! Why can't you do anything right?" screamed Toni. Then her mind seemed to snap in a completely new direction. "What am I going to do for money?"

Sally hesitated. "I thought you were going to ask Popsi for money."

"You stupid idiot! Didn't you hear me asking him? Didn't you hear me say I would accept the plane ticket to come to visit him?" Toni glared at her.

Sally was silent. Like many Hollywood hangers-on, she put up with constant abuse just to have the opportunity to be near the famous. It was a price she was willing to pay.

"I leave the day after tomorrow for Phoenix. I will be gone for a few days. I'll call Detective Merlin, in a little bit, and let him know that I absolutely have to see Popsi because he is so old, frail and upset about the murder - and he misses his son, Saul, soooo much," cooed Toni. She took another pull on her drink. "Merlin will agree to it because he will know where I am."

"Will Popsi give you money?" asked Sally.

"Of course he will. He always does. And besides, how can he resist when he has a look at this! I've paid dearly for all these lifts and tucks!" smirked Toni, as she admired her figure in the long mirror over the couch.

"But he is married…" said Sally.

"And what should that matter? He is on his sixth wife. He took his first three wives for *their* money to make *his* fortune - and then the last two gold-diggers thought they would get his money; the joke was on them because they both died suddenly, and he cashed in on *their* large life insurance policies he had taken out on them."

Toni took another drag on her cigarette and took another gulp on her drink. Going to the mirror to admire her face again, arranging a few strands of her red hair she glanced in Sally's direction to see if she, too, was admiring what she saw.

"Saul and I made out great because Popsi laid a chunk of change on us when each wife snuffed it. This new one is a nasty, vicious, seventy-three year old alcoholic with an alcoholic daughter; they think they will take ol' Popsi and cut his children out of their part of the inheritance." She finished the drink and held the glass out to Sally for another refill.

"Ummmmm, shouldn't you slow down before calling the police detective?" asked Sally.

"Ummm, shouldn't you slow down before calling the police detective?" mimicked Toni. "You are an IDIOT!" she screamed.

Sally ran into the kitchen to make another drink while Toni lit another cigarette. "You listen to me, baby cakes. I'm packing my best. At the very least Popsi will leave all of his estate to his granddaughter, Jennifer, and me. And I WILL be the administrating guardian. I will make sure Sarah and Jim are cut out of the will. But if I have my way, that codger will divorce the old bat he is with and marry me. Then I'll cut out little Miss Stupid, Jenny, from her inheritance; I'll have all his money for me!"

Toni's eyes were starting to cloud from drinking since she had woken up. She was starting to weave and slur her words.

Her eyes fell on the sable and white corgi cowering in the corner. "Come here, Grace. Did Jennifer's little baby think mean, ol' stepmamma was yelling at her?"

The corgi looked at her doubtfully, her big, warm brown eyes searching Toni.

"Come, little baby, come to momma," Toni cooed.

Grace, nicely groomed, with a pink bandana, and a matching pink, rhinestone collar, pricked her ears forward and moved doubtfully toward Toni. The nub of her tail moved slightly to the left and right. "That's it, babykins, come to momma…" said Toni.

The corgi straightened up and walked towards her. Toni took aim and tried to land the toe of her shoe into Grace's side. With that force it would have sent the dog's short-legged, compact body across the room, but she dodged with a yelp and skedaddled behind the couch.

Toni laughed. "That stupid thing! I'd cut her throat! But right now she is the ticket I am using to get Jennifer back here!"

* * *

The air wafting through the window was fresh and clean; waking, Jennifer couldn't remember having dreams. Rubbing her feet together she heard thumping - it had to be Luna's tail. Opening her eyes she found Luna's nut-brown nose a few inches away from hers. She reached out and rubbed her head.

When they went downstairs the table was set with a platter of grilled cheese sandwiches and a bowl of blackberries. Propped on the milk bottle was a note:

Dear Jennifer,

Uncle Jim and I got a phone call last night after you fell asleep. We had to go to the lawyer in Burlington early this morning to sign some papers to counter a legal motion your stepmother has made with her lawyer. At the same time we are going to make another motion to have your dog, Grace, brought here. Please try not to worry - all of this is just legal formalities. Dale, Monty and Peter, the employees, are over at the barn working with the dogs. Wave hello to them and feel free to help them with chores and the dogs. I packed you a water thermos, trail-mix, sandwiches, fruit, cookies - and biscuits for Luna – so if you want to explore - go ahead! Put Luna on her pink leash so she doesn't run off. I packed a wind-up flashlight and your camera –

Have fun!
Your Aunt Sarah

Jennifer sighed. She and Luna were alone. Her father and stepmother often had left her alone for hours without a housekeeper or sitter. She was used to it. But somehow this felt different, like Aunt Sarah and Uncle Jim trusted her. She guessed that the employees had been instructed to watch her, but her aunt and uncle were giving her freedom.

Still, she was disappointed. She did not feel hungry despite the good food on the table. A light knock came at the door. A young, handsome man stepped in. Tall and solidly built, he had longish brown hair and hazel eyes. He smiled warmly. "Hey, Jennifer, I'm Monty. I work with your uncle."

Luna scooted across the floor to him as he tossed her a treat he took from his pocket. "Hey, Luna! You taking care of Jen?"

"I didn't want to bother you but I'm going to take a family on a dog tour soon. Dale, Peter and I will be in the barn and around the farm all day and evening until Jim and Sarah get back. You are welcome to hang out with us."

Jennifer looked at him shyly, then down at the floor. She wished she could at least say hello. Not being able to speak felt so awkward.

"Sarah said you might prefer Luna's company to ours – I don't blame you!" Monty hesitated then tossed Luna another biscuit. "Well, come on over to the barn if you feel like it!" Smiling, he turned and left.

Jennifer sat and picked at some food. She fed the bulk of it to Luna, tossing pieces high in the air and giggling as Luna jumped here and there to catch each morsel. After washing the dishes and placing them on the drain board next to the sink, they went out to explore.

The morning was bright and fresh. At the pond Luna went for a swim and paddled after treats that Jennifer threw into the water for her. Except for Luna's strong, white body swimming through the water, the surface was smooth, mirror like. The fluffy white clouds above in the clear blue of the Vermont sky reflected on the still water.

"As above, so below." That was a line from something archeologists had found written on stones they called the Emerald Tablets that were supposed to be three thousand years old. Jennifer loved to read everything she could find on archeology. She also loved to watch the documentaries on YouTube of Richard Dolan, Graham Hancock, David Wilcock and others who spoke of history being older than scientists had previously thought, and possible ties to ancient civilizations on other planets. They also talked about UFOs, ETs, portals to alternate realities and bridges across time to other planets.

She loved to study maps of the universe and look at photos of other galaxies on the Hubble Telescope website. With Grace by her side she would look at the beautiful photos and dream of being able to travel to them. Now she wondered if her father was somewhere up there in the sky, or on another galaxy, looking down on her. A tear slipped down her cheek.

"Woo-woo!" A dripping wet Luna stood before her. She brought her face close to Jennifer's, cocking her head as she studied her intently. She seemed to be trying to tell her something.

Luna woofed softly again, turned and started off at a trot, dragging her pink leash behind her in the tall grass. Jennifer picked up her blue backpack and ran to snatch the leash. "*Goodness*," she thought, "*I can't lose her. Aunt Sarah warned me that she might try to escape. What would I tell her if they got back and found I have lost Luna?*"

Tugging on the leash, Luna led Jennifer to a trail that ran along the side of the large field into the forest. As they entered the woods, the bright light of the morning faded through the filter of the leaves. The trail stayed level for a while and then descended to the old, heavily rutted road that Sarah had mentioned.

They followed the dirt road to a bridge that spanned a rapidly flowing stream below. Jennifer was surprised to find such a large, concrete structure in the forest; massive, it was twenty feet wide and thirty feet long, with no guardrail. With Luna beside her, Jennifer sat near the edge to watch the water as it danced over the rocks twenty feet below. As she watched and listened to the water, it seemed to pull the tension from her stomach and chest. Feeling a slight sense of peace, she leaned against Luna and shut her eyes.

Suddenly she fell onto her side as Luna lunged away. Jennifer scrambled to her feet as Luna's white, curled tail disappeared in the underbrush next to the bridge. Surprised, she tried to call Luna's name, but her throat tightened - no sound came out.

Luna's alto, 'woo-woo,' came from below. Peering over the side of the bridge, Jennifer could see the white dog standing there. Luna stared up at her, wagged her tail, woo-wooed again and sat down. Jennifer motioned with her hand for Luna to come. Luna gave her a short woof. Jennifer showed her a cookie, thinking Luna could be lured back. Luna simply sat and looked up at her.

Jennifer stomach did flip-flops and then squeezed tight. She could not return to the farm without Luna. On the other side of the bridge she found an opening in the brush to a path that dropped sharply down. Inching her way down, branches and brambles pulled at her hair, face and clothes. Trying to steady herself she grabbed a branch that broke and she slid to the bottom.

Jennifer felt her heart tearing. She would never see her father again. Who knew what Toni would do to Grace and if she would ever hug her again. She started crying. Life just never seemed to get better. Now if she lost Luna, her aunt and uncle would send her away for sure.

Pushing herself up, she found the path leveled out. She followed it towards the sound of the water. Luna was standing in the middle of the stream. No matter what Jennifer did with hand signals and offers of treats, the white dog refused to come to her.

She took off her new sneakers, put them in the backpack, and edged herself into the water. It wasn't deep but the water was cold; the bottom was covered with large, rounded, slippery rocks. Jennifer slowly worked her way towards Luna, hoping to grab the pink leash that dangled from her collar into the water. Each time she thought she could reach the leash, Luna hopped merrily upstream. Jennifer gingerly followed her, trying to keep her balance. On and on they went until they were almost under the bridge.

Peering through the darkness of the tunnel, Jennifer could barely see the sunlight and stream on the other side. The water under the bridge looked black; she couldn't see into its depths. Luna turned and started to walk through the darkness towards the other side. Jennifer swallowed hard. What might be living in the water under the bridge? She had never liked dark places. And when she would see her father acting in B horror movies, she would cry and cry when the dark scenes came on the screen because usually there was an ugly monster lurking. She would be afraid her father would die, and often he did in those movies. And now he was really dead.

"I have to be brave!" Jennifer jumped. Had she spoken out loud? No, surely she imagined it.

"I have to get over this! I have to catch Luna." She heard her voice but now knew it was in her mind.

Taking a big breath, she tried to hold down her fear. Slowly she inched into the tunnel. Her breath came sharp and shallow. She hoped she wouldn't fall over, getting the new backpack soaked, and even more that her toes didn't find something horrid and squishy on the bottom. But losing Luna was worse, so she followed Luna's white tail.

Breaking into the sunlight on the other side, Luna jumped onto a stretch of sand, shaking a spray of water from her fur. She lay down and started to roll back and forth, stretching her legs happily in the air. Jennifer rushed to climb out of the water, hoping to finally grab the pink leash while Luna was occupied.

Luna jumped up and danced away. "Not so fast, Jennifer!" came an alto voice. Laughter followed, echoing off the boulders at the edge of the stream and cement of the bridge. Jennifer jumped. She looked around to find who was speaking. There was no one there.

More laughter filled the air, but Jennifer still couldn't see where it was coming from.

Luna came back towards her and sat about fifteen feet away. Her eyes twinkled. She seemed to be humming. Jennifer felt her head spinning; she sank to her knees.

"Hey, don't pass out on me!" Luna came over wagging her tail. Her lips seemed to be moving. Could it be possible that she was talking?

"Yes, Jennifer, it's me. I am speaking." Luna sat and appeared to be smiling. Jennifer sat down, bringing her face to the same level as Luna's. She squeezed her eyes together and then opened them. Luna stared back.

"I'm still here and I'm still talking. Shutting your eyes is not going to make this go away." She smiled. At least Jennifer thought she did.

"Yup. I am smiling. And yes, I'm reading your thoughts." Luna smiled again.

"Would you like to speak to me? There are no other humans here who can hear you." Luna tilted her head while arching the white eyebrow over her right eye.

Jennifer shook her head.

"Hmmmm. I didn't think you would. But now I can hear your thoughts fairly clearly. On the other side of the portal, I can only get the general gist of what you are thinking. We are now in a land called Solaria. I can talk here. We got here by the tunnel under the bridge." Luna stared intently into Jennifer's eyes.

"Want to experience something cool?" asked Luna. Jennifer thought that maybe she was dreaming. Maybe she had fallen asleep on top of the bridge and would wake up from this.

"No, you are not dreaming. I'm really talking. But look! I am not moving my lips! I am thinking straight into your head." Luna laughed.

"Try it! Try thinking in words back to me!" She finished with a woof.

Jennifer looked at her. She rubbed her nose and considered. "*I don't know what to say to you,*" she thought.

"There you go! It's a start. You are probably a bit confused speaking with a dog. It simply isn't done on the other side of the portal, on Earth, by most humans," Luna said. "In Solaria, dogs are equal with humans."

Jennifer looked at her.

"On Earth, we dogs try to speak to you through your intuition, but most humans have that channel shut down in childhood." Luna rose and stretched.

"We can talk about this while we walk. Put your shoes back on. The morning is half over and we have a lot of traveling to do." Luna started off down a path next to the stream, her white tail curled tightly over her back.

Jennifer put on her sneakers and followed. The trail sloped upwards gently and then became steep. Luna walked easily but Jennifer had to lean forward, using her hands and arms to balance. Finally they emerged onto a grassy knoll. Luna sat. "How about a cookie? If I am not mistaken I also smell some sandwiches – almond butter and homemade cherry preserves with sunflower sprouts on Walnut flour bread, and Vermont Cheddar, honey mustard, Romaine and tomatoes on millet bread. Some of my favorites!"

Jennifer shrugged off her backpack. She wondered if Luna was right. Could a dog's nose be that exacting? Opening the pack she found Luna's nose had been correct. Jennifer found she was really hungry. Together they enjoyed a delicious lunch.

Luna stood and gave Jennifer's face a lick. "I am really glad that you are hearing me. I'm excited that you are my new friend. Come on, let's get going." Jennifer shouldered her backpack and walked across the field beside Luna.

Jennifer felt shy. Suddenly being able to communicate with

someone after being in silence for so long was strange. *"Ummm, where are we going?"*

"Jen, we are on an adventure. My talking is likely the least of the surprises you will be getting today," Luna said as she looked across the long field.

Jennifer nodded. She wanted to ask Luna if Aunt Sarah and Uncle Jim would be mad to find them missing, but she didn't want Luna to think she didn't trust her. So she tried to keep her thoughts on this quiet.

Jennifer saw a row of forms in the distance where the forest met the grass of the knoll. As they got closer she saw large, adobe ovens. Black smoke billowed from them. Small voices yelled, "Help! Help! Help us!"

Bass voices insisted, "Help us! Our bread is burning! Help us!"

"Hurry Jen! They need help!" Luna took off at a gallop. Jennifer pursued as fast as she could.

They arrived at seven ovens that looked like the coal-fired pizza ovens Jennifer had seen in Los Angeles. "Help! Help! Help us, pleaassse!" yelled little high voices.

"Jennifer – it's the loaves of bread baking! They are starting to burn! Quick, you have hands! I don't! Grab that bread paddle and get them out!" Luna shouted.

Jennifer threw off her hat and backpack. Grabbing a wooden paddle, she ran to the first oven. Shoving the paddle in she scooped out the loaves. Placing them on a nearby table she ran to the next oven, and then the next; finally she had seventy loaves out of the ovens safely.

"Ohhhh, thank you!" said seven ovens in their bold, bass voices. "The Keepers of the Ovens ran off when the shadows attacked them. Our bread would have burned."

"Thank you!" said seventy tiny bread loaf voices in unison.

Jennifer turned to Luna and thought, "*What is going on*?"

"Trouble," said Luna. She turned to the ovens. "You said that the shadows were here?"

"Yes, Luna," answered one of the ovens. "The shadows have been lurking since you were last in Solaria."

"I am sorry to hear that; for centuries this area has been undisturbed. This is my new friend, Jennifer. I will have her take the tarp and cover the loaves to protect them. Hopefully the Keepers of the Ovens will be back soon," said Luna.

"Hello, Jennifer!" called seventy high, and seven bass, voices. "Thank you!"

Jennifer took a tarp and started to cover the bread. "Luna, these are Talking Loaves, as you know. We are sure the Keepers of the Ovens will return – but please take seven of the loaves with you to Zumulia for safe keeping," asked one of the ovens.

"Jen, choose seven of those loaves and put them in your backpack," said Luna. Jennifer felt strange picking up talking loaves of bread and tucking them away like her lunch. "Don't worry, we won't be eating them," laughed Luna.

"I was afraid to ask what we are going to do with them," thought Jennifer.

"I'll explain it to you later. We must get moving if the shadows have been around," said Luna.

Luna said goodbye to the ovens and then led Jennifer on the trail into the forest, setting a quicker pace than before. Soon they came to a large clearing where they heard more voices, "Help, help, help us!"

Jennifer saw trees with branches filled so heavily with ripe apples that they were touching the ground. It was the trees that were calling out.

"Quick, Jen!" Luna ran to a tree and jumped on one of the branches, shaking some of the apples free. Following her example, Jennifer ran to a laden branch and started to shake it to knock more apples loose. Branch by branch they worked together until the branches were upright on all the trees of the orchard. Jennifer filled the bushel baskets, stacked nearby, with the apples.

Exhausted, Luna and Jennifer collapsed to the ground. Luna

had an apple between her paws and took a bite out of it. Jennifer was horrified.

"Don't worry," sighed Luna. "The trees were the ones calling. Not the apples; they don't talk. Delicious, by the way!"

"Thank you," called the trees.

"You're welcome!" said Luna. "What is going on? Where are the Keepers of the Orchards?"

"The shadows attacked them - they ran to hide," said the trees.

"The Keepers of the Ovens were also attacked." explained Luna. "Do you have any news?"

"Just whispers through the trees of the forest. Sometimes the winds brought tales that gave us fear and doubt. We didn't know if the tales of animals being attacked or disappearing were true," said the apple trees.

Luna added, "We are traveling on to Zumulia's Keep. We are carrying seven Talking Loaves to her for their safety. We will tell her of the trouble here and see if she knows more."

The apple trees shivered. "Bring her our news and give her our 'Hail!' Please take her as many apples as you can carry. There are some burlap bags under the tables."

Luna supervised Jennifer as she filled four bags and tied them by their necks by twos. She had Jennifer sling a pair over her shoulders, tied by twine to her collar. Jennifer slung the other set over her right shoulder, steering clear of the backpack. They said their goodbyes and set off again. Soon they entered a pine forest.

After a half hour's walk, the forest opened into a very large clearing. In front of them stretched a field of grass, enclosed by stone walls. To the right was a field of corn. Further on rose a two-story cabin, with a thatched roof, surrounded by a profusion of flowers. On a bench in front of the home sat a tall, older woman.

Luna bounced towards her happily, despite carrying the sacks of apples on her shoulders. Her white tail curled tightly over her back, waving back and forth as she got closer to the lady who rose to meet her. There was a frenzy of patting, woofing and praising.

As Jennifer drew close the woman looked up and watched her approach. She was tall, large boned, and seemed physically strong, despite her age. Her steel-grey hair hung in thick braids down her front, tied at the ends with ribbons that held heavy silver ornaments. Her shirt and pants were faded denim. She wore a battered straw hat that couldn't hide her large, emerald-green eyes; other than her own, Jennifer had not seen such green eyes.

"Hello, Jennifer." The woman's voice was deep. "I have been expecting you. I am glad that my friend Luna has brought you along."

"How did this woman know we were coming?" thought Jennifer to Luna.

"I have known for years that you would visit here," came the woman's voice into her head. *"I am Luna's friend, Zumulia. Welcome to my Keep."* Her eyes seemed kind.

Jennifer looked at her, surprised. She nodded, then quickly pulled the bags of apples from her shoulder and offered them to Zumulia.

"We have brought you apples from the orchards and seven infant Talking Loaves from the bread ovens. The ovens have asked that you keep the loaves safe," said Luna. "The shadows have attacked the Keepers of the ovens and apple orchards."

"Come inside." said Zumulia. "We can speak safely."

They entered a dark, cool home. The floor was made of large red-clay tiles covered with woven rugs. Stuffed chairs, couches, and wood rockers surrounded a stone fireplace that was so large an adult could walk into it. On the far wall sat a sink, counters and brick ovens. Drying herbs hung in bunches everywhere from the rafters, like at Aunt Sarah's. The home seemed centuries old.

After washing up, Luna and Jennifer sat in stuffed chairs pulled up to a massive dining table. Zumulia dished out bowls of vegetable stew and placed a plate of scones next to pitchers of fresh-pressed apple juice and water. The spoons, knives and forks had carved, silver running dogs for handles, their eyes set with gemstones.

As they ate, Luna and Zumulia spoke quietly about the shadows' attack on the Keepers, the whisperings that had been heard through the trees and rumors that the animals and birds of the forest brought to Zumulia. Afterwards they went out to a grape arbor where they drank mugs of steaming tea made of ginger, cloves and cinnamon, laced with honey.

Balancing her mug on the chair arm, taking occasional laps of tea, Luna listened to Zumulia. Jennifer felt sleep coming on as she rested in her chair. Suddenly she remembered her aunt and uncle; she panicked and sat upright.

Zumulia turned to her. "It's alright Jen, your aunt and uncle are not worried yet. You have entered a land called Solaria. Time is different here; sometimes faster and sometimes slower than on Earth. Right now it is much slower so you do not have to be concerned. For the present, you may spend the night here and rest; only a few minutes will have passed on your uncle's Vermont farm. Finish your tea and Luna will show you up to your room where you can spend the night."

Luna led her up the carved, wood staircase to a cozy, airy room with a four-poster bed covered with quilts. Just like the drying herbs, this reminded her of Sarah's home in Vermont. "You'll find pajamas in the dresser. I'll come curl up with you later." Jennifer knelt down and hugged her tightly.

"Jen…"

"Hmmmm?" Jennifer moved back to look at Luna.

Luna looked into her eyes, gently. "I know about Grace and how much you miss her."

"You do? . . . How do you know? How is she?" Tears started to well in Jennifer's eyes.

"I don't know Grace. But dogs have ways of knowing about things that many humans on Earth do not. I know that Grace loves you and misses you. For now she is safe. Your Uncle Jim and Aunt Sarah are good people. Trust that they will do all they can to bring Grace to Vermont as soon as they can."

Jennifer buried her face in Luna's soft furred neck and didn't let go until she stopped sobbing.

When Luna went downstairs, Jennifer changed into soft cotton pajamas she found in the top drawer of the oak dresser. She thought about this surprising world with talking dogs, ovens, trees and bread loaves. Time being different just like Albert Einstein and other scientists said it could be. Luna had given her news of Grace and now real hope that she would see her again. Soon she fell asleep.

* * *

Luna was not in bed when Jennifer woke. For a moment she felt frozen with fear that Luna had not returned last night. Then she saw the pillow next to her imprinted with Luna's round, curled form and a few stray white hairs. Hearing a soft buzz, she turned to see humming birds hovering in mid-air, waiting their turn at a bright red, glass feeder outside the window.

When Jennifer came downstairs; she found the table in the great room set with silver, covered platters. One held sweet-smelling carrot muffins, another scrambled eggs, and the last held a melody of cooked peas, zucchini, and butternut squash. Pots of honey, butter, maple syrup and yogurt sat next to a bowl with apples and pears and a pitcher of carrot juice. She was fascinated by the handles on the platter covers: large, standing dogs, made of silver with sparkling jeweled eyes, they were like the handles of the silverware, but much grander.

"Mmmmmm, isn't this a delicious feast?" came a high voice.

Through the dim, morning light Jennifer saw one of the rescued loaves of bread. It was perched on a wrought iron stand hanging from one of the beams. It had grown eyes, ears and a nose on one corner of its rectangular, loaf form.

"Luna says you are new to Solaria. I guess you don't have Talking Loaves where you come from. We develop slowly. My face developed overnight. The legs and arms won't be here till tomorrow," said the loaf.

Jennifer continued to stare.

"My name is Millet. I am made with millet flour, sunflower seeds, walnuts and dill. But the main ingredient that my bakers use is love! I hope we get to be friends," he smiled sweetly at her.

"You'll start to get used to differences here in Solaria. Soon you won't be surprised," said a voice from behind her. She turned to see a boy, perhaps of fourteen or fifteen. Tall and lanky, he had long, dark-blond hair hanging to his waist. A lock on the left side was braided with silver bells and trinkets hanging along its length. His eyes were large and blue, set wide over an aquiline nose.

Smiling, he crossed the room and sat himself in the stuffed chair across from her. He reached for a carrot muffin. Jennifer's eyes followed his arm as it reached – he looked strong, the muscles of his arms were long and ropey. He carried himself with a dignity and wisdom beyond Earth-born boys of fourteen; yet there was a wildness to him, as if he had spent his life running through the forest and fields, freely, without rules. "I'm David, by the way; Zumulia's grandson. I'm told you're Jennifer, Luna's friend."

Jennifer nodded. She took another bit of her muffin. Did he know she could not speak? Could he read thoughts like his grandmother and Luna?

"Luna and Zumulia have gone to see if they can find out more about the trouble you ran into yesterday." David took a bite of the carrot muffin. Like the one she was eating it had visible chunks of carrot, walnuts, and pineapple. "My grandmother is a great cook and baker. She says that we can't have a good life unless we have natural, homemade food from happy plants and trees."

David tapped on the lids of one of the silver platters. "Get some veggies into you because you'll want to keep growing that body of yours. In case you haven't noticed, you are a bit short and scrawny." His blue eyes twinkled; his pursed lips held back a grin.

Jennifer studied her plate as she blinked back tears.

David drew in his breath. "Hey, I'm sorry. Luna said you have had some tough times - and Solaria is new to you. I am sorry about your father by the way..."

Jennifer nodded. She willed herself not to cry. She tried to breathe deeply. David was trying to be nice. She wished she could answer him.

David cleared his throat. "I am sorry if I was too abrupt. We don't get many visitors, so sometimes I speak what's on my mind. It's been awhile, but both of my parents are dead, which is why I live with my grandmother."

Jennifer nodded.

"Let's eat!" David finished his muffin and started on another.

They sat in silence as they ate. Millet hummed softly from his perch in the shadows. Jennifer ate the eggs; they had been cooked with fresh chives, black olives and herbs - they were delicious. Jennifer took a second helping.

After finishing several platefuls of eggs and muffins, David stood. "Fill your thermos with water. We are going out in the gardens. There is lots of work to do before Zumulia and Luna return."

Jennifer grabbed her straw hat from a peg by the door and followed David out through a covered porch. When they reached an area with rows of corn he stooped to pick up baskets and handed her one.

"Don't worry. This corn does not talk. If you are someone with plant sensitivity you might be able to communicate with it, but it won't speak out loud like Talking Loaves do. And not all bread speaks here, by the way. Some of it we eat." He chuckled.

Jennifer nodded. She had been worrying that she might have to eat talking food.

David showed her how to slightly open the husk around the ears of corn to see if they were ripe enough to pick or if they should be left for later. "I can't read your mind like Zumulia and Luna can. If you want me to stop just raise your arm and wave it back and forth. Okay?" he asked.

Smiling, Jennifer looked at him, raising her arm straight up in the "yes" sign that her uncle had taught her.

David laughed. "Well, someone's been teaching you to communicate. Must have been a dog person. Maybe that Uncle Jim of yours?"

Jennifer raised her right arm in an animated salute again. She laughed. She felt happy standing under the blue sky in the corn patch with her new friend. She was thousands of miles away from Los Angeles and the trouble there. She stopped smiling when she realized that she was also in a new world and did not know how to return to her aunt and uncle's farm.

David and Jennifer spent the afternoon gathering ripe vegetables, weeding and caring for plants. David tried to share as much knowledge as he could; he was a patient teacher. Finally, tired from leaning over, squatting, digging and carrying, they went to a nearby pond to swim and cool off.

* * *

Luna and Zumulia were seated in front of the cabin when they returned. A platter of tomato and lettuce sandwiches, zucchini soup, green salad, figs and sliced apples sat on the table. Jennifer eyed the cheesecake topped with wild strawberries for dessert.

"Sit down, you two. We have many things to talk over," said Zumulia.

They each sat down and waited quietly. Although the food looked good, Jennifer felt anxiety clutching her again, chasing away her hunger.

"We traveled to the Lake of Sleoden. A group of Wisdom Runners live there: a man named Samuel and twenty-six dogs," Luna began.

"What are Wisdom Runners?" asked Jennifer.

"Jennifer, Solaria is in a parallel reality to the one that your planet, Earth, and your universe exist in. You came through a portal, one of many from Earth, that lead here," Zumulia explained. "The Order of Wisdom Runners are a group of humans, dogs and horses that are dedicated to protecting Solaria. It takes years of training to enter the Order; only very special beings are chosen to become members."

"Are you and Luna Wisdom Runners?" asked Jennifer.

"I am, Jennifer," said Luna.

"And I am not. I am a Seer. The Order of Seers works closely with the Wisdom Runners. We specialize in seeing the future, interpreting dreams, communicating across distances; we also work with plants and herbs and the Healing Arts. Both of our groups are dedicated to seeking truth and preserving the presence of light and love in Solaria," explained Zumulia.

Jennifer considered and then looked at David. "*And David?*"

"My daughter, Tumilia, was David's mother. She and her husband, Zarcourt, were both Wisdom Runners and Seers, a rare combination. They were killed, fighting for our safety, eight years ago. David has not yet started training in either Order," said Zumulia.

Jennifer looked at David. *"He can't hear me. Please tell him that I am sorry about his parents."*

Luna relayed Jennifer's sympathy. David nodded to her. Then he asked, "How is Samuel and the pack?"

"We don't know because they weren't there," answered Luna.

"His place was swept clean and not in the usual disarray that Samuel leaves when he is out foraging for the day or visiting a friend for a few days. All of his gear, winter and warm weather, was gone. The dogs, the harnesses and the winter sleds were gone, too," said Luna.

"But it's summer!" said David.

Luna looked down at the mug of tea in front of her.

"David, there was something far worse. On our way there we found Glacier, Luna's brother," said Zumulia. "He was dead. It looked like he had been in quite a fight before he died. He must have gotten the best of his attackers because his collar was still around his neck with a case and a note inside."

"Glacier was never the brightest of sled dogs," said Luna. "Jim gave him to a neighbor when he was a year old because he never got the hang of pulling a dog sled; Jim wanted him to have a good home. Then Glacier's jaw was shattered, almost killing him, when a hunter accidently shot him. Peaberry, Lioness and members of our pack got him through the portal to Zumulia, who was able to help him heal. But he was never able to learn to speak. Although he understood what was being said to him he could never speak audibly or intuitively to humans, dogs, or other beings here in Solaria." Luna paused for a moment.

"Glacier had the biggest, kindest heart; he loved it here. He would do anything for Samuel, the dog pack and Solaria. He died trying to get a message to us," Luna said.

They sat in silence. Jennifer was sad that Luna's brother was dead. She wanted to hug her but felt frozen, the sadness for her father ached in her. And what of the man, Samuel, and his dogs disappearing? This was very bad news.

"What does the note say?" asked David.

"I wish we had it to show to you but it burned completely as Zumulia read it. Samuel used some of his herbs and oil on it so that if it did get into wrong hands, it would not stay there," said Luna.

"I read it as fast as I could. Samuel said that the shadows had been lurking nearby. He thought they had killed some of the friendly squirrels and beaver. He wasn't sure, as he could not find them or their bodies. There have been strange whispers coming from the lake and he and the dogs had forebodings. They received warnings from the Keepers of the Ovens and Orchards that they were in hiding - fearing to return to their work," said Zumulia.

She continued, "Samuel wrote that after Glacier came to us with the note, he was to find him to give any instructions or news that we might have. The dogs and he were going to search for Contalia and Dohanos."

"Jennifer, about fourteen months ago two of our Wisdom

Runners left Solaria, to a conference hosted by beings called The Servers of Light; they are in another alternate reality. They have not returned," Luna explained.

"Their names are Contalia and Dohanos. The Servers of Light, whom they were meeting with, dedicate their lives to bringing light and love to all creation through all planes of existence. We believe that something happened to our Wisdom Runners when they tried to return to Solaria," said Zumulia. She paused to sip on her tea, considering.

Jennifer gripped her toes tightly and looked at Luna. Although Luna had just found her brother Glacier dead, she was steady and appeared focused on what seemed to be the bigger picture of what needed to be done. Jennifer took a deep breath and wished she could be as steady.

"There have been strange happenings in Solaria. There has been darkness growing on the planet Earth and the universe that your planet lies in. This darkness is evil that has been leaking and infiltrating into our parallel reality. This should not be happening. The whole balance of order in creation is shifting because of what is happening on Earth. It has reached a point where we now fear for all life in all parallel realities..." said Zumulia. She gazed off across the gardens.

Luna continued. "There is a saying, 'As above, so below.' The opposite is also true: the negative or positive in the "below" can effect the above. This parallel reality vibrates on a higher, more positive level than what is found on Earth. Solaria has been mostly trouble free - except when things have been their darkest over the centuries in your reality."

Jennifer shivered. That phrase, "As above, so below" was the one she had been thinking of when Luna and she had been at the pond on Uncle Jim's farm before this adventure to Solaria had begun. What did that mean?

"Jennifer, in the private school your father sent you to, you had tutoring in mathematics and physics. Did you get a certain understanding of the difference between Einstein's physics and Quantum Mechanics?" Luna cocked her head to the right.

Jennifer nodded. It was strange to be discussing physics outside of school. One of her favorite documentaries was "What the Bleep?" She loved the idea that the physics theory, called the Theory of Everything, said that there were eleven planes of existence, or more, beyond what humans knew on Earth; and that at the level of particles, which were finer than atoms or electrons, the past, present and future all happened at once. She also knew of studies that there were parallel realities to what people on earth lived in.

Luna continued, "Jennifer, we really thought that there would be time to explain to you about Solaria and train you before we asked you to take part in any protective action that we felt was necessary here. Certainly we hoped that you would have had time to heal from the trauma you have lived through with your father's death," Luna said.

"But we have to take action right now; I am a Wisdom Runner and I must try to find Samuel because he is a fellow Wisdom Runner, as are his dogs. I hope that I will be able to fill in the details as we journey and give you some of the training that you and David need," said Luna.

Luna studied both of them. "Jen, I know that you are worried about Jim and Sarah, but as Zumulia started to explain last night, time does not work the same here. It can be faster and it can be slower; right now it is much slower. But even if time passes so that both of us are missed on Earth, and even if we never make it back, you have to believe me when I say this is more important than ever seeing Jim and Sarah again."

Luna's eyes held Jennifer's.

Something shifted in Jennifer. Suddenly she knew deep inside that she had to be here. It was beyond her mind's rational comprehension. Her heart seemed to have grown a voice; it was speaking to her and she could hear it and understand it, just like Luna and Zumulia could hear her. Her heart was saying, "YES! YES! You must do this!"

She did not know why, but somehow this mission that Luna was asking her to go on was tied into something bigger than her. It had something to do with "as above, so below," and the fascination she had had with the stars, archeology, the Egyptian pyramids, physics and the many phenomena about UFOs and things that could not be explained. It might also give her some answers about her father's death and where he was now. She had to be here and do whatever she could to help her new friends.

Looking back into Luna's eyes, she thought the one word her heart was shouting, "*Okay!*"

Luna woofed. "Great! Now we can make plans to leave early in the morning, before the sun comes up."

"I will prepare food, tools and equipment for the three of you," said Zumulia.

"Isn't Zumulia going to come with us?" asked Jennifer.

"I am the Seer that guards this corner of Solaria and the portal to Vermont. From here I can aid you in ways that I could never do if I was traveling with you. And I must be here if others need aid, send messages, or if Samuel and the dogs come back," said Zumulia.

"Why don't you go back to Vermont to bring Peaberry and some of the other dogs here? They are skilled Wisdom Runners. Some could stay to protect and aid my grandmother, and some could go with us," asked David.

"There is no time for this. The time differences between Earth and Solaria can fluctuate suddenly and greatly. Samuel could travel months ahead… or be hurt or dead by the time Peaberry gets here. We cannot risk it," said Zumulia. "Trust me, I know I will be okay and will somehow get word to him if it is necessary."

"Okay. Agreed. Where are we going to go?" David asked.

"We should track Samuel north because we sense that is the direction he has taken. We will head towards the Keep of Justin Valor where we think that he will go first. If we don't find Samuel we will relay our news to Justin Valor, Tuvalla, the Seers and Wisdom Runners at their Keep," said Luna.

Zumulia explained, "Communicating by intuition – Jennifer, you may have heard it called psychic communication or distance communication - is clouded right now. Messages don't get through, or the growing dark forces can attack and invade the communicators. This is why Samuel tried to send Glacier with a written message."

They spoke on as Zumulia prepared and packed food and supplies. She finally shooed them to bed so that she could spend time in prayer and meditation, trying to get guidance, receive or send communications to Samuel and the lost Wisdom Runners.

* * *

Chapter Three

There are times when Wisdom Runners are called to go forth and find the truth when life is endangered. But darkness confuses us; often there is a rift between the facts before our eyes and what we sense in our hearts. If we choose to journey it must be with faith that our devotion to truth and light is guiding us. Thus we pray to know when the knowing in our hearts needs to be pursued - and the courage and sense to follow it.

Book of The Wisdom Runners

It was dark when they arose. Zumulia had not received any messages from Samuel, other Seers or Wisdom Runners during her long vigil the previous night. She had perceived that a thick sense of confusion was growing on Earth and Solaria; it clouded individuals' judgment and ability to make wise decisions. Readying for the journey, they ate, then gathered their packs and sleeping rolls. Luna had a special pack with a chest strap that easily released to free her should there be danger and a need to defend them.

David carried a bow and three quivers of arrows, a slingshot, a hunting knife and a short sword that fit in a scabbard at his waist. He also brought a beautiful harmonica that he pocketed and a shepherd's lyre that he attached to his pack. "We can have some great entertainment on our journey and at the campfire at night," joked David. He winked at Jennifer.

Zumulia brought lighter versions of David's weapons and tools for Jennifer. "I know you don't know how to use them, but David can teach you some basic skills while you are on the trail."

Jennifer ran her fingers over the slingshot, knife and short sword. She had only ever seen the guns her father loved to own. A gun had killed him. It had not crossed her mind when she agreed to the adventure – the mission – that weapons would be involved. She had known that there would be danger, but now, in the early hours of the morning, she did not know if she could learn to use weapons. But the knowing in her heart that she had to help Luna was still strong; she would just wait to see about the weapons.

Outside the cabin Zumulia hugged them and laid her hands on their heads; she pronounced blessings in a language that Jennifer did not understand, but found tonally beautiful. They left by the trail behind the cottage; Zumulia's tall figure fading into the darkness as they entered the forest.

They walked for an hour in silence through the darkness. Luna led, with Jennifer in the middle, and David a few paces behind. Slowly, as the sun came up, the light filtered through the high treetops, allowing them to see the trail ahead of them. When they came to a fast-moving stream, Luna broke stride and went to the water's edge. After carefully sniffing the ground and the surface of the water, she pushed her white muzzle in, taking a long drink.

David bent to the stream to drink and motioned to Jennifer to do the same. When their thirst was satisfied, Luna spoke. "If my directional sense and calculations are correct, the trail that Samuel and his dogs may have followed will meet with this trail about an hour's walk from here. I haven't seen, smelled, or sensed anything dangerous or amiss."

A high-pitched sneeze brought them to attention; David and Luna carefully scanned the woods around them. Then two more sneezes rapidly followed, coming from Luna's pack. A small hand reached out, undid the buckle holding the pouch strap, then a loaf of bread emerged; it was Millet. He jumped to the ground on his newly grown legs and feet.

"How did you get in there?" asked Luna in her lowest alto tones. She crouched down so that she was muzzle to nose with Millet.

"I could tell you that Zumulia packed me but you would know I wasn't telling the truth. All of us heard you from the pantry last night and I got elected to sneak into your pack," said Millet.

"We can't protect you out here! Zumulia is going to be very angry with you and your brothers and sisters. The Keepers of the Ovens can only bake Talking Loaves at special times when the energy is right. With all the dangers around you never should have done this!" said Luna.

"Oh, I know. But really, I will try to be good. And you know Talking Loaves have always gone along for adventures in the past. We are very important!" pleaded the Talking Loaf.

Luna turned to Jennifer. "Three years ago all of the Talking Loaves in Solaria suddenly died. No one knew why or how. These are the first born since that time."

Jennifer looked at Millet. He smiled, then wiped it from his face as he turned back to Luna with pleading in his eyes.

"Enough! You are a very bad, young rascal!" Luna growled. "When Talking Loaves are grown they know all the recipes for baking the food that is eaten in Solaria. On journeys they know where to gather wild food. No house goes hungry when they are with us and no traveler ever lacks for a nutritious meal. But that is when they are mature and you, youngling, are not!"

David was chuckling. "I know why you are angry, Luna."

He turned to Millet. "You are a very bad little bread loaf, Millet. You could easily die out here and the people of Solaria really need you and your knowledge. However, we can't take you back right now, so we will have to make the best of it."

Millet smiled. "Can I ride on your shoulder, David?"

"We should make you ride in the pack so that no buzzard comes down and absconds with you!" said Luna.

"No, please, no!" pleaded Millet. "I promise to be good. Besides, I can learn lots by riding on David's shoulder.

David put his arm out to Millet as one would do inviting a parrot to perch. Millet climbed up and ran onto David's shoulder and took hold of a lock of his long, blond hair to stabilize himself.

"Luna, I think that he knows what he has done is wrong. Let him ride along with me? I don't mind." David asked.

Luna cocked her head to the side. "Okay. Millet, just try to stay safe. If anything happens you are to run for cover and not come out until you are absolutely certain that it is safe. Understood?"

"Yes!" said Millet.

"Okay, then let's get going," said Luna.

The four set off across the stream. Millet chattered away, sending the travelers into giggles and laughter.

* * *

When the trail from the Lake of Sleoden met the main trail, they stopped. Luna had them take off their packs for a stretch and a meal before the trailhead. She did not want them to go further as a group because they might track their scent onto any scent or physical clues, like foot or paw prints, which could tell them if Samuel and the dogs had passed through the path they were traveling.

When they felt rested, Luna rose. "Okay, Jennifer and Millet sit here while David and I do some tracking. David, let me go first and then you can start to look for visual clues when I get about thirty feet ahead." Luna, nose to the ground, went off slowly as if walking a grid.

They watched as Luna sniffed the ground on the trails and five feet on either side. She carefully examined each spot, spending extra time on some. Carrying his bow, fitted with an arrow at ready, David followed behind her. Finally Luna sat down and called to them. "Nothing so far. I'll keep searching the main trail and then

I will search in the forest to see if they were trying to cover their tracks."

Millet and Jennifer watched them search. Luna continued tracking scent down the main trail and then disappeared into the underbrush. David, tall and lithe, moved like a dancer as he scanned the ground, plants on either side of the trail, and up into the branches of the trees.

"Mmmmm, I know you don't speak right now and I'm not intuitive for human thought yet. But would you like to know about plants?" Millet asked.

Jennifer nodded. Her green eyes watched him curiously.

"Do you see those plants over there? The brown ones with the white flecks?" he asked.

Jennifer peered into the underbrush and then nodded.

"The powder on the underside tastes like cheddar cheese; it's really good on greens and salads." Grabbing a lock of Jennifer's black hair, as if it were a strap on a metro bus, Millet leaned out to make eye contact. He grinned.

"I really like you, Jen! Why don't we go gather some food so we can surprise them at dinner? I want Luna to know that I can be useful, too," said Millet.

Leaving the packs on the trail, Jennifer and Millet waded into the forest. The plant powder did taste like cheddar. Jennifer filled her pockets.

"Oh, look! Those are blackberry bushes. Let's get some!" Millet was excited.

Jennifer lined the inside of her straw hat with her bandana to use as a bucket. The berries were huge and very sweet. A few minutes into picking she thought she saw something moving to the left of her. She looked carefully, but could see nothing.

"What's the matter?" asked Millet.

Jennifer shook her head. Then the air seemed to move again to their left.

A crash came in the branches above; Jennifer went into a crouch.

The air suddenly felt very cold. Her pounding heart whispered to her that something was very wrong. Dropping her hat, she reached up for Millet and clutched him to her chest.

Another crash came from above. Jumping up, Jennifer ran towards the trail, cradling Millet with one arm, as she fended off the branches, snapping at her face, with the other. Something heavy landed behind her with a thud and gave chase. An opening ripped through the blockage in her chest and throat - she started to scream.

Gaining the trail, Jennifer and Millet fled in the direction Luna and David had taken. Still screaming she saw David turn to face her. As Jennifer ran, his arrow flew over her head, making a whizzing noise. Whatever was pursuing her was getting closer. Another arrow flew over her head and then another. And another.

Luna broke out of the underbrush, teeth bared, growling almost to the level of a roar, she ran past Jennifer as David continued to loose arrows with his bow. "Keep running, Jennifer!" Luna yelped and then resumed growling.

Jennifer ran past David and then turned. Directly in front of Luna was a deep, deep darkness. She couldn't see through where it was and yet it was not completely opaque; it shimmered strangely – it was as if the trail behind it had disappeared. It rose until it was upward of fifty feet taller than the treetops. A strange sucking, whirling sound came from it. The sound made Jennifer's stomach churn.

Luna held her ground, appearing to grow larger, her white fur sending off luminous sparks. She began howl-singing in the same language that Zumulia had used in her blessings when they left in the dark of the early morning. Rising up on her hind feet as she sang, streams of rose and golden light poured from her mouth as her fur continued to send off sparks.

Suddenly the darkness seemed to vibrate. It drew back from the touch of the light that Luna emitted. Then it grew smaller and seemed to disappear all at once, leaving behind an eerie silence.

Luna's fur continued to stand up along her spine, as she appeared to shrink to her normal size. She kept staring at the place where the darkness had been. Finally, she turned and walked toward where David, Millet and Jennifer stood. David lowered his bow as his eyes continued to search the branches above them.

Luna looked around carefully and then sat down. "Jennifer, are you and Millet alright?"

Jennifer nodded. Millet seemed frightened into silence.

"Did you two go off the trail?" Luna demanded.

Jennifer nodded again. Millet shook.

"I assumed you would know to stay put. I should have thought to warn you," explained Luna. "We are in danger, now, more than before; that shadow has gone to warn whatever controls it. David, see if you can find your arrows on the trail because we are going to need them."

David walked down the path, still scanning the woods as he looked for his arrows. He found all but one.

"Jennifer, where is your hat?" Luna asked.

Jennifer pointed into the woods in the direction that she and Millet had walked. Millet stayed quiet.

"We can't leave it out there; we don't want anything else to find it and track us. David, stay here close to them; fit an arrow to your bow and be ready. I will find Jennifer's hat and see if I can detect anything that was traveling with the shadow," Luna said. She walked off into the underbrush sniffing carefully. She returned with the hat, still filled with blackberries.

"Millet, did you convince Jennifer to go off on a food hunt?" Luna asked.

Millet peeked out from Jennifer's arms. "Yes, ma'am."

"Do you understand why that was dangerous?"

Millet was quivering. "Yes, ma'am."

"Okay, let this be a lesson to both of you," said Luna. She seemed calm for all that had just happened.

"David, please take Millet from Jennifer," Luna asked. "We have to keep going. There are still a few hours before dark, and I would like to make it to the Plain of Vendona. I don't like that we have found no traces of Samuel and his dogs. And now, whatever is controlling the shadows will soon know where we are."

They gathered their packs and started off.

"Jennifer, please walk with me," Luna asked. They fell into a steady pace along the wide path.

"I miss having fun with you," Luna started. "I wish we had had more time to be friends before being called on this journey."

"It's okay. I feel like I am supposed to be here," thought Jennifer. *"Somehow all of this makes sense."*

Luna looked up at her. "How so? How does it make sense?"

Jennifer took a deep breath. *"I can't explain this, but I feel as if I know you, and I know Zumulia, David and Millet. I also feel like my heart is speaking to me and it is telling me I have to be here, that this is right even though it is like being in a live fairytale."*

"Okay. Good. Go on," said Luna.

"I haven't ever met any of you. I mean, how would I forget you if I had met any of you?" asked Jennifer.

"But you just sense that you know us? We are familiar to you?" asked Luna

Jennifer took another breath. *"I can't remember you being in my dreams but it feels like that is where I have known you… sort of… but I also feel like I have always known you… like I have known all of you forever."*

"Well, maybe you have. There is much more to life and existence than most humans are taught on Earth. You do know us at the level of soul and spirit; we are connected at those places and now we have come together in linear reality," explained Luna. "Zumulia has been watching for you since you were born," said Luna.

"How? How did she know about me?" asked Jennifer.

"Several decades ago Zumulia sensed trouble coming to Solaria in her dreams and meditations. Other Wisdom Runners had the same sense of coming trouble," explained Luna.

"Her visions told her that certain humans, not yet born, would aid in healing the darkness spreading across the earth. A dream told her that you had been born. She had a strong premonition that you would come to Solaria through your Uncle Jim and Aunt Sarah," said Luna.

"But my father did not have contact with Uncle Jim and Aunt Sarah when I was born. My father was not nice to them – he sold drugs and ran scams, stole their inheritance from their mother – so they stopped contact with him. I have just met them," thought Jennifer.

"Outer facts often have nothing to do with what is trying to happen on a higher, spiritual level. Zumulia just got the 'knowing' that you had been born and would come to her through the Vermont portal. I was one year of age when I first started coming here; she asked me to watch for you. Peaberry, Lioness, Stormina, Rose and the others have been looking, too," said Luna.

"But how can a person have intuition that strong?" asked Jennifer.

"Well, it is a matter of innate talent; and then training to use that special ability. Not everyone is good at math, basketball or singing. Each individual has gifts. Some people are born strong intuitives," Luna explained.

"Okay, that seems obvious," thought Jennifer.

"It seems obvious to you because you were born with the ability to see the potential and gifts in humans, plants and animals. One of your gifts is the ability to see that each person is unique; many people don't have that ability." Luna paused and stretched. "Would you mind scratching behind my ears as we walk?"

Jennifer laughed and reached over to scratch behind one of Luna's short, white, pointy ears. *"Grace loves this, too!"*

Luna sighed and cocked her head. "Of course Grace loves it! It feels so good! Besides, it's good for you. People often think that dogs are just begging for attention. We dogs have known for centuries that when humans pat us they lower their blood pressure, release stress and generally get healthier!"

"I wish I had been able to talk to Grace like we are talking. She is very brave." Jennifer bit her lip.

Luna stopped and looked up at her. "Of course you miss her. If Grace could have spoken out loud to you, she would have. But she loves you, and communicated that love by the way she played with you, kept you company while you read and cuddled with you at night. Dogs don't have to speak out loud; humans need to learn to listen to them in a different way."

Jennifer nodded. *"If more humans could spend time talking with you they would learn so much. I am so glad I know you!"* thought Jennifer.

"Thank you!" Luna leapt away, spinning in a circle, chasing after her white tail that was curled tightly above the green backpack she wore. She came to a bow, white forelegs stretched in front of her, chest to the ground, bottom in the air, in front of Jennifer; then she leapt up to resume walking by her side.

Jennifer laughed. *"Why did you do that?"*

"I just wanted to remind you that we dogs are about fun and enjoying life no matter what challenges we face. Part of true wisdom is knowing how to enjoy the moment and to honor the ones that we love," said Luna.

Luna sighed, "We have had enough serious talk for right now."

"No! Wait… I need to know more about who I am and what I am supposed to do in Solaria!" thought Jennifer.

"You must learn patience. We have a few hours before we must find a den to spend the dark hours safely. I want David to show you some basics of using a slingshot," Luna said.

"David," she called. "Would you please show Jennifer how to use her slingshot?"

"I want to learn, too!" came Millet's voice as he peered out from a curtain of David's hair. He had been nestled under David's ear, taking a nap.

"Why don't you pass Millet over onto my shoulders, so that he and I can have a discussion while you are teaching Jennifer," said Luna.

"But I want to learn, too!" pouted Millet.

"Millet! Talking Loaves historically are in charge of food wisdom, not of weaponry. You and I have much to discuss so please stop being obstinate!" said Luna.

Millet looked reluctant.

Luna sat down. "Millet, you can practice opening to the energy of plants. I will give you some guidance with it while they are practicing with their slingshots. We can find roots to bake, some greens and herbs for a salad and some seasoning for the rice we will have for supper tonight."

"I really am looking forward to dinner. I'm really hungry," said David as he rubbed his stomach. His blue eyes lit up as he smiled. He winked at Jennifer.

Millet jumped up and down on David's shoulder. "Good! Good! Good! David, please let me go with Luna!"

After placing Millet on Luna's back, David readied his slingshot as Jennifer found hers. Walking ahead on the trail they heard Luna's alto tones interacting with Millet's high-pitched, excited chatter.

David smiled. "Slingshots are not easy to use effectively. To develop skill it takes practice, practice, practice."

"The most important thing to remember about using any weapon is that we never aim at a person, animal, bird, or live being unless we are absolutely certain that they pose a real threat and we need to hit them," explained David.

Jennifer nodded. Holding the slingshot in her hand, she could sense that it could be dangerous.

"The second is that you must learn good form." With a rock in the sling, pulled back, he planted his feet, focused on a target, became very still and then released the sling. The rock flew thirty feet, hitting the center of a large boulder to the left of the trail. He loaded another stone into the sling and hit the same place on the boulder. A third attempt was also a direct hit.

"Okay, now you try," he said.

Jennifer raised the slingshot as she thought she had seen David do. Taking a rock, she fit it in the sling, pulled back, then released it. The rock flew into the bushes a distance from the boulder.

"It's not easy, Jen," called Luna from about twenty feet behind them.

Jennifer tried again and again. Each time the stone went wide. Finally she lowered the handle, frustrated. She turned towards Luna, took a breath and thought, "*I can't do this. It's impossible.*"

Luna, with Millet holding to her collar as he balanced on her shoulders, trotted towards them. Millet looked like a cowboy riding a gigantic, white dog-horse.

Luna skidded to a halt. "Good riding, Millet!" She laughed.

Millet was grinning from ear to ear.

"Jennifer, you are learning to focus when you communicate intuitively. It works with using weapons, too. Learning the technical skills takes lots of practice. But practice is only one side of the equation. The other is focusing: see the rock going exactly where you want it to go and also see it having hit the target. You vision the present and the future as if they are one, happening at the same time," explained Luna.

David showed Jennifer how to stand in relation to the target, how much tension to use in the pull back of the sling and where to look with her eyes.

"Good, now you are close to ready," said Luna. "Jen, take a slow, deep breath, and see the rock flying to the target in the path you want it to take. At the same time try to see in your heart that it has hit the target exactly where you wanted it to."

Jennifer released the rock from her slingshot. It went past the boulder but this time it was much closer.

"Good!" said David.

Jennifer turned to Luna. "*But it didn't hit.*"

"No, it didn't. But this is your first lesson," said Luna. "You must continue to visualize hitting the target and at the same time seeing that it is already hit. This is a duo focus that brings the future and the present together as one."

"But it is also important to relax about learning. Let's just have fun with the slingshots as we walk," said David. "I started doing this from the time I could walk. My parents and Samuel helped me with my form but they also made a game out of it. I never thought of it as work."

Luna continued to help Millet explore the world of plants as David helped Jennifer learn to aim and hit her intended targets. The late afternoon was sunny and cool which made the walking easy. They made steady progress along the trail.

* * *

The trail meandered out from under the thick forest canapé onto a grassy bluff. The green valley below stretched northward for miles until it met the mountain range in the distance. Dotted with the blue of lakes and ponds, the floor of the plain was several hundred feet below them. There was no evidence of a trail to take them down.

"This is the Plain of Vendona. The mountain range is the Nordana, home to Justin Valor's Keep," explained Luna. Luna stretched her back and then sat. "We need to gather dry tinder, branches and wood for a fire later. The trail down is a ten minute walk west from here; off of it is a hidden side trail that leads to a cave that should be safe to stay in tonight."

"Where do you think Samuel and the dogs are?" asked Jennifer.

"I'm perplexed. I don't know of any other trail that they could have taken. Perhaps they didn't go to Justin Valor's Keep. Perhaps they took a portal to Earth or somewhere else," Luna answered.

Jennifer took a napping Millet from Luna's back. She cuddled him close like a baby, loving how he snuggled close to her. "*What do we do?*"

Luna rose and stretched. "Rest for the night and then travel on to Justin's Keep. Tonight I will try to contact Zumulia to see if she has heard from Samuel."

Jennifer placed the sleeping Millet in one of the pockets of Luna's pack, then helped David gather fuel for their fire.

* * *

Luna led them on the steep descent. Halfway down she turned off the trail and led them up over a ledge. From there they dropped down, two feet, to a rock outcropping. Skirting around a lone pine, they came to a small opening in the ledge rock.

"Here we are," said Luna. "Please help me take off these saddlebags. I want to go in to sniff out any danger, and then I will return for you."

After ten minutes she returned. "I think it is safe. Jennifer, follow me through the entrance. David, please pass Millet in, and our packs, and the firewood, then you follow. Where is the glow weed that Zumulia packed?"

David produced a pouch. Reaching in he pulled out a large tuff of blue fibers and handed them to Jennifer. "Take them in with you and then blow on them gently. They give a soft light for about twelve hours. They are cool to the touch, even when they are lit, so you don't have to worry about getting burned. They produce no smoke; there are no fumes."

Luna went first. Jennifer followed carrying the glow weed; inside she blew lightly on the fibers. At first faint, the light increased as she continued to blow gently; finally it lit the tunnel.

Millet scrambled in on his own, taking a place between Luna's forelegs. Jennifer pulled the backpacks and firewood in as David passed them to her. Then David crawled in to join them.

David showed Jennifer how to divide the glow weed so that they each held a light. With Millet riding on Luna's shoulders, they followed the widening tunnel until it opened into a rounded cave. The light of the glow weed grew in radiance, revealing that the ceiling domed at about twenty feet above them. The space was dry and clean; a fire ring of rounded stones sat in the center of the cave.

"There is a natural air shaft above us that allows for a fire; the smoke will go upward and escape. Once the sun sets no one will see the smoke; we can cook and get enough heat to sleep comfortably without the danger of someone finding us," explained Luna.

Jennifer and David laid out the bedrolls around the ring of stones. Then Luna and Millet supervised the preparation of the herbs, roots and vegetables that they had gathered. The blackberries were reserved for dessert. David showed Jennifer how to make a fire and cook the roots by wrapping them with herbs in wet leaves that they pushed under the burning logs to roast.

As they waited for the dinner to cook, David sat back, wrapping his arms around his legs. "I'm always grateful to the Creator after a day like this."

Jennifer reached out to stroke Luna's head. "*What does he mean*?"

Luna nodded. "David, Jennifer would like to know why you say that."

"Well, we have started on a journey; journeys are always something that I am thankful for. We had an unexpected guest, Millet, join us; he has become a great member of our group. We safely got away from a shadow attack. We have had opportunities to learn new things. We will have a good supper from food that appeared along our way. And now we have a fire and a safe place to spend the night. I feel thankful to our Creator for supplying us with friendship, protection, adventure, good food, and good rest," explained David. The silver trinkets in the braid in his hair reflected in the dancing firelight.

Jennifer pondered for a moment. *"My father and stepmother said religion was a bunch of hooey. My father made a show of going to church and told people that he was a Christian. But at home he said it was just a ruse to keep up his image; he said that he knew better than to believe in any form of God. He used to say, 'God, if you are there, then strike me dead!' Then, when nothing would happen, he would laugh and say, 'See, there is no God."*

Luna relayed to David and Millet what Jennifer had said, then turned her eyes to the girl again. "From what I know of your father's childhood, he was very abused. Trauma can cause people to hate the Creator; or think he, or she if that is a more comfortable word for you, doesn't exist. Instead of doing the work necessary to heal their minds and spirits, they blame the Creator. Deep inside themselves, they fear their pain from childhood wounds that have not healed. But that causes them to fear themselves; especially their soul and spirit that link them to the fabric of oneness that connects us all. Instead of connecting to what will really heal them, they often turn to addictions, harming and controlling others."

"But that is silly! Of course there is a Creator who is Divine. How else would our food grow?" asked Millet. "Who created us? My Keepers put the ingredients together to make me in the ovens, but our Creator used those things to give me life."

"My stepmother made a big deal of having an altar in the living room. She loaded it with shells, beads, pictures of gods and goddesses from around the world, candles, rocks and crystals. People were impressed with how beautiful it was. Toni told them that you could get whatever you wanted if you meditated everyday and asked for it. She said she meditated everyday, but she never did. And she was always yelling because she said she never got what she wanted," thought Jennifer.

Luna again relayed to Millet and David what Jennifer had communicated. "She sounds like she is very sad – very angry," said Luna. Both Millet and David nodded.

Millet toddled over to the fire. "Dinner's ready! Don't let it burn!"

The roots were soft and delicious; they tasted akin to potatoes, yams and carrots. The blackberries were scrumptious. Heating water in a copper pot, they had spearmint and chamomile tea to relax with after the meal.

Millet cuddled with Luna and began to hum. His voice was high but calming. David joined in with his harmonica. Together they produced a soothing melody.

Jennifer looked at Luna. *"I sense Millet can read my thoughts."*

"Of course I can; I'm maturing. It started while we were running from the shadow. I felt a link with you grow inside of me. At first I could just hear the thump of your heart and then I could hear you thinking," said Millet.

"I suspected he would be able to eventually. Talking Loaves have many special abilities. Jennifer, I let you choose the seven we took to Zumulia because I knew that you would naturally gravitate towards the ones that resonate with your heart energy," said Luna. "I sensed you would be good friends."

David stopped playing his harmonica; he looked perplexed. "Now all three of you are communicating intuitively and I'm not."

"Since we are wakeful, let's take this occasion to try some learning." Luna shifted her body as she lifted her head. Millet adjusted himself against her.

"Jen, move your blanket so that you can sit facing David. I want you to be three feet apart while you sit cross-legged," said Luna.

They moved so that that they were facing each other. Light from the fire flickered and danced on the walls and ceiling of the cave.

"Okay. When you were practicing with the slingshots we spoke of using the breath to help focus the intention," continued Luna. "The breath is a very important starting point for any action. It allows you to access your center where your real power and strength is stored."

Jennifer and David nodded.

"Now close your eyes. Focus on your breath as it goes in and out of your body. Don't force it. Just feel it as it naturally comes in and out," said Luna.

David and Jennifer closed their eyes and began to focus on their breathing. Jennifer was glad to close her eyes; she felt self-conscious having David looking directly at her. She wondered if David felt the same.

"Now, start to feel your breath go deeper and deeper with each inhalation and exhalation. Don't force it, just allow it. Invite your breath to go all the way to where your body is sitting on your blanket and out again," directed Luna. "Of course, it isn't really doing that, but it feels as if it is."

As Jennifer focused, indeed her breath deepened. Within moments she felt a sense of peace softly replacing the tension that was often in her belly. When the breath reached deep to where she sat, the sense of peace radiated out into her legs and feet, then her arms, hands and fingers. Finally it filled her back and then neck and face. She felt both relaxed and alive.

Luna's voice came as if from a dream, "When you feel a sense of deep relaxation lift your forefingers of both hands so that I know that you are ready."

Jennifer lifted her fingers. Her hands felt both familiar and yet totally new.

"Good," said Luna. "Keep focusing on your breath while you listen to my instructions. If at any time you feel overwhelmed or confused - try to immediately bring your focus back to your breath."

The peaceful energy was becoming stronger inside Jennifer's body as it radiated out from her breath.

"Okay, now maintaining focus on your breath, I want you to open your eyes and gently look at your hands in your lap," said Luna.

Jennifer found it was hard to open her eyes. Once she did, her hands looked familiar, as she knew them, and yet different. They seemed to be filled with energy that she had never detected before; it was as if they belonged to her and yet did not.

"Keep focusing on your breath," came Luna's voice. Jennifer realized that she had lost that focus; as she resumed feeling her breath she felt more connected to her own hands. The inner peace that had somewhat diminished started to rebuild.

"Now, slowly lift your sight to take in each other's faces. Keep focusing on your own breath as you softly gaze at each other. Don't look intently; allow the peace that is coming from your breath to soften your normal vision," said Luna.

David's face was the same as Jennifer remembered and yet

different. There seemed to be a soft glow of aliveness that she had not detected before. She felt kinship.

Luna's voice came again, "Now look into each other's eyes. Make sure that you are feeling your breath go in and out, very deep, as you do this."

Jennifer looked into David's eyes as he gazed back. At first the ice blue of his eyes seemed too alive; as she focused on her breath she found she could maintain a soft focus. His face continued to have the glow of aliveness. Gradually she could see soft white energy swirling around him; she knew it was his life energy – the energy of his spirit.

"Okay, keep your focus on your breath AND on each other's eyes. As you are breathing deep into your center, feel your chest at the level of the heart. As you focus and gaze into each other's eyes you will feel a tingling in your chest, and then you will sense an opening as if light is moving in a clockwise manner and then outward," said Luna.

It was true. As Jennifer focused on her breath, allowing her eyes to soften their gaze, she felt an opening in the midline of her chest that seemed to swirl with light. Somehow it felt natural, as if she had done it all of her life.

"Now, Jennifer, since you have more experience sending intuitive communication, focus on your breath as you think of something that you want to say to David. Try to send the message out from your chest center towards David's chest center," said Luna.

"*What should I say?*" Jennifer took a longer breath. She formed a word in her mind, seeing all the letters clearly, and then sent it out through the opening of the light center in her chest. "*Hello*!"

David didn't respond. "*Try again*," Luna's voice came into Jennifer's mind.

Jennifer took a deeper breath, feeling it as it passed through her nostrils, into her belly, down to the tip of her spine and out again. "*HELLO!*"

David's eyes slightly widened. A smile flickered on his lips.

"*Hello*!" came his voice into her mind.

"Very good! Keep focusing on your breath and try a simple conversation," said Luna.

"*I feel both relaxed yet very, very alive.*" David's voice came into Jennifer's mind.

"I do too. It is as if I am awake for the first time. I didn't even know that I was asleep," sent Jennifer.

"I have felt this way momentarily when I practiced breath relaxation. Also, when I have played my harp, or sang the chants of the Wisdom Runners, I have felt this; and when I have been mushing one of Samuel's dog teams, or when Peaberry and the Vermont pack visit and we go mushing, I have felt this sense of aliveness," thought David.

"This is the first time for me. It feels as if all of my life I have lived with tension within me. It's gone now," thought Jennifer.

David's face seemed a bit more serious. *"I am sorry for the pain that you have lived with."*

Jennifer felt her cheeks heating. She had tried again to focus on her breath more intentionally. Except for Luna, she had not had this level of closeness in communication with someone else she cared for. It was both wonderful and frightening. The feeling of fear creeping around her sense of peace reminded her to focus on her breath.

"The other times I have felt this sense of aliveness has been practicing with my weapons," thought David.

Jennifer nodded. *"You focus intensely when you use them."*

"Yes," David thought. *"When I have had to face danger, like with the shadow that was chasing you, I enter this state, too."*

"You just enter into it?" Jennifer asked.

"Immediately. I feel as if the attacker and I are related. Time slows. There is a great sense of peace. I only care that goodness comes of our interaction. I don't feel concern as to whether I live or die; I just want what is best for all concerned," thought David.

Luna's voice came into both of their minds, *"David, that is because you have trained well: you do not think about your body or how to use your weapons. At the time of danger – your heart, soul and spirit take over; you step into this higher state of awareness. It is in this state of higher consciousness that you meet your attacker and know them as being related to you, in the oneness that we all actually exist in. Because your heart is pure you lose your caring for your physical safety and commit yourself to action that is for the good of all beings in creation."*

"I seem to know what you are saying. But I don't really understand in my mind," thought Jennifer.

"This will come to you as you have more experience. Have patience and focus on what you are experiencing right now. Listen to those who guide you and use it as direction until you have inner knowing," thought Luna.

Luna switched to voice communication. "You are both doing well; you have innate talent with communication – enough to train to be Seers, if you choose. Let's go further; I want you to help me open a communication channel with Zumulia. Move slightly back from each other so that your bodies form a triangle with mine. Then lift your eyes to the air right above us."

Luna rose and nudged the drowsy Millet with her nose, gently guiding him to a place closer to David and Jennifer. She sat on her haunches, letting Millet recline between her front paws.

Gazing upward Jennifer and David saw nothing at first, except a certain vibrancy of the air as they had seen in their hands and around each other. Then a soft, luminous white light started to come forth from Luna's chest. It gathered density and started to glow.

"Okay, make sure that you keep feeling your breath. See the white light in your chest area rising outward to support the light that I am sending out," said Luna.

Jennifer felt a tingling in her chest that grew stronger, producing pressure; gradually she felt the energy flowing from her, rising up to meet the light that Luna had sent forth. Light emanated from David's chest, joining the light that Jennifer was producing; their combined columns of light were underneath the cloud that Luna had formed, energizing and supporting it.

"Now, think of Zumulia; feel your good feelings for her as you see her face," instructed Luna.

As their light streams merged, David and Jennifer felt the molecules of their bodies glow with energy. The light above them became a large, pulsating orb. Slowly its surface became opaque. Then a vision within it formed, coalescing into Zumulia's face; behind her was the great room of her Keep.

"Luna, you have done it. You have managed to open a communication channel," Zumulia chuckled.

Luna's spoke into the orb. "We are in a deep cave at the edge of the Plain of Vendona."

Zumulia nodded. "I know the one. We have stayed there together. It has a very secure channel for sending."

"I have been working with David and Jennifer to open their ability to intuitively communicate with each other. They did well on their first try and now they are lending their energy to support the communication orb I am using to send to you," said Luna.

"Oh, Millet is here with us. He was a stowaway in my saddlebag pack; we didn't discover him until we were far from your Keep," added Luna.

"I know. I heard the loaves whispering and tittering excitedly in the pantry all morning. I went in to quiet them down and found him missing. They explained to me what they had done. I let them know that they had plotted a very dangerous thing. They will be happy to know that he is safe," said Zumulia.

"We were attacked on the trail here by a shadow. David stood his ground bravely, sending his arrows into it. His courage gave me time to make a stand to confront it with singing and light; it hesitated for but a moment and then vanished. But whoever is controlling it will know that we have set off from the direction of your Keep," said Luna.

Zumulia eyes narrowed; she looked troubled. "I am glad that you evaded it. And I am very thankful that you are now in the safety of the cave."

"We have found no trace of Samuel or his dogs along the trail. I cannot understand this. Have you any news?" said Luna.

"No. I have gotten no messages. We had a very strong storm pass through that should have chased and dispelled the darkness and blocks to intuition; but unfortunately it did not open up the communication channels. The trees have no new knowledge; they still hear whispers from afar that carry warnings - against what, they do not know. You are the first one that has gotten a communication through in three months," said Zumulia.

"That is good news and it is bad. Jennifer and David are potentially strong Seers, which is why we are getting through to you right now. But both are young, untrained, and there are dangers in intuitive communication," said Luna.

"I trust that you will give them the warnings that they need. And I trust that they will heed your teachings. Good friend, it is best to stop here so that the light of the communication channel does not draw danger to you," said Zumulia.

"Yes. Be well, my good friend," said Luna.

"Please let David know that I am proud that he is my grandson. Please tell Jennifer that I am honored to finally have her acquaintance. And tell Millet that he is a rascal! Again, dear friend, till we meet, travel well!" said Zumulia.

The clarity of Zumulia's face and the great room of her Keep faded, and then vanished. The orb of light that emanated from Luna went to opaque and then translucent as she sent less energy into it.

"Okay, both of you bring your focus onto your breath and feel your feet," Luna spoke audibly. "Feeling your feet will allow you to pull your energy back into your body. Once your energy feels like it is fully in your body, I want you to lay back onto your sleeping rolls and continue to follow your breath as it flows in and out."

Although it seemed like it took hours to bring the light back into her body, Jennifer knew it had been less than a few minutes. As she lay down she felt exhilarated, exhausted and peaceful - all at the same time.

"Are they going to be alright?" came Millet's high voice.

"Yes, they are just tired," explained Luna.

"Hey buddy, I'm fine," said David.

"*Me, too*," thought Jennifer.

"Hey, I am still hearing you, Jen," said David audibly.

"With practice the two of you will be able to forge a channel between yourselves that will stay open when you want to communicate. Presently, it may fade after you have slept, but we can work on strengthening it," said Luna. She shifted onto her side so that Millet could nestle more comfortably.

"Did you both hear Zumulia?" Luna asked.

"I heard her loud and clear the whole time. I also saw her; I felt her right here with us. That was amazing," said David.

"*I heard and saw her, too,*" thought Jennifer.

"Thank you both for helping with the transmission. When I sensed how strong your innate intuitive gifts were, I took the opportunity to try to contact Zumulia. Until you are much stronger I will not attempt to communicate in the open country; this cave lessened the risks," said Luna.

"*What are the risks*?" asked Jennifer.

"The greater the ability of the sender, the greater the risk of his or her light being seen by a dangerous force; Seers must learn how to shield themselves. First you have to learn to use your intuitive gifts and then you learn to protect yourself as you use them. Right now, with the shadows and some sort of great trouble on the way, a person who is new to opening their channels of communicating over a distance can be easily seen and attacked," explained Luna.

Luna rose to her feet and stretched; Millet toddled over to Jennifer's blanket and curled up in the crook of her arm. "David, please throw some more wood on the fire. We should all try to get some sleep," Luna said.

As they got themselves ready for the night, Luna instructed David and Jennifer to focus on their breathing gently as they waited for sleep; she said that it would help their body, mind and nervous systems adjust to the changes that were growing in their intuitional abilities. Relaxed, stretched out in the small cave, they fell asleep listening to the crackling of the fire.

* * *

Chapter Four

When we answer the call to journey, often we are rewarded with surprises. With our eyes open we find real magic: there is more to see and experience in our lives than we imagined - even in the small moments. These times of wonder, sent to us by the light, strengthen our hearts, souls and spirits for challenges that also come our way. Thus we pray that our eyes, ears and hearts be open, even in what seem to be mundane times, so that we may enjoy the journey and be up to whatever crosses our path.

Book of The Wisdom Runners

Jennifer was pulled from her sleep by the soft humming of Millet accompanied by a melodic, gentle strumming. She lifted her eyes from the cradle of her arm to see David playing his harp; the tune was sweet. She stretched and sat up.

David put down his instrument and passed her a bowl of hot rice and a mug of mint and ginger tea. "Luna has gone out to scout the trail. We thought we would let you rest until she returned.

"*Thank you,*" Jennifer thought.

There was no response from David. She realized that the channel of communication between them must have closed as they slept.

Luna came in. "Good morning Jennifer. The trail seems to be

safe - I can find no scent of danger. As soon as Jen finishes eating, let's pack and be on our way. There is a small lake about forty-five minutes from here where we can take a morning swim to freshen up for the day's journey."

They emerged from the cave into day with a mixture of tangerine and apricot clouds against a sky that was a brilliant, turquoise blue as the sun rose from the east. The Plain of Vendona that stretched before them was green; the lakes and ponds dotting it mirrored the clouds and hue of the sky. The morning felt full of goodness as they set off to find the main trail.

Taking turns sitting with Millet on the bank of the first lake they came to, they swam and bathed. The water was on the warm side of icy; it was refreshing. Masses of fragrant water mint grew on the banks; taking handfuls they rubbed it over their skins and into their wet hair. Jennifer massaged the mint into Luna's fur as she stood in shallow water; they both plunged into the deeper water to rinse themselves.

"There is nothing like a good swim!" said Luna as they donned their packs and started off.

"The mint is cleansing, relaxing and stimulating," beamed Millet.

"Very good, Millet. You seem to be increasing in knowledge with each passing night," said David.

The group started walking in earnest towards the line of mountains far to the north of them.

* * *

By midday, with the sun directly above them, it was bright but not hot. Jennifer had lent Millet her straw hat for a parasol; she donned the rain hat she had stashed in her pack. Riding on Luna's shoulders, balancing the wide-brimmed straw hat above his head as he held Luna's collar, the loaf of bread looked a peculiar sight. Jennifer thought that none of her father's Hollywood writer friends could have imagined such a pairing. She wondered what he would have thought of her current life; but then she willed the thoughts away because she did not want to think of him as dead.

They stopped next to a large lake for another swim and lunch. The meal consisted of cold rice, left over from the morning, and vegetables found along their early walk. Millet found greens to make a salad and small, scallion-like roots that, mixed with water, made a lovely dressing.

David had been quiet during the morning. He had not suggested lessons with the slingshot. He did not seem to be hearing Jennifer's thoughts nor could she hear his. After lunch he walked a short distance off to sit against an oak tree, playing his harmonica softly; it was a sad melody.

"Luna, why is it okay for us to be walking in the open like this?" thought Jennifer. Millet was curled asleep in her arms.

"During the day the shadows should not be able to follow us here. In the forest the shadow took advantage of the deep shade," answered Luna. "I believe if we continue at the pace we have set, we should make the northern foothills by evening.

"I cannot hear David and I don't think that he hears me," thought Jennifer.

"It's natural. Opening intuitive channels of communicating with others is a slow process," said Luna.

Jennifer considered. *"David has lived in Solaria all of his life. Why wasn't he taught to communicate before?"*

"Astute question, Jen," said Luna. His parents died when he was six. Zumulia's daughter, Tumilia, was his mother. The Wisdom Runners could tell that he had a special, deep sight and ability to resonate with others; this brings with it the ability to feel past, present and future pain of others. David's guardians did not want to chance him tapping into the agony that his parents felt as they died. The guardians decided to delay training until he was older."

"*How did his parents die*?" asked Jennifer. Millet whimpered as he shifted in his sleep.

"They were Wisdom Runners and Seers; a combination that few individuals are capable of becoming. There was great darkness coming in from Earth through one of the portals far to the east. His parents infiltrated the group that was raising the darkness. They were able to stop the darkness from doing further damage here and close the portal; they lost their lives in doing so," said Luna.

Jennifer looked at Luna. The great peace she had been feeling dissipated as the anxiety she had known since she could remember gripped her belly again.

Luna's eyes held Jennifer's gaze. "You are letting the past disturb your peace. The way to honor our loved ones who have died is to make an honorable stance for goodness in the present - in the now. It is not possible unless you have peace within."

"*But how*?" asked Jennifer.

"Practice watching your breath as we walk. The more that you work with your breath, focus on it during the day, the more you will grow a stable center of peace within," said Luna as she rose. "David, Millet, it is time to move on. Let's try to get to the mountains before nightfall."

* * *

The tangerine and magenta clouds of the early morning were now giant puffs of white swirls against a sky that was azure. From high above a bird would see a white dog, wearing a green backpack, her tail curled over her back, with a large-brimmed straw hat that seemed to float above her neck, but worn by a curious creature that rode on her shoulders. The bird would see the white dog leading a tall, blond, long-haired youth followed by a black-haired, petite girl - both young humans carrying large packs and bedrolls. A curious bird might swoop down to have a look because the group was keeping a pace that only those on a mission would set on a gorgeous summer day, made for swimming and enjoying.

Suddenly dozens of long shadows traveled over the ground and surrounded the journeyers. Jennifer screamed and dropped into a crouch as David grabbed for a quiver of arrows and readied his bow. Luna swung around to look skyward as bizarre calls filled the air. The breeze seemed mad as it came from all directions at once.

"Sit!" yelled Luna.

The rushing air and shadows confused David and Jennifer; they didn't know where to look or run.

"Sit! David, put down your weapons!" yelled Luna's alto voice through the din of the moving air.

Luna sat with Millet clinging with both hands to her collar. He had released the straw hat, which, tied to Luna's collar by its chinstrap, flopped wildly in the ever-changing currents of air. Defying their own logic that told them to run or defend, David and Jennifer sat close to Luna. Jennifer put her hand out to steady the frightened Millet.

The earth shook repeatedly, as if hit by five hundred-pound meteorites; the air continued to move violently; every wash of air making Jennifer's panic rise. David searched the sky and their surroundings with his weapons-trained blue eyes. Luna seemed placid in the midst of the tumult.

Suddenly there was silence. Before them and surrounding them were one-foot thick orange poles.

"Don't move," came Luna's alto voice softly.

Looking upward they saw the poles were in pairs attached to the bodies of huge, bright, multi-colored birds. Their large bodies held fifteen–foot long necks, atop which sat round heads with a high-crested hat of feathers, bobbing this way and that. Their hooked beaks, shaped in the manner of a puffin's, matched their orange legs. From the base of their tailbone grew eight separate plumes of long feathers - each in a different color. However, the profusion of colorful feathers could not compete with their eyes – a kaleidoscope of continuously swirling blue, gold and purple.

As they sat frozen Luna cautioned, "Do not move no matter what!"

Suddenly, as if of one mind, the one hundred feathered creatures elevated onto their toes, commencing to leap about like ballerinas on point shoes. With wings extended they danced together as an ensemble, in small groups, pairs and in elaborate solos. Leaps Baryshnikov would have been hard-pressed to attempt, pirouettes and bounces skyward were graceful despite the size and obvious weight of the birds. The whole time they exclaimed, "Ga-gooo – Ga-goooo – Ga-gooooooooony! Ga-gooo – Ga-goooo – Ga-gooooooooony!"

Then, just as abruptly as they had started, they came to rest in front of the wayfarers. Jennifer's eyes were wide, she wondered if they had gone through another portal to a kaleidoscope world. David grasped his slingshot but didn't raise it. Millet, gripping Luna's collar tightly, shook as he peered out between her small white, perked ears. Only Luna sat calmly.

"*What are they*?" asked Jennifer.

Luna sniffed. "Goony Birds."

"*What*?" asked Jennifer. She looked to David and saw a faint smile cross his lips.

"I said they are Goony Birds. Take Millet from me and undo the buckles of my pack as unobtrusively as you can. But stay sitting and don't stare at them," said Luna.

Luna's directive was hard to follow as the creatures were mesmerizing. Jennifer took the quavering Millet into her arms and cuddled him. David loosened the pack from Luna as she slid from it.

Luna ran towards a bird directly in front of them. He had a triple crown, like a hat, of feathered plumes above his head in aqua, circus red and school-bus yellow. Stopping ten feet in front of him she doggie bowed with her front legs out, stretching her chest to the ground as she looked up at him; she then righted herself into a sitting position, gazing calmly at him.

The towering bird eyed her, then placed his pole-like right leg in front of his left leg, spread his brilliant peach and green wings, shimmering with gold dots, and lowered his body as if making a curtsey. Straightening up he lowered his neck, like the boom of a crane, to bring his giant head to Luna's level. The irises of his eyes swirled blue, gold and purple like a cartoon imitation of the red and white barbershop poles of yesteryear. She pushed her white muzzle forward to touch her brown nose to his beak.

The other birds stepped back a few paces as they watched. Suddenly the giant bird bounced into the air, landed and proceeded to roll onto his back, wiggling the three toes of each foot in the air atop each pole-length leg. The white dog jumped this way and that as she bounced off of his body, nipped at his tail, pulled on the feathers of his crown, and barked loudly, sounding her characteristic, "Woo-woo."

"Gooo – a-hoooo- a- oooony!" called the bird, repeatedly.

Jennifer was alarmed, but David started giggling and then laughing so hard that he fell over. "They are playing," he said finally, when he could catch his breath.

"Gooo – a-hoooo- a- oooony!" called the bird in a final gasp and then fell on his side with his long legs and neck stretched along the ground.

Luna walked over to where the tip of his beak rested and sat. "Gifford, my friend! So good to see you!"

"Likewise. What a spot of fortune when I saw you from the air. I might have missed you with that green pack because it camouflages you against the green of the valley grass. But your white head and curled tail, carried just so, gave me a sense that it might be you! And indeed it was." The giant bird turned his head to peer at Jennifer, David and Millet with his improbable eyes. "We must have given your friends quite a scare!"

Turning slightly towards them, Luna said, "King Gifford, this is David, grandson to Zumulia. Beside him is Jennifer, who came through the portal with me from Vermont. In her arms is Millet, a Talking Loaf."

King Gifford pushed himself up with his wing into a low perching position, bending his long legs at what Jennifer supposed must be his knees. He brought his head down near where they sat. "Goooooooooooooooood to meet you!"

The three nodded at him and smiled. Jennifer found it hard to center on her breath.

"I remember you from when I was much younger," said David.

"Indeed," said King Gifford. "I was a friend of your parents. We spent much time together and I remember you well. I have not seen you since they have died as I was in the east and then, for the last year, in the west. I did not know if you would remember me or my flock."

David smiled broadly. "King Gifford, you are hard for anyone to forget! But it has been eight years, so I was not certain it was you and not another flock of Goony Birds. I remember the antics of your tribe that always brought smiles to all you met. As a child I looked forward to your visits. And how can I forget the dawn, day and twilight flights when you carried my mother, father and me? I have often remembered and hoped to see you again."

"If I weren't so many colors already I might blush!" laughed King Gifford. "But David, please just call me Gifford." The bird turned his head and seemed to be trying to focus his wildly swirling eyes.

"Luna, did you say this was a Talking Loaf? What a blessing if this is true!" King Gifford said.

Luna explained how Jennifer and she had rescued the loaves from the ovens; the situation at the orchard and ovens with the shadows; Samuel's departure from his home with his dogs; finding Glacier dead; the message in the note that burned; and how Millet had stowed away in her pack.

The swirling in King Gifford's eyes slowed. "I am glad to meet you, Millet. I wish you a long and worthy life. Solaria needs the knowledge that your tribe carries; it is good to know the Oven Keepers have succeeded in bringing your kind forth again. But in the future please heed the words of elders like Luna and Zumulia because your safety is of great importance."

Millet bit his lip. "Yes, King Gifford; I made a mistake. But I am glad to meet you, too."

"Luna, this is very worrisome news that you carry. Combined with the news that I have brought back from the west it does not bode well," said King Gifford.

"I am glad to see you back. I knew if anyone could get through the barrier of darkness that has cut us off from the west, it would be you," said Luna.

"Aaaa - gooooooooony - ahhhhh," King Gifford seemed to be clearing his throat. "Where are my manners?" he asked as he bent his beak to the ground and pushed his large eyeballs forward towards Jennifer.

"*Jen, get up and make a bow,*" Luna's thought came into Jennifer's mind.

Jennifer rose slowly, holding Millet, and proceeded to make a slow bow from her waist.

"She does not now have her voice," said Luna.

King Gifford pulled his head back a bit. "Someday, perhaps? But for now it is very good to meet you. I will not communicate intuitively with you as our Goony Bird thoughts vibrate painfully in human heads when we are this close. When you learn the muffling technique perhaps we can try a conversation? I am glad that you are here with such a great teacher."

Jennifer nodded and bowed. She wished she could answer him.

"Luna, I sense you are on your way to the Keep of Justin Valor?" asked King Gifford.

"Yes. Zumulia and I thought that Samuel and his dogs were headed there. Now I have doubts because there has been no trace of them along the trail," said Luna.

"I am troubled that you are traveling in such a small group. These humans are too young; you need the aid of at least one Wisdom Runner. Where are Peaberry, Stormina, Lioness, Buttercup and Lily? And that is not enough, surely. If you don't have Samuel's dogs then you must also have Bear, Barney, Hosta, Fuchsia, Rose, Amos, Lucky, Rainbow, Rose and Maple!" said King Gifford.

"There was no time to send for them. I really hoped to have met up with Samuel by now. As for other Wisdom Runners – you know that we have not had word from the east or south for months; and the west has been cut off completely for years. You are the first to return," said Luna.

"We are flying east right now to find King Saul. Even for us it is a long flight. The Court of the Wisdom Runners should be convening soon and I have grave news for them from the western cities," said King Gifford.

King Gifford righted himself up to full height and stretched his neck as he fluffed his wings. "Luna, I am enjoying this wonderful, unexpected meeting; but I cannot delay the flock any longer. I can fly you to the foothills of the mountains yonder to shorten your journey to Justin Valor's Keep – hopefully you can then reach it by nightfall so that you don't have to spend another night without protection. I cannot take you further as snow is coming and I must get to the east before we fly south. I will explain our news on our flight so that you can relay it to Justin and hopefully to Samuel, Contalia, Dohanos, the Seers and Wisdom Runners of the Keep."

"Snow?" asked David and Luna in unison.

Jennifer looked around. "Surely snow is impossible with all the green and how warm it is?" asked David.

"I know, I know," said King Gifford shaking his giant head. "It does not seem possible. But times are changing and the weather here is not easy to predict as Earth's environment shifts. When you are aloft you will be able to sense what we have intuited - there is snow coming."

Luna nodded. "Then, as much as I, too, am enjoying your dear company, we must make haste. I welcome your offer to fly us to the foothills. I feared that we would not reach them before dark, but I did not want to worry my young friends."

King Gifford turned to his flock. "Giffa – oodoo, snatiffalooo!"

he said. They waggled their crest feathers at him and nodded in unison. Four stepped forward.

"They will open their beaks for you; jump into one of their lower mandibles so they can lift and place you on my son's back. His name is Prince Bartholomew. He will carry you so that I may fly close and speak with you as we journey," explained King Gifford.

Prince Bartholomew crossed his right leg in front of his left and made a curtsey with his bright turquoise and gold wings spread wide.

"Well met, Prince Bartholomew," greeted Luna as she returned his bow. "Gifford, I have not had the pleasure of meeting this son."

"No, indeed. As you know it takes five years for our chicks to mature. He was still in his mother's care, with our female flock in the south, until just before I flew through the barrier of darkness to the west. It was his first official mission. I am pleased to say that his mother is a great queen who has trained him well."

Bartholomew bowed to his father.

"We will talk on the way. Let's get aloft!" said King Gifford.

The three birds accompanying Prince Bartholomew lowered their heads down to where Luna, David and Jennifer, with Millet still cradled in her arms, stood. David bent to help Luna on with her pack.

"No, don't do that," advised Gifford. "In fact it would be best, Jennifer and David, if you remove your packs for the flight. Some of the flock will carry them and return them to you when we land."

The waiting birds hoisted the travelers in their large mandibles to the flat back of Prince Bartholomew. Luna led them to settle in on a magenta patch of feathers just below where his neck attached to his body; the patch of down was soft and fluffy, giving off a scent of roses.

King Gifford brought his mesmerizing right eye level with them. "Comfy?" he asked.

They nodded.

"Okay, now hang on tight to the tufts of down around you.

David, you might want to put Millet into your tunic so that he can look out; he will be more secure," said King Gifford. David obliged and then took hold of tufts of feathers, and Jennifer followed his example, marveling at the softness in her hands. Luna took hold of a tuft in her mouth and nodded at King Gifford's eye.

"Okay, off we go!" King Gifford said. "OOOOOOOO –eeeeee – ooo - wooooooo!"

"OOOOOOO - eeeeee – ooo – wooooooo! OOOOOOO – eeeeee – ooo – wooooooo! OOOOOOOO - eeeeee - ooo-wooooooo!" called the flock back at their leader. Jennifer, David, with Millet in his shirt, and Luna held onto their magenta feather tufts, swaying as Prince Bartholomew and his flock mates prepared to get airborne. In groups of ten abreast the giant birds started running across the green grass of the plain, flapping their outspread wings. Gradually the power of Prince Bartholomew's wings caused them to rise gently. Soon the ground was far below them as they rode in a sea of wonderful, brightly colored birds, with the azure sky and white clouds still higher above them.

Fully aloft, the Gooney Birds broke their take-off formation. A number moved out to fly to the front, sides and behind Bartholomew; his wings moved gently up and down as his long neck and head stretched twenty feet in front of them. Jennifer turned to see his colorful tail feathers fluttering gently between his long, orange, pole-like legs that trailed behind his body.

The wind against their faces and bodies felt like a gentle breeze. The magenta patch of feathers, where they sat, rose and fell gently as Prince Bartholomew flapped his wings. Luna planted her feet and let go of the tuft of feathers that she had held in her mouth.

"I love flying like this!" she said. She was smiling.

"Wow, it's beautiful up here!" exclaimed Millet from the safety of David's shirt. His left hand reached out to hold a long lock of blond hair. David bent down and kissed what might be perceived as the top of Millet's head; in fact it was a corner of his loaf-shaped body.

"I have missed flying with King Gifford and his flock! I have dreamed of this for years. Thinking about it made me so happy!" said David.

Jennifer enjoyed watching the wondrous birds flying around them, the sky and clouds above, and the green plain, dotted with its blue lakes and ponds, below. To the south she could see the great forest that they had left the night before; and in front of them, to the north, the Nordana Mountains, with their high, snow-covered peaks. She knew that even if she had tried a week ago, she could not have ever imagined such beauty. Her life in Los Angeles seemed a nightmare that had faded to nothingness as she woke to the wonders of real life.

A bright orange beak appeared next to them and then floated forward as King Gifford's right eye came abreast of them. His triple-plumed crest of aqua, circus red and school-bus yellow wafted magically behind his head. He was flying ten feet above them, but had lowered his head on its giant neck to be level with the voyagers.

"Beautiful, eh?" he asked.

"Yes, incredible, my good friend!" said Luna. "But then I am a dog. I love to run but I also love to ride. Cars, trucks, boats, dog sleds – anything as long as I can see out and watch the scenery. Better yet, to feel the wind blowing against my face!"

King Gifford chuckled. "You aren't comparing us to Earth vehicles are you?"

Luna smiled. "Certainly not! Of all rides in Solaria and on Earth, this is the best I have ever had."

"Thank you, Luna," said Gifford. "Coming from you, this is the highest compliment. How are the rest of you faring?"

"Gifford, since I was a child I have longed to fly with you again. Thank you," said David.

"I love it!" beamed Millet.

Jennifer looked into King Gifford's large eye with the iris swirling blue, gold and purple. She felt her heart stir in resonance with his energy; the great creature was flowing with love and compassion. A smile came to her lips as her right arm and hand rose in the salute that Uncle Jim had taught her meant, 'Yes!"

Gifford chuckled. "I'll take that as compliment. Do you like the scenery?"

Once again Jennifer saluted, freely laughing aloud. She surprised herself; if the others found anything amiss they said nothing. She wondered if they had heard her.

"Luna, I wish we could dwell on the beauty of this flight. However we will be at the foothills too soon for me to give you a full account of our mission to the west. I will give you a short version to share with Justin Valor, Tuvalla Seer, Samuel and the others at the Keep," said King Gifford.

"I agree," said Luna.

"As you know, years ago a veil of darkness started to form between east and west in Solaria. At first travelers could easily get through but they reported being dizzy and confused as they traversed the five miles that it covered," explained Gifford.

Luna nodded.

"Then it darkened and travelers were sick, depressed and weak for months. Some lost their minds and never recovered," said King Gifford.

"The veil got darker and some who tried to pass through never returned. Others who made it through, after a period of horrible illness and madness, told of horrors that no one could comprehend. Finally the darkness became impenetrable; we lost touch with the west, from the far reaches of the north, to the ends of the south. We have had no contact with the inhabitants of the west for three years, since Contalia and Dohanos left their canine Wisdom Runner companions there, to return to us in the east via portals to Earth and back."

David shifted uncomfortably. Jennifer wished that she could still read his thoughts. Holding on to a tuft of feathers with her right hand she reached the forefinger of her left hand out to touch Millet's hand grasping David's shirt; he smiled up at her.

The movement drew David's attention and he smiled; Jennifer felt his smile was covering worry as he turned back to listen to King Gifford.

"When the Wisdom Runners and the Seers, east and west of the veil of darkness, failed in all attempts to lift it, or find a way to keep communication open, we knew that very serious measures were necessary. Losing all contact with those on the other side could bring complete destruction of Solaria and beyond. It would have devastating consequences on all levels of existence. As far as we know all of the portals from Earth into the west are now sealed. That is why Contalia and Dohanos, both highly gifted Seers and Wisdom Runners, left through the Portal of Nordon to attend the conference of the Servers of Light in the higher plane of existence; they were looking for wisdom and aid to help us," said Gifford.

David turned to Jennifer, "It is rare for people to be both Seers and Wisdom Runners. My parents were both, as are Dohanos, Contalia and Justin Valor, whose Keep we are traveling to. Only highly gifted beings ever make it through the training to become Seers or Wisdom Runners; but those who pass both trainings are truly exceptional."

King Gifford continued, "When Dohanos, Contalia and Justin's dogs did not return after two months, the Seers and Wisdom Runners knew word had to be gotten to the western lands. They called on our flocks. I assembled the best of our Goony Birds to make up this battalion of one hundred. Although we chose a few young birds that showed promise, like Prince Bartholomew, most were seasoned fliers who had experience traveling to all eleven dimensions, known by your Earth physicists, as well as parallel realities. Individually we are visionaries, but as a flock we form a unity that can perform feats that many consider impossible."

"A year ago we flew in formation, uniting our intuitive, visionary powers. We opened a hole in the veil of darkness that now separates east and west and flew through it. All of the flock got through safely and we were able to tour huge portions of western Solaria," explained King Gifford.

"What did you find?" asked Luna.

"We found Contalia's and Dohanos' dogs alive and well; they send their 'Hail!' to you and all here. In the major cities, villages and the Keeps that were intact, we found the inhabitants in good spirits. But there are whole cities and countryside that have been destroyed - they are now held by darkness. When we penetrated into these dark places we found no one alive. We only found the crumbling structures of buildings, tools, clothes and belongings left behind," said King Gifford.

"Did anyone know if any of the inhabitants survived? And if they did, where were they?" asked David.

"No one knew anything. Family and friends had disappeared in the towns, cities and Keeps," said Gifford. "Contalia's and Dohanos' dogs told us that shadows had been seen about; then darkness grew over the now dead places, as had the veil that separates the east and west," said King Gifford.

"Was there any sense as to why those particular cities, towns and Keeps were subjected to the darkness?" asked Luna. "Had the inhabitants done wrong, or special good deeds… or something out of the ordinary that drew attack?"

"Nothing that anyone knew or could intuit. When we penetrated into the dark places there was a strange feeling. It felt like an angry buzz in our heart center - only that does not quite describe it adequately," said King Gifford.

The iris of King Gifford's eye slowed its swirling as his pupil dilated and then contracted again. "There is something more, but I do not want to frighten the young ones."

"I am no longer a child!" said David. He clenched his teeth and looked away.

"David, he knows that. But you have not started your Wisdom Runner training," explained Luna.

"That is because you and Zumulia have held me back!' said David.

"Zumulia and Luna are very wise. They have consulted with

others; what they have done has been with your best interest at heart," interjected King Gifford.

David clenched his jaw but kept his silence.

"There is more, David. Because your parents were Seers and Wisdom Runners you also have the potential for being both. With that potential comes a drawback in that you are still very connected to their energy. When Zumulia consulted me, I agreed at the time that your training should be delayed until you were eighteen. Your nervous system would be more mature, allowing you to heal from any pain resonating from the death of your parents. It would also allow you to block anything evil that was attached to them at the time of their deaths," said King Gifford.

David turned back to face the bird, but with a different, softer look. He wiped a tear from his eye.

"Luna, I have changed my mind. Consult with Justin Valor and his daughter, Tuvalla Seer, when you arrive at their Keep. Tell them that I am recommending for David's training," said King Gifford.

Luna shifted slightly so that she could look at David. She turned back to King Gifford. "I agree with your assessment. In the past few days I have had the same sense. I will consult with Justin and Tuvalla. Now, what were you going to relay?"

"Our flock senses the darkness has grown on the planet Earth since the advent of the First World War in the early 1900's. The two World Wars and further war actions on the planet, the mass extinctions of animals and birds, the selfishness that has led to distressing weather events, earthquakes and volcanoes, the growing focus on materialism and corruption of many politicians and business corporations is directly involved with causing the growing darkness here," said King Gifford.

"But what can be done?" thought Jennifer.

"Jennifer, I hear you," said King Gifford. "We don't know yet. We believe much of the solution must come from Earth. Perhaps that is why you are here, to learn how you can aid healing by finding new ways of living for your planet. Perhaps you will teach others," said King Gifford.

"Now, dear friends," said King Gifford. "Time is too short. We must land; please hold on very tightly."

King Gifford pulled his head up and floated backward to give Prince Bartholomew more room to maneuver for landing. The foothills were indeed just below. The snowcapped mountains loomed purple in front of them as the sun sat low to the west. They descended gently in large, sweeping circles. Luna was again holding tightly to a tuft of magenta feathers with her mouth and bracing with her paws. Jennifer looked back over the green Plain of Vendona, towards the place in the south from which they had come; it seemed impossibly far off with the great forest appearing as a line of darkness.

Prince Bartholomew and the rest of the one hundred landed gracefully on tiptoes. When they came to a halt, three Goony Birds came forward with King Gifford to help the travelers down. When the group was on the ground they stepped backward to be replaced by three birds who set their packs in front of them.

"Thank you, Prince Bartholomew, for the wonderful and pleasant flight!" said Luna.

"Yes, thank you!" said Millet and David at once. Jennifer smiled and waved at the feathered prince, and then reached out to David to take Millet back into her arms.

Prince Bartholomew waggled his large head back and forth on his long neck. "Ga-gooo – Ga-goooo – Ga-gooooooooony!"

"He is pleased that he had the pleasure of serving you!" said King Gifford. "Except for a few words, he does not speak any human tongues yet."

"He is a fine boy. I am sure that he will give great service to the all beings in existence. He will make you, his mother and all Goony Birds very proud," said Luna.

With right long leg in front of left, King Gifford and Prince Bartholomew gave the curtsey-bow of the Goony Birds.

"Thank you, Luna. My son and I will take that as a prayer and a blessing from you for the future," said King Gifford.

"And now I am afraid that we must part. We cannot get you any closer to the mountains. Could you smell the promise of coming snow when we were aloft?" asked King Gifford.

"Yes, my friend. You were correct. This is very strange," said Luna.

"The darkness is disrupting the weather. Our flock must try to get to the Court of King Saul and the convening Court of the Wisdom Runners and Seers before we fly back to the south," said King Gifford. "Please relay our 'Hail' to Samuel if you find him and to Justin Valor, his daughter, and the many who bide with them. I hope that you find Contalia and Dohanos – my heart tells me that they are alive."

"I will relay your news to Justin. We will try to communicate intuitively to you through the Court of the Wisdom Runners," said Luna.

"David, remember that you are your parents' son. I know they would be proud of you now. Please give my 'Hail' to your grandmother," said Gifford.

David placed his hands over his heart and bowed to King Gifford.

"Jennifer, learn well. May we fly again soon!" said Gifford.

She smiled at him and raised her right hand and arm in the sign of 'Yes!'

Gifford lowered his bright orange beak to Luna. She touched her brown nose to it. The giant bird and white dog stood nose to beak for almost a minute as the flock, David, Millet and Jennifer watched in silence.

"Dear one, till soon," said Gifford as he raised his head.

"Till soon," said Luna.

The birds moved into a formation of lines of five. As one they started a chorus of, "OOOOOOOOeeeeee-ooo-wooooooo! OOOOOOOOeeeeee-ooo-wooooooo, OOOOOOOOeeeeee-ooo- wooooooo, OOOOOOOOeeeeee-ooo-wooooooo!" as they ran towards the breeze coming from the east. One hundred pairs of wings whooshed through the air as they pushed themselves into flight. Aloft, the huge mass of color circled as King Gifford separated himself from the flock. He flew a figure eight, tipping his wings to them. Then, with a flourish of his triple-feathered crest, he took the lead of the flock as they straightened their flight path to the east. The four journeyers watched till they could see them no more.

"Come," said Luna. "The light is fading fast and we must try to make it to Justin's." There was a huge sadness in her tone.

David buckled her saddlebag pack onto her. They followed Luna to a narrow, well-worn path leading into the foothills. David kept his bow fitted with an arrow as they traveled in silence; Luna stopped repeatedly to sniff the air and the trail. They hiked over three hillcrests as the light lessened. Pine and spruce were sparse at first and then gradually thickened into a forest. It was night.

Luna sat down. "I know that it is dark but we are less than forty-five minutes from Justin's Keep."

"What do you want to do?" asked David.

"I'm hungry," said Millet. They looked at him and realized it had been hours since they had eaten.

"We cannot take time for a meal right now, Millet. I am sorry. We must try to get to Justin's where I am sure we will be given a good dinner; I promise," said Luna.

"Should we get out the glow weed?" asked David.

"I have the wind-up flashlight that Aunt Sarah packed for me," thought Jennifer.

"Jennifer, wind it up but don't turn it on unless I tell you to. Put glow weed in your pockets so that it is handy if we need it. But for now we will have to travel close, in the dark, so we are not spotted," said Luna.

"Jen, put Millet in your shirt so he can hang on and allow both of your hands to be free; I want you to walk between David and me. You can hold onto my tail for guidance," said Luna.

With Luna leading they made steady progress. Occasionally

the treetops thinned so that they could see the waxing moon in the dark sky overhead. When they came to the forest edge, a vista, lit dimly by the moon, stretched before them; high, outcroppings of rock were scattered across it. Two thousand feet in front of them rose massive walls and rounded towers that glowed cream in the pale moonlight. Long banners, on poles rising from the walls, flew in the light breeze.

Jennifer's breath caught in her chest. "*What is that?*" she thought to Luna.

Luna looked towards her. "The Keep of Justin Valor. We must make our way across this open area to the front gate. Hopefully someone will recognize me in this light as we cross. But first, I will try to signal them."

"David, we must risk using three arrows now. I want you to wrap glow weed around their tips. Send two rapidly, as high aloft as you can aim, to the left. Wait one count, then send the third aloft to the right; it is my special signal. We will wait to see if they answer us," said Luna.

Doing as he was instructed, David fitted the tips of the arrows with the glow weed. Jennifer helped him blow on the tips to light them. He then sent the first two aloft, waited, and then the third.

"Good," said Luna.

They waited for several minutes. Suddenly seven arrows, shot at once, lifted off the high walls. They arced slightly away from where the travelers stood.

"Good!" said Luna quietly. "Justin is there. The seven arrows are his sign. But we must cross the field quietly and swiftly to the main gate; it is not safe for them to be opening the entrance at night.

They started off at a rapid pace. The light from the moon made finding footing easier than in the forest. Mid-way across the field, as they passed the largest of the rock outcroppings, they quickened their pace.

"Psssss! Psssss!" sounded from above them, on the rock, and behind. Luna spun and looked up.

"Pssssss! Pssssss!" came from their right.

"Pssssss! Pssssss! Pssssss!" from the left.

David crouched with an arrow in his bow. Jennifer drew her arms around Millet; her elbows jutted out defensively.

Luna started to growl. "Hissing Cats! Stay close till we know where they are!"

Around them appeared pairs of luminous yellow eyes. "Pssssss! Luna, we meet again!" came a low hiss from behind them.

"Stand with our backs to one another!" growled Luna. "Natab, could that be you?"

"Pssssss! What do you think, sssstupid dog?" came a hiss closer now.

"House cats have good sense. Lions, tigers, bobcats and mountain lions have good sense. But you, Natab, have no sense!" said Luna. "Jennifer, David, Millet blow on your glow weed."

They did so. In the light they saw ten huge, tailless, tiger-sized cats crouched around them.

"Pssssss! Whatssss do we have here? Luna, ssssssince when are you traveling with children?" hissed Natab. Her head was twice as large as the Hissing Cats with her. In the light their large hindquarters and stubby, bobbed tails were visible.

David placed his glow weed on a rock in front of him; he raised his bow. "I am hardly a child now. My parents told me tales of your evil deeds *when* I was a child."

Natab moved closer. "Pssssss! Brave boy! Do I ssssssense the child of the cowardsssss Tumilia and Zarcourt?" she twitched her head slightly as her gold eyes brightened.

"My parents were not cowards!" said David.

"David, hush. Don't let her twisted mind rattle you!" growled Luna.

"And who issssss thissssss girl with you? Sssssssomehow I think that I know her," said Natab almost in a purr.

"Never mind, Natab! What foolishness to threaten us less than a thousand feet from Justin Valor's Keep!" said Luna.

Natab's fur bristled out as she raised her back slightly. "Psssss! You know nothing! Thingssssss are changing in Ssssssolaria. Your rule will be over momentarily!"

"Pssssss! Pssssss! Psssss!" the cats all started to hiss at once. A bright light appeared from the great gate of Justin Valor's Keep.

"Luna, our meeting is being cut sssssshort. Give my 'Hail' to Jussssstin and let him know that I will be sssssseeing him sssssss-hortly if the sssssshadows don't take him afore. Let him know that I no longer fear him," said Natab. "Oh, and boy, your parentsssss died ssssscreaming for mercy!"

David drew his back his bow and let fly an arrow straight between the eyes of the cat nearest him. It fell to the ground dead. The Hissing Cats all started to howl and hiss, backing away before they turned and ran, except for Natab who stood her ground.

"SSSSSTupid boy! I sssshall not forget thissssss! I will take a ssspecial interest in bringing you a death far more painful than your parentsss had!" Natab turned and disappeared into the night.

When she vanished they found themselves surrounded by the light of torches held high by seven riders on horseback. Wearing armor and helmets, they carried shields, torches and reins in one hand as they brandished swords in their free hands.

"Luna, is that really you?" called one of the riders on a dark horse with long mane.

"Yes. Hail and well met, Justin Valor! It is me and three friends," called Luna.

"Wonderful friend, I only see three!" said Justin.

"Here, sir! I am a small Talking Loaf!" called Millet from the safety of Jennifer's shirt.

"Justin, greetings later! Natab was just here. She is gone, but David has killed one of her cats; its body is just to the right, there. We best be behind the safety of the walls as soon as possible!" called Luna up to him.

Justin handed his torch and shield to another rider, dismounted and bent to Luna, greeting her with a quick placement of his hand on her head. "Hail, dear friend! Well met!"

He sheathed his sword. "For expediency it is best if you consent to ride. We did not have time to bring extra horses, so each of you must ride with one of my comrades. I will help you mount."

Grabbing Jennifer by her waist he placed her behind a tall rider on a bay horse. He cupped his hand to give David a leg up, mounting him behind a rider on a grey gelding. He boosted Luna onto the saddle of his own horse and swiftly mounted behind her.

"Move out!" Justin commanded. The seven horses seemed to fly over the path and moat bridge to the gate of the fortress wall. A word from Justin brought guardians, carrying swords and bows, from smaller doors in the wall as the entrance gate opened. Their horses entered into a tunnel lit by torches; at the far end another huge gate opened after the first had closed behind them. Once through the second gate, it too closed behind them. "All safe," came the hail of male and female voices from the wall above them.

They found themselves in a large, enclosed, cobblestone courtyard. Windowed buildings of stone were four stories above them on three sides; the massive, six-story buttress, guarding the Keep, completed the enclosure. Grooms ran forward to take the reins of the horses as the riders and aides helped the travelers to dismount. Orders were shouted as Luna, Jennifer and David were helped off with their backpacks. Smiling, Justin Valor led them through a massive door, down a corridor and into a great hall with blazing fires lit in the stone fireplaces at both ends.

Aides helped Justin divest of his helmet and armor as he led the group to the hall. He now stood before them in a room lit by many candelabras and wall sconces. Tall and handsome, he looked to be in his fifties. His hair was as dark as Jennifer's, long, streaked with white, hanging down past his waist. His green eyes sparked as he smiled, revealing deep crow's feet. He wore a soft grey tunic of woven knit, over black trousers that tucked into grey, felted boots.

"Ahhhh! Luna my friend, spectacular entrance!" he laughed. His voice was soft now that he was not giving orders.

"Woo-woo!" Luna laughed. She then bowed her doggie bow, with forelegs stretched out as she lowered her chest to the stone floor. Justin flourished a non-existent hat, returning a bow from his waist.

"Have you traveled from Zumulia's Keep?" Justin asked. "If so, you must be tired and famished."

"It is good to see you! But yes, we have come from Zumulia's these last two days. We are very tired and hungry," said Luna.

"Then let me get you food and drink. But first, was anyone hurt by the Hissing Cats?" asked Justin.

They all shook their heads.

"I don't think that Natab had any intention of actually harming us. I think that she was playing with us as many cats do with their intended prey; they can't help themselves. But she has become so twisted from her life of malicious actions, that she is making mistakes in judgment. In this case it was stupidity on her part, as we are now warned that she has evil intentions towards us. And a further stupidity because David's arrow took down one of her troops," explained Luna.

Justin looked David over for a moment and nodded. "Well done, David! Introductions once we get all of you seated to some food and drink."

Jennifer cuddled Millet to her as she gazed about the huge, stone hall. Even her father's Hollywood movie sets were dwarfed by this room. She wanted to spend as much time as she could examining the details.

Justin turned to the three aides standing near and spoke with them in low tones. They quickly went off; soon others came with warm basins of water, soap, towels and bunches of fresh mint to rub onto their hands, faces and hair after they had washed. Feeling revived, they were seated at a great wooden table where tureens of soup, platters of vegetables and rice dishes arrived. Pitchers of ice water laced with lemons and mint and apple-raspberry cider were poured into their glasses each time they emptied them. Without introductions and led by Luna's example, Millet, David and Jennifer started eating rapidly as their hunger won out over their manners.

When they were full, they stopped and looked up from their plates. Justin sat at the head of the table with one leg hooked easily over the arm of the large, carved wooded chair that he sat in. A smile played at the corner of his lips as he watched them.

"Luna, when did you and your young friends last eat?" asked Justin.

Luna pushed her muzzle towards the ceiling as she pulled her shoulders downward in a good stretch. "Ahhhhhhh," she said.

Returning to a relaxed sit on her chair next to Justin's, she looked at him. "Sorry about that. Sometimes the doggie instincts get the better of me, even in Solaria. My young friends were following my example!"

"Excellent food! The seasoning was wonderful and had the added benefit of being reviving. Someone here knows their herbs and plants!" exclaimed Millet.

"Hello, little one. I am Justin Valor. I am very glad that you are here; we have missed the Talking Loaves in their absence."

Millet beamed. "I know who you are! Thank you for letting me come to your wonderful table!"

Luna explained how Jennifer and she had rescued the seventy Talking Loaves from the bread ovens when the Keepers of the ovens and orchards had been attacked by shadows.

"Before I go on, let me introduce my other friends," said Luna as she turned to David and Jennifer.

"Luna, if you feel it will not upset them, allow me?" Justin asked.

Luna smiled. "Go ahead. It will be a good introduction for them to see how you work."

Light from the fireplaces danced on the walls as the candlelight played softly on their faces. The shock of the frightening caper with Natab and the Hissing Cats faded with their bellies full. Memories of the beauty of the day and the enchanted flight with King Gifford and his flock drifted back for the four travelers. Justin held a goblet of cider as he studied them.

"I will start with David," he said. "I know you are not surprised that I know your name as I heard Luna using it."

David's blue eyes met Justin's emerald green eyes. He nodded calmly.

"You and I met when you were a child. Do you have any memory of this?" asked Justin.

David considered for a moment and then shook his head. "I am sorry, Justin, I do not. I know of you from my grandmother; from her I learned that you kept me several times when I was small. I do not remember being here or of you visiting my parents and grandmother's Keep."

Justin considered. "Indeed, you were here as an infant when your mother, father and grandmother had a mission together. You were also here just after the death of your parents – but you were ill, so you would not have a memory of it; we cared for you until Zumulia could safely have you at her Keep. You have no memories of my visits because I have not been to your grandmother's since your birth."

David nodded.

"You have been trained well by shepherds and hunters in the ways of bow, knife and slingshot use. Traveling Wisdom Runners have taught you the use of the sword and handling teams of dogs. Your grandmother has taught you the ways of planting, harvesting, herbal use and managing a forest Keep," said Justin. "Zumulia has kept you from learning the ways of intuition and distance communication for fear that you might be harmed by those that follow and give allegiance to darkness," said Justin.

David nodded again.

"You are very loyal and dedicated. You have a pure heart that does not understand why there are those that choose to deliberately harm others. Even less do you understand those that outright choose to align themselves with evil. This inability to understand the malicious heart, combined with an impetuousness of spirit and quick temper, led you to your rash killing of one of the Hissing Cats when Natab insulted your parents," said Justin.

David looked at him. "She had no right to call them cowards!"

"She was probing you," said Justin. "She found an easy way to provoke you to anger. Now, I promise you that she will not rest until she has avenged your rash act," said Justin.

David looked down. His chest heaved visibly.

Jennifer felt Millet shivering in her arms. Until this moment the importance of what had just happened to them with those nightmarish cats had escaped her. *"David is in danger?"*

Luna fixed Jennifer with her eyes and shook her head slightly. *"Ssssssh. Don't interrupt, Jen. Just listen for now."*

Justin placed his goblet down on the table and leaned forward. The light glimmered on his dark, white-streaked hair. "David, I am not criticizing you. You have a temper that can be provoked when those you care about are being attacked. This is also part of the reason that Zumulia and Luna did not want you to begin training earlier. However, I sense a great strength within you that will help you overcome this. You are ready to start the Wisdom Runner training and the beginning levels of Seer work."

David looked up at him. "Am I?" he asked. "I am honored. But these are troubled times. The schools of training for the Court of the Seers and the Court of the Wisdom Runners are many days journey in the East. I cannot leave my grandmother alone, at her Keep, for the seven years that training requires."

"No, you cannot. But you can apprentice with my daughter, Tuvalla Seer, our companions here at this Keep, and myself. Here you are but two days journey to Zumulia's. You can go home often. With Luna and others I will try to open a safe intuitive communication channel with your grandmother to seek her permission," said Justin.

"There is no need to seek Zumulia's consent," came Luna's alto voice. Her white fur glimmered pearlescent in the candlelight. "We discussed David's readiness. Zumulia and I decided that when we found Samuel, and made plans with you for more protection of her Keep, I was to leave David here if you felt that he were ready."

David nodded. Jennifer noticed that he did not seem to have any resentment towards these elders who were making major life decisions for him. She wondered if it was because he trusted the hearts and minds of those who cared for him. Both David and she had had horrible things happen in their lives; she envied David the goodness of the people – dog and human - that he found himself with. She hoped that Grace would soon be with her and that she could eventually have trust like this with Uncle Jim and Aunt Sarah. And of course, Luna.

Justin's eyes fell on Jennifer. She tried to return his gaze as steadily as she could. What would he see?

"You are Jennifer. You are twelve but you feel a lot older at times. Your life is not stable; many challenges have taken place and you feel helpless. On Earth, in fact, in many ways you are helpless," said Justin. "Choices seem to be in the hands of others for your wellbeing. You have come to trust no one."

Jennifer did not move. She searched to find stability inside of herself by focusing on her breath as Luna had taught her. She tried not to have a thought so Justin would not see more of her inner self than she knew herself.

"Jennifer, you have gifts. No one in your life on Earth recognized these gifts until you met Luna. We have sensed you coming for some time. Now here you are," said Justin. He shifted in his chair as he took a sip of cider. "I imagine that it must be unnerving for you to meet Luna, Zumulia and me and have us tell you that we have been expecting you. You also have to make huge adjustments in your perception of reality as you experience our life in Solaria; it is vastly different from the life that you have grown up with. Things here turn all that you know of as reality upside down, sideways and inside out."

David chuckled. His laugh was infectious and the group started to laugh with him. Jennifer felt some of the tension melt. She smiled along with them.

"But Jennifer, if you think back you will see that your coming here has been hinted at previously in your life. Look at your interests. Two years ago you pestered your father for the movie, "What The Bleep," because you wanted to know more about intentional thought and what science said about other levels of existence within the framework of theory in the new physics. You searched for any information on the use of intention and prayer in medicine and science. You read books from the library on energy medicine, psychology, archaeology, the world's religions, ghosts, demons and anything that might explain something that you could not define but knew you had to search for; your school teachers said you read years beyond your age level. Your stepmother made fun of your reading and serious intent; but your father indulged you when he actually took time to notice you," said Justin.

Jennifer felt frozen. Who was this man? How could he, living in this parallel reality, know anything about her life on earth?

"*Relax, Jennifer. I mean you no harm*," came Justin's voice quietly into her mind.

Jennifer's eyes widened. She swallowed hard.

"Jennifer, I am a Grand Master Seer of the Court of Seers. I am also a Wisdom Runner. I, like Luna and Zumulia, want to aid you in finding your gifts and developing them as you find your purpose in life," said Justin.

He turned to Millet who sat on the table next to Jennifer. Jennifer felt her breath soften as Justin no longer centered his gaze upon her.

"And you are Millet. I am so pleased that the Keepers of the Ovens have been able to bring you forth. I am not sure what they used for leavening; you seem to have more of an adventuresome bent than any of the great Talking Loaves that I have known in the past."

Millet peered at Justin. He seemed not to know whether to smile or be nervous.

"Only a few days old when you and your siblings decided you should come along on Luna's journey. I admire that," smiled Justin. Millet puffed himself up and smiled back.

"However, little one, there is great danger in our world right now. We lost all of your kin a few years ago; we cannot afford to lose you because you are being fool-hardy," said Justin. Millet looked crestfallen.

Justin smiled and shook his head. "I am not scolding you, young friend. Now that you are here, you will stay at my Keep and learn from our master bakers, herbalists and cooks to hone your gifts. You are welcome here!"

"Thank you, thank you, thank you! Justin Valor, it is such an honor for me!" Millet was dancing in place on Jennifer's lap. She giggled and reached out to steady him.

Justin stretched. "All of you are welcome here. I want to hear about your personal concerns and your journey here. I also invite you to speak with me about any questions that you might have about what I have just said, your lives and anything that troubles you. But it is late and I think that Luna and I should talk privately while my aides show you to your sleeping quarters."

Luna agreed. "I will join you after Justin and I have had some time to catch up."

Justin gave directions to a few of the young men who were waiting in attendance. Like Justin and David they had long hair that fell past their waists. They were dressed in pale green, woven tunics over dark pants tucked into soft, woolen boots. Silver buckles in the shapes of running dogs held belts from which hung scabbards; the protruding knife handles were silver, carved intricately with swirling shaped patterns.

After David and Millet thanked their host, and Jennifer nodded to him, they left Luna behind as they followed the aides out from the great hall. The wide corridor had walls and a floor of stone; intricately patterned carpet runners muffled their footsteps. Candelabras holding thick, beeswax candles sat on massive wooden carved tables. Higher up on the walls were bronze wolf heads; in their mouths they held baskets of glow weed that gave off soft light. The aides spoke amicably as they led the way to the entrance of a staircase at the far end of the hallway.

The stone stairway curved in three ascending spirals before they reached the corridor above. To the right were windows that reached to the ceiling; they could see down into the courtyard where they had arrived. The hallway was lit with candelabras and glow weed. A line of massive oak doors ran along the inside wall. The aides led them past six doors before opening the seventh.

The shortest of the three turned to them. "Justin wanted you to have a suite of rooms for your stay with us; this way you can spend time alone together, receive visitors and have privacy when you choose. This door leads into your shared receiving chamber."

The young man led them into a large room furnished with comfortable couches and armchairs covered in thick burgundy velvet. A long oak table and chairs stood to one side. Next to the table sat a carved oak sideboard set with a large, silver teapot; teacups and saucers were neatly arranged on one side and a glass-covered platter held bread and muffins on the other. The far wall was filled with tall windows; each sidewall held a fireplace with a carved oak mantel. The stone floor was covered with a deep blue carpet patterned with trees, flowers, dogs and birds around its border. A huge chandelier hung from the ceiling in the center of the room with matching sconces on the walls; they held beeswax candles that filled the room with a faint, warm scent of honey.

As with the giant hall where they had had supper, Jennifer had never seen such a room, except in her imagination when she was reading fairytales and myths. Her heart told her this was even better.

Walking past the fireplace on the left, the aide led them to another door that opened into a bedchamber. Luna's and Jennifer's backpacks sat on a burgundy velvet bench at the foot of the bed. "We hope that you will find this room comfortable. There is a bath chamber through the far door. The armoire holds clothes and bedclothes that you are welcome to use while you are here." He paused to see if the three had questions.

"We thought that Luna and Jennifer would be comfortable in this room," said the aide. He then led them across the living room to a door opposite where they found another bedchamber; David's pack lay on an upholstered bench. "We thought the boys would find this room to their liking. You will find your own bath chamber through the door on the right."

"Is there anything that I can get you before you retire?" he asked. David, Jennifer and Millet looked at each other and then back at him and shook their heads.

"If you have need, just open the door to the corridor and hail us; someone should come to you within moments. Until you know the Keep, please do not wander on your own. It is not that it is forbidden - but this is a very large compound; it holds a maze of corridors where newcomers can easily get lost," he explained.

He hesitated, "Forgive my manners, my name is Lacino. I am a Seer and one of Justin's aides." He joined his two companions in the hall; bowing their heads in a salute, they closed the door.

David took Millet from Jennifer's arms and collapsed into the comfort of one of the huge couches. "My goodness, we have had quite the day!" said David.

Jennifer smiled. Her body ached; in the time since coming to Vermont, and then Solaria, she had had more exercise than she had ever had in her whole life. She realized she just wanted to shed her dirty clothes, take a quick, hot bath, don fresh pajamas and climb into the nice bed Lacino had just shown her.

"This place is incredible. My grandmother has told me stories of it many times. I hear the gardens, apothecary, training centers and craft shops where they work with iron, precious metals, wood and fibers are some of the best that can be found in Solaria. And then there are the caves…" said David.

Jennifer looked closely at him. She took a deep breath and thought, "*What caves?*"

David looked at her quizzically. "I felt a stirring in my mind but I got no words. I hope that we can learn from Luna further how to open a channel of communication between us. If you were asking about the caves – I know very little. Hopefully Justin or Luna will explain them to us tomorrow."

* * *

Chapter Five

Dreams are messages from our heart, soul, spirit, friends, loved ones who have died, other beings who are trying to communicate with us, and our Creator. There are no bad dreams; there are no good dreams. When we fail to examine our dreams, we lose the wealth of insight that we might use in our lives to gain wisdom. Thus we pray for the courage to value our dreams, discern their meaning, learn from their messages, and follow their wisdom.

Book of The Wisdom Runners

Jennifer is in a dark cramped space. Her chest feels bound by metal straps. Something terrible is happening. She must be quiet. Close by are sounds of scuffling, yelling, swearing and banging. A loud shot, a thud - then silence. Her cramped arms and legs start crawling forward on their own – she can't stop them. Her limbs pull and push her out from the darkness from where she is hiding.

In the center of the room sits the giant Hissing Cat, Natah. The many striped markings on her large face ripple and pulse. The cat's gold eyes gleam as she flashes her teeth in a grin from ear to ear. Bringing her large right paw up to her mouth she gives it a few lingering licks and then smoothes her whiskers. Toni, Jennifer's stepmother, is standing in the doorway with a gun.

"Pssssss! Come here, Jennifer. Don't jussssst lie there like a corpssssse," Natab glowers.

The force that first pulled Jennifer from under the bed now lifts her into a standing position. She tries with all of her might to stop her legs – they move her across the room on their own. Her father is lying on the floor. Blood is pooling on the white carpet beneath his head. Her stepmother snarls and throws the gun across the room at Jennifer's feet.

"Pssssss! Pick it up, little Jen!" whispers Natab.

Jennifer cannot stop her body from leaning over… her hands reach out – her fingers close over the gun. It is heavy and black. Her father's limbs are akimbo. This is not right. Deep within her a feeling starts to rip upward and out. A scream breaks free from her chest… trying to make the room and everything in it go away, she screams and screams and screams…

Jennifer's eyes flew open as her screams shattered her sleep. Luna was standing over her, a forepaw on her chest, pushing her back and forth. "Jennifer, wake up!"

A rapping knock sounded on the door of the bedchamber. "Luna, Jennifer, what is wrong? Can I come in?" came David's voice.

"Come in!" Luna shouted to him.

"What's happening? What's the matter?" asked David as he crossed to the bed.

"She's waking now - she was having a nightmare. Help her to sit up," said Luna.

David pulled Jennifer up, plumping the pillows behind her so that she could lean back on the carved headboard. Her arms and hands trembled; her breath came shallow and hard.

"Are you alright?" asked David.

She nodded, trying hard to focus on the room, telling herself that she was not in Los Angeles. Her black hair was in disarray around her face.

"David, could you get her a glass of water from the bathroom?"

asked Luna. He nodded and returned with a large tumbler; her hands trembled when she took it from him.

"Jen, I think it will be awhile for the dream feelings to leave you," soothed Luna. "David, why don't you get us all some tea from the pot on the sideboard? And some muffins, too." He nodded and left the room.

"Do you want to tell me about it?" asked Luna.

Jennifer shook her head. No words formed in her mind.

A knock came at the outer chamber door. They heard David telling someone that everything was okay. He came back carrying a large tray with a teapot, mugs and zucchini muffins. A sleepy Millet toddled in after him. Taking an extra pillow, David propped Millet into a sitting position on the king-sized bed. He handed Jennifer a mug, placed Luna's in front of her, gave Millet a doll-sized cup, and balanced plates of muffins on the bed near each of them.

Luna found a comfortable position, cuddling near Jennifer. "I like a tea party when someone needs comfort in the middle of the night."

Jennifer felt herself smile. She sipped the chamomile and mint tea with honey; the fright gripping her chest and stomach began to melt as her friends sat with her.

Luna took a few laps of tea from her mug. "Mmmmmm, just right. Thanks."

"Mmmmmmm, yes, delicious!" said Millet.

Luna cocked her head. "Jennifer, was this dream like the one that you had at your Aunt Sarah's when you first came to her home?"

Jennifer looked at her and nodded.

"Jen, have you been having nightmares since your father's death?" asked Luna.

Jennifer nodded slowly.

"Has it been the same dream, recurring over and over, since his death?" asked Luna.

Sitting up straighter, Jennifer nodded.

"Did you have nightmares before his death, too?" Luna cocked her head to one side.

Jennifer shrugged her shoulders; letting out a sigh she nodded.

"Many?" asked Luna.

Jennifer nodded in assent.

"But they were different from the recurring dream that you have had since your father's death?" asked Luna.

Jennifer slowly nodded her head; the anxiety in her stomach starting to grow stronger again. Looking into Luna's, David's and Millet's eyes she felt their concern; she sensed David knew what nightmares could be.

"Was anything different tonight in this dream from the others like it?" asked Luna.

Jennifer nodded. The dream had been coming to her every two or three nights since her father had been murdered; it was always the same until tonight. Although she had always felt there might be another presence in the room, she could never see who it was. This was the first time that Natab had been there, or at least visible. The Hissing Cat's glowing yellow eyes started to form in her mind's eye.

Luna cocked her head, reading Jennifer's mind. "Natab was there?"

Jennifer nodded. The knot of anxiety in her stomach felt like it was the size of a basketball.

David looked at Luna, questioning.

"Jen, try not to worry about this right now. Given Natab's attack on us just hours ago, your unconscious mind may simply have added the stress of the fright to the repeating nightmare," said Luna. "And Natab tried to rattle you by inferring that she knew you."

"But dreams have meaning! And they can tell us about the past, tell us the truth about the present, and foretell things for a person for the future," said David.

"Yes, they do that too." Luna licked the last crumbs of the muffin that David had given her. "Dreams are complex. The books on Earth that claim that there is an exact meaning of symbols in dreams, easily looked up in a book, make shallow and trite what is a wonderful mystery. Everyone's symbols are unique to the individual, just as every individual is created an exceptional, wonderful being by our Creator."

Jennifer took another sip of her tea. She knew dreams could have meaning but she had never been able to figure them out, even though she had read as many books as she could find in the library and bookstores.

Luna continued, "One of the purposes of our dreams is to communicate messages from our soul, heart and spirit to our conscious mind – our day mind that we use when we are awake. Our night dreams are like postcards and letters from our deeper, true soul and spirit self, to our waking selves telling us things we need to know in our life."

"We have our own, unique language and symbols that are trying to communicate to us?" asked David.

"Exactly. Our heart, soul and spirit try to communicate messages about what we need for healing and growth, how best to use our time and our innate gifts, and how we should best live our lives – but these messages are communicated in symbols. It is up to us to learn our own individual symbolic language so we know what we are being told," said Luna.

"But what are nightmares?" asked David.

Luna considered for a moment. "All dreaming is complex. You will begin to learn the art of dream interpretations in Wisdom Runner training, and more, if you enter into Seer training. But for now a basic understanding would be that nightmares that repeat themselves are coming from a wise part of you that is trying to bring about healing from an ongoing, stressful situation, or a past trauma in your life."

Jennifer, David and Millet nodded. They were trying to understand.

"There are many things that we just don't want to acknowledge in our waking life, especially if it involves our parents or people we love. Most of us have good hearts and feel, wrongly, that just knowing the truth about our loved ones who have hurt us, and their wrongful actions and deeds, will bring harm to them. This is especially true if our parents have done something bad to us or others," explained Luna. "We often would rather have painful lives than to see the truth of what people have done to us."

"Can't we know the truth, so that we can heal, and still love our friends and loved ones? Even if they have done wrong things?" asked David.

Luna looked at him and then at Jennifer. "Yes, of course. And that is part of the path of wisdom. To be able to see that deeds and choices are wrong, and may have done terrible damage - but that we can, and must, separate the person from their actions. The person who has done harm must be accountable for their actions; they must be stopped from harming again. But a person of honor and wisdom sees that the wrongdoer has a soul, spirit, and was created to be good – whether or not they have chosen to live a good life."

They sat for a moment in silence. "David, please carry our dishes out and then come back so that you, Jennifer and Millet can do a breathing exercise before we return to sleep," asked Luna.

"But I would like to talk more about this," said David. "And I sense that Jen does too." Jennifer nodded.

"Me, too," said Millet. "I want to learn all about dreams."

"David, Jen, Millet - real mastery of dream work takes many years to accomplish. But there are practical aspects that can be learned by all; I am going to teach you one right now," said Luna. The three nodded. David took the tray outside and returned to sit in the armchair next to the bed.

"Okay, now we are going to work with the breath again," said Luna.

"When you wake in the night with a dream, pleasant or harsh, it is best to write notes about it; when you wake in the morning you will remember enough of it to write down the whole dream. Writing dreams in a dream journal will help you learn your unique dream language," said Luna.

"With a nightmare, it helps to tell them to trustworthy friends or family members if they are there when you have them; it will help to relax you. Sipping on a cup of chamomile tea, or milk with honey, is calming, too." Luna shifted her weight.

"The most important thing is to tell yourself that you have written notes or told the dream out loud; and that you will not think about the dream for the rest of the night. You promise yourself to think about the dream in the morning; but for now you make a decision to think only on good things while you fall back to sleep," said Luna.

The three nodded.

"Then you stretch your arms and legs slowly and gently," said Luna. Each of them stretched in place several times.

"Now take in some big breaths and slowly release them," said Luna. The three took ten long breaths.

"Okay, now think of something that you really love. Perhaps it is a place with a beautiful garden, or the seaside with waves gently lapping at the shore, or a meadow with a view of a mountain. It could also be a beautiful flower with a smell and color that you love, like a rose or chrysanthemum. Or it could be a color of light that helps you feel happy when it surrounds you. Just find something that you find happiness in when you call it up in your mind's eye and focus on it," said Luna.

"What if it changes?" asked Millet. "At first I was seeing the beautiful garden with daisies at Zumulia's; then I was in her rose garden seeing the many pinks and reds of the roses, while inhaling the wonderful scents there; and then I was flying along with King Gifford and his flock in a beautiful sky, like we had when we flew with him."

"Good question. If what you are seeing changes, then just allow it to – if it brings you joy. If it becomes negative, change it to something you love. Enjoy the color, smells, textures and sounds," said Luna.

"Once you are seeing something beautiful and calming, you can start to focus on your breath as I taught you in the cave for communicating with intuition. Only this time it is a much more gentle focus because you are also allowing the beautiful scenes, smells and sounds to drift in your mind as well," said Luna.

"As you sit or lay down in a comfortable position, you allow your breath to go deeper in and out, as if it is floating inside of you. Eventually feel it go all the way down to your toes and out again," explained Luna. "If you keep allowing the breath to be gentle, as it floats in and out, and continue seeing beautiful scenes and things that bring you happiness, you will be relaxing your nervous system. This will allow you to have sleep that will restore your mind and body so you will wake well and refreshed in the morning.

Luna was resting her head on her paws as she watched the three starting to nod. "David," she said quietly. "Carry Millet back to your bedroom. We will see each other in the morning."

* * *

Daylight splashed through the tall windows as Jennifer opened her eyes. Luna's head was on the pillow next to hers. She reached out her hand to rub the soft white, thick fur. Luna opened her eyes and twisted around so that her belly was up in the air. Jennifer moved her hand in circles up and down Luna's chest and tummy.

Luna stretched her forepaws forward and her rear legs backward as far as they could go. "Ahhh, you have no idea how good this feels. There is nothing like a good belly rub in the morning!"

Jennifer alternately stretched her legs, feet, and toes as she continued to rub Luna. She felt calm inside; her body relaxed.

"Luna, that breathing exercise you taught us last night really worked. I feel good this morning, thank you," Jennifer thought.

Luna rolled over to look at Jennifer. "I'm glad. There are many things that you can do to help yourself heal and have a good life. It's your responsibility to learn the tools and then to use them when you need them. Try doing that exercise each night, as you are falling asleep – it will always help you to sleep well."

Luna rose and jumped off the bed and shook herself vigorously. "Jen, why don't you wash up? I will go and rouse David and Millet." Luna went to the door, jumping up, hitting the levered handle with her paw; the heavy door opened a crack, which allowed her to open it wider so she could pass through. Jennifer pushed from the comfort of the quilts; after bathing she dressed in soft, black pants and a soft, woven tunic of magenta cotton that she found in the intricately carved, free-standing closet. Unlike its predecessors, the nightmare had left no residue of fear and bodily aches in its wake.

Jennifer padded barefoot into the main room of their suite. David, Millet and Luna were perched on a window seat that looked out onto a huge common, filled with brick pathways, gardens, stone fountains and places to sit. Further on lay a great field where a number of horses and dogs were interacting with humans and each other. On either side stood a long row of three-story high buildings. Luna explained that the buildings held shops and artisan studios for producing the clothing, tools, and many items needed at Justin's Keep. The Keep was the largest outpost between the east and the west; it served as an advanced training and gathering center for both Seers and Wisdom Runners. The group could see the massive outer walls of the compound, which curved around and away from them until they attached themselves on each side to the mountain behind.

Luna hopped off the window seat and opened the door to the outer corridor. They followed her to a stone staircase that descended to a dining chamber. A long oak table was laid out with breakfast things.

Lacino appeared immediately. He was dressed in faded corduroys and a purple tunic. In the daylight they could see that the running wolf on his belt buckle had emerald eyes. The carved handle of his dagger was also set with emeralds. "Did you have a good sleep?"

"Yes," Luna said as she jumped onto the upholstered seat of the chair that Lacino held out for her. Jennifer took a chair next to her.

David sat across from them; he placed Millet on a velvet tabletop cushion that had been provided for him.

Going to a doorway opposite the staircase Lacino spoke to some aides. Within moments they brought out pitchers of freshly-squeezed carrot juice, a hot beverage made of roasted dandelion roots, and plates of poached eggs on a bed of spinach and amaranth, a grain, topped with butter.

"Mmmmmmm! Jen, this dandelion root tea is good for your liver, which cleans our blood!" said Millet. "And amaranth has a delicate, nutty taste if you have never had it before. It is filled with all the B vitamins, calcium and good nutrients that you need for your nervous system." His knowledge of food had increased during the night.

Lacino stepped near Jennifer. "I am sorry that you had a disturbing nightmare. How are you this morning?"

She looked up at him and wondered if he could enter into her mind. She nodded, hoping that it communicated that she was well.

"I will not enter your mind unless you ask me. I am a Seer of the Order of Seers. As my group sat together last night we felt the disturbance in the energy of the Keep. When we came to give aid, David confirmed that you had had a nightmare," Lacino said. He was genuinely concerned.

"Jennifer has only been in Solaria a few days. I gave my young friends their first dream work instruction last night," said Luna.

Lacino turned to Luna. "I did not mean to interfere," he said. "You are a great teacher, Luna. If Jennifer stays here, the Seers can work with you to give her further aid and instruction. I know that you will speak to Justin about this, as well as his daughter."

"Where is Tuvalla?" asked Luna.

"She and a number of Seers spent the last few days in the Cave of Dreaming Children. If all goes well we expect her back today," answered Lacino.

"Good. Then perhaps we will see her before we search for Samuel," said Luna.

"You are seeking Samuel?" asked Lacino.

"Yes, that is why we have traveled from Zumulia's Keep. As you know, distance communication is not safe so we weren't able to send you advance notice of our arrival," said Luna.

A smile flickered across Lacino's lips as he looked beyond them.

"It's about time you found us!" came a deep, booming voice from the door behind them. They turned to see a tall black man, smiling broadly; a large gold front tooth sparkled in the morning sunlight that streamed through the windows. Numerous braids of dark hair, twisted with beads and figured trinkets, hung to his waist. His tunic was of deepest midnight blue with sprays of stars woven into the fabric. In front of him stood many large furry dogs; they had massive heads and shoulders, twice the size of Luna's. The dog pack members were white, black, and a combination of black and white shaggy fur with blue, brown, and bi-colored eyes; they stood proudly with ears and eyes at alert. Slightly behind Samuel stood Justin Valor.

Luna looked up at the ceiling as if watching for errant flies. She yawned and stretched, then settled back down on the chair, again studying the ceiling.

Laughter echoed off the stone walls as Samuel crossed the room to Luna. She jumped up, placing her paws on his chest as he bent his face down to her, holding her white head between his dark, massive hands. They stood nose to nose as Samuel continued to laugh.

"Hail and well met! Oh sweet friend, it is so good to see you," said Samuel. "And still a clown, despite the gravity of our circumstances!"

"Hail and well met, yourself! We must not lose our humor or all is lost," said Luna.

"Truer words have not been spoken," said Samuel. He turned to reach his hand across the table to David who was smiling. "My good friend, I am so glad to see you."

Justin, surrounded by Samuel's dogs, came closer to the table.

Samuel turned to Millet, still sitting on the table. "And you must be the wonderful young Talking Loaf!" said Samuel.

"Yes, my name is Millet."

Samuel turned to Jennifer. "I won't stand on formalities! You must be Jennifer, the human that Luna has brought through the portal from your Uncle Jim's farm. I am pleased to meet you." He held out his hand, which Jennifer shook.

"Ahhhh-hemmmm!" came a voice from behind him. Samuel stepped back and turned slightly.

"As I said to Jennifer, no formalities! Introduce yourselves!" he said to the large dogs behind him.

The largest male with thick, black fur came close to their table and boomed in a base voice, "Nicco!" He saluted with his front paw to his brow, then bowed low with his front legs to the floor and his bum in the air, laughed loudly and paraded back to his pack.

A black and white female walked forward as if she were a queen in front of her subjects, "Tundra!" then turned, wiggled her bottom and tail at the group and giggled before returning to her pack.

A sable and white female raced forward, "Woooo – ooo – Wooooooooo, woo! I'm Honey!" turned and raced back to her group.

The introductions continued with much canine silliness as Rampart, Alex, Rock, Buck, Libby, Jose, Hannah, Topi, Thorn, Lawrence, Brazil, Coal, Hermi, Angel, Fred, Sweetie, Thomas, Sylvia, Calli, Umbra, Sookie, Bunny and Daniel proclaiming their names in a variety of voices ranging from low to high, raspy to clear. The group continued to dance, clown and prance as they did so; Jennifer could not stop laughing at their antics.

Luna jumped down and went nose to tail with each bear of a dog as the rest milled around. Fur raised into hackles at their shoulders; they barked, growled and yipped as they interacted and postured. Samuel, with a wide smile showing his gleaming, gold front tooth turned to Jennifer, "Nothing to worry about – they are just saying hello, canine style. They may be Wisdom Runners, but they are also dogs; they go through this every time they meet. They are all good friends."

Luna returned to sit up on her chair as most of the dogs moved close to one of the walls to observe the action without being in the way. Nicco, the large black dog with a chewed left ear came to sit in a chair next to Samuel. Next to Nicco, the piebald female, Tundra, sat; she looked regal and wise. They were obviously Samuel's close confidants. Justin took a seat at the head of the table. Lacino brought dandelion-root coffee for Justin and Samuel while aides placed bowls of tea and plates of biscuits and muffins in front of the dogs.

"Samuel, we came up the main trail seeking you. We found not a trace, and now, here you are!" exclaimed Luna.

"He arrived last night shortly after you went upstairs. I told him as much as I could of what you shared with me," said Justin.

"Luna, I know that Glacier is dead. He was your brother and to us he was a great friend and a pack member; we shall always honor him in our hearts," said Samuel. All of the dogs, including Luna, started to sing-howl like wolves. The mournfulness in their voices tugged at Jennifer's heart. Finally the song softened until there was silence in the room.

"Samuel, it is good of you to honor him. Glacier will be missed; but one day we will all run together again in the light. You were an exemplary friend to him; he could not have served a better human or dog pack. I was more concerned for you as I know of the bond that you had," said Luna.

"Luna, your brother knows I dearly loved him. I still do. I, too, know that death is simply a curtain that one day will part so that we will be together in the light. Glacier understood how much danger Solaria is in, and will understand now if we do not spend time in mourning, but move forward to counter the darkness taking our land," said Samuel.

"Well spoken," said Justin. The dogs gave woofs of assent.

"Then let us move on. How did you arrive here? You were not ahead of me?" asked Luna.

"No. I will back up a bit. The Keepers of the Ovens and Orchards near Zumulia's Keep sent word when they went into hiding after the shadows attacked them. Many of our animal neighbors started disappearing; the dogs and I found homes destroyed or left with uneaten meals on the table, laundry hung out to dry, chores half done with tools scattered about," said Samuel as he paused to sip his dandelion coffee.

He continued, "Soon eighteen of our neighbors' homes were abandoned. Then some of the dogs were attacked by the shadows. One night Brazil was cornered and nearly had her soul taken from her when the shadows tried to suck it out; she escaped with the shadows close behind her. Nicco, Tundra and the pack intervened but it was a close call," explained Samuel.

"These times call for caution, no matter how experienced a Wisdom Runner is," said Justin.

"Exactly," said Samuel. "My Keep is not as sheltered from the attacks of darkness as is Zumulia's. I knew Zumulia needed to stay at her Keep to hold that part of Solaria; I knew that she has the power to do so. She is a Seer; I am a Wisdom Runner with two teams of the best canine Wisdom Runners in all of Solaria! We felt it best to get here, parlay with Justin, and then come up with a plan to search for Contalia and Dohanos to see what healing solutions they may have from the Servers of Light."

"But how did you get here?" asked Luna.

"Glacier was sent to you with the note. It was a ruse of sorts. I knew that you or Zumulia could read his mind, where most, even the best Seer, shadow or demon could not," said Samuel. "You would know that we did not travel the main trail."

Nicco lifted his head. "I should have gone!" He groaned in his low, bass voice.

Samuel turned to him. "Glacier would not hear of it! He knew that I needed all of my team, and especially my best leaders, if we are to find Contalia and Dohanos."

"Glacier was right. He may not have made the ranks of Wisdom

Runner, but he was a great dog and died doing service for Solaria," said Luna.

The dogs chorused into singing again for Glacier's courage.

"He was never able to see how much we valued him; but he will always have a place in our hearts," said Nicco. His blue eyes stood in sharp contrast to the black of his furry head.

"He is now in the light, and he now knows how much we loved him, and love him still," said Samuel. "But to continue, we did not set out on the main trail as the note said we would – it was meant as a ruse should Glacier fall to an evil force. We sensed that Luna had crossed into Solaria with Jennifer. We knew that Glacier, had he reached you, would let you know that we were planning to follow a different route. When he did not return to us, we knew that something terrible had happened." Luna nodded that she understood.

"We accessed the caves under the Lake of Sleoden," said Samuel.

"But those caves were flooded and cut off more than fifty years ago, of Earth time, when the Americans were testing the atom bomb on the Bikini atolls on Earth. The nuclear explosions shattered through to this parallel reality," said Luna.

"Yes, the accesses were blocked years ago. The dogs and I used visioning techniques to repair some of the damage; we have been working on it in secret for several years. We also used some old-fashioned doggy digging," laughed Samuel. Then his face became more somber. "We found the entrance to the underground Swinburg Trail."

"A spur of that trail used to come out in a deep part of the cave where we spent the night, at the southern edge of the Plain of Vendona," said Luna.

"And it still does. The dogs found your scent when we broke through into the main part of that cave. We were an hour behind you," said Samuel. "We were resting under some trees, after a swim, when we saw King Gifford and the Goony Birds fly over. We tried to get their attention but it was too late; they didn't see us."

"It was good that King Gifford cut so much time off of your journey," said Tundra. "It would have been bad business had Natab and her Hissing Cats found you on the trail in the forest when it was dark."

"Peaberry, Lioness, Buttercup and Stormina should have been with you; you needed Wisdom Runners," said Nicco. "These young ones are not trained, brave though they may be."

"I know. With Glacier dead, I feared for your safety; the fear clouded my judgment," said Luna.

"These are strange times, Luna," said Justin. "There is a cloud over all of our senses that we use to guide us; none of us are making the best decisions. Without being able to intuitively communicate safely at a distance, with the fear that seeps into our lands, with the shadows and darkness - we fall short of what we have trained to be."

Samuel, the dogs and the aides in the room nodded sadly. "When my daughter, Tuvalla, returns we must sit in counsel," said Justin. "We can make plans."

"We must try communication with Zumulia, King Saul and the Court of the Wisdom Runners and Seers convening in the east," added Samuel.

The group fell silent. Jennifer studied the faces of the adult dogs and humans as they seemed caught up in their own thoughts.

Finally Justin looked up from his mug. "I will ask the Seers to call their groups together for a meeting when my daughter returns. We need to use the Wisdom Cave of Dreams to try to communicate with the courts in the east and Zumulia before we lay our plans. It is possible that Dohanos and Contalia have somehow traveled to the Court of the Wisdom Runners and are there now," said Justin.

Justin called his aides to him. After conferring in quiet tones, a number of them left the room. Justin turned to the group. "Why don't we show Millet, David and Jennifer around some of the Keep? The morning is long, and no doubt you dogs would like to take a few runs at the snow trails."

Except for Luna, Nicco and Tundra who continued to sit

placidly on their upholstered chairs, the pack of dogs jumped up and became a moveable sea of fur, leaping, yipping and dancing. "Snow! Play! Hurray!"

Jennifer turned to Luna, "*Snow*?"

"Yes, Jen. Snow. The Seers are able to manifest things and events when they are united in vision. Justin's Keep is situated against a special mountain, with massive protective walls, that give safety and shelter. Within this Keep the Seers' powers of visioning and manifesting have not been lessened by the darkness affecting the rest of Solaria. For training and fun they have trails with snow, even in the warmest months," explained Luna.

"We would be honored to have you ride with us," said Tundra. Samuel and Nicco both nodded as the cavorting pack gathered around Jennifer.

"YES! RIDE WITH US!" they sang together. "Come Jennifer! Ride with us!" Their exuberance was infectious.

"Luna, may I?" asked Samuel as he reached out a hand to Jennifer.

"Absolutely, if Jennifer wants to," said Luna. "Jen, what do you think? If you are going to spend time in Solaria you must learn the basics of mushing with a team of dogs."

"Jennifer, we are not just dogs," said Tundra. "We are Wisdom Runners!"

The group of bouncing dogs cheered happily, "We are Wisdom Runners!"

Samuel stood as Tundra, Luna and Nicco jumped to the floor from their chairs. David rose and took up Millet from his pillow on the tabletop. Samuel offered his hand again to Jennifer. "Jennifer, the dogs are explaining that they are equal members with the humans of the Order of the Wisdom Runners."

Luna moved to her side. "We have advanced training in healing, visioning the future, knowing events that are taking place across distances and non-verbal communication. We know how to work as a team pulling a sled - but we are also instrumental in missions of our Order that serve the good of all living beings."

"Wisdom Runner training is vigorous; it takes talent and skill to pass the examinations," said Justin. "But above everything, one must be dedicated to truth and love for all, above one's own needs."

"In Solaria, which is only one of many worlds in this plane of existence, the Wisdom Runners and Seers have kept light, love and service to others as the guiding principals for our life here," said Luna.

"Enough!" exclaimed Tundra. One side of her face and muzzle was white, the other black. Each side had a patch of the opposite color just where her eyes were; on the black side, a patch of white held a brown eye, and on the white side, a black patch held a blue eye; she looked like a canine rendition of the Chinese Tao. "Jennifer is a child of twelve. Wise and gifted, yes! But she cannot learn all of who we are in one sitting!"

All black, blue-eyed, massive Nicco moved closer. "An important aim of the order of the Wisdom Runners is to support and participate in bringing forth joy and love into life. We dogs bring balance to the Order because humans can easily sink into despair. So come, now, let's play!"

Justin and Samuel laughed. "They are right," said Justin. "The morning is waiting for us!"

Justin led them out into the large courtyard that they had first seen from the windows of their suite. The water in the stone fountains splashed pleasantly. The scent and color of the many flowers and flowering bushes invited walkers to take a seat on one of the elaborately carved benches to rest, read, reflect, or just enjoy the day. Justin took them through some of the shops and studios that lined the courtyard. He pointed out the stories above that held rooms and apartments for Seers, Wisdom Runners, aides, apprentices and artisans. Wrought-iron fenced balconies ran the length of the two upper levels; filled with large pots and window boxes growing a profusion of flowers and hanging ivies, poles with banners, chairs to sit on, sculptures, and wind chimes - the effect was festive. The humans and dogs they met along the way were pleasant and cheerful.

On the green beyond the buildings they found themselves watching horses running through paces. Individually and in groups they jumped barriers, did figure eights and serpentines, charged at full speed, and then came to a full halt as their hind legs slid under them. They were magnificent to watch.

A bay mare with flowing mane and tail broke from the group, trotting over to stand in front of Justin. Placing her face and forehead to Justin's chest, she nickered softly, and then stepped back a few paces. Her dark eyes were intelligent and shy, her delicate nostrils flared as she took in the group. "Sooka," Justin said softly. "These are good friends."

"Hail! Well met!" said Sooka. Her voice was low and modulated.

"Hail! Well met!" chimed the dogs, Millet, and the humans. Jennifer looked up at David.

"Horses talk in Solaria, too. They were not speaking last night because they are shy with strangers," explained David.

"Sooka, we are on our way to the snow trails," said Justin. "Please carry on with your training." She bowed her head slightly to them, turned and trotted back to the group she had been working with.

"Beautiful horse, Justin," said Luna.

"Sooka was in the east at the schools of the Court of the Wisdom Runners for many years. She was born here, of one of my favorite horse companions, Rainia, who has gone on to the light. Spelia, her father, is on a mission to the west and has not returned. Perhaps I will learn something of his whereabouts or fate from King Gifford," said Justin.

"I am sorry, Justin," said Luna. "Gifford said nothing to me. But we had little time together."

Without warning, the dogs, including Luna, suddenly took off at racing speed. They sped this way and that, leaping over each other, nipping at each other's curled tails and breaking into small groups that tried to outrace each other. They woofed and sang joyfully as they played.

"Now there is one of the most joyous teams of dogs that I have ever known!" exclaimed Justin.

"We are fortunate to be with each other in this life," said Samuel.

David looked like he was about to run straight to them and join in their play. "Samuel, may I drive one of the teams? It has been months since I have been on snow."

"Yes, you may," said Samuel. "Justin, David here is really progressing with his mushing skills. The dogs love him. He can navigate over very rough terrain, keeping the sled balanced and upright; he is skillful at hitting targets with both the slingshot and bow from a fast-moving sled. He will do even better once he starts the Wisdom Runner training and learns to communicate intuitively with the dogs."

"Can I drive, too?" asked Millet.

David laughed. "I don't think so. You are a bit small to be handling a sled. But you could ride tucked into my tunic."

"Millet, you have much to learn about cuisine and herbalism. And I will speak to the herbalists and chefs to get your apprenticeship started," said Justin. "I think you can learn the dog mushing commands, and the sledding procedures, so you can assist a Wisdom Runner on a mission as Talking Loaves have done in the past."

Jennifer looked at Millet. He was excited about riding with David; but she sensed that given a chance he would be off with a dog team of his own. Millet did not seem to understand his own limitations until trouble was upon him.

Justin's dogs ran into a long, low building; they bounded back out with brightly colored harnesses in their mouths. They ran straight to Jennifer. "Jennifer, would you please harness us?" asked Tundra.

As David, Justin, Samuel and Millet watched she took the bright blue harness that Tundra held in her mouth. Holding it as her Uncle Jim had shown her, Jennifer slipped it over Tundra's large white and black head, pulled each of Tundra's front legs through the proper loops and then pulled the back of the harness towards her black, fluffy, curled tail.

"Thank you! You have learned well from your Uncle Jim on Earth; he is a great musher!" Tundra bowed, front paws forward, chest lowered to the ground; she smiled up at Jennifer, each of her eyes, one brown and one blue, glimmered in the sunlight.

"Now, if you would honor me?" asked Nicco, in his base voice. He weighed twenty pounds more than Jennifer, and as she helped him into his harness, she could feel his strong muscles under his mass of black fur. He, too, doggy bowed and smiled when she finished.

Then the rest of the pack started shouting, "Now me! Now me!" In the mass of happy, dancing, furry dogs, David, with Millet perching on his shoulder, Jennifer, Justin and Samuel helped them into their harnesses.

Now ready, the dogs ran to the sleds sitting in a thick carpet of snow in the midst of the green, summer grass. "Jennifer, come help us get hitched to the sleds!" called several of the dogs. Once hitched, they jumped in the air vigorously, trying to pull the anchored sleds forward as they howled cheers of excitement. "Hike!" "Yahoo!" "Let's go!" "Whoopee!" "Smokin'!" mingled with yelps, howls and yips of pleasure.

Justin, David and Samuel took their places standing on the long runners behind the sleds. The three men pulled their long hair into clasps at their necks and each put on goggles. David tucked Millet in front of his tunic so that he could stay warm and view the team. Justin motioned for Jennifer and Luna to hop into his sled.

Samuel took off with his team of twelve dogs, led by Nicco and Rampart; the dogs' paws and sled runners blew sprays of powdered snow as they dashed onto the trail into the wooded area. With Angel and Fred in the lead, David's sled took off, also spraying snow as they seemed to fly along the ground.

"Hike!" yelled Justin as he pulled up the sled's snow hook anchoring the sled. The earsplitting cacophony of barking, yelping, baying and vocal cheering slipped into silence as they took off. The dogs galloped along the trail of snow as the summer green foliage of bushes and trees glided by. In unison, the team of dogs sparkled with the spirit of joy; Jennifer felt their magic filling her heart.

After ten minutes of mushing, Justin called loudly, "Whoa, doggies!"

"You don't have to shout at us!" yelled several dogs back to him. "You can communicate with us intuitively!"

"It was for Jennifer's benefit!" laughed Justin. "Indeed, with Wisdom Runners, a musher only needs to think the commands to the dogs; but I wanted you to hear the verbal command." The dogs started to slow and then came to a halt; Justin slipped the snow hook into the snow, stepping hard on it to anchor the sled.

"Come with me, Jennifer," said Justin as he held out his hand. He led her forward, up the line of dogs, checking their harnesses and towlines for frays; the dogs happily asked her how she liked the ride so far.

At the front of the team Tundra looked up at her, "I think it's time that you take a lesson on the sled runners with Justin. No time like the present."

"How about it, Jen?" asked all black, blue-eyed Umbra, who stood next to Tundra in lead.

"Learn to mush! Learn to mush!" came the cry of the rest of team members.

They were so joyous, Jennifer started laughing. She raised her right arm in the signal of, "Yes!" The pack cheered.

With Luna riding as a passenger, Justin had Jennifer stand with a foot balanced on each runner of the sled, her hands holding the curved handgrip that formed the back. After showing her how to brake and steer, standing behind her on the runners, he pulled the snow hook and shouted, "Hike!"

The team took off again. Jennifer remembered to focus on her breath as she hung on tightly. This was a whole new sensation; a bit like being on cross-country skis – but being pulled by the dogs. She felt free, yet connected to the dogs and nature.

"*Do you like it?*" Luna asked into Jennifer's mind.

"*Yes!*" thought Jennifer. Justin laughed behind her.

"There is nothing like a dog team. I am a bit older now and actually like riding in the sled more than pulling…" said Luna.

"*Lazybones!*" came Tundra's voice into Jennifer's head. Somehow she knew that Tundra had sent it into both Luna's and her mind.

"Watch it, young lady; one day, you too will be a middle-aged dog!" laughed Luna out loud.

"*Isn't this great, Jen?*" "*Yahoo!*" "*Splendid job!*" "*You're on your way to being a musher!*" and a host of doggie communication flooded Jennifer's mind.

"Knock it off, you dogs! Jennifer is just learning to communicate intuitively; let's not overwhelm her!" commanded Luna.

Justin patted Jennifer's shoulder. "Jen, the team communicates intuitively with their human musher and each other. One of the differences between Solaria Wisdom Runners and an Earth dog team is this communication; many Earth mushers love their dogs and do communicate empathically with them, but not on this direct level. We don't have to shout our commands. The dog leaders can communicate what they are seeing to us and give advice as they go. We are a real team when we are on a mission."

The trail led to a large field that was filled with snow trails criss-crossing it in wide loops and turns. Justin taught Jennifer how to use her weight on the runners to balance and turn the sled. He also showed her how to help slow the sled, or stop it, so that it would not run into the dog team.

As they practiced turns and handling, they could see David and Samuel with their teams playing in the distance. They were taking turns driving past targets that they hit with arrows from their bows, or stones from their slingshots. With each bull's-eye their dog team would cheer and verbally tease the other team. "I think they are having too much fun," said Justin.

"Never!" shouted Luna, Tundra, Umbra, Thomas, Sylvia, Buck, Rock, Lawrence, Thomas, Brazil, Calli, Daniel and Bunny in unison.

When the morning was over the group walked back to the main manse of the Keep while most of the dogs ran off to swim. The great hall was set with a grand buffet for their lunch. David and Jennifer made plates for everyone while Luna and Millet took seats at the table.

Millet was thrilled. "This is the best combination of herbs and spices on zucchini that I have ever tasted."

"How much zucchini have you had?" teased David.

"Well, not much," said Millet. "In fact, this is the first. But I seem to have some sort of genetic memory. Like I have for dog sledding!" This brought laughter to many in the room.

"How did he do out there?" asked Luna.

"He did well. I tied a pouch on the handlebars so that he could stand and hold on to balance himself. He couldn't work the brakes or steer because he isn't big enough; but he learned the commands of 'Gee,' 'Hah,' 'Hike,' 'On by!' and 'Whoa!' readily. Soon he was communicating with the dogs intuitively, which is something that I have not learned yet," said David.

"You will start soon," said Samuel.

"Jennifer did well, too," said Luna. "Someday she will handle a sled well. The dogs were able to communicate with her almost immediately."

Justin returned from his errand into the kitchens. With him was a tall, willowy woman of about twenty-five. She was dressed in a tunic of green, black pants tucked into soft, felted wool boots. Dark black hair cascaded in waves down her back, caught away from her face with a silver clasp. She surveyed the room with large green eyes; they were the same emerald as Justin's.

"This is my daughter, Tuvalla," said Justin.

The group stood, "Well met!"

"Thank you. Well met to you, as well," said Tuvalla. Her voice was clear with honeyed tones. "Please, sit back down. Hello, friends Samuel and Luna!"

"And hello to you, dear friend," said Luna.

"And as always, my Hail to you! The dogs will be very pleased to see you again," Samuel gave a flourishing bow.

"As I will be pleased to see them. I have missed their courageous hearts, energy and humor," said Tuvalla. She took the cup of tea Lacino handed to her and sat next to her father. "And hello to new friends, David, Jennifer and Millet – I look forward to knowing you. However, right now, I must be brief and expedient: We need Samuel, Luna and the dogs working with us if we are to communicate through the darkness to Zumulia, the Courts of King Saul and the Wisdom Runners."

"We will convene a planning meeting of Seers and Wisdom Runners this afternoon after our meal," said Justin. "The Seers have readied the Wisdom Cave of Dreams where we will all meet, including David, Jenifer and Millet as soon as the sun sets."

"Is there any way that we can be of service while you are gathering to plan?" asked David.

"Well, our staff are Seers or Wisdom Runners so I cannot spare them to teach you or show you around further. With the shadows and Natab lurking you cannot go outside the walls of the Keep, nor should you wander around on your own until you know your way," said Justin.

"May I take Jennifer and Millet out to the target range to practice with slingshots and shooting arrows? Afterward we can come straight through the door here to spend time in our rooms."

Justin nodded. "That sounds productive and fun. I will have some books and maps of Solaria sent up to your rooms that you might enjoy looking over when you finish with your practice. I am sorry for the inconvenience."

"There is no inconvenience. I will be happy to teach Jennifer how to use the bow and slingshot," said David.

Samuel, Justin, Luna and Tuvalla quietly watched the three: a silent, traumatized, slip of a girl with black hair running wild with curls, gazing back at them with luminous green eyes; a tall muscular youth with wisdom beyond his years, and a mischievous Talking Loaf, with a face reflecting kindness of heart. The group spent the rest of the meal telling Tuvalla of the morning fun she had missed with Samuel's dogs and Justin's canine apprentices on the snow trails.

* * *

The target range lay beyond the snow trails. Jennifer found the large, straw-stuffed bull's-eye targets were easier to hit than grey rocks in the woods. She made progress using the slingshot. "To be good one has to spend hours practicing. It may take awhile before you get a feel for it. Just keep seeing and feeling yourself hitting the target as Luna taught you," David told her.

When they began shooting arrows, Jennifer surprised herself. David demonstrated proper form, holding the bow firmly but not rigidly. He reminded her to breathe, feeling the arrow as it was pulled back on the taunt bow in the now, and seeing the arrow hitting the center of the target at the same time. Present and future as one.

Jennifer drew the arrow back, held it for several long, deep breaths, and then released it. It flew in a slight arc, sailing past the target a few inches to the left. David handed her another arrow and helped her to adjust her form.

Jennifer took her time. As she followed her breath, felt her feet on the ground, and saw the future of the arrow hitting the target as happening now, she started to find herself in a timeless place. It was vibrating with a feeling of awareness and aliveness that she had experienced in the cave when Luna led them through the intuitive communication work. She released the arrow and watched as it arced through the air, hitting the target three inches to the left of the center bull's-eye.

"Good. Breathe, and erase this experience from your mind. You must start with a fresh image of success with each release," said David. He handed her an arrow. "Put the past aside now and start over."

Jennifer felt the brightness of the day around her. As her breath flowed in and out, simultaneously she sensed the beauty of her surroundings and the immediate task of shooting the arrow into the target. At one with her goal, and with greater life pulsating within and without her, she drew back the arrow, feeling the present and visualizing the future. Releasing the arrow, it sailed to the center of the target.

She felt a tingle of pleasure in her heart; it was as Luna and David had told her it would be.

"Wow! Great shot!" cheered Millet. He sat on an upside-down bushel basket David had found for him. "I wished I was big enough to shoot a bow!"

David looked at him thoughtfully. "It might be a tall order but I will see what I can do. Jennifer, you are moving in the right direction. Erase the shot from your mind and try again."

Jennifer nodded. What he said made sense in her heart; even with past success one must start afresh each time. Again focused on her breath, she saw the arrow hit the target as she pulled back the string. Releasing the arrow, she watched as it flew into the center again.

Jennifer spent the next hour shooting arrows. David gave her occasional suggestions but for the most part kept quiet as she learned from her own practice. Finding some suitable wood and line, he formed a small makeshift bow for Millet. Forming arrows the size of darts from wooden skewers, he sharpened the ends to points with his knife, then fitted them with feathered ends from a few obliging ducks who wandered near. Setting an apple on a stick a few paces from where Millet stood on the bushel basket, David coached him. Millet seemed to catch on immediately and jumped with joy each time he hit the apple with his tiny, dart-size arrows. The ducks murmured encouragement, rapidly flicking their tail feathers with each of Millet's successes.

Tired from the morning of mushing with the dogs and their early afternoon weapon training, the three said goodbye to their new duck friends and made their way back to the main manse. Once in their common room, they found the table piled with books and rolled maps; the sideboard laden with fruit, tomato and zucchini sandwiches, green salad, biscuits and a pitcher of fresh-squeezed carrot juice. The large teapot held lemon balm and raspberry leaf tea. After washing and changing into fresh clothes, they settled into the large, burgundy couches for a snack.

"The lemon balm in this tea is good to refresh the mind and body, and the raspberry leaf restores iron and micronutrients which all athletes need," said Millet. "And this carrot juice has a hint of lemon and basil in it. Very nice! Justin must have a special green house for tropical fruits here at the Keep."

David teased him, "And just how do you know all of this? By my calculations you are just a week old."

Millet looked thoughtful. "I don't know. I just know. Must be genetic."

"Well you certainly did well with hitting the target, as did Jennifer. I will have to speak to Justin and Samuel about having one of the expert bow makers here at the Keep crafting you a real bow," said David.

"I would love that!" said Millet.

The three snacked and chatted before turning to the books and scrolls containing maps. David found one that contained an old map of all of Solaria.

"Jen, Millet - look at this. Here is the west of Solaria before it was divided by the wall of darkness." He slid his finger over the area showing the mountains. "The wall starts here, just west of Samuel's Keep."

Jennifer looked at the map; it was like nothing she had ever seen. She reached out to touch its soft surface. Her father had helped her find and look at maps of the stars and galaxies. When he was sober and paying attention to her they would pour over copies of old maps of Earth, in particular the Mercator map from 1569 and the Piri

Reis map from 1513. She loved the mystery; modern mapmakers were baffled by them because they showed in detail the continents before they had been mapped by modern European explorers from Columbus on, including the details of the land under the ice of Antarctica that had not been properly mapped until the 1950's with modern methods.

As David and Millet studied the map, Jennifer wrapped her arms around herself and sighed. She loved watching documentaries about the researchers Graham Hancock, Robert Bauval, Andrew Collins and others exploring land and submerged temples and ruins around the planet, and their relationships to the constellations of stars in the sky. The maps of Mars and the structures that might be pyramids, and a Mars stone structure that looks like a face akin to Earth's Egyptian Sphinx; all of this pointing to past civilization. The mysteries of it all was something that she often thought about as she and Grace, her corgi and best friend, lay in bed waiting to fall asleep at night.

Jennifer shivered. This was real, not a dream, not a movie her father was in, not a video about possible life on other planets on YouTube. She was here with her new friends studying a real map of a land that was not a fairy tale, but in parallel reality. She looked up at David, his blue eyes serious as they studied the map. And Millet, a talking loaf of bread, yet as real as she was and everyone else here. She took in a deep breath; she was not dreaming, Solaria was real, and except for Grace, they were the first friends she had ever felt close to.

David raised his eyes and looked into hers, then shook his head as a quick smile flittered across his lips. She felt her face blush and looked away. Rolling the map up he searched the pile and found another. "Look at this, it is the old Swinburg Tunnels and cave systems that Samuel and his dogs found!" The three quickly became absorbed in trying to figure out how Samuel and the dogs had traveled to find them and where else the tunnels might lead.

"Do some of the tunnels lead into the west?" asked Millet.

"They seem to." David traced his finger along a branch from the main tunnel. "Here is one in the south, and another in the north. I wonder if they are open or if the Bikini Nuclear test caused them to cave in, like the entrances that Samuel and the dogs were able to dig through…"

"I wonder if the darkness goes into the tunnels and blocks them," Jennifer thought.

"That's a good question," Millet answered her out loud. David and Jennifer looked at him.

"Jennifer, I just heard you clearly," explained Millet. "David, she is wondering if the darkness that is blocking the west goes into the ground and blocks the tunnels that lead there."

David nodded. "Good question."

* * *

Chapter Six

All beings are blessed with gifts and abilities. We nourish these gifts by seeking proper training and mentoring by those who are accomplished and known for their goodness of heart, courage, dedication to truth, justice, and lives devoted to the betterment of all creation. With the gifts of intuition and healing we must train diligently because of the danger of evil coming in to cloud and possess our rational minds. Thus we pray for the skilled mentors that we need and the wisdom to use our gifts prudently –for light and goodness of all.

Book of The Seers

The Wisdom Cave of Dreams lay many meters below the manse of the Keep. Used by generations of Seers and Wisdom Runners, one reached it by numerous tunnels, gates and flights of wide, gentle stairs that allowed the horses to pass as easily as the humans and dogs.

Tuvalla and her father, Justin, held large rings of keys that opened stone doors and gates hidden in the stone walls of the passages. The dogs, horses and human group that followed them were gifted with intuition and had many years of training and experience in the Wisdom Runners and Order of Seers; but few knew their way to the great cave on their own.

Millet rode on David's shoulder as he and Jennifer followed close to Luna.

Luna spoke softly to the three. "These are very special caves that are deep under the Keep. They are protected from psychic attack and spying by dangerous ones, like Natab and her gang."

"We looked for them on the maps this afternoon but couldn't find them," David answered softly. Jennifer nodded.

"No. Many things are not on the maps, even the old ones. The passages of these caves are complicated and have not only twists and turns but unique locks and doors that can only be opened and remembered by unique individuals; in all of Solaria only a few are born in each generation who can learn them."

"Can you?" asked Jennifer.

"I can, but I do not have hands to work the keys. I have to have a human with me. Justin, his daughter Tuvalla, Lacino and a few others were born with the ability."

The final passage brought them to twelve-foot high metal doors. They were carved with the sun, moon, stars, great horses, sled dogs, wolves and humans standing together under a massive oak tree. A carved banner adorned the rock above the doors that read: "Peace to all who enter these doors. May peace be the intent of all communication emanating from here and received here. Peace to all who leave through these doors."

Jennifer followed Luna as they entered the Wisdom Cave of Dreams. She felt her breath catch as she looked around the hall. It was two hundred feet long by one hundred feet wide. The carved walls rose into a dome high above. Shallow clefts in the rock held glow weed and more than one thousand pillar-candles of beeswax that lit the space. Soft mats and rugs lined the floor.

"Makes me feel so small," she thought to Millet as she looked around in awe. She reached for him and settled him closer in her arms. As the group gathered in a circle, the dogs and humans sitting, the horses standing, it felt good to be cuddling Millet. She also felt safe between David and Luna with Justin, Samuel and Tuvalla to their left. The group gathered itself and grew quiet.

After a moment Justin spoke. "We all know of the trouble in our land. Much of it has been stirred from Earth; we have been working for years to bring back the balance and order that once reigned. Over the last few decades Wisdom Runners and Seers have died defending Solaria in our efforts to turn the tide. Many of our bravest and most dedicated have gone to the light; we have not been able to replace them, so our numbers are dwindling."

The group listened quietly as Luna and Samuel explained what they knew. Members nodded at the news and asked thoughtful questions; though in the end, no one felt they could add any new insight that might be of aid.

When silence came over the group, signaling that there were no further questions, Justin spoke. "As a group we will attempt to open a channel of communication to the Court of the Wisdom Runners in the east; we will ask if King Gifford has landed safely, if they have word of Contalia and Dohanos, and we will share our news with them. We will also try to contact King Saul at his Court. Depending on their news, and any directives that they may have for us, we should then contact Zumulia.

Jennifer shrugged her shoulders back to release tension. Millet followed suit. She felt him deepening his breath as she did the same.

Around the circle, everyone nodded. Soon white light drifted from each one's heart region towards the center of the cave where the light streams mingled. Gradually, as each one fed it, the center grew into a large, luminous orb that shimmered as it rose towards the top of the cave. Hovering above their heads, it increased in size and brightness as it sent streams of light back to the head of each horse, dog and human. Loops of energy moved through each individual until the orb became opaque.

Images slowly formed: several large dogs and three humans appeared. The dogs had markings in black and white. The two men wore their grey hair in braids; the woman had mahogany hair, hanging loosely around her face. "Hail Seers and Wisdom Runners of the Keep of Justin Valor and Tuvalla the Seer!" came their voices along with many others from somewhere outside of the view of the orb.

"Our Hail to you!" said all in unison in the Wisdom Cave of Dreams.

Jennifer and Millet joined in a slight beat behind the group. She tried to listen and keep up as she focused on her breath at the same time.

"We have been hoping that you would be able to open a channel to us. We knew that Luna had traveled to you because King Gifford and his flock are here," said Riana, the woman with the red hair.

"Hail to you, Riana!" the group chorused.

"And my Hail to you all!" said Riana. "I don't know how much of our group you are able to see. We are about four hundred gathered in the Hall of Eternity under the Lake of Keewa. We feel it is the only place that we can safely meet together, and send and receive communications.

"What news have you of Dohanos and Contalia?" Luna asked.

"We have had two communications from them. They came through the Portal of Nordon a week ago. They said they had been detained for months; they have been battling with shadows and Ice Beings on the third plane of existence. They had been pursued since they left the meeting with the Servers of Light; they are carrying crystals, given to them by the Servers. They feel the crystals will help to dissolve the curtain of darkness dividing east from west. They were coming to you before they traveled to us." said Riana.

"But they are not here!" said Justin.

"We know," said Riana. "They said they had to go back through the Portal of Nordon to bring the dogs through. We heard nothing for two days; then Dohanos, with twelve dogs, opened a channel to us. They said that Contalia and the other twenty-eight dogs were somehow stuck in the portal. They were going back to try to free them; they urged us to warn you as soon as we could."

"The channel of communication was fuzzy and quickly

dissipated. We had hoped that they would be with you by now," said Teelee, a large, mostly white, blue and brown-eyed female dog.

"Perhaps we have time to get to the Portal of Nordon and give them aid. Samuel is here with his dogs: with them and some of my stronger, retired dogs and apprentices, we will leave as soon as possible," said Justin.

"Is it wise?" asked Riana. "Many say that you should be running Solaria soon. King Saul's health is not good and many here feel that there are members of his court that can no longer be trusted."

Justin took a moment to think. "We will go with caution. We should be there in less than two days."

"King Gifford's news from the west is terrible. We need to make plans to stop the veil of darkness and the shadows from spreading. The crystals Dohanos and Contalia are carrying may be instrumental in dissolving the darkness," said Teelee.

"And what of Zumulia?" asked Riana.

"We are going to try to contact her after trying to speak with King Saul. She promised Luna that she would call in Peaberry and some of the others from Vermont, if she needed the help," said Justin.

"We feel she needs the aid, sooner than later. If you were not going to the Portal of Nordon we would tell Samuel to travel there now," said Teelee.

David shifted next to her. Jennifer wondered if he was as worried about his grandmother as she was. Millet reached over and patted his shoulder.

"Agreed. When we return we will send Samuel and his dogs to protect her," said Justin. "I must mention the matter of the training of Zumulia's grandson, David. If the Court agrees, he can train with me so that he can visit his grandmother's Keep regularly. I realize it is a diversion from our normal Wisdom Runner training protocol – but in these times I feel it is best."

"We have all been waiting for David, the son of Tumilia and Zarcourt, to train. His parents live in our hearts and eternity!" said

Teelee. Howls and cheers came from around her. "Let him begin when you return."

"David has just killed a cat from Natab's pride on his journey here. It was a short distance from the walls of Justin's Keep," said Luna.

"Then he is brave and skilled already. However, he is now marked," said Teelee. "It is not good that Natab is on the prowl, so close to Solarian holdings."

"When I return from the Portal of Nordon we will have to deal with her," said Justin.

"Well said, Justin!" came a huge cheer from the orb of light.

"We will wait to hear from you. Till soon!" said Teelee. She held her paw in the air; then the images of the court faded from the orb.

Jennifer studied Justin's face and the faces of the animals and humans of the large group. They trusted him. She had only known him for a short time but she felt she would do what he asked her to do. She trusted him too.

The group began visioning for King Saul. The form of an older man started to come into the orb and then faded quickly. They tried again, and again he came and then faded. They tried again and got nothing.

"Courage. The channel does not seem to open up. King Saul's court must not be in a safe receiving chamber just now. We will try again after we try Zumulia," said Tuvalla.

Jennifer adjusted her back and started breathing deeper again. Millet cuddled deeper into her lap and grabbed hold of her sleeve. Almost, but not quite as good as having Grace. She wished her corgi was here with her, and even talking, too. She wondered if this could be possible.

The orb above them grew bright and opaque as they breathed into it in unison. Then Zumulia appeared in the great room of her Keep. "Ah, my dear friends," said Zumulia. "Hail and well met!"

"Hail and well met!" came the voices of all in the cave. Jennifer tried to project her intuitive voice as loud as she could.

"Dear friend, we are in the Wisdom Cave of Dreams," began Luna. "Samuel and his dogs got here just after we did. They traveled the old, underground Swinburg Trail and came out just behind the cave we stayed in when I last communicated with you."

"Ah, Samuel, you did the Swinburg Stomp! You ol' Fug, you!" laughed Zumulia.

"Zumulia, you are showing your age! Few would understand that reference," said Samuel. "But we do not have time for joking. The dogs and I were an hour behind Luna when King Gifford flew over, having just pierced the veil to the west. He took Luna's group to the foothills so we did not meet up until the next day at Justin's Keep."

"Gifford is back! I thank the Divine Creator!" Zumulia clapped her hands together. "What news has he?"

"We had little time to exchange news," answered Luna. "He said that there is snow coming. He needed to report to the Court of the Wisdom Runners before he and the Goony Birds could fly south to join their great flocks."

"Snow?" asked Zumulia.

"Yes, snow. I was able to scent it when I was aloft with him," said Luna. "He said that many in the west are doing well. However there are cities, towns and Keeps that have been surrounded with shadows so thick and dense, no one could pass in or out. When the flock penetrated those places, there were no living beings and no signs of bodies. Gifford had no answer for what is happening."

"This is bad," said Zumulia. "But still, Gifford is back; we no longer have to worry if he is lost to us. And what of Jennifer, David and Millet?"

"They traveled well. Millet is a handful!" said Luna.

"Millet! Well, I can imagine, if he is anything like his brothers and sisters!" A crash came from behind Zumulia. Four Talking Loaves swung into view as they rode past on ropes of garlic, hanging from the ceiling of the Keep's great room. They wore little woven hats and sweaters and were waving merrily.

Millet jumped out of Jennifer's arms and started jumping up and down, waving his hands at his siblings. Jennifer grabbed hold of him. *"Please sit down and behave!"* She spoke intuitively as she heard herself giggle audibly. It was strange to hear her voice; maybe it was coming back?

Many of the group in the Wisdom Cave of Dreams stifled laughter as they tried to hold their focus on sending light into the orb. A few did smile and muttered, "As much trouble as children, puppies and colts!"

"My hands are full trying to keep order around here," chuckled Zumulia. "I cannot imagine what secret ingredients the Keepers of the Ovens used in baking them, but Talking Loaves were never like this! I don't know how they are handling the other sixty-three loaves, and managing to stay in hiding, at the same time!" Another crash sounded from behind her.

"Unfortunately, we must hurry along as we have grave news," said Justin. Zumulia frowned for the first time as Justin described Natab's harsh words and how David had shot and killed one of her pride.

"Natab holds a long grudge against my daughter and her husband. She has transferred her twisted hatred onto David."

"Well, the good news is that he is an excellent shot. He is brave and handled himself well. The Court of the Wisdom Runners has accepted that he start training with me. You have done well in raising him," said Justin.

"Thank you. But Samuel, Tundra, Nicco and the rest of their pack, Luna, Peaberry and many members of their Vermont UN-Chained Gang have shared raising him," said Zumulia. "And other grave news?"

"Contalia, Dohanos and the dogs are in trouble at the Portal of Nordon," said Justin. "When we finish here, Samuel, Lacino and I will leave with the dogs to search for them."

Zumulia sighed. Another two crashes sounded behind her as a Talking Loaf swung by with a wig of spinach, swinging a carrot as a sword. Stifling a laugh, she said, "With the trouble at the Portal you must be fast. I will look forward to your news. Hail and travel well!" Zumulia disappeared from the orb.

The group tried again to contact King Saul but got nothing. Jennifer tried to add as much energy and intent as she could; she wished she could see him. Saul was her father's name and other than her father she had not heard the name used often.

Failing to contact the King, they started a search for Contalia, Dohanos and the dogs.

At first they were not able to find a trace of them. Patiently they continued to scan until finally a clear vision of the Portal of Nordon came into the orb. Cut into the rock face of a mountain, the door of the portal stood open, showing only blackness. Heavy snow lay on the ground. Just beyond the door sat a dog, chained to the trunk of a tall pine. Two large, black dogs were chained to the front of a sled nearby. The three dogs searched the surroundings and the air above with their eyes and noses.

"Denali! Tonka! Hunter!" yelled Tundra. All of the dogs in the Wisdom Cave of Dreams started howl singing. The three chained dogs continued to search the air around them, unable to hear or see the senders of the communication.

"Focus more!" Luna told the group. In the orb, Denali, Hunter and Tonka continued to scan.

"Someone is looking for us," said Tonka. "It may be the Court in the east, or Justin and the Seers at his Keep. I sense it is Justin's group." Although the Seers and Wisdom Runners could see and hear them, the three dogs could only sense their presence.

"Help us!" called Denali. "But be careful! There are shadows everywhere! We cannot get loose, we are chained!"

"I know it's you, Justin! Dohanos, Contalia and the other dogs are trapped in the portal. If we don't survive we will see you on the other side, in the light. But try to help them! The Ice Beings have frozen them. And there is another force in there - we don't know who or what! An invisible being has chained us here!" yelled Tonka.

All of the dogs in the Wisdom Cave of Dreaming sang and

howled back at them, to no avail. The three chained dogs did not hear or see anything of their searching friends. Then the vision went blank.

After a few moments of silence, the group spoke quietly together. They made plans for Justin, Samuel, Lacino and the dogs to depart for the Portal of Nordon.

Wrapping her arms closer around Millet, Jennifer watched the group of horses, dogs and humans conferring. Where many on Earth would jump to the task in haste, the Wisdom Runners and Seers knew that time spent in proper preparation would best serve their comrades.

* * *

After leaving the Cave of Dreams they went to their rooms and had a snack of carrot soup, flax crackers and apricot-walnut bars. Luna joined a small group with Justin, Samuel, Tuvalla and others to make plans for the rescue mission.

"I love the sound of your harp," Millet closed his eyes happily as he and Jennifer listened to David play. They were sitting with tea after looking at the maps again and leafing through several of the books.

David stopped playing. "Hey Jen, we have not worked on communication since the night in the cave with Luna. Maybe we could practice now, before bed?"

Jennifer immediately nodded.

"I could help you by supervising," offered Millet.

Both Jennifer and David nodded their ascent. They quickly found three cushions to place in a circle on the thick, patterned carpet. They stretched as Luna had instructed and began their breathing.

"Okay," said Millet. "When your breath is deep, allow the energy to build within you." He continued, quite well, the same instructions that Luna had given them in the cave. Soon they were bathed in a sense of connection, peace and timelessness as they gazed into each other's eyes.

"*Hello again,*" David sent his thoughts towards Jennifer.

"*Hello,*" thought Jennifer.

"Now that we are connecting again, I don't really know what to say," thought David.

"*I don't either,*" said Jennifer.

"Have you always been shy?" asked David.

Jennifer started to nod and then stopped, switching to intuitive communication, "*Yes.*"

"Even before your father died?" asked David.

"Yes," thought Jennifer.

"*Do you miss him*?" asked David.

"*Yes… and no,*" thought Jennifer.

David took in a deeper set of breaths. "*What do you mean*?"

"I haven't really thought about it… I loved him but he really wasn't a nice person. Sometimes he was mean; he was often drunk and took drugs."

"I'm sorry."

"Me too. Sometimes he was nice; I really loved to be with him then. He sent me to a special private school with really good teachers. He would take me to a bookstore and buy me all the newest science and archeology books that I wanted. He also let me buy books online… I don't know if you have the Internet here?"

David nodded. *"I know what it is. I'd love to see a computer! Luna and the members of the UN-Chained Gang from your Uncle Jim's have told me about it."*

Jennifer looked at him, her eyes widened. She could not believe that Luna knew about the Internet! And as she thought about it, she had not seen a computer since she had arrived in Solaria.

"After all Luna has taught you, and all you have seen her and the other animals doing here, are you really surprised that she knows about the Internet?"

Jennifer looked at Millet and back at David. Stifling a giggle, she shook her head. *"You mean we have things on Earth, like computers, that you would like to see?"*

"Oh yeah! Someday maybe I will find a way to visit! . . . But what else did you like to do with your father?"

"He took me camping in the Redwood Forest a few times, and that was fun. He would promise that things were going to be better for us because he was going to change his life; he said he would stop drinking, leave my stepmother and we would buy a ranch in Montana where I could have a horse, my corgi, Grace, and a much bigger telescope. But then we would get home and he would start doing cocaine with my stepmother. Things just didn't change, no matter how many times he promised," thought Jennifer.

"*That's very sad,*" interjected Millet.

"Millet, you can hear both of us?" asked David.

"Yes," said Millet out loud.

"I know you hear me, Luna and the dogs, but do you always hear David?" asked Jennifer.

"Well, only sometimes when I really want to," thought Millet.

David smiled at the loaf wryly, *"Next time you hear me, let me know?"*

David looked back into Jennifer's eyes. *"Do you have a corgi?"*

"Yes. Her name is Grace. I miss her very much. Uncle Jim and Aunt Sarah are trying to bring her to Vermont but my stepmother is lying, insisting that Grace belongs to her."

David thought a moment. *"That is not good. After Justin leaves tomorrow let's speak to Luna and Tuvalla. Maybe they can do something."*

The three sat in silence. Jennifer hoped that maybe there could be some help in Solaria to bring Grace to Vermont.

Millet jumped up to his feet. *"Why don't we try to communicate with Zumulia? I would love to see how my brothers and sisters are. I think that she might be happy to hear from us."*

"Okay," thought Jennifer.

"Mmmmmm... I am not sure," thought David. *"Luna and Justin told us not to go outside of the Keep."*

"But we are not leaving the Keep. We are right here in our rooms, where they told us to stay while they prepare for the rescue mission," thought Millet.

"Isn't Justin's Keep protected like the cave we communicated with Zumulia in and The Wisdom Cave of Dreams?" asked Jennifer.

"Well, I think so. But I don't know. The Wisdom Runners and Seers are very careful of what they are doing these days. That is why we met in the Wisdom Cave of Dreams this evening," thought David.

"Oh, let's try! Pleeeeease! We will just be visiting! We won't be sharing secrets like the group did in the cave..." begged Millet.

"What do you think, Jen?" David asked.

"I am new to Solaria and intuitive communication. I don't know," thought Jennifer.

"*PLLLLEEEEEEEEEEEASE*!" Millet's intuitive screech almost knocked Jennifer and David over.

"Wow! Millet! Not so strong!" thought David. *"Okay, let's try it."*

Together the three took a few breaths in unison, then started to send out light from their chests to form an orb. Millet laughed happily as it became luminescent. All three could feel waves of peace flood into them as they watched it turn opaque.

"Now how do we send communication?" asked Millet.

"I don't know," thought Jennifer. *"Luna was directing it in the cave. David and I were just helping. And this afternoon the Wisdom Runners and Seers were directing it, we were just helping."*

"Maybe if we each imagine my grandmother at the same time," thought David. *"I think that might be how the Seers and Wisdom Runners do it."*

"Okay, let's try that!" thought Millet.

Zumulia, with her grey braids was an easy picture to imagine. The three sat for several moments visualizing, but nothing happened.

"Ummmm, perhaps we have to also feel what she feels like to us," suggested Jennifer.

"*What do you mean*?" asked Millet.

"Well, she has a big heart and is very wise. For me, when I am with her, she 'feels' a certain way..." thought Jennifer.

"You mean like energy. Like each dog and person that I know, each tree, each plant emit their own particular energy... I get a certain feeling when I am with each one. Like that?" asked David.

"Yes, I think that is what I was trying to say," thought Jennifer.

"Okay, let's see a picture in our minds of Zumulia and try to feel her energy," suggested David.

The three sat breathing energy into the orb, imagining a picture of Zumulia and trying to feel her as if she were present with them. The orb started to vibrate and then a hazy vision of Zumulia came into it.

"Who is there?" Zumulia asked. Her eyes moved warily as she scanned the air around her.

"Grandma, it's me, David," thought David.

The vision of Zumulia was still blurred in the orb. She continued to look about her. "Who is there? Luna, Justin, Samuel, Tuvalla? I can't see you," she said cautiously.

"Speak to her audibly. That's what Luna was doing in the cave and what Justin and all were doing this evening," thought Jennifer.

"Grandma, it's me, David," said David.

"David, is that you? I can barely hear you but I sense you," said Zumulia. "Where are you? Let me speak to Luna or whoever you are sending with!"

"Grandma, it's just Jennifer, Millet and me. Luna and the others are at a meeting making plans to rescue Contalia, Dohanos and the dogs. We are just practicing," said David.

"You three must never do this unless it is a dire emergency. Never send without a Seer or Wisdom Runner aiding you. This is dangerous. Find Luna or Justin as soon as possible…" Despite the fuzzy image the three could feel Zumulia's panic.

"Grandma, I am sorry…" pleaded David.

"Child, I am going to try to clear this channel from here. Do not be frightened! I am angry because I am afraid for your safety. Close the channel as fast as you can but keep focusing on your breathing. Find someone to aid you as soon as you can, so that they can protect your energy channels," said Zumulia as she faded completely away.

Jennifer felt her stomach clutch in fear. Her chest started to constrict. She tried to focus on allowing the orb to fade from opaque to luminescent and then to dissipate.

Suddenly an explosion burst through the orb. The center flashed to black. Within the darkness, Natab's gold eyes stared out. With her were two more Hissing Cats.

"Psssss! Ssssoooo! We meet again, you three. Of course, Jennifer, I have been sssssseeing you for years, haven't I?" said Natab.

"*What do you mean?*" asked Jennifer.

"We have been meeting in your dreamsssss. You ssssssaw me at your father'sssss home in the mirror the night he died. So did Gracsssssse, your corgi. You finally met me in perssssson lassst night," crooned Natab.

"You get out of here!" demanded David.

"Ssssstupid boy! Killer boy! It won't be long before I finissssssh you! That ssssstupid dog cannot protect you… I told Luna that it would not be long before I entered Jussssstin's Keep and here I am!" said Natab.

"GETTTTTTTTT OUTTTTTTTTT!" screamed Millet.

Natab and the Hissing Cats crouched down with their paws on their ears, closing their eyes. Finally she straightened. "What is that?"

"E E E E E E E E E E E E E E E e e e e e e e e e e e e ! EEEEEEEEEEeeeeeeeee!" screeched Millet.

The two Hissing Cats with Natab fell over screaming, "Stop, Stop!" from behind her. She held her ears, screaming in pain.

David, Jennifer and Millet were not able to disconnect their energy from the orb. Natab rallied, screaming in rage, "What is that!"

Millet screeched again. Jennifer joined him in the loudest note that she could hit, as the fortress in her chest broke, allowing her to push sound from her throat and mouth. Just then, Luna burst through the outer door, followed by Tuvalla, Justin, Samuel, Nicco, Tundra and several of their pack. More Seers and dogs raced in after them.

Silently the group surrounded Jennifer, David and Millet. The humans drew their daggers and held them sideways over the heads of the three, unschooled visioners. The rays of black energy emitting from the orb bounced off the mirrored surfaces of the daggers, reflected back towards the image of Natab. The dogs planted their paws into the wool of the carpet and began singing a chant; ropes of white and pink light started to emanate from them towards the orb. Luna stepped closer and rose onto her hind legs. "Out of here, right now, Natab!"

Natab hissed at her as the cats behind her continued to cry in pain.

"Thisssss Keep is not yoursss for much longer, Jussssstin!" hissed Natab as the energy from the dogs wove to wherever she was and began to touch her. She hissed and screamed as the blackness in the orb dissipated and then disappeared, leaving mists of white energy coming from David, Jennifer and Millet in its wake.

The dogs continued to sing, sending ropes of white and pink energy through the room. Justin, Samuel and Tuvalla swiped their knives through the energy and then sheathed them. As the dogs sang the humans knelt down, placing their hands on David, Millet and Jennifer. Speaking softly, they guided them to breathe and bring their energies into their bodies. After some time, Tuvalla worked to clear their nervous systems of negative energies that Natab and her Hissing Cats had attached to them.

When Tuvalla finished they led the three to the couches and

handed them mugs of chamomile tea to sip. The group asked them questions about their ill-fated vision journey.

"This is very bad, you three," said Justin. "Zumulia was absolutely correct. You should not have attempted such a thing. None of you have enough training. Even apprentice Seers and Wisdom Runners must have mentors, who are members of our Courts, aid them until they become full members."

"David, I am most displeased with you. Your parents died in action that involved psychic attack. You know the dangers," said Samuel, shaking his head as he sighed.

"Yes, sir," answered David. "It was my fault.

"Please, sir," asked Millet. "I am the one who pleaded with David when he had reservations. It is not his fault." The Talking Loaf quietly looked at all assembled.

"Millet, I am not reprimanding David. But I am asking him to be fully accountable," said Justin.

Jennifer sat up and took a deep breath. *"If you please, sir. And all here, especially Luna. It is not just David. We all agreed to this and participated. It is all of our responsibility."* Her thoughts were heard clearly by all present.

The group of humans and dogs looked at her. Justin searched her face for a few moments. "Thank you, Jennifer. Wisdom Runners must take responsibility as individuals and as a group. I admire your coming forward like this."

"A mistake holds no value if we do not look back at our actions, fearlessly, to learn from them. In truth, you did not know the real dangers; I trust that once you know the rules that you will follow them. Do not attempt feats in the unseen realms that you have not learned and practiced with mentors; this is for your own sake, and the safety of all of us." Justin looked at all three. "Do you understand?"

They nodded.

"Samuel, the dogs and I will leave you with Tuvalla and Luna; we must prepare to leave now for the Portal of Nordon. We will be honored if you come down to see us off," said Justin. He, Samuel, Tundra, Nicco and the other dogs rose and left. A number of Tuvalla's Seers stood at the open door; she motioned them in.

Tuvalla turned to David, Jennifer and Millet. "What you did was both inventive and creative; but it was lacking in proper preparedness. We do not want to curtail your curiosity and creative initiative, because they are important qualities," said Tuvalla. She took a moment to allow them to consider her words.

David spoke first. "Tuvalla, Luna and all here, I am very sorry for my actions. I realize that I lacked wisdom; I put this Keep in danger." His blue eyes were solemn.

Millet nodded, "Me, too."

"I apologize both for my actions, and for not trying to hold the group back until we could ask Luna or one of you for guidance," thought Jennifer *to the group.*

The group nodded. Looking thoughtful, Luna was silent as she gazed at each of them.

"From now on I want at least one adult Wisdom Runner or Seer with the three of you. We may not have fully closed down the channels of communication that Natab may use against you; the three of you are open to attack."

"This is not a punishment. We will try to instruct you and answer your questions. I will try to spend as much time with you as possible so that we can plan the course of further studies for each of you," said Tuvalla.

"Jennifer, we need to test you further. I sense that you are a Seer candidate, but Luna feels that you have the abilities to be both a Wisdom Runner and a Seer. If you wish to start training we will see what abilities emerge. We know that you have suffered trauma from events in your life on Earth, but we will work with you so that you can heal," said Tuvalla.

Jennifer was struck by how this woman's green eyes seemed to reflect, somehow, so much of what she didn't even know she felt.

"But what about my aunt and uncle? And what about the situation

in California over my father's death and my stepmother's custody battle for me? And what about Grace, my corgi? My aunt and uncle could be in trouble if I don't go back to them and I don't want to lose Grace," thought Jennifer. She bit her lip and looked away from Tuvalla's gaze.

Tuvalla put her hand on Jennifer's arm. "As Luna has explained to you, time in Solaria is not the same as on Earth. Hopefully they will not miss you, and there will be no trouble, but it will be awhile before we can return you safely."

Jennifer nodded.

Millet stood up, "What about me?"

"We would like you to start training with our herbalists and chefs," explained Tuvalla. "Once we feel it is safe, we will transport your brothers and sisters from Zumulia's Keep here, so that you can all train together."

Millet sat up as tall as his bread loaf shaped body allowed, "But I would like to be a Wisdom Runner – I want to help protect Solaria."

"This is an admirable wish. But you should first explore your own unique gifts. Talking Loaves are very necessary to our life in Solaria – we have greatly missed your kind," said Tuvalla.

"You think that I am too small to handle a dog sled," Millet pouted.

Tuvalla shook her head. "There are other ways of the Wisdom Runners – you could ride a horse. For now it would be best for you to start in the gardens and kitchens to develop your important talents. I am sure that David and others will be happy to let you ride with them so that you can continue to learn to work with the dogs."

"What of my grandmother?" asked David.

"I have great concern about Zumulia's safety; Natab and the shadows cannot be trusted," answered Luna.

"I have concern, as well. Once we see Justin, Lacino, Samuel and the dogs off we must attempt to contact her," said Tuvalla.

"I sense that she is okay," Luna assured David. "As soon as Justin and Samuel return from the Portal of Nordon, I will take Jennifer back to her Keep and then back through the portal to Vermont. Samuel and his dogs can accompany us and arrange to protect Zumulia."

Tuvalla stood. "It is late now. In the morning I will have you moved to bigger rooms so that we can have guards with you at all times. For now some will sleep in this main room with others close by in the hall while you sleep."

Luna and Tuvalla then introduced David, Millet and Jennifer to the Seers in the room who would be keeping them company and instructing them over the next few days. Looking out the windows, in the torchlight of the grand courtyard, the group saw that snow had begun to fall.

* * *

They woke early to light snow blanketing the grounds and trees of the Keep. Looking out the window Jennifer shivered and wrapped a blanket over her shoulders as she padded out to the main room to find the others. This was not L.A. and it certainly was not even Vermont in summer.

They had a quick breakfast of fruit and hot tea in the rooms. Aides brought Jennifer and David snow hats, mittens and parkas. For Millet they supplied little woven boots, mittens, leg warmers, a sweater of red knit that was made specifically to fit his loaf-shaped body, and a red-knit hat. Luna walked with them to the dog sled trails; two of the women Seers, that Tuvalla had assigned to protect them when Luna was elsewhere engaged, followed a few paces behind.

"Luna, again I am sorry," said David. Millet and Jennifer nodded.

She stopped a moment and looked up at them. "Your apologies before were sincere. All of us have accepted them. Once apologies are taken, then you must let your guilt go and learn from the mistakes."

Millet was waddling in the snow alongside Luna in his new suit of clothes; his legs appeared to be growing quite sturdy. "Are there many masters here?"

"Yes. Although they may act in servant roles, they are all members of the Seer or Wisdom Runner Orders and quite accomplished on their own. Right now there are few Wisdom Runners here, most are Seers. The only real apprentices are some of the young dogs and horses who have not been to the east to train," said Luna.

"Luna, are we allowed to speak to Jennifer intuitively?" asked Millet.

"It would be best if she uses the intuitive communication to you and David, but you should speak audibly to her, unless one or more of us are here to aid you," Luna suggested.

"*Why*?" asked Jennifer. She could see that all three could hear her.

Luna turned to the two Seers walking near them. "Could you hear her speak intuitively just now?" The women nodded. She turned back to Jennifer.

"I thought so. You are quite loud because your communication channel is open from what you did last night. David and Millet, please say something intuitively to us,"

"What did you want me to say?" asked David.

"Me, too. What should I say?" asked Millet.

Luna turned back to the women. One was short, with a powerful body, white hair, and bright blue eyes; her name was Kaarina. The other was tall, with short, blond hair -Brigitte. "Did you hear the boys?" asked Luna.

"Quite clearly," nodded Brigitte.

"That is what I thought," said Luna. She turned back to the three. "When you worked without a mentor, your communication channels opened up very wide; now you are easily heard by both good and bad-intentioned individuals."

"What can we do?" asked David.

"Right now, nothing. But it is another reason that I want you to speak to Jennifer audibly. Three of you communicating intuitively, at this intensity, could create an open, easily-detected channel. You could draw Natab or other darkness again," said Luna.

Luna halted, looking at the sky. The snow had started to fall again. "I don't have to tell you that this is not good for July. On the positive side, Justin can make much better time because they can use the dog sleds instead of carrying the supplies and portaging the sleds to the trails on the other side of the mountain."

"They always take the sleds, Jennifer, when they are going through the Nordana mountain trails to the Portal of Nordon," explained David. The mountains behind this Keep always have snow, even during the summer."

In the main grounds they found a bustle of activity. Three sleds were packed with tents, blankets and supplies. Bows, quivers of arrows, shields and sheathed swords were stowed for quick access. Nicco, Tundra, Rampart, Alex, Rock, Buck, Libby, Jose, Hannah, Topi, Thorn, Lawrence, Brazil, Coal, Hermi, Angel, Fred, Sweetie, Thomas, Sylvia, Calli, Umbra, Sookie, Daniel, Honey, Bunny, and fourteen of Justin's canine Wisdom Runners - Betty, Cocoa, Elvis, Cash, Creflo, Taffy, Stanley, Price, Kenneth, Gloria, Robinson, Beth, Lance and Bandit - were in harnesses; they sat in a tight circle, facing inward, singing softly.

Luna ran to them, followed by young, unharnessed dogs. The circled dogs stood, opened their ranks to Luna, who touched her brown nose to each of her fellow Wisdom Runners while the young dogs watched from a distance. She sat in the center and sang an alto note, holding it, as one-by-one the dogs in the circle joined her, each with their own individual chosen tone. Outside the circle, human Seers started to play deep, resonating drums while others joined in with bagpipes. The snow floated down in huge, beautiful flakes, clinging to all they fell upon, making the formerly green summer landscape, with its trees and bushes laden with leaves, seem surreal.

Justin, Samuel and Lacino drew their carved-handled swords as Tuvalla, her hair loosed and flowing black around her, appeared with another drawn sword. They saluted the dogs with their swords held high in the air; then in pairs touched the blades, point-to-point, forming a canopy. Opening the circle, Luna, flanked by Nicco and Tundra, came forward as the rest of the harnessed dogs formed threesomes in a line behind them.

Together the dogs bounced up and down on their paws, turning their heads from side to side, matching the rhythm of the pounding drums. Each group in the line danced towards, and then under, the upheld swords. Emerging, the dogs danced into a circle around the humans; sparks began to fly from their fur. Tuvalla lowered her sword, leaving the circle followed by Luna. The three men brandished their swords above their heads and danced with the dogs.

Jennifer picked up Millet so he could see better; they were transfixed as they watched the group. David's face held a sense of wonder. "I haven't seen this since I was a child, when my parents would go off on a mission," he said. He turned back to watch.

The music continued as the circle of dogs broke and aides helped hitch them to the sleds. There was none of the barking, jumping or zaniness of yesterday's morning run. Sparks of light continued to fly from the dogs as snow fell about them. The mushers sheathed their swords and took up their positions on the runners of their main sleds with the cargo sleds trailing behind. The teams took off down the trail, running straight for the mountain.

A huge boulder rolled from the sheer rock directly in front of the racing dogs, opening a passage. Without breaking pace, the teams sped into the darkness and disappeared. Seers standing on each side of the cave opening raised their hands and sang; the giant rock rolled back into place, leaving no trace of the tunnel.

After the music stopped, Millet, Jennifer and David crossed the field and courtyard to the manse. Inside the small eating hall they took off their snowy outer garments. Millet wanted to keep his boots, sweater and leggings, but was pleased when Brigitte brought him soft slipper-boots and a matching purple sweater to wear instead. They sat down to lunch of soup, steamed broccoli and cabbage, and cornbread fingers. Hot apple cider, mulled with cinnamon sticks and cloves, steamed in crocks on the table. Strawberry shortcake for dessert was the only real taste of summer.

After lunch Kaarina and Brigitte led them up the stone staircase to their new rooms. David picked up his harp and settled into one of the couches as Jennifer and Millet snuggled in the one across from him. The main difference from their previous suite was that instead of burgundy, the furniture was upholstered in deep blue velvet. Also, there were two extra bedrooms.

Kaarina's bright blue eyes twinkled brightly at the three. "Luna and Tuvalla said that they would be here as soon as they could; they are trying to contact Zumulia. Is there anything else you need now?"

They shook their heads.

"Well, we will be here by the window until Luna returns. If you need anything, just ask," said Kaarina. She settled with a book and Brigitte reached in a richly decorated bag and pulled out skeins of multicolored yarn and long wooden knitting needles.

David played his lyre as Millet cuddled in Jennifer's arms and began humming.

"I didn't know there was a path through the mountain," thought Jennifer.

"It's hidden normally," said Brigitte as she looked up over her knitting. "It is very protected from intuitive detection. Seers on this side opened the stone with the help of the dogs' energy that you saw rising. Seers on the other side of the mountain opened the outer, hidden gate and closed it after the dog teams passed through."

"Do you have to have the dog's energy open it?" asked David as he continued to play. His fingers seemed at home on the strings as he strummed them.

"Yes," Kaarina said, "the big stones move only for the teams. The humans and single dogs can open and get through smaller passages."

"I have been with Samuel and his dogs, Luna, Peaberry and the Vermont dogs when they have been dancing for fun. But I have not witnessed the mission ceremony since I watched my parents taking off with their dogs when I was small. The music and dance helps them build their shared vision and the energy necessary to go out on a mission," said David.

"Samuel and his dogs dance for fun?" asked Millet.

"Some people say that Samuel and the dogs have too much time alone in their Keep on the Lake of Sleoden. They can get up to some crazy things with their music, singing, tall tale telling and dancing. Most of the Wisdom Runners stay with the traditional music, but Samuel is from Earth originally, so he brought his favorite music. Once they start playing and singing Earth poets like Ian Anderson, Bob Dylan, and others - things can get wild," David laughed. You should see Nicco do his version of MC Hammer's, "Can't Touch This."

"*You are joking!*" thought Jennifer.

"No, actually I am not," said David. Kaarina and Brigitte grinned as if agreeing with the truth of his statement.

"They do Earth music?" asked Millet.

"Yes. But they are not the only ones who have great fun," said David. "Jen's Uncle Jim's dogs, in Luna's pack, are really wild. Some of them even play instruments while singing and dancing. You should see Rose, Lily and Rainbow playing the piano; Buster, Lucky and Flint on the drums; and Stormina, Buttercup and Lioness playing silver flutes at my grandmother's Keep."

Jennifer looked at him incredulously. "*They don't have hands. We have to carry Luna's mugs around for her and break her food into pieces; she likes us to throw food to her when there aren't other human adults around. How can they play the piano or the flute?*"

"Well, there is some sort of transformation that happens when most dogs are in Solaria. Some have a gift that gives them abilities to make musical instruments work and play beautifully. Luna does not have the gift, she has other important abilities. Jen, isn't being able to speak and carry on conversations a gift you never imagined dogs could have?"

Jennifer looked around the room at each person as she considered

David's words. He seemed so earnest. If they were putting her on they were great actors.

David continued. "For playing piano they work as a team. Each one has their favorite keys. Dogs are actually really talented musically. You have heard them sing; they each have their own notes and no one steals another pack mate's note," said David. "You should see Peaberry play his violin. My grandmother keeps it for him in a special case in one of the window seats so that he can play when he is visiting from Vermont."

"That's ridiculous! You are making fun of me!" thought Jennifer.

David stopped playing the lyre and sat up. "No, I am not, Jen. It is a gold violin. It has a strap on the neck so that he can slip his paw through to his wrist to hold it as he uses his toes and intuitional intent for making notes. If you look at his feet his front toes are much longer than a lot of the dogs in the pack because he has greyhound in him. The bow is also gold and has a strap on it, to fit his right paw, so that he can fiddle. He stands up on his hind feet, dances and plays it. He sings, too."

"That is impossible!" thought Jennifer.

"What he is saying is true, Jen," said Brigitte. "Just as with being able to speak, many dogs have the ability to make instruments work, it is more with the powers of their intention than actually with their toes. Peaberry is legendary in Solaria; he is quite a good fiddle player. All of your Uncle Jim's dogs love playing and dancing to fast, bluegrass music. It is said that Peaberry took that gold fiddle from the devil himself."

"And bit him on the bottom as we chased him out the door!" said Luna as she entered the room laughing. She jumped up on the couch beside Jennifer and Millet.

"Now that part may be doggie humor," said Brigitte. "Most dogs have great senses of humor and play. Sometimes it is hard to know the actual truth, Jennifer. Your Uncle Jim's dogs love the Charlie Daniels fiddle tune about a golden violin won from the devil. Most of us assume that is where this story comes from; none of them, even Luna, will definitively tell us the true facts."

Luna looked at the ceiling as she hummed a traditional Solarian ditty. Smiling, Brigitte and Kaarina rose to their feet as two male Seers, Donal and Michael, entered from the hall. Four more Seers stood outside the door, looking in.

Donal seemed in charge. "Luna, Tuvalla spoke to us when you came from your work. For extra protection with Justin and the others gone, Kaarina and Brigitte will take one of the smaller bedrooms at night; Michael and I will stay in the sitting room while you are sleeping. Seers and Wisdom Runners will take shifts outside the door to stand guard; we are to call for Tuvalla if any of you wake with dreams, or there is any trouble."

"This is well thought out. Thank you, Michael," said Luna, serious again. "A group of Seers, Tuvalla and I went into one of her small, well-guarded Seer caves. We were able to contact Zumulia, who seemed well. She was concerned with this second attack by Natab, but was glad to know that we had all of you under our protection now. She is taking further precautions for the Keep. I told her that Jennifer and I would go to her as soon as Justin, Samuel and the others return here."

"This is good news," said Kaarina. Brigitte, David, Jennifer and Millet nodded.

"Oh, yes," said Michael. He handed Millet a small parcel. "One of the weavers sent you a sleeping shirt he has just finished."

Millet opened the package to find a soft purple nightshirt. "This is so nice! Thank you! I can't wait to supervise making some cookies to send him to show my appreciation!"

They all laughed.

"With all that you are now capable of, that will be soon, I think," said David.

Luna stretched and jumped down from the couch. "Now that we have protection, let's have a nice walk in the fresh air and enjoy the snow because here in Solaria it could be gone by morning. Then we will have an early supper, wash up for the night and get some sleep."

When they were finished with their day, the Seers took up their places in the sitting room, outer bedchambers and hall to take turns to keep watch over the group for the night.

Chapter Seven

We must be aware of the cost of our choices; we must be willing to pay their price. Good choices, devoted to the well-being of all, will result in more light in our lives and those around us; choices for good strengthen all aspects of our character, heart, soul and spirit. Choices that appear to give us personal power, especially when they harm and manipulate others, open the door to evil. Evil waits to be invited in with promises of power and fulfillment of wishes; later we find that the price is greater than we could ever imagine.

Book of The Seers

A woman was sitting at the mahogany table in Toni's dining room in Los Angeles. She was strikingly dark and pretty, hair in dozens of braids; sparkling, multi-colored glass beads interwoven in her hair made soft clicking sounds as she smudged the air of the room with a feather and burning sage incense. Toni sat on the woman's left wearing a flowing caftan and gold jewelry; her red hair glimmered in the light of the numerous candles sitting on pedestals on the table. The candlelight reflected off the polished surface of the table and the many mirrors in the room. Two wax figures lay on the table; one of a woman with a wig made from Toni's red hair; the other, a man, had white hair. The two women were unaware of the gold light that was growing on the ceiling above them.

"Are you sure that this is what you want?" asked Marie La Blanc. Her voice was low and husky.

"Oh, for Pete's sake, I have paid you enough money; let's get on with this!" Toni said, trying to contain her temper. Taking a cigarette, she lit it with a red lighter matching her blood-red nails.

Marie La Blanc looked at her steadily. "You have asked me to bind you to a man who has a wife. This is why I am asking you to consider what you truly want. I am not sure what you worship and whom you serve; the gods and goddesses that I serve do not take lightly to those who are not serious when they ask for something. Marriage is a soul and spirit covenant that should not be broken by a jealous or envious outsider."

"That woman is nothing! She is in the way of what I want and need! I will have his money!" screamed Toni.

"And do you really know what it is that you want and need?" asked Marie La Blanc through narrowed eyes.

"Listen, I am going to see this man in two days! I want to be married to him yesterday! Do you understand me? I paid you! Now you make your gods give me what I paid for!" Toni's face was pinched tightly in her fury; her brown eyes dull from the afternoon spent drinking.

"As you wish, lady. As you wish!" responded Marie La Blanc. Taking rose petals from a bowl, she threw them gently on Toni and onto the dolls. Picking up a whip of braided leather, holding a long stream of horsehair, she dipped the tips into a bowl of salt water and whisked it around herself, Toni, the dolls and the room. She mumbled prayers in a language Toni didn't understand.

"My gods are ready to hear your petition! Speak to them now!" commanded Marie La Blanc.

"I want to marry Popsi as soon as possible! And I want Dodi, his stupid idiot wife, dead!" slurred Toni vehemently as she glared at the candles.

The candle flames flickered and jumped; the gold light on the ceiling grew in intensity.

"Lady, you be careful of what you are asking! All requests have a price. When you ask for something that the great Creator has not willed, then you are playing with the forces living on the Earth that are dark and evil. The price you pay is three times that of what you demand of others; if you bind others you will be bound triple, in ways that you cannot predict. If you demand the death of another – well, consider carefully," said the priestess.

Toni stood up in a rage. "I get what I want! Now just do this!"

"Sit yourself back down, lady. Sit yourself back down," said Marie La Blanc. "I will summon the soul of the one to whom you want to bind to yourself. I have warned you that someday you will pay. The consequences are on you, not on me, lady. But I will not ask for a death; I will ask that his wife leave him for another."

"Oh, do whatever you please! Just get that stupid woman out of Popsi's life! Don't give her a cent of his money because it's mine!"

The priestess started muttering unintelligible words as she looked towards the candles. She reached for red thread and bound the dolls together. Then she went back to muttering. Toni looked on, tapping her brightly painted nails on her hips.

A dim light appeared above the candles. An image of Jennifer's grandfather, Popsi, materialized. White hair, puffy face, grey skin with old-man moles, he stared out at them with dull, cold eyes. Darkness throbbed around him. The same darkness began to pulse around Toni.

Marie La Blanc stood slowly; cautiously she studied Toni and the materialized image. "Lady, this is not a good man; he has given his soul to evil. Ask me to stop this now, before you lose your soul and spirit."

"Shut up! Do what I paid you for!" Toni snapped.

The gold light, directly below the ceiling, started to pulse, growing in the air above them. It grew until it became solid gold in the center, emitting strong rays of white and rose-colored sparkling light. The image of Popsi grew darker as it throbbed above the two women, as if threatened by the brightness of the golden orb.

A giant thud sounded to the right of the two women; a large, golden-eyed, bob-tailed cat had appeared before them. Then two more giant cats came through the mirror hanging over the couch; they stood behind the first. Glaring at the priestess and Toni, the first cat tilted her head, opening her mouth; dark clouds sprayed forth, spinning out and into the image of Popsi and then entering Toni.

Marie La Blanc pulled a crucifix from her robes; holding it in front of herself she made the sign of the cross as she backed towards the door. "Lady, save yourself. Come with me now. The gods and goddesses that I serve are of the Earth; some consider them dark and greedy. But this is pure evil; they serve a master that I dare not have anything to do with!"

Natab hissed at her, fangs bared. Marie La Blanc turned and fled.

"I order you to come back here and finish!" Toni screamed after her.

Natab approached Toni; her Hissing Cats close behind. Popsi's image grinned as it hovered in the air.

"Toni... Toni... Toni... I will help you. All you have to do isssss to asssssk me to help you," crooned Natab. She leered up at the orb of golden light, still hovering at ceiling height, before turning back to Toni.

Toni blinked hard and wondered if she had taken drugs earlier. Talking to hallucinations was not new but something seemed real about this. "And who are you?" she spat. "Did my stupid friend Sally slip some LSD into my margarita?"

"I'm no figment of your imagination. Jusssst asssssk me and I will help you," soothed Natab.

"Okay, stupid cat. Help me," said Toni. "I want to be bound to that man. I call him Popsi and I want his stupid wife out of his life for good! In fact, I want Dodi dead!"

"Oh, I know what you call that man. And I know his wife. I know their names," said Natab with no hint of her hissing lisp. "Swear allegiance to me and I will give you what you ask."

Toni took a long sip of her drink, wiping her mouth with the back of her ring-encrusted fingers. "Oh, whatever! I swear allegiance to you, stupid cat!"

Natab started to purr. "My name is Natab. Say, 'Please, sweet Natab, I swear my allegiance to you.' Then I will get you what you want."

Toni rolled her blood-shot eyes. "Whatever!" She screwed up her face, "Please, sweet Natab, I swear my allegiance to you! Now bind Popsi to me and kill that idiot of a gold-digging wife of his!"

"Thank you," purred Natab. "Ssssstretch your arm forth and I will draw your blood."

Without hesitation Toni stretched out her right arm. Natab slashed with her claws deeply and quickly. Darkness swirling from Natab's wide open mouth swirled into the cuts on Toni as blood streamed out. "Pour your blood onto the two bound figuresssssss," said Natab.

Toni showered the dolls with her blood.

"Now, let me sssssssee your arm," said Natab. Toni reached out again to Natab, who opened her mouth wide again and hissed. Darkness poured from her jaws into Toni's arm as her body shook and swayed; Toni gasped. Natab's tongue flicked out from between her large, white fangs and licked the length of the wound which knitted together until no blood flowed; all that was left was healed flesh, with an angry looking scar, from Toni's elbow to her wrist.

"Look at what you have done! No plastic surgeon will be able to fix that!" screamed Toni.

"That issssss the leasssssst of your worriesssss now," hissed Natab. Popsi's image slowly faded into nothingness; but the golden orb above them grew brighter. The other cats hissed as they looked up.

"Sssseen enough?" asked Natab as she gazed up at the orb.

"You'll never win! I'll take you too, ssssssoon!" Turning, the Hissing Cats disappeared into the dark rent in the surface of the mirror that they had appeared from; it closed behind them with a dull pop.

The glowing orb hovered in the air above Toni and then slowly faded, leaving her in the candlelight with the blood-soaked dolls on the table. She looked for her drink. Under an end table cowered the sturdy corgi, Grace. Rising, Toni took a running start, giving the dog a solid kick.

* * *

David, Millet and Jennifer woke feeling rested. At bedtime, Tuvalla had administered a syrup she called a tincture, of valerian root and a chamomile and chocolate mint tea, that had provided deep, restful sleep. Luna led them downstairs where Kaarina ordered them fresh green drinks and muffins from the kitchens. Several more Seers gathered in the room.

The drinks arrived, deep emerald in color; they looked vibrant and alive. David and Millet grabbed theirs and started drinking immediately, swishing the green liquid in their mouths before swallowing. Luna lapped delicately at hers. As Jennifer looked around the room she saw all of the Seers were drinking large tumblers of the green liquid.

David's eyes were bright turquoise in the morning light as he looked over his glass at Jennifer. She felt her heart jump; suddenly she realized he was handsome - more handsome than any of the young teen idols she had gone to school with in Los Angeles. And unlike them, he wasn't dreaming of being famous when and if he got a coveted part in a popular movie or wrote a hit song; he had a life that was full of real adventure. She was beginning to hope she would never have to go back to Earth.

"Hey Jen, you aren't drinking your emerald elixir," teased David. She realized that all of the Seers were watching her. Her glass stood full on the table in front of her.

Millet finished his smaller glass and looked at Jennifer from his tabletop pillow. "Jen, it's really good for us. It has fresh-picked greens put through a blending machine: dandelion, mint, romaine and beet tops mixed with fresh ginger, apples, pineapple and honey. You'll love it!"

Jennifer looked at the green drink doubtfully. Salad and green vegetables were one thing, but a green drink?

Kaarina brought a pitcher to refill David and Millet's glasses. "Jennifer, you must drink this. Tuvalla has insisted that you have green drinks four times a day to strengthen and heal your nervous systems from the shock of the encounters with Natab."

Jennifer raised the glass to her lips and tasted the liquid. It was sweet and smelled good – not like the grass taste that she expected. It was like the delicious fruit smoothies that she had had in California, despite the green color. "*It's really good*!"

Luna looked over. "The live enzymes and the vitality of fresh chlorophyll will both cleanse your body and help it to grow stronger so that you are able to learn to vision better."

"And it matches your eyes!" said David.

Jennifer glared at him and finished her drink. She could feel its strengthening effect starting to flow in her body within minutes.

The group turned as Tuvalla entered the room; her dark hair gleamed as she walked towards them. A dark-haired man, dressed in white, followed her. "Good morning. How are our three intuitive communicators? Any bad dreams or feelings from your late evening adventure?" Her green eyes sparkled and danced as she surveyed them; a smile played at the corners of her mouth.

The three shook their heads.

"Kaarina, Brigitte and I checked them through the night and they seemed well. I don't think we have anything to worry about," said Luna.

Tuvalla nodded. "Okay, then let's get started. First, let me introduce the Master Keeper of our kitchens, Vesper." She motioned for the man behind her to come forward. He smiled in greeting.

"Millet, Vesper is going to give you a tour through the kitchens, gardens and green houses. He is our Master Chef Seer over all the kitchens; he will personally be in charge of your apprenticeship – which starts today," explained Tuvalla.

Millet jumped off his cushion. "Really?"

Vesper came forward offering his hand to Millet. "I'm excited too. We have not had Talking Loaves at the Keep for three years. I am looking forward to helping you learn to use your natural talents." Millet climbed into his arms and waved goodbye to the group as he went off to the kitchens.

Tuvalla turned back to the table. "Now that you have had your green drinks and muffins, let's be off. Some of the Seers, Luna and I will take you to the Cave of the Dreaming Children."

Luna and Tuvalla led Jennifer and David out into the courtyard behind the Keep's manse. Joining them were male Seers Jonathon, Donal and Michael; and the women Seers, Kaarina, Brigitte, Adelita, Valerie, Bethany, Carol and Joyce. They made their way through the outdoor gardens, now covered in snow, and past the workshops, the training fields, and dog sledding trails to the mountain forming the back of the Keep. They found themselves in front of a smooth, flat, vertical surface in the face of the mountain.

The Seers formed a semi-circle with Tuvalla. Humming together, they held their hands in the air. White energy flowed from their chests and hands onto the surface of the rock. Its surface changed from dark grey to white; then it slid to the right revealing a passage. Tuvalla lowered her hands and motioned for Luna, David and Jennifer to follow her into the tunnel. The Seers, still humming and emitting light, followed behind them, turned and waited until the door slid back into place before lowering their hands.

The tunnel was well lit with glow weed and pillar candles sitting on niches in the rock. They followed it through to a door of black onyx; the Seers opened it by humming a low, sweet melody. They continued along the passage through six more doors: red set with rubies, orange set with tiger's eye gems, green set with emeralds, sky blue set with tourmalines, purple set with turquoise and the last, gold, set with diamonds.

As the golden door closed behind them, they entered into a huge, domed cave. The surface of the walls and ceiling were lined with amethyst crystals. A lake the size of three football fields lay in the center; a stone walkway circled the perimeter. Aerial walkways made of clear, shimmering fiber woven in a spider web pattern hung five feet over the surface of the water. An orb of pink light, hovering high above the lake, provided soft visibility for the Seers who moved along the walkways and sat focusing on the surface of the lake. Around the lake and at juncture points in the web sat Seers playing harps and stringed instruments in soothing melodies. Numerous lights, like stars, shimmered in the water.

Tuvalla turned to Jennifer and David and put her finger to her lips; she smiled. *"Focus on your breath and think pleasant thoughts here. Try not to speak unless necessary."*

One of the dark-haired Seers in their group, Adelita, handed David and Jennifer helmets and capes woven of a light, silver-colored, gossamer fiber. Dressed, they followed Luna and Tuvalla on the wide stone path around the lake. Midway they came to a recess in the wall of the cave; it was furnished with cushions on a rug intricately woven in a pattern of stars and bright flowers. Tuvalla motioned for the group to be seated.

Jennifer looked over the lake; it was an entrancing sight. Her heart was trying to whisper something to her. The Cave of Dreaming Children felt like a place that she had been coming to all of her life; yet she knew she had not been in the cave, nor did she remember seeing it in any of her dreams. In all of her research she had never read of such a place. Watching David, she thought he seemed at home here as he sat studying the surface of the lake.

"The hats and capes that Adelita gave you to wear shield your outgoing negative thoughts," came Tuvalla's voice into their heads. *"You do not have training in shielding your thoughts – so you must wear these until you do."* David and Jennifer turned and nodded to her.

"We have brought you here so that you could experience one of the many places our Keep has in its trust," said Tuvalla.

She continued. *"I am the Master Seer here; this is my main trust. The Order of Seers have many duties in Solaria and this is one of them. Wisdom Runners guard Solaria so that Seers can do their work in safety."*

David nodded. He raised the index finger of his right hand as he looked towards Tuvalla.

"Yes, good question," said Tuvalla. Jennifer had not been able to hear David's thoughts – the caps and capes were doing their work. *"This is the Cave of the Dreaming Children. There are several of these caves across Solaria in very guarded Keeps, like ours, that are in the trust of Master Seers."*

David nodded. Tuvalla continued, *"The lights that you see on the surface of the lake come from children on the planet Earth. They are ones who have unfortunate hardships in their lives, often with no one to love, comfort and aid them."*

Jennifer cocked her head and tried to ask Tuvalla a question from her heart.

"Jennifer, I sense I know what you are trying to ask. We cannot directly intervene in their lives. But we watch their dreams, send healing energy, and pray for their wellbeing. We pray that guidance comes to them through people, places and animal companions so that they have the strength to find the goodness in themselves to grow to be the fine people they were created to be."

David raised his finger again. Tuvalla nodded. *"With terminally ill children, the murdered, the ones who have horrible accidents – we pray light around them so that they can ascend to the Creator in peace, free from their pain."*

Jennifer raised her finger and gazed hard at Tuvalla with her question. Tuvalla laughed softly; it sounded like a burbling brook in Jennifer's head. *"No, Jennifer, we are not angels. Angels are infinite beings; they serve the Creator across all dimensions and parallel realities, bringing messages, interventions and aid in healing. On Solaria we are finite beings who live in a parallel existence to your life on Earth; most of us are serving good, but others like Natab choose to serve darkness. Angels, by their nature, are infinite goodness."*

Jennifer sensed it was more complicated than she could understand at present. She took a breath and tried to relax with what she was able to take in.

"I wanted both of you to see and experience this important work. David, now that you will be starting Wisdom Runner training you can begin to understand why the service you will render is so important to Solaria. This is one of the works of goodness that you will be protecting." Tuvalla rose and beckoned them to follow her.

They continued around the lake. David admired some of the large, standing gold and silver harps that the Seers played; placing his ear near one of their sounding boards he smiled at the clarity of tone.

Tuvalla watched him calmly; her bright green eyes sparkled despite the dim light of the cave. "*You are a very talented harp player. Perhaps in your Seer training you may elect to learn about the healing power of music and train to play these – they send healing and comfort to many children who need it, who think they are all alone."*

Adelita took the helmets and capes from Jennifer and David as they were leaving. With raised hands their group of Seers hummed until light emitted from their chests and hands, opening the gold and diamond encrusted door to allow the group to pass through.

* * *

The wind blew cruelly against them as the dog teams tried to break through snowdrifts along the trail that they traveled north towards the Portal of Nordon. The snow, mixed with bits of ice, came hard. The dogs pulled harder; the mushers squatted low on the sled runners to minimize the air drag. Justin Valor and his team, with Betty and Bandit in lead, held up his hand to stop, "*Whoa! Whoa*!" he intuitively commanded to the teams and mushers.

Justin, Samuel and Lacino set their snow hooks to anchor their sleds. Each checked in with each of the dogs of their team and then carefully examined them physically and intuitively. Everyone was in good shape, no cut paws, frostbite or strained ligaments.

"We could cut the cargo sleds we are pulling behind us," suggested Justin. *"It will make our loads lighter and we'll move faster in this storm."* The wind howled around them.

"Justin, there could be wounded at the portal. We may have to carry home many of our comrades," said Betty, a white dog with a black face that had served with Justin for many years.

"I agree," sent Nicco to all. *"I don't mind the extra load. It should not be that much further."*

"*Well said*!" called the canine Wisdom Runners together.

Samuel cleared his goggles. *"It's up to you dogs. You are doing the work. But I agree with all of you. If there are wounded we need to be able to carry all of them quickly to your Keep."*

"Again, it's up to all of you," sent Justin. *"Don't be heroes so that you lose the energy that will be needed to try to free our comrades."*

"Onward! Hike!" howled the dogs audibly against the wind and snow. The mushers jumped to their sleds and pulled their snow hook anchors. They were off again.

* * *

Tuvalla and Luna led the group through a cave tunnel. After passing through several doors, the Seers used light and tone to open a door of silver, carved with swirling, geometric patterns. Passing through the doorway they found themselves in a twenty-foot oval cave whose walls were lined with amethysts, as the Cave of Dreaming Children had been. A bright patterned rug and velvet cushions lined the floor; glow weed and beeswax candles gave light that danced as it reflected from the amethysts.

"This is the Amethyst Cave. We can talk audibly here," said Tuvalla motioning for the group to sit. They sat in a circle with Jonathon, Donal, Michael, Kaarina, Brigitte, Carol, Adelita, Valerie,

Bethany and Joyce. Jonathan and Donal brought out harps of gold and silver; seated they began to play softly.

Jennifer felt her body relaxing. It felt as if her heart and more were being soothed within. The amethyst crystals of the room energized the sound so that it vibrated pleasantly into the bodies of those sitting in the circle.

"This is one of our special healing rooms where we bring those who are seriously wounded or sick. The harps produce healing energy, as do the crystals of the room. Amethyst is very cleansing," said Tuvalla. "This cave also gives healing and aid to those who have been traumatized."

Luna spoke for the first time in an hour. "Jennifer, we wanted you to come here with these Seers who specialize in healing. You were very traumatized when your father died. We suspect that you suffered abuse by your father and stepmother, earlier in your life, as well."

Jennifer bit her lip; she nodded.

Tuvalla took over. "You saw the lights in the Lake of Children Dreaming. Each one represents a child who has no real support from the adults around them in their lives. We are watching over them, sending them our good intentions and praying for them."

David looked to Jennifer, then down at his hands.

"One of the lights that we have been tending was yours," said Tuvalla.

Jennifer's breath caught in her chest and then eased. "*That's why I felt like I knew the cave . . .*"

Luna nodded. "We hoped you would recognize it."

"*When I sat in the cave it was like I have known it all of my life. I felt like it was a safe place that I knew... in my heart*," thought Jennifer. An inner barrier in her chest, that had been there since before she could remember, started to dissolve. The Seers in the circle suddenly seemed more trustable to her – she could feel their kindness.

"The Seers here have been watching over you since you were born. We confirmed Zumulia's 'knowing' that you had been born on Earth. We have tried to send you guidance and comfort," said Tuvalla.

David shook his head. "But she has had terrible nightmares, a horrible stepmother, her father cared more about drugs and celebrity than her… now he is dead. Jen has had such a hard life."

Tuvalla nodded. "We know that. I told you that we cannot directly intervene in a child's life. But most children feel the love we send them."

"Before my father's death, I did feel at peace when I was with my corgi, Grace. We read science books and novels, sat on the beach watching the waves, walked in the park, watched the fish in my aquarium. I loved to look at flowers or see the stars. I loved how Grace was so curious about the world and would spend hours enjoying it. Whenever I was with most cats or dogs – I felt like they cared about me. When my stepmother and father were mean to me – I'd be under the covers crying, hugging Grace, and sometimes I felt a sense of peace that felt so… loving," thought Jennifer. *"Was that you?"*

"We hope that we are having an effect in getting you the support you need," said Tuvalla. "All goodness comes from the Creator. We can only try to send healing through our prayers."

"I just know that you got through. I know that the goodness I felt was you caring about me," thought Jennifer. *"Did you bring me here?"*

"Not directly. We only pray for the highest good of a child. We pray that good, helpful adults, animals, and life circumstances come to them," said Tuvalla.

Luna turned towards Jennifer. "I sense that their prayers aided you in getting to your uncle's farm because it is a steady place for you to live and heal."

"And Grace?" A tear slid down Jennifer's cheek.

Tuvalla placed her hand on Jennifer's shoulder. "Grace was there for you in California. A comfort and a good friend. It is sad that your stepmother's meanness has kept you apart. It is our hope that your aunt and uncle's efforts will reunite you."

Tears started to flow freely. Jennifer tried to brush them away. Sometimes she missed Grace more than her father.

"Understanding the power of prayer is a lifelong pursuit," said Tuvalla. "Luna and I wanted you to come to the Amethyst Cave to try to vision the time of your father's death. With the support of the Seers, we hope that you will get some clarity, guidance and healing. Maybe the nightmares will stop."

"Are you willing to try?" asked Luna.

Jennifer nodded as she took a soft handkerchief someone passed to her and wiped her eyes. "*I trust you. I trust all of you.*"

"Good," said Luna.

"We will focus on our breathing as Luna has taught you. We will then raise an orb of light. As we do that, Jennifer, start to visualize yourself back to where you lived in Los Angeles with your father and stepmother," Tuvalla instructed.

With the gentle melody Jonathan and Donal played upon the harps the group closed their eyes. Jennifer felt her body respond quickly as she focused on her breathing. The relaxation spread and soon the light started to form within her with each deep, soft breath she took.

"When you are ready, open your eyes. We are going to allow the light to go out through our heart center into the space above the group," came Tuvalla's voice.

Gradually the white light came from each one's heart center and pooled into the space above them. An orb formed slowly and became opaque gold.

"Jennifer, start to see your Los Angeles home in the orb. See as much detail as you can. Tell us of any concerns. I will give you guidance through this journey," said Tuvalla.

The living room of the house started to come into view in the midst of the orb: the crème leather couches, dining table and yards of white carpeting. The vision was from above, as if they were on the ceiling looking down. Fear gripped Jennifer's center as she viewed the room where her father had died. Her breathing started to constrict.

"Jennifer, we are right here, with you," said Luna.

She nodded and swallowed. "*I don't think I can do this.*"

"Jen, try to place more focus on your breath than on the vision," said Tuvalla. "It should lessen the fear that is trying to hold you." Tuvalla held up her hands, sending rose-colored light directly at Jennifer's chest; it felt soothing. Allowing her breath to go deeper, she looked around the living room in Los Angeles.

Suddenly the vision switched from day to night. Although blurred, her stepmother appeared, sitting at the table with a woman whose hair was done in tiny braids, interwoven with many colored beads. Dozens of lit candles flickered; in front of the lady were two dolls: one had red hair the same color as Toni's and one had shorter, white hair.

"*Ummm... this isn't the night my father was shot... that is Toni, my stepmother, and I don't recognize the other lady . . .*" thought Jennifer.

"Perhaps your heart is showing us something that we need to know for your healing or your protection," said Tuvalla. "We are with you. Let's just watch..."

Jennifer felt her heart jump and tears started to flow again. "*The corgi hiding under the table by the couch is Grace.*"

"Let's send Grace our prayers," said Luna. The Seers murmured quietly in accent and silently offered prayers.

Jennifer dabbed at her eyes and watched as the vision became clearer. The two women were arguing; the woman in braids urging Toni not to go forward with something. Toni got nasty and the woman reluctantly began to mumble in the direction of the candles. A dark cloud appeared with the face of an elderly man.

"*That's my grandfather; my father's father. We call him Popsi,*" explained Jennifer.

Suddenly Natab and two of her Hissing Cats appeared in the vision. The woman pulled a cross from her robes and held it towards Natab as she backed out of the room, crossing herself, warning Toni.

Natab looked directly at them, leering, before smugly turning back to Toni.

"We will pray for Jennifer's stepmother, now!" came Tuvalla's voice. Jennifer did not know what to say or how to pray. She heard Luna, David and the others softly speaking as the orb above them grew brighter, as did the vision of the living room in Los Angeles.

Jennifer's body tensed. She wanted to jump through the vision, into her living room to grab Grace and run. Instead she watched as Natab mesmerized Toni into giving her allegiance in exchange for binding Popsi to her and killing Jennifer's step-grandmother, Dodi. When she slashed Toni's arm, causing the blood to flow over the red haired and white haired dolls, the room began to fill with dark energy pouring from Natab. After Natab filled Toni and the image of Popsi with darkness, she and the two Hissing Cats looked up at them.

Jennifer's stomach knotted, she felt paralyzed looking into those cold, gold eyes. "Ssssseen enough?" glowered Natab. "You'll never win! I'll take you, too, sssssoon!" The three cats jumped into the rent formed in a wall mirror, and were gone.

Jennifer started to shake. She could not take her eyes off her stepmother who was gazing about smugly. When Toni kicked Grace a scream tore through her throat, but no words would come audibly. *"I hate her! I hate her!"* vibrated over and over in her head.

"Close the orb, NOW!" ordered Tuvalla. As the Seers worked, Luna and Tuvalla moved to Jennifer.

Tuvalla hugged her, speaking softly. Luna put her paw on Jennifer's lap and hummed forth rose-colored light. Gradually Jennifer stopped shaking.

"Please open your eyes and look at me." Tuvalla's voice gently pulled at Jennifer and she wiped her eyes before looking into Tuvalla's; it was like looking into a mirror, they were so green, so like her own.

"You are angry and upset because you have been hurt by your stepmother for many years. You sense she may have killed your father and now is plotting something with your grandfather. And now she has hurt Grace and you cannot protect her," said Tuvalla.

Jennifer felt wooden inside.

"What we saw is frightening. We understand that," said Tuvalla. "But hate will get us nowhere. It does nothing to stop a person that is hurting us or protect the ones we love; it sucks us into the power of darkness and we become paralyzed and powerless."

Luna nodded. "You may not believe this, but Toni was once a child who was also very hurt. She had no guidance for healing, so her hate and bitterness has drawn her to hurt others."

Jennifer looked around the Amethyst Cave. The Seers and David were singing softly as they focused on her. She looked up at Tuvalla, "*What you are saying makes sense in my heart. But what do I do?*"

"You choose, no matter what, to believe in the power of goodness. You devote yourself to love, truth and doing what is right," explained Tuvalla.

"Does that mean that Toni and Natab can't be stopped?" asked Jennifer.

"No," said Luna. "You saw David shoot and kill one of the Hissing Cats. He was angry at what Natab said about his parents. But he shot the Hissing Cat without rancor in his heart."

"*I don't understand,*" said Jennifer. Tears flowed again.

Tuvalla gently brushed Jennifer's face with her fingers. She offered her a sip of herbal liquid from a small, blue glass bottle. "Breathe deep and listen to the Seers singing. All of this is hard to learn. But you are a strong person, Jennifer. Your heart, soul and spirit will lead you to know, learn and make right choices in your life."

Taking another sip of the herbal medicine Tuvalla offered, a gentle relaxation spread from her chest and then into her arms and legs. Jennifer took in the peaceful beauty in the crystal cave; she could feel the care that flowed from the singers around her. She looked over at David and then at Luna before her eyes closed as she slipped into a deep sleep.

* * *

The beautiful harp music and humming seemed to continue softly as Jennifer opened her eyes again. It seemed she had only closed them for a moment, but confusion gripped her mind as she saw late afternoon sunlight streaming into the sitting room of their suite. Struggling to sit up, she found herself on one of the deep blue upholstered couches. David sat across from her, strumming his harp as he and Millet hummed a gentle melody. Kaarina and Brigitte were sitting on the window seats.

"How did I get here?" asked Jennifer. *"We were just in the cave . . ."*

White-haired Kaarina got up and poured a mug of tea from a pitcher on the sideboard. She handed it to Jennifer. "Tuvalla wants you to drink this. Sip it slowly; it's chamomile and lemon verbena. It is good for relaxation."

"Jen, I carried you from the cave five hours ago," said David. He put down the harp and accepted a mug of tea from Kaarina. "Tuvalla asked that you be allowed to sleep until you woke on your own. We have been sitting with you."

"How do you feel, Jen?" asked Millet.

"Okay. Well," Jennifer said. *"Natab was in Los Angeles with my stepmother . . ."*

Luna and Tuvalla entered the room from the corridor. "Yes," answered Luna. "But first, how do you feel?"

"Surprised to be back here: I have no memory of leaving the cave," thought Jennifer. *"But I feel... soft inside, relaxed."*

"We spent time praying for you in the Amethyst Cave. The herbal drink allowed you to sleep so that you could heal at a deep level while we worked on you," said Luna. "Our hope is that your trauma is greatly reduced."

Tuvalla accepted a cup of tea from Brigitte as she sat near

Jennifer. "Although seeing Natab and Toni together, and the orb with your grandfather, and what happened to Grace was frightening to you - you faced it with us. That took courage. I sense that much of the fear you have lived with will no longer grip you as it has in the past."

"But Toni has done something terrible..." thought Jennifer.

"Yes, Toni has. We are praying that she finds the courage to turn from this very bad course of action in her life," said Luna.

"But she is nasty. She loves to hurt people," thought Jennifer. *"She wants Popsi's wife dead and she wants to marry him. I am afraid for Grace!"*

Luna jumped up next to Jennifer and leaned her compact, strong body solidly against her. "We know that. But even the furthest gone - even Natab - has the choice of turning his life around towards good."

Tuvalla nodded. "It is what we tried to explain to you in the cave. It will make more sense in the days and years ahead of you."

"For now we are concerned about how Natab has managed to enter the Earth and find her way directly to a person who is so closely associated with you," said Luna. "Three, actually - Popsi, Toni and Grace. Although we are not sure she saw Grace."

"*What can I do*?" asked Jennifer.

"Right now you can relax," said Tuvalla. "I have arranged for a good supper for the three of you after you have your fresh green drinks!"

David and Millet started laughing when they saw the look on Jennifer's face.

"Jen, taking care of yourself and growing strong is part of being a Seer or Wisdom Runner," said Tuvalla as she, too, smiled. "So is relaxing. It is all about balance. Luna and I must work with the Seers tonight in the Wisdom Cave of Dreams to send healing prayers for Samuel, Lacino, Justin and the canine teams; they must be near the Portal of Nordon. We will also try to contact Zumulia and the Court of Wisdom Runners in the east to see if they have news; they need to be warned of Natab's venture to Earth. We feel that the darkness on Earth is getting worse."

Jennifer nodded and sighed.

"We have arranged for some entertainment. Jonathan and Donal will bring harps to play for you after your supper. Adelita makes beautiful, healing crystal jewelry; she is going to show you, David and Millet how to bead. Carol is a marvelous storyteller; she will come to tell you tales from the lore of Solaria. How does that sound?" asked Tuvalla.

"The truth is," said Luna as Jennifer hugged her, "Jennifer has had no evening fun in her stay in Solaria."

David laughed again. "It's true. We have been traveling, talking about trouble, learning, recovering… that's all she has known here."

"We went dog sledding and we practiced with slingshots and bows . . ." thought Jennifer.

"You have television, radio, DVD's, Internet, YouTube and mp3s on Earth for evening entertainment," said David. "Our dog sledding is fun, but it is part of our work. In Solaria we spend many of our evenings telling stories, playing instruments, singing, dancing and eating together. People knit, bead, sew, or read while enjoying the company of others. Life here is about companionship and fun – not just working against darkness!" David laughed and the group joined in. Jennifer loved his laugh, it was infectious.

"It's true, Jen," said Luna as she rose and stretched. "Tuvalla and I will leave you now. Relax, drink your green drinks and enjoy the evening.

Tuvalla and Luna left them in the capable hands of other Seers.

* * *

Kaarina woke them in the morning, handing each a freshly made, emerald green vegetable and berry drink. The night before had been filled with extraordinary music from standing harps, good food and homemade fudge, beading lessons and fairy tales that were like none that Jennifer had ever heard.

She could not have ever imagined such fun. In L.A. her father and stepmother had gatherings that seemed to hinge on drinking and drugs. No one was happy and no one really liked one another; everything was about status. But here dogs, horses and humans had been genuinely happy; she had never had such a relaxing, fun evening. She had even tried dancing! Alone in the room she tried a few of the steps of the circle dances they had taught her and ended up whirling round and round till laughing, she fell back on the bed in a heap.

Sobering thoughts about her father, Toni and Grace brought her back to her feet. After washing and dressing she put on the necklace that Adelita had helped her make: real amethyst beads alternating with gold. Adelita had explained that the beads promoted healing and could help to protect her from negative energy, including bad intentions of others. But Adelita had also said, "Jennifer, please remember that ultimately it is the goodness in our hearts that allows goodness to come to us. Crystals have healing energy, as do herbs and plants. But if you lose this necklace or someone tries to take it – let it go and trust in higher goodness that something better will come to you."

Jennifer lingered on Adelita's words as she touched the beads of the necklace. Then she pushed open the great wooden door of the bedroom to join the others in the sitting room.

"Where's Luna?"

Brigitte looked up from the book she was reading. "Luna, Tuvalla and a number of the Seers and Wisdom Runners are trying to contact the Court in the east again. They did not get through last night."

"Early this morning, before she left, Luna said we are to get some fresh air," said David. "She suggested we take a sled out with the yearling dogs to get some practice mushing. Then she thought we should work further with bow and arrow practice at the outdoor range."

"Oh, I wish I could come," Millet perked up. "But Vesper, the Keeper of the Kitchens, will be teaching me basic pie making. I'm excited!"

"Millet, you look very cute in that magenta tunic, tiny white chef's cap!" Jennifer thought.

The evening before he had been so happy – telling them about his tour of the greenhouses with all of their fruit and berry bushes and trees, many vegetables in raised beds, the outdoor gardens where the Seers had melted the snow, and the many kitchens of the Keep. He was looking forward to learning how to make fresh vegetable and fruit dishes and jams, jellies, herbal tonics, pies, bread, cakes, stews, medicinal teas and other healing concoctions. They were also going to teach him how to preserve fruits and veggies for both winter times and taking on journeys.

"Well, let's go down for breakfast and then we can get going!" David stood, gathering Millet up in his arms. Jennifer, Brigitte, Kaarina and several Seers followed them down the corridor.

* * *

The young canine Wisdom Runner apprentices were excited to go out as a team with Jennifer and David. Many of them were big, roly-poly versions of Nicco, Tundra and many of Samuel's dogs; they shared close and distant dog bloodline relatives. Twenty of them took turns making a twelve-dog team; what they lacked in the stamina, endurance and skill of their elders, they made up in exuberance and innocent joy. The morning was spent listening to their jokes, teasing and laughter as the young dogs pulled, fell over each other and accidentally tangled the team lines.

The Seers watched the antics. Kaarina jumped up and down and clapped when the young dogs got a maneuver right. Brigitte and several other Seers stomped their feet, laughed and encouraged them. David patiently helped the yearlings and Jennifer learn commands of "Gee" and "Haw" – right and left - and the art, skill and magic of gliding through the snow as a team.

After lunch the Seers went with them to the archery field. Standing in the snow, side-by-side, they sent arrows into their targets. Jennifer watched David, all grace in his form and precision. She was surprised as arrow after arrow she shot hit the bull's-eye of her target. After retrieving their arrows they stopped for hot mugs of mint tea that Kaarina handed them.

"Kaarina, I don't understand this. This is only the second time that I have practiced archery, but all of my arrows are making target exactly as I vision them to do," thought Jennifer.

David didn't let Kaarina answer. "Jen, you were hitting the center repeatedly when we first practiced. You have natural talent." He grimaced an apology at Kaarina who waved it away. "Luna said it was partially because you have powerful gifts of intuition and visioning and also because your body is flexible and strong – it responds well to what your mind asks of it."

The small, older woman looked at her thoughtfully. "What David says is true. Has the archery changed since your Amethyst Cave experience?

"I don't worry about 'doing it right,'" thought Jennifer. *"It was the same on the dog sled this morning. Everything felt... alive... as if it was exactly what I was supposed to be doing right then and there. I didn't have thoughts; just a sense of aliveness."*

Kaarina's blue eyes sparkled, set off by the whiteness of her skin, hair and the snow on the ground around them. "Jennifer, you faced your past, your current life and your fears with courage yesterday."

"But I got very frightened and passed out," thought Jennifer.

"No, the herbal medicine brought sleep," said Kaarina. "While you slept we administered prayer for the traumas of your life. The healing would not have been possible if you had not been willing to face your fears."

"But what does that have to do with archery and dog sledding?" asked Jennifer.

"As we face our traumas our real skills can emerge, unfettered by fear," said Kaarina.

Jennifer considered this. Although it did not seem quite logical, it felt right.

David looked towards the young dogs playing in the distance. "Zumulia, Samuel and the dogs taught me that often we have to turn off our thinking. Things that don't make sense to our heads make sense in our hearts. It may not make sense that facing past trauma helps us do better in our present – but it does."

"*I'm sensing that*," thought Jennifer.

* * *

Luna and Tuvalla were waiting for them after their practice. Millet had a banquet ready that he had helped to prepare. While Jonathon played his harp for them, David, Jennifer and Millet shared with the group what they had learned during the day; they spoke and intuitively communicated with animation, hand gestures and laughter. The white dog and the Master Seer listened intently, asking questions, sharing their merriment.

After the meal, Luna stretched and then sat again. "I am glad you three had a wonderful day. We also have news to share, though not so joyful as yours."

Tuvalla began. "We have not been able to communicate with Justin. They should have reached the portal by now. We were able to get through to the Counsel in the east and they, too, have had no news."

"*What do we do*?" asked Jennifer.

"For now, we pray and continue to try to contact them," said Tuvalla. "But we have bad news from Zumulia."

Jennifer felt jolted from the light reverie the activities of the day had produced.

"What has happened?" asked David.

"More shadow attacks. The neighboring animals have had to hide in their homes," said Luna. "We believe that the darkness that allowed Natab to slip through a portal to Earth is escalating."

"There is no snow in the capital city of Tacha on the far eastern reach of the Plain of Vendona. Geoffrey and Sebastian rode to the plain, just south of us where we crossed it to come here from Zumulia's, and found no snow either," said Luna. "King Gifford was about to depart for the south, but has agreed to fly here first, ahead of the snow, to take us directly to Zumulia's."

"The Master Weavers are preparing special parachutes so that the Gooney Birds can drop us just above the treetops," said Luna. "We will leave in the dark hours of the morning - so I suggest we get to bed soon."

"Good!" said Millet. "I can't wait to see my brothers and sisters!"

Tuvalla put her hand out to him. Her dark beauty and green eyes were enhanced with the candlelight. "Millet, you will be staying here with us for now. You must continue your studies."

"But..." said Millet.

"Millet, we cannot risk losing all the Talking Loaves again," said Luna. "We have not heard from the Keepers of the Ovens. For all we know, you and your brothers and sisters at Zumulia's may be all of your kind alive."

Vesper came from the kitchen. "Millet, you must be brave. Trust the judgment of Luna and Tuvalla. Besides, staying here, you will have more knowledge to share with your brothers and sisters when you meet again."

Millet nodded. "Can I stay with David one more night?"

"Of course you can," said Luna. "Now let's be off to bed. Jonathon is going to serenade us on the harp until we go into dreamland."

Jennifer was awake most of the night. Thoughts of Natab, Toni and the darkness kept tumbling through her mind. Were Justin, Samuel and the dogs lost? Dead? Had they saved Contalia and Dohanos? What more was going on at Zumulia's that they would leave Millet behind? Luna and Tuvalla were hiding their real concern, she could just sense it. Not wanting to wake Luna, she tried the deep breathing and a cup of herbal tea but nothing helped. Her thoughts just whirled away.

Chapter Eight

When Wisdom Runners serve Solaria and creation with truth, light and love in their hearts they are like the dawn light when the sun rises on a cloudless morning – they bring clarity to all of creation. The service rendered in a single courageous action sows seeds of light across all planes of existence. Thus we pray to always serve with love, light and truth in our hearts – no matter what the consequences to our incarnate form.

Book of The Wisdom Runners

It was snowing hard as the three dog teams came to a halt in front of the portal of Nordon. Justin, Lacino and Samuel set their snow hooks to anchor their sleds and began to free the canine Wisdom Runners from their lines and harnesses. Three piles of snow lifted and crumbled as three black dogs emerged from them; two chained to a sled and one to a tree. The freed dogs and humans ran to them with concern, bringing food and herbal tonics.

"We knew you would come!" said Tonka. "We knew it was you searching for us!" Denali and Hunter nodded their black, shaggy heads; they were weak from being without food for three days.

After asking the dogs where they hurt, Lacino and Samuel checked them carefully for wounds and frostbite. "We saw you and heard you when we visioned for you from the Cave of Dreams," explained Justin. "Tell us what has happened."

"The Servers of Light gave us twelve crystals to bring to Solaria to combat the darkness; we hope they will aid in dissolving the veil of darkness dividing east from west," said Hunter. "When we left the conference we were attacked by Ice Beings but managed to drive them off. It took us months to reach the Portal of Nordon in the parallel reality that we were traveling in. At the entrance we were attacked again, so we sent Contalia and Dohanos through the portal, with several dogs, to contact the Court of the Wisdom Runners."

Tonka continued, "After they made contact, they came back through the portal for the rest of us. In the tunnel, the shadows and Ice Beings attacked. Contalia and some of the dogs were frozen as they fought. We contacted the Court to warn them and then went back in to try to free them."

Finished with their ministering, Samuel and Lacino found that the three dogs were weak but unwounded, with no sign of frostbite. "How did you get chained out here?" asked Justin.

"We have no idea!" said Tonka. "We were singing behind Dohanos, protecting him from anything that might come from this side of the portal. Suddenly all three of us were lifted into the air. We were transported here, chained to the sled and tree, and abandoned."

Denali nodded. "It felt like invisible hands. We didn't smell or hear a thing. Then, all noise in the tunnel ceased. We expected to be attacked, but nothing returned for us."

Samuel nodded. "The Ice Beings came through with you from the parallel reality you were in?"

"Yes, probably as we transited," said Hunter.

"They bite with their ice fangs and suck energy. Then the shadows have an entrance into the body to finish the job. They make their victims into servants of darkness; once bitten with the shadows within the only hope we know of is to pierce the heart of the victim before they actually die," said Tonka.

Justin considered this. "How did the dogs and Contalia get frozen?"

"We had our backs to the action most of the time," said Tonka. "We could see that the dogs' singing energy, and the energy that Dohanos sent out, drove the Ice Beings back, as it does the shadows. But when the Ice Beings surround us, the energy we send out is bounced back, so that it freezes and encases us."

"The Ice Beings can't get in, but we can't get out, move or think," said Hunter. "Contalia and the dogs were immobile inside the ice that enshrouded them. We could not communicate with them intuitively."

"Okay," said Justin. "We will carry swords and arrows tipped with glow weed. The one time I fought the Ice Beings, I was with David's parents. We found that when we had the dogs sing as we sent three arrows at once, we were able to bring down the Ice Beings."

"Samuel and Lacino will walk abreast with me, arrows ready," said Justin. "Denali, Hunter and Tonka will walk directly in front of us, to lead and show the way. Alex, Rock, Buck, Libby, Jose, Hannah and Topi will make a frontline. The rest of you make up three more lines and a rear guard. Angel, Fred and Sweetie will take over and guard the left flank when we enter the larger room of the cave. Umbra, Tundra, Nicco and Rampart will wait out here, guarding the entrance; as soon as we find the first group, I want Hunter, Denali and Tonka to leave us and join the dogs who are guarding the entrance – you are too weak to be in the midst of the fighting that will take place."

The dogs agreed. The humans and canines entered the cave in formation. Three dogs carried the broad shields on their backs as others carried extra quivers of arrows. Lacino raised a white light in front of the group to light the way and lead them.

They found Dohanos when they entered the main cave, sword raised, seven dogs ringing him, encased in clear ice. Alex, Buck and Libby, all white, stepped forward to sniff and sense the frozen group. The dogs started to sing a soft, Solarian chant, attempting communication with the frozen Wisdom Runners.

Buck turned, "Justin, we aren't getting through to Dohanos or the dogs."

Justin nodded. "Samuel, Lacino and I will join your effort. Second line, go forward and ring us, and sing up a shield of protection while we work."

Fifteen dogs made a ring and began singing as the humans and frontline dogs tried to communicate with Dohanos. The ice surrounding human and dogs was crystal clear; Dohanos' blue eyes, graying and dark hair and the eyes and fur of the dogs were magnified in their ice crystal prison – the effect was startling.

Buck stopped again. "There are no signs of life."

Libby focused, cocking her head, "But there are no signs of death, either."

Justin glanced around the cave, "Let's go forward. Hunter, Denali, Tonka – return to the cave entrance." The three canine survivors turned and left as the rest of the dogs and humans gathered and proceeded into the second tunnel cautiously. They came upon Contalia frozen, bow and arrow raised, his dogs singing around him. The group tried to get through to him intuitively.

After a twenty-minute effort, Justin held up his hand. "We are not able to communicate. Lacino, do you have any idea how to melt the ice?"

"It would be better to have them working with us. This is not real ice – it is their energy turned into a frozen field. If we unfreeze the energy, it could turn on them," said Lacino.

Topi looked up at them. "Work on one of the dogs, first. We always stand ready to lose our lives for our human comrades."

Justin clenched his jaw, hesitated and then nodded at Lacino. "Do it."

Lacino knelt next to the frozen form of a white dog, Franco. "Sing a healing chant, very softly. Don't go louder unless I ask you.

Once we unfreeze the energy – immediately surround him with pink light. Samuel, be ready to resuscitate him. Let's start."

With a circle of dogs watching the cave, the inner circle hummed softly with Angel, Fred, Sweetie and Bunny singing lyrics in an old Solarian language. White, gold and rose energy surrounded the ice imprisoning Franco. Kneeling, hands in the air in front of his heart, Lacino sang. The ice started to vibrate, gradually becoming mist that lifted away from Franco; freed, his body slumped limply to the stone floor of the cave. The nearest dogs moved forward, sending pink light that engulfed his body as Lacino cleared the dog's throat and administered CPR. Justin administered healing to the dog's heart.

Franco coughed, shook and coughed again as he attempted to rise. "You're here," he said. Looking up at his frozen companions, he moaned. "We tried." He collapsed again.

Samuel lowered his bow. "We need to carry him out of here, he's too weak to be in battle if we are attacked."

Pops and bangs sounded behind them in the main hall of the cave. The ring of dogs holding protection growled as seven-foot, willowy figures appeared; visible in the light reflecting from them, they rapidly shimmered in and out of vision – their silvery human-like features and long, spiked fangs were hard to focus on.

Justin jumped to his feet with his bow ready. "*Don't sing. Bring the shields forward – stay behind them.*" The dogs did as they were intuitively told, propping the three great shields in front of the ring of guarding dogs as Justin, Lacino and Samuel readied their arrows.

"*Second line, sing up at the Ice Being closest to us and then duck when you see the arrows pass over your head*,' ordered Justin intuitively. Three arrows flew from their bows as Lacino, Justin and Samuel sang in tones together. Hit at chest level, the Ice Being nearest to them shrieked, flowed into a puddle on the floor, and then disappeared.

"*Again!*" ordered Justin. The dogs sang, then ducked; the Ice Beings who were struck shrieked and disappeared. Volley after volley of triple arrows felled the twenty-three circling, shimmering beings.

The dogs and humans looked around cautiously. "*Do we move?*" asked Samuel.

Justin held up his hand in caution. Suddenly Franco yelped. The group spun around to see an Ice Being sinking fangs into the white dog's neck. A second one loomed, standing on the frozen figure of Presley. The dogs nearest growled furiously.

"Silence! *Back up, slowly,*" Justin demanded as he fitted an arrow into his bow. As the dogs backed off the Ice Being took his fangs out of Franco. Two shadows dropped from the ceiling above them and entered the wound; he shook violently and then went still.

"*Turn the shields and everyone get back behind them,*" commanded Justin. As the humans sang in tones that spun forth gold energy, two volleys of arrows felled both Ice Beings.

"We're surrounded!" growled black and white furred Bunny. The group looked out to see the main room of the cave and both portal tunnels filled with Ice Beings.

"If we start shooting one group, the other two will get us," thought Samuel.

"Humans back up to the cave wall; we will ring you in three rows of half circles," thought Angel, an all white dog.

"Face one shield towards each group of Ice Beings," thought Justin. *"Creflo, Taffy, Stanley and Price watch above us; send violet light into any shadows you see."*

"Triple arrow on each bow?" asked Samuel.

"*Try it. Dogs, don't sing,*" ordered Justin. The arrows struck and passed through the beings.

"*Two dogs sing, then duck behind the shield,*" thought Justin. Two dogs on each front sang, then ducked as the arrows whizzed over their heads. The Ice Beings fell and disappeared. Volley after volley felled a number of Ice Beings.

"Justin, we only have one third of our arrows left," thought Angel.

The humans stopped shooting. "*What do we do?*" asked Lacino.

"If we use full, singing energy they will freeze us," thought Justin.

"*We need to get the crystals*," thought Samuel. The three men were backed against the wall, each watching the group of Ice Beings they had been shooting at.

"Contalia was holding them. We need to shoot our way out of here, get more arrows from the sleds so that we can shoot our way back in, unfreeze Contalia and gain the crystals if he still has them," thought Justin.

"Then we can return with reinforcements from the east to free the rest," thought Samuel.

The group agreed and began moving away from the wall towards the entrance tunnel. The humans had triple arrows fitted to their bows as the dogs formed a double circle around them. *"I will shoot four volleys to each of yours, to clear our retreat. With luck, your arrows will hold the two rear groups off,"* said Justin.

Slowly, working together, the group cleared the Ice Beings from the exit towards their sleds. They halted where Dohanos and the frozen canines stood in eerie tableau. Justin whistled towards the entrance where Tundra's group was guarding. Hunter and Denali appeared behind them. *"All clear outside the port tunnel?"*

"Yes," answered Hunter.

Suddenly, Samuel and Lacino wailed; they were being lifted towards the ceiling of the cave. As the dogs and Justin watched, the two men flailed in the air with their bows, striking out at the invisible force that held them.

"What do we do?" demanded several dogs. *"They're in horrible pain; we can't communicate intuitively to them."*

The two groups of Ice Beings merged to the center of the cave, elevating towards the dangling Seer and Wisdom Runner. They were followed by shadows.

"*As many as can, shield yourselves*!" ordered Justin as he dropped his bow, pulling his sword. The dogs moved in groups behind the three shields as Justin turned his back to the two dangling men. Raising the mirror surface of the sword broadside into the air at an angle, he sang towards it. White energy bounced off the sword into the air between Samuel and Lacino. Bolts of white electricity exploded outward as the two men dropped down to the floor in the midst of the Ice Beings.

Justin and the dogs watched as the fighters went back to back, unsheathing their swords. Holding the swords aloft, they sang onto the surfaces, sending their energy out backwards, over the shoulder of their companion. Their energies hit Ice Beings behind them, who screamed, backing away. Justin turned backwards, again sending energy into the surface of his sword, outward into the Ice Beings blocking Samuel and Lacino's retreat towards the exit of the cave.

"Almost there, keep going," thought Justin.

Just then a force knocked into Samuel and Lacino, sending them sideways towards the other side of the cave. The dogs broke ranks, splitting into three groups to surround each man. The dogs holding the shields, not being able to move rapidly, stayed flanking Justin.

Leg broken, Lacino slumped against the wall behind him. Two Ice Beings loomed above his group of canines. Lacino focused into the shimmering, but lifeless eyes of each. *"Justin, Samuel, dogs, these beings have no joy, no humor. It's a missing energy frequency for them."*

Samuel, in pain from his fall, started to laugh. The trinkets and beads in his hair made soft sounds as he shook. The Ice Beings, directly surrounding him, vibrated, shrank, then backed off. "What's the matter, don't like that?" he asked in his deep, smoky voice. Then he laughed more, his gold tooth flashed as he smiled. The Ice Beings backed off further. "Well, I'll be! They don't like laughter!"

"Justin, Samuel - Lacino has passed out!" thought Buck. *"He's bleeding! There are shadows above us! We are surrounded by Ice Beings!"*

"*Sing! It may be your only chance. Wisdom Runners from the east may be able to unfreeze and save us later*!" ordered Justin. The group of canines snarled at the Ice Beings and shadows; then they began to sing. Their icy adversaries turned the dogs' energy onto them, encasing the group in clear ice.

"Now what, Justin?" asked Samuel. As if prompted by his

question, a rock flew though the air, hitting him square in the chest. Blood flowed from his nose and mouth.

"Sing!" ordered Justin to the canines surrounding Samuel. The dogs sang; soon they were immobile, encased in ice.

Ice Beings surrounded Justin's group. Suddenly three of the dogs - Fred, Sweetie and Angel - started bouncing together on their toes, waggling their tails behind the dogs holding the shields. "La, la, la! Ho, ho, ho! Yip, yip, yip! What silly clowns we are!" The Ice Beings in front of them actually seemed to stare, then vibrated and backed off. The other dogs took up the chant. Seeing the reaction, Justin started laughing; as his laughter echoed off the walls of the cave the seven-foot tall beings began to shrink.

"*Keep it up*!" thought Justin. "*Lacino and Samuel were right, they don't like humor or joy.*" The dog pack chanted silliness as the beings continued to shrink. Abruptly, three Ice Beings shrieked and turned black, becoming solid, and flew at Justin. They knocked him past Samuel before they shattered into pieces on the cave floor. The dogs dropped their shields and ran to ring Justin, growling as he lay dazed.

Hunter and Denali were holding their position at the exit tunnel. Seeing Justin down, and Samuel, Lacino and their dogs frozen, they turned and ran to the mouth of the portal to the dogs guarding the entrance. "Almost everyone is frozen," they yelled. All seven dogs ran back into the cave.

Entering the main dome area they saw Justin, his back against the wall. "Sing!" he shouted out loud to the dogs ringing him. "*Go for help! Freezing is our only chance now*! *Tell Tuvalla that these beings have no humor or joy*!" he telepathically commanded Nicco's group.

As Justin's group sang they were imprisoned in the ice. The Ice Beings then circled in the center of the cave, hovering in the air. As they started to move toward the group of the last standing dogs, Hunter, Denali and Tonka dropped low and began to sing.

"*Run*! *Get to Tuvalla*!" commanded Tonka intuitively.

As Rampart, Nicco, Tundra and Umbra watched, the energy of

their singing comrades encircled the three dogs, turning them into a monument of ice.

"Retreat!" yelled Tundra. As they ran the Ice Beings gave chase. Two hundred feet outside the tunnel the four dogs turned to face the opening. They saw and heard nothing but the wind around them.

"We have to get help," panted Nicco. "There is nothing we can do here."

"We will try to contact Tuvalla on the way," said Tundra.

The four dogs started down the trail at a furious pace. The wind howled as it hurled snow and ice pellets at their retreating forms.

Chapter Nine

The winds of grace are always blowing but you have to raise the sail.

Ramakrishna - Earth Visionary as quoted
in the Book of The Wisdom Runners

After a tearful goodbye with Millet, Tuvalla led Luna, Jennifer and David out of the manse. In the courtyard the horses and sled dog apprentices readied themselves in the dark of the early morning. The cold air held a scent that promised the snow King Gifford had warned of earlier.

Justin's horse, Sooka, stepped forward to Tuvalla. "Well met, Tuvalla Seer and Luna, our comrades."

"Well met," said Silver Birch, Traveler, Buttons, Mando and Layla, the horses standing just behind her.

"Well met, to you," answered Luna and Tuvalla.

Fully clad in light armor, helmets, shields and swords, Wisdom Runners Geoffrey and Sebastian stepped forward. "Well met!"

Luna and Tuvalla returned the salute.

"It is best we depart now if we are to meet King Gifford at the appointed hour," said Geoffrey.

Jennifer was fascinated by how formal her friends could be, but with great heart; she found it strangely comforting, especially in such a troubled time. While David mounted Silver Birch, Jennifer was helped onto Traveling Man. Luna was mounted onto a special canine seat, with "paw-holds" that she could slip her feet into to steady herself, on Buttons. A spare horse, Layla, had a packsaddle loaded with their backpacks and supplies for Zumulia's Keep. After handing David's bow and quiver up to him, Geoffrey mounted Sooka, and Sebastian mounted Mando.

Tuvalla called the twelve yearling dogs to her. "This is an important mission. You will be guarding the riders and horses. It is a test of your ability to be Wisdom Runners. You must be quiet and there can be no mischief, joking or playing. Stay near the horses but out of their way. Report any trouble to Luna, Sooka, Geoffrey and Sebastian immediately. Do you understand?"

Sitting as attentively as young dogs could, they answered, "Yes, Tuvalla Seer."

"Go forward with love and courage!" called Tuvalla to the group.

Jennifer tried to set Tuvalla's image, the remaining Seers, Wisdom Runners and the courtyard of the Keep firmly in her mind's eye and heart. She did not want to leave this safe place; but should she never return she did not want to forget a single detail about these incredible beings and this place.

"Hail!" said the departing group in unison as the first gate opened. Once inside the passage through the massive outer wall, the gate closed behind them. When the outer gate opened, they moved swiftly onto the shallow snow on the path leading from Justin's Keep towards the forest beyond.

Luna, Jennifer and David rode between Geoffrey and Sebastian. The horses were quiet, watching the trail around them. The yearling dogs walked respectfully, heeding the warning Tuvalla had given them. David rode easily on his mount and Luna sat comfortably on her canine saddle. Jennifer, having only ridden ponies at carnivals, held tightly to the pommel of her saddle.

They emerged from the forest to the rendezvous point on the Plain of Vendona in less than an hour. The twelve dogs formed a ring of safety around the horses; they faced outward as they watched for danger. After dismounting, David, Geoffrey and Sebastian helped Jennifer and Luna down and took the packs and bags from Layla. The three travelers put on the parachutes that Gifford had asked them to wear. Their baggage had been attached to cargo chutes at the Keep.

The sun was just beginning to rise to the east. A low-flying mass came towards them; soon the magnificent colors of the Gooney Birds became visible. The flock of ninety-five huge birds circled above them as five descended; the earth shook as they landed.

"Hail and well met!" said King Gifford, Prince Bartholomew, and the three Goony Birds with them.

"Hail and well met," called the group of horses, humans and dogs.

King Gifford bent his giant, colorful, tripled plumed head to Luna who ran forward to him, touching her nose to his bright orange beak. "We have little time for our formalities and fun. Please let yourself be lifted onto Prince Bartholomew."

"Our friendship is forever and needs no polite manners in times like these!" Luna bowed her white body and quickly righted herself.

Jennifer felt her heart flutter, she loved the warmth of the friendship between the two.

Luna, David and Jennifer jumped into the three waiting Goony Bird lower beaks and were raised to the magenta patch of feathers on Prince Bartholomew's back. Without the noisy fanfare of their previous flight the huge bird took off running as his father turned to the waiting horses, dogs and humans.

"Give my 'Hail' and the 'Hail' of my flock to Tuvalla and all at the Keep, and to Justin, Samuel, Contalia, Dohanos, Tundra, Nicco and all the dogs when they return. Tell Justin that his horse, Spelia, still lives and runs free in the west! Sooka, your father sends his 'Hail' and encourages you to run bravely and do all to free Solaria!"

Sooka ran forward. "Thank you, dear King Gifford, for such wonderful news!"

The dogs, humans and horses bowed as King Gifford and the three Goony Birds, holding the baggage within their beaks, ran in formation after Prince Bartholomew, who was already lifting off the ground. Soon the five giant birds joined their flock and flew towards the south.

Jennifer felt the strong north wind blowing behind them. Their speed was triple that of the original flight towards Justin's Keep. Looking over her shoulder, behind her she saw David hanging on tightly and Luna bracing herself, with a tuft of Bartholomew's down feathers in her mouth.

King Gifford's head came close, aqua, circus red and school bus yellow head plumes flowing in the strong north wind. "I am sorry about this, my friends. The wind is with us which is good, as my flock must not be caught in the snow that is following us south. But it is bad for talking. We will get you close to the clearing at Zumulia's and let you float down. There should be no trouble. It is early in the day so the shadows should not be about - they will be afraid of the sounds of our wings if they are near."

"*It is okay, Gifford. We will be fine,*" Luna's voice came into all of their minds. She continued hanging onto Bartholomew's magenta feathers with her mouth.

"I can't speak intuitively because Jennifer and David do not have the training to filter and soften the power of the energy of our Goony Bird thoughts," said King Gifford, "but any of you may speak intuitively to me. In the meantime I must shout at you!"

Jennifer laughed out loud but the sound was swept away by the wind.

"When you see Zumulia, and when you meet again with Samuel, Justin Valor, Contalia, Dohanos and all the dogs and horses of the Keep, please let them know that the Council of Wisdom Runners has concerns. There is evidence that one or more at the Court of King Saul have turned to the darkness. No one can prove anything. And all on the Council are cautious as it may not be true; this may simply mean that *we* are allowing the darkness to invade our minds and it is playing on our own fears so that we doubt each other," said King Gifford.

"We must guard against this. The worst damage of darkness is when it turns honest people against honest people," transmitted Luna.

"We see what the darkness is doing here and we know that our weaknesses bring us to entertain fear. We must affirm the greatness of light, goodness and love no matter what we see before our eyes, ears and senses," said King Gifford.

Jennifer held on tightly. Her arms were tiring with the force of the wind and from the speed of their flight. Luna and Gifford switched into a language she couldn't understand. She listened to the tones of it but could only sense their concern. From her heart she wished that some day she could be a member of the Wisdom Runners so that she could bring aid to Solaria and Earth and whatever else called her for higher purposes.

The warmth of Prince Bartholomew's body coming up from beneath his down feathers felt reassuring; the gentle rise and fall of his body was comforting as his wings propelled them forward. She shivered at the magical sight as she looked around at the sea of giant, colorful birds flying around them. The sun had risen and was now reflecting off the bright colors of their feathers, making them appear like a magical patchwork comforter aloft. Intuitively she felt the goodness of their brave, beating hearts. This was so far from life in L.A. No amount of reading about parallel realities, fantasy books or listening to scientists and historians speak about higher realities prepared her for this goodness. In her heart she knew this was real and somehow all the suffering her father, stepmother and friends lived was a bad dream. She wished she could stay awake like this forever.

Finally King Gifford spoke to everyone again. "We are almost at Zumulia's Keep. First, a few of the flock will circle to look for shadows; so far, they sense none. Then we will drop your packs, and then you. It is a short drop; with the sailing parachute you will just float down and should land gently."

Below them Jennifer could see the clearing and the cabin, barn and small buildings of Zumulia's Keep. Five of the jewel-colored birds flew two circles at the level of the treetops.

Their leader, Simon, sent intuitively to King Gifford, "Simon says that they sense safety right now. No shadows, darkness, Hissing Cats or other dangers," he relayed.

Then the birds carrying the baggage in their beaks flew close with flock mates who pulled the strings to open the parachutes on the backpacks and parcels. White sails billowed out as the birds released the bags.

"Okay, my dear friends, this is it," said King Gifford. "Please give my 'Hail' and love to Zumulia, Peaberry and the dogs of the Vermont pack. Until we meet again, fly and travel well!"

"Rest well in the south. Give my 'Hail' to your Queen and all of the greater flock. My heart is with you until we meet again!" said Luna.

"Hail and fly well, until the next time!" said David.

"*Thank you, kind King*," thought Jennifer. King Gifford winked his swirling, colored eye at her. "Prince Bartholomew and I will fly close. When I say, 'NOW', pull the cords on your parachutes."

The two great birds circled down. Jennifer gulped and tried to take a big breath. "NOW!" shouted King Gifford.

Pulling the cords on their packs, white, gossamer tissue billowed out and above them; when they caught the wind Prince Bartholomew gently sank from beneath them. They floated towards the green meadow below where they saw the grey-haired figure of Zumulia waiting. Landing softly the gossamer fluttered over them.

Pushing out from the gentle folds of fabric Jennifer looked skyward. The bright, colorful birds circled above as King Gifford and Prince Bartholomew descended till their wings almost touched the treetops, the feathers of their crowns and tails were like giant banners flowing behind them. Then they sailed upward to join the flock and circle once more. For the first time in their flight, they called, "Ga-gooo – Ga-goooo – Ga-gooooooooony! Ga-gooo

– Ga-goooo – Ga-gooooooooony!" The flock disappeared south in the grey sky.

Jennifer was surprised as tears started to flow down her cheeks. Until she came to Solaria she had always felt herself to be tough. Now it seemed like she was always crying. She quickly wiped her eyes with her sleeve.

"They are the heart and soul of our world," said Zumulia softly. "As are we." She turned to her grandson and hugged him to her. And then Jennifer and Luna. As they walked to the cottage David gave Jennifer a sudden smile, then jogged away to gather their packs.

Over tea and tomato sandwiches Zumulia told them more about the shadows. The six Talking Loaves listened with surprising restraint as she told of the birds, squirrels and smaller animals that had been threatened and how she made the Keep's barn and cabin available to all of them for safety. Luna then relayed the details of the dogs, Justin, Lacino and Samuel's departure for the Portal of Nordon; Jennifer's vision of Los Angeles where Natab had again threatened her and her concern for Grace; and what King Gifford had told her of the meeting at the Court of the Wisdom runners and the suspicions of the Council regarding the Court of King Saul.

Zumulia blew on her tea to cool it. She looked up at Luna. "So now the plans are for David to stay here with me while you and Jennifer go to Vermont to get Peaberry and the others to help here until Samuel and his dogs are back?"

"Yes," answered Luna. "But first, now that we are together, we need to let Tuvalla know that we have arrived safely.

Zumulia shooed the Talking Loaves into the pantry over their protests. Jennifer pressed her lips together so that she would not laugh. She missed Millet already. David tapped a forefinger on her wrist, to get her attention, while stifling his infectious laugh.

Zumulia locked the door behind them and put the key on a hook. "I don't like doing this but you cannot imagine the mischief they get into! If they figure out how to send intuitive communication I shudder at what sort of trouble we could have." Putting her finger to her lips she smiled.

Luna nodded. "Having traveled with dear Millet, I think that we have had a good taste of what they can cook up."

Zumulia turned to David and Jennifer. "We are going to ask the two of you to sit with us while we try to contact Tuvalla. Do not add your energy to this, as I don't want to endanger you further until you learn how to communicate safely, just breathe quietly and think positive thoughts of her."

Within minutes Luna and Zumulia had raised an orb of light above their heads. Tuvalla appeared clearly in the center. "I am so glad to see you. I have been waiting."

"We are here at Zumulia's Keep," said Luna. "The flight was successful and fast. It is cold here but not snowing. Zumulia is safe; while David stays with her, Jennifer and I will travel through the portal to Vermont and return as soon as we can with Peaberry and as many of the others that we can round up, to protect Zumulia's Keep. King Gifford has warned that there may be some at the Court of King Saul that can no longer be trusted."

"Luna, I am glad that you traveled swiftly and that Zumulia is safe for now. We have bad news. Umbra, Nicco, Tundra and Rampart have returned. Samuel, Justin, Lacino and the dogs are all trapped after a terrible battle with shadows and Ice Beings. Justin's group found Contalia, Dohanos and their dogs frozen in ice inside the tunnel of the Portal of Nordon. Ice Beings and shadows attacked Justin's group - they were all, but these four, imprisoned; they managed to escape, unharmed."

Jennifer took a deep breath. She locked eyes with David. She could feel his fear for Justin, Samuel and the dogs, too.

"Umbra says that Denali and Tonka told them, before they were imprisoned in the ice, that Contalia is still carrying twelve healing crystals from the Servers of Light; these crystals should help bring healing and balance back to Solaria. Six are to stay in the east and six to the west when we can pierce the dark veil again, as King Gifford has done. The Servers of Light will try to help our Seers activate a protection for Solaria through the crystals. The Ice Beings chased Dohanos, Contalia and the dogs from the parallel reality to steal the crystals."

"What can be done?" asked Zumulia.

"We are trying to contact the Court in the east. When we get through it will take days for them to get here and travel north to the portal. Our horses cannot get through the deep snow and we are mostly Seers here, not Wisdom Runners. With Justin's and Samuel's dogs at the portal, we have no more able and trained canine Wisdom Runners – all are apprentices, pups or retired because of age and disabilities. Umbra, Nicco, Tundra and Rampart have volunteered to lead the apprentices, but feel that it will be dangerous and useless – a waste of lives," explained Tuvalla.

Jennifer shifted uncomfortably. *"I don't understand. If the canine Wisdom Runners and Seers can open passages through the mountains, why can't they melt the snow to make a trail for the horses and others?"*

"A good question, Jennifer. Although gifts and abilities are different here, there are some things that we cannot do. Easily opening trails through deep snow is a gift we do not have." Tuvalla's emerald eyes sparkled, even in the orb of distance communication.

Luna considered for a moment, "If Peaberry and most of the pack come through the Vermont portal it will be more than a day before we can reach you and then at least two days to the Portal of Nordon."…

"The Seers and I have gathered with the dogs to consult the old books and maps. On the underground Swinburg Trail we found a portal that leads directly into the tunnel of the Portal of Nordon. Samuel's dogs remember seeing it in the passage when they were traveling through the trail," said Tuvalla.

"Okay. The old portal is risky because it may not still lead to the Portal of Nordon, but it feels like a necessary risk," said Luna. "We get to the Swinburg trail through Samuel's?"

"The dogs say yes. In the cellar. However Umbra, Nicco, Tundra and Rampart want to meet you there. They will cross the Plain of Vendona and take the underground Swinburg Trail to their home;

if they leave now, they should be at Samuel's Keep by the time you return with Peaberry and the Vermont gang," said Tuvalla.

"Tell them 'Hail' and swift journey!" said Luna.

Umbra's shaggy black head and bright blue eyes appeared in the vision. "And to you, Luna! Hail! We will see you soon! Tell Peaberry he must bring the golden violin!" He disappeared from the vision.

Tuvalla laughed, her voice, like a musical brook, lifting some of the concern from her face. "Umbra, Tundra, Rampart and Nicco insist that you must bring your musical instruments. Justin's last words before he was frozen was to tell me that the Ice Beings have no joy or humor. The dogs are positive that Peaberry and the gang have a way of raising joy with music from Earth, and it may be the key to freeing Justin and the others."

She grew serious. "Luna, the time delays between Earth and Solaria can be quite disparate. Our Seers are meeting to vision you into a time similarity so that you, Jennifer, Peaberry, and the pack return here the same day that you leave. We don't know if we will succeed - but try to spend no more than a night in Vermont. We are also praying for circumstances at Musher Jim's farm that will allow most of the pack to get loose and escape to access the portal to Solaria with you."

"I understand. Peace to all of you. Jennifer and I will depart now," said Luna.

"Peace and swift journey to all of you," said Tuvalla. Her image faded.

After spending a few minutes to breathe and ground their energies, Luna and Zumulia rose. Jennifer looked from one to the other waiting for their instructions

"Should I get the scooter for you and Jen?" asked David.

"Yes, David. That would be best. I am older, but Jennifer is so light that it shouldn't be a problem for me to pull her on it. Peaberry and others can pull her on the way back."

David left the cabin to get the scooter, dog harness and tug lines for the return trip ready.

Zumulia got Jennifer's pack and helped her into it. "Do you have my pink leash?" asked Luna. Jennifer had forgotten all about it. Walking Luna on a leash no longer felt right. She checked the pockets of her jacket.

"*Yes, here it is*," said Jennifer.

"Good, let's remember to put it on my collar before we go through the portal; your Uncle Jim and Aunt Sarah will believe that you really used it on me. They will think you tried to chase me on one of my adventures and couldn't catch me… which is true, at least in the beginning until I lured you here," said Luna. "This way, if we have been gone too long, they will blame me, not you. We need them to trust you."

Zumulia helped Luna into a harness and handed Jennifer several more for the return trip with Peaberry and the others. Outside the cabin, David was holding a large scooter fitted with fat, knobby tires. He showed Jennifer how to stand on it and use the brakes. "It's sort of like mushing on wheels."

"I have ridden a scooter and I have been on Uncle Jim's wheeled sled," thought Jennifer.

"She will be fine. I will communicate with her as we go," said Luna. David hooked the line from the ring on the front of the scooter to the tug line loop at the back of Luna's harness.

Zumulia put Jennifer's straw hat on her head and pulled the chinstrap tight. She bent and hugged her. "You will do fine." She backed off a step. "Good and speedy run, both of you!" Her green eyes flashed and Jennifer felt a jolt of courage fill her heart; this wise woman trusted her.

Luna took off down the trail away from the Keep at a trot. Jennifer found her balance on the scooter and practiced with the brakes. "*I can do this*!" she thought to Luna.

"Of course you can!" called Luna back to her.

Luna progressed to a lope as the trail widened out. They passed the apple orchards and empty bread ovens, waving 'Hail' as they sped by. Eventually they were at the top of the ravine trail leading to the stream through the portal to Vermont.

Jennifer dismounted and helped Luna off with her harness. They found a place to hide the scooter, other harnesses and equipment under some bushes. Sliding down the steep trail of the ravine, they finally arrived at the stream and tunnel under the bridge – the portal to Vermont. Luna sat down and looked at Jennifer.

"There are a few things that I have to explain before we go back through the portal. I will not be able to talk verbally or intuitively to you when we get back to Jim's farm. I completely lose the ability to speak out loud. Some dogs are special and can speak audibly on both sides, but so far none of Jim's dogs have ever been able to." Luna sighed.

Jennifer was perplexed. *"Okay. But you and I can communicate like this…"*

"No. That is the second thing. I will not be able to read your mind the way that I can now. If you are very sad, happy or distressed I will know. If you need to tell me something you must get my attention and see a picture of what you are trying to communicate. Try to make it simple and the most concrete example of what you want to tell me. For instance, if Jim is in danger, you could picture his face with a black monster trying to eat him. Or, if there is trouble at the cabin you could picture it on fire. I'll know that is not exactly what you are trying to tell me, but that something is wrong," she said.

"I will not fully understand words you think at me. But if you have strong emotion I will know you are in trouble. Try hard to watch me; if you pay attention you will know when I'm trying to lead you somewhere or communicate something." Luna bent her muzzle down to scratch it with her paw.

Jennifer took in a deep breath to center herself. She hoped she would remember all of the instructions.

"And lastly," Luna continued, "I will be much more like a dog on the other side. My attention span will only be about thirty seconds, so I will often forget what I am doing. I will be much more controlled by my instincts. I will be prone to chasing squirrels, getting into squabbles with the other dogs and not seem at all like the friend I am to you on this side."

"That hardly seems possible. Why don't you stay in Solaria with Zumulia and the Wisdom Runners?"

"I really love Jim, which is the only reason that I have not taken up permanent residence in Solaria. My mother, Licks, and my father, Flash, lived long and happy lives with your uncle. I knew the moment that I was whelped that I loved him, even though my eyes did not open for a whole week. He has the most wonderful heart and is a real dog-sensitive human. Until my spirit is called to the light I will always try to return from Solaria to your Uncle Jim," she said.

Jennifer felt her stomach start to knot. *"Luna, I don't think I can do this."*

Luna came close and Jennifer put her arms around her. She did not want to let go.

"Jennifer, it is going to be alright. Now, snap my pink leash on my collar. I don't know how much time has passed on Earth, but I suspect we will walk into late night of the same day that we left. If so, then tomorrow morning we have to somehow get the attention of Peaberry and the others and get them free. Zumulia, Tuvalla and the other Seers will be trying to aid us," said Luna.

The white dog jumped up and walked directly into the stream, looking over her shoulder for a moment before entering the darkness of the tunnel. Jennifer quickly pulled off her shoes and socks and followed.

It was dark on the other side. The air seemed thicker and harder to breathe. Jennifer followed the white of Luna's body till they emerged from the stream and she sat to put on her socks and shoes.

"Oh, good Lord!" she heard her Uncle Jim exclaim. "There you two are!" A bright light shone at them from a few feet away.

Luna ran to him and started chasing her white tail.

"Don't you dare make a joke out of this! Do you know how late it is? You are naughty, Luna! I told you not to take Jen on one of your walkabouts! You are bad!" yelled Jim.

Luna crouched down in front of him in a mock bowing position, wagging her tail.

"Jen, are you okay? Monty, Peter, Dale, Gary, Sarah and I have been searching for you for hours," Jim said.

Her uncle bent down near her. She backed up, afraid. Her father had sometimes hit her when he was angry. Her stepmother, Toni, often had.

"Jen, I am sorry. I don't mean to scare you. I'm not angry at you. I'm angry with Luna because she led you off. You don't know your way around and we were afraid that you or Luna were hurt," Jim spoke gently.

Just then a group of sled dogs crashed in from the underbrush. Flint bounced up, almost knocking Jennifer down as he tried to kiss her. Buttercup ran up and then flew off chasing a moth. Peaberry came to sit right at her feet, regarding her with his luminous blue eyes, reflecting from Jim's flashlight. A number of others came to gather around them, trying to get close to Jennifer, demanding patting and ear scratching.

Jim pulled a walkie-talkie from his belt. "Hey everyone, I found them over by the bridge near the old logging road that goes over the mountain to Albany. Jennifer and Luna are both okay so we'll walk back to Sarah's cabin."

A number of 10-4's came to acknowledge his radio call.

"Alright you two adventurers. Let's get you back home so I can feed the pack. Luna, your punishment is no people food tonight – you get sled dog kibble and meat and that's it!" said Jim. Luna looked up at him and then frisked off after Stormina.

Jennifer felt numb. It was hard to believe that Jim was so kind, even when he was angry. She felt bad that she and Luna had deceived him and were planning to do it again.

* * *

Sarah seemed relieved and happy to see Luna and Jennifer. She did not scold or yell as Jennifer was used to with her stepmother and father. She had a nice late supper of clam chowder and a fresh green salad from the garden ready. Jennifer was surprised to find how hungry she was, taking a second bowl of soup. She watched Luna go through her dog food as if vacuuming it down and then come to the table to beg with soulful eyes. When Aunt Sarah nodded consent, stifling a smile, she tossed Luna pieces of the homemade flax crackers. Afterwards they sat out on the porch with glasses of iced mint tea while watching fireflies and the stars.

"Jennifer, we worried when we got back from Burlington. Gary, Dale and Peter started to search at four o'clock because they had not seen you while they were out running the dogs or doing chores. Not finding you, they were so concerned they called Monty at home to come to help search. When Jim and I got here at seven o'clock, and Luna and you had not been spotted in any of Luna's favorite places to go exploring, we joined the search," she explained.

"There are bears, bobcat, raccoons and moose in the woods. Luna might have gotten hurt and you might not have known how to get back here," Sarah said.

Jennifer shifted in her chair. She wanted to try to show her aunt her concern but it was dark and she knew she could not see her face. *"Luna, can you hear me? How do I let Aunt Sarah know we are sorry?"* Luna did not look at her. She could not hear her.

Sarah considered for a moment. "I think from now on you should have at least three dogs with you. I know it takes away from the fun of exploring with one best pal. But with two other dogs, if one of you gets hurt then at least one will be there to protect you and one will be able to come back here to let us know there is trouble."

Jennifer could not believe her luck. *"Luna! I didn't know how I could get Uncle Jim to let me take more dogs out with us tomorrow!"* Luna still could not hear her. Now the hurdle would be getting most of the pack through the portal for the daunting journey ahead of them.

Sarah lit a citronella candle and placed it on the patio table between them. "Did you and Luna take any pictures?"

Jennifer shook her head slowly. She had forgotten all about the camera.

"Really? I put the camera and extra batteries in the backpack for you along with the sandwiches and snacks. I thought we could figure out where you had been if we looked at the pictures." Sarah said.

Luna looked directly at Jennifer. "*You heard that!*" Luna did not respond but Jennifer was sure that she was warning her not to say a word about their adventure and future plans.

"Well, okay. But try to use the camera if you remember. The pictures you took yesterday show you have a good eye. Did you have enough to eat? You and Luna ate all that I sent. If you go out tomorrow I will send more, although I thought I packed enough for an army!" Sarah laughed.

If only Aunt Sarah knew how long Luna and she had really been gone. Solaria no longer seemed real, but more like a vivid dream, rapidly fading, as Jennifer sat on the porch of the log cabin in Vermont, watching the stars. Growing tired, she reached out to stroke Luna's head. She hoped they could pull their plans off tomorrow. They had to get Peaberry and the UN-Chained Gang to Zumulia's. They had to try to save Justin, Samuel and the rest. They had to help save Solaria. She worried that she would fail to help get the dogs through the portal.

Chapter Ten

When we are really following a calling from the Divine, the supernatural will arrange our circumstances in ways that we cannot predict in our rational mind. We are called to focus on the target - the greater good of all - and have faith that what we need will be provided. If, despite seemingly impossible circumstances, our needs are provided, then we know that we are truly following a quest. Thus we pray for the faith we need to see beyond what seems to be true to our rational minds...

Book of The Wisdom Runners

The phone rang on and on, pulling Jennifer from her dreamless sleep. As she lifted the receiver on the extension she heard Aunt Sarah also pick up downstairs. It was her stepmother, Toni.

"Sarah, put Jennifer on the phone now. I have something to say to her," commanded Toni.

"Toni, she is still sleeping. You know that she is currently mute, and the murder investigation rules forbid you to speak to her," explained Sarah.

"That little brat is a liar and pulling a fast one! There is nothing wrong with her voice, the doctors have said so. I don't give a damn about what the courts say. Put her on right now!" the other woman slurred.

"Toni, listen to me. We were at our lawyer's yesterday; he was in touch with the caseworker for family services, the judges, and my brother's executor. Right now, while you are a suspect in my brother's murder and Jennifer is a witness, you are not to have direct contact with her. In any case, Saul was in the process of divorcing you and having your parental rights terminated," said Sarah.

"Listen to me, BABE!" Toni screamed. "I want you to know something! I am her legal mother! When all of this is done I am going to sue you, and I am going to make sure that you and your friggin' brother never see her again, BABE!!!!!" Toni sounded like she was spitting poison-coated nails.

"I am hanging up now. I am calling the lawyer so that he can have the courts deal with you!" Sarah banged down the receiver. Jennifer hung up feeling sick all over. She was afraid for Grace. After seeing Toni with Natab in the vision in the Amethyst Cave, and now, with this phone call, her arms and legs felt like putty.

Just then Luna came up the stairs and through the doorway. As Jennifer sank to the floor, trembling, Luna ran to her. Jennifer buried her face in the white fur of Luna's neck, wrapping her arms around her. A moment later Sarah came in.

Sarah got down on the floor with them. "Honey, did you hear us? You never should have heard that. I know that Toni is the only mother you have ever known - but she is mean and very sick. No matter what she says, it is not about you. It's about her. She is very ill and an alcoholic. When she says bad things about you or me it isn't about us, it's about her illness and alcoholism. This illness makes her want to destroy anything good." Sarah hugged Jennifer and Luna as they sat on the braided rug next to the bed.

Finally Sarah moved back from Luna and Jennifer. "I have to call the lawyer in California. Jen, please don't worry. Your uncle and I have good lawyers. Your stepmother legally adopted you, but she has a history of drug and alcohol abuse and assault convictions. The courts will not let her have you."

"Please Aunt Sarah. Please, Grace is not safe there. Please get her!" Jennifer pleaded, hoping that somehow Sarah would hear her.

Sarah rubbed Jennifer's back gently and then rose. "I am going to call the lawyer now; then I will join you and Luna for some breakfast. I set up a table in the gazebo in the wildflower garden. Why don't you wash up, dress and meet me out there?"

* * *

The gazebo sat in a meadow of wildflowers, daisies, purple irises, lavender, white and pink lupines. The slope of the field fell gently away to the forest below. In the distance the peaks of the Lowell Mountain range led the eye towards the horizon.

Jennifer sat down to a plate of poached eggs on a bed of shredded broccoli; spears of asparagus were arranged over the eggs, with Vermont cheddar sauce over the top of it all. There were similarities between Solaria and Uncle Jim's sled dog center: the fields of flowers; quiet, natural beauty, caring people and good, home-grown food. And sled dogs. Both Solaria and the Vermont farm were light years in difference to Los Angeles.

Luna lounged on the floor, occasionally snapping at a passing fly. When Jennifer started eating, Luna eagerly came over to beg for tidbits. *"It's so strange to have you acting like a normal dog. We have just spent days together on an adventure!"* Although Luna didn't seem to hear she felt she should try to communicate anyway. Jennifer had come to rely on Luna's wise direction and companionship. She was also used to Luna sitting on chairs, drinking tea from mugs and being in charge.

Jennifer needed Luna's counsel now. The threats and accusations her stepmother made frightened her. What could Toni do to her aunt and uncle? Would she hurt Grace, give her away, or worse, kill her? Her stomach knotted. Even if she had her voice, she didn't know how to get her uncle to let her go on a hike with Luna and most of the sled dogs.

Sarah came out to the gazebo with a mug of coffee in her hand. She sat down and gazed over the field of flowers. Finally she asked, "Hey, how are you doing?"

Jennifer nodded to indicate she was okay now.

"Listen, I hate to do this to you. We haven't spent much time together except for the shopping trip when you first came. But Jim and I have to go to speak to the local police chief about a restraining order against Toni calling here and then go back to Burlington to sign more papers for the lawyers to courier to Los Angeles. We have also gotten two of the doctors who evaluated you in L.A. to make written statements to the courts stating that in their opinion Grace needs to be here with you to support your recovery of your voice."

Jennifer bit her lip and threw a piece of egg to Luna who snapped it out of the air.

"Honey, this is not your fault. You just remember that, okay?" Sarah leaned forward, her eyes searching Jennifer's eyes and face.

"I am going back to the cabin to get changed. I packed your backpack with lots of sandwiches, fruit, cookies, and extra dog treats for you to go out with today." Sarah stood up, piling the extra dishes and containers onto a tray. "I'll take these things back to the kitchen now and you can drop off your plate and glasses when you finish. If you and Luna go over to the barn, Gary will find you some nice dogs that you can take exploring."

* * *

Uncle Jim and Aunt Sarah, with four of the Lion Brother puppies - Leonard, Aslan, Mufasa and Simba - drove down the tree and flower-lined driveway in their blue pickup truck. Luna stood next to Jennifer as she waved goodbye to them. Taking a deep breath, Jennifer clucked to Luna who happily followed her to the barn.

"Hey you two! You gave us a scare yesterday. We couldn't find you anywhere!" Gary was smiling, but Jennifer could tell it covered concern.

"Jim said you would take Peaberry, Stormina and Llewellyn with you today," said Gary. "We don't want you to get into any more trouble without backup."

Luna looked up at her. All of this was great, but how was Jennifer going to get Gary to give her the other dogs as well?

The door burst open. A handsome, wild-eyed man charged in. "Gary, the dogs have dug a hole under the far pasture fence; they have escaped! We have to go after them!" he said with a heavy accent. "Hey, you must be Jennifer. Pleased to meet you! I'm Peter, from Switzerland. I help Jim with the farm and the dogs. You gave my ulcer a workout yesterday trying to find you!" He laughed as he motioned his arm at Gary to hurry up. Jennifer liked his energy.

"Okay, Jennifer," said Gary. "I have to go. Have fun and try to be back here by five o'clock this afternoon so we don't worry." Grabbing dog leashes Gary ran out the door with Peter.

Luna woofed, spun around in several circles, and then trotted to the door on the other side of the barn.

"Luna, you understood them!" Luna looked back at her and then at the handle on the door. Peaberry, Stormina and Llewellyn followed as Jennifer pulled on her straw hat and opened the door. The four dogs galloped out past Sarah's cabin into a stand of pines. Jennifer ran as fast as she could to catch up. In the cover of the trees, she found them standing with Lily, Rainbow and Rose. At a trot Luna led the group out of the pines towards the pond.

Jennifer had trouble catching her breath. *"Luna, I can't keep up!"* Luna and the group stopped for a moment, looking back at her. Had she understood her?

In a thunder of paws, Flint, Amos and Lioness came whizzing by on the trail; then just as suddenly, they turned and came back to join the group. Along the way others joined in until they had a pack. Together they moved with a sense of purpose, seeming to know where they were going. When they reached the bridge on the old road they dove into the underbrush. Sliding down the steep path, Jennifer found the dogs were in the water walking upstream towards the darkness of the tunnel under the bridge. She slipped off her sneakers and socks and waded in after them. Emerging into the sunlight on the other side of the tunnel, Jennifer found a sled dog party. Voices shouted and sang with exuberance and abandon as they danced and twirled.

Jennifer climbed out of the water onto the sandy spit of beach. Peaberry jumped over, looking at her in a manner that was both goofy and intent. "I say there, darlin,' it sure is great of you to bring us all on an adventure to help our friends! Would you be willing to lend me your sunglasses until we get to Zumulia's? These blue eyes of mine can be seen at a distance in Solaria; the pair of glasses I left here are not under the rock where I buried them."

Jennifer placed her sunglasses on Peaberry's muzzle with the elastic, sport strap behind his floppy, soft brown ears. With his freckles, white and brown markings on his face, greyhound-like head, with elongated muzzle, he looked quite silly.

"Spectacular!" he shouted and bounded away.

"Hi!" a semi-high voice said from beside her. Llewellyn was sitting at attention, chest held out, small ears that stood up, and then flopped over at their tips, looking up at her. "Umm, I'm Llewellyn. I will be one year old on July 25th. My brothers and I are called the Lion Brothers because we were born under the sign of Leo. My name is Welsh Gaelic for lion-like."

Jennifer thought he was possibly the cutest and handsomest young dog that she had ever met. He had pretty white markings on his brown and black face, tan dots on the fur above his eyes, and white socks on all four legs. The fur on his body was brown and black, longer, and softer than most of the other pack members. She reached out to touch his head.

Luna appeared on the other side of Jennifer. "This is my nephew. He is one of Stormina's litter of boys. Peaberry is his grandfather. His brothers are remarkable, too, but I could only risk having one pup on this mission."

"I am very glad you chose me, Aunt Luna." He tilted his head toward Jennifer. "This is the second time I have been here. The first time was only for a moment when my brothers and I got loose and found this place. Aunt Luna and Peaberry immediately caught us and herded us back to Vermont." He cocked his head to the side.

"You are still wet behind the ears. There are many dangers that a dog faces, young man, and you have much learning ahead of you – on both Earth and in Solaria!" Luna was forceful.

Llewellyn bowed deeply, his hindquarters in the air, front legs stretched forward, head between them. Then he stood on all fours. "Aunt Luna, I know you are the queen alpha dog – the leader of our pack with Peaberry - and very, very wise. I am honored that you singled me out to start my training here."

"Dearest, you are going to be an incredible dog one day, as are the rest of your littermates. I didn't mean to be sharp. Why don't you play with Flint while I speak with Jennifer and then meet with Peaberry?" asked Luna.

"Yes, Aunt Luna!" Llewellyn stood and trotted off.

"Well, we are back! What a stroke of good fortune! I am sure that Zumulia, Tuvalla and the Seers of Justin's Keep were instrumental in getting us here. They visioned us an opening in the time differences and circumstances that allowed most of our pack to get loose to come to Solaria. It is so good to be able to speak again. I hope I didn't do anything too doggy when we were back on the farm?" Luna asked.

Jennifer got down and hugged her. *"Luna, I kept trying to speak to you!"* she thought, showering Luna's face with kisses.

Luna laughed and then pulled back. "Well, good! I love you, too! But it seems your stepmother has caused your aunt and uncle quite a stir on Earth. Darkness is causing trouble in both of these parallel realities."

"But all the dogs seem happy," thought Jennifer.

"We are always happy to serve. And no matter what we face we must preserve our humor and our joy," said Luna.

Finished with dancing and jumping about, the dogs came to sit attentively in front of Jennifer and Luna. They shouted their names happily to Jennifer: Peaberry, Llewellyn, Flint, Lioness, Buttercup, Rose, Rainbow, Buster, Lily, Lucky, Fuchsia, Bear, Stormina, Maple, Gretel and Amos. Luna filled the pack in on the trouble with the shadows; the dire situation Justin, Samuel, Lacino, Contalia, Dohanos and their dogs were in; and all that had transpired on their last journey through Solaria.

When Luna finished, black and white, blue-eyed Rainbow offered, "Rose, Lily and I can stand guard for Zumulia and the Talking Loaves while you travel to save Justin Valor and the others.

"And I will, too, because I am bigger than the gals and strong," said Buster. A son of Peaberry's, he was several inches taller than the largest of the others; strong, he had blue eyes, pliable ears that hung down from his broad head, and the softest brown fur, that had people hugging and patting him for hours. Like his father, he was an alpha male – a born pack leader.

"Good. You are incredible singers and should be able to keep the shadows and evil at bay," said Luna. "And someone strong should be with you and Zumulia until we get the situation sorted out at the Portal of Nordon, so that Samuel and some of his dogs can be with her full time.

"Let's be off, then," said Peaberry. "It is sunny but I smell snow in the air."

The pack sniffed the air and confirmed that snow was on the way.

"We left a scooter, equipment and some harnesses in the bushes just above the ravine here," said Luna.

"What are we waiting for?" asked Buster. "Jennifer, hold onto my collar and I will pull you up this steep path."

"Thank you!" Jennifer reached out to take his collar with her left hand as she balanced herself on his shoulders with her right hand. The top of his back came up to her chest; he easily assisted her up the steep incline.

The group was soon up the trail. Jennifer helped Peaberry,

Buster and Maple, another of Peaberry's sons, into their harnesses. She attached lines from the scooter to the tug-line loops of their harnesses.

"I say there," said Maple with a British accent that went remarkably well with his stately demeanor. He was almost as large as Buster, with shorter, reddish-blond fur, and large, stand-up ears. "You really have learned some sled dog basics! Smashing, really!" Jennifer felt her face flush as the pack cheered for her, barking and woofing.

"Okay, enough!" barked Peaberry. Despite the sunglasses, all signs of goofiness had vanished as he assumed his leader role. "Jennifer, hold on tightly to the handlebars. I will warn you if there are any bumps, but we will be going fast, so tie your hat on tight!"

In a moment they were off and running. The pack fanned out around Peaberry, Buster and Maple as they pulled Jennifer on the scooter. Clinging tightly to the handgrips of the handlebars, working the brakes on the downhill, Jennifer was surprised how natural riding behind the powerful dogs felt. Flint, imitating Uncle Jim, kept singing, "Ta-da-ta-da! Charge!" as if they were the cavalry. Gretel, who had a pointed muzzle, ran beside her, periodically looking up in a big grin that bared her front teeth, as she merrily pronounced, "Eeeeeeeeeeee!"

Although it did not seem possible, they were at Zumulia's in less than an hour. The snow was just starting to fall. The pack emptied bowls of water and then helped themselves to the vegetable stew and corn muffins that David dished out into bowls for them. Raspberry cheesecake brought woofs of glee.

"Our musher, Jim, feeds us well, but not like this!" said Lucky as he had a third helping of cheesecake.

"Smashing! Exquisite! Really, Zumulia, I have missed your cooking," praised Maple. "Jim really needs to hire us a chef."

Zumulia sat down next to Maple and hugged him. "I have had incredible help from the six Talking Loaves. They are real rascals but they are already teaching me things about cooking and baking!"

The Loaves, seemingly sedate from a day of cooking and baking to be ready for the Vermont gang, hung from perches in the rafters, waving and saluting.

The gang sang a howl cheer for the cooking. Zumulia laughed and shook her head. "Please don't anyone let them out. In some ways I would be more worried for Solaria's safety with them running wild than the trouble the shadows are causing!"

Jennifer put her arm around Luna and fed her bits of cookie with her other hand. *"Luna, I am really happy to be back here with you. I really like Peaberry and the rest of the gang. And I feel like this is my real home. I can't explain it…"*

Luna put her nose to Jennifer's cheek, "I think you have."

Around the big dining table Bear, Buster, Flint, Amos and Buttercup laughed as they told private jokes, happy to be able to speak again. Lioness, Lily, Rose and Rainbow smiled ear to ear as they nodded their heads in agreement with the compliments to the cuisine and traded pleasantries as they caught up with David and Zumulia.

Stormina, Maple's sister, with her extraordinarily big ears, ate her dinner demurely. "I really appreciate being able to sit at a table again; and yes, I agree with Maple, this is wonderful." She had a hint of a British accent, like her brother's.

Sipping lemon-mint tea, Peaberry shifted to business. "David, are you up to handling a sled? The snow is getting deep."

David nodded. "The Vermont gang, Samuel, his dogs, and you have taught me well. I have my bow, several quivers of arrows, and slingshot ready."

"Good. Get the sled gang-line out to hitch us to. I will lead with Lucky. Everyone else choose your positions. Jennifer, my grandson, Llewellyn and Luna will ride in the sled. Please pack plenty of glow weed for the underground Swinburg Trail," said Peaberry.

"What about your gold violin? And the silver flutes for Stormina, Buttercup and Lioness?" asked Zumulia.

"Absolutely, but before we go we will have Rainbow, Rose and Lily play a bit on that piano of yours – with Buster on the bass drum. I'll play my fiddle and all of us can dance up some healing, protective energy with music for our adventure!"

The dogs pushed the furniture out of the way while David went to ready the sled. Jennifer helped Stormina, Bear, Fuchsia, Llewellyn and the others into their harnesses. Zumulia consulted with Luna and then went to her window seat where she kept Peaberry's violin. Using her fingers, she helped him tune the strings to his satisfaction as he flexed and stretched the toes of his forepaws.

When David returned he joined Peaberry and his grandmother. "Peaberry, Jennifer thought we were teasing her when we told her that you are a great violin player."

Peaberry looked up to where she was standing nearby.

"That so?" he chuckled in his southern drawl.

A blush colored Jennifer's cheeks. *"I just couldn't imagine how it is possible. But they explained to me that you and many dogs can make the instruments work through the power of your intention."*

"Well, that's partially so. Something happens to the toes of some dogs' paws here in Solaria, blended with focused intention and love of music, the instruments do seem to work almost on their own." He batted the eyelashes of his big blue eyes. "But why not just watch and see for yourself!"

Jennifer could not believe her eyes as Peaberry rose onto his back legs, standing almost like a man. Zumulia helped to strap the violin to his left paw and the bow to his right. He then raised the violin to his chin and started tuning on it as he walked on his back legs, gracefully, to the other side of the room.

Lily, Rose and Rainbow jumped onto the piano seat and started to warm up; hitting the keys with their toes, they worked as a team to produce the chords they wanted. With Peaberry playing fiddle, mimicking bag pipes, and Buster beating the bass drum with his tail, they played a Celtic Earth tune that got the others dancing as Jennifer had seen the dogs do at Justin Valor's Keep. Zumulia and David held swords in the air, tips together, as the dogs danced in pairs. They held their heads high, moving them in unison left and then right; bouncing on their toes, they went under the swords, broke from pairs, and formed a circle of dancing dogs. Zumulia left the center of the circle as David held his sword over his head, dancing in the elegant style Jennifer had seen Justin Valor, Samuel and Lacino dance before they had left the Keep on their rescue mission. Sparks of energy flew from the dogs fur and the room brightened as the energy built.

When the music stopped Peaberry stepped back into the center with his golden fiddle. "Okay, now let's get some real hootin' on for the trail!" He launched into a version of Charlie Daniels classic, "The Devil Went Down To Georgia." He added hilarious personal twists in the lyrics: Georgia became Vermont and Johnny was Peaberry – but the gist was the same. In a fiddle contest with the devil and a band of demons, Peaberry and the Vermont sled dogs had defeated the devil; the singing dogs claimed that Peaberry had won the violin of gold.

Jennifer laughed as she took in the scene. Peaberry really was playing the fiddle. The dogs not only were playing instruments, singing and dancing, they were amazing, even by human standards on earth. Soon she joined in.

Stomping his feet and clapping his hands, David danced over to where Jennifer was trying to do a jig with blue-eyed Gretel. "Told you!" he laughed over the loud din.

"*They are amazing!*" she thought. When he laughed more and whirled her around she knew that they were still able to connect.

The dogs whirled in jigs this way and that, sang fast harmonies as an ensemble and in small groups as Peaberry fiddled, sang and danced. Stormina, Buttercup and Lioness played flutes with the passion of Ian Andersen from Jethro Tull; although they did not appear to have good forepaw-toe dexterity, the silver keys indeed seemed to move by their focused intention. Rose, Rainbow and Lily banged honky-tonk on Zumulia's piano. Buster, Lucky and Flint played drums and cymbals with their paws and tails. The cabin started to shake as the music continued to build; it felt like it would rock off its foundations from the speed and intensity of the energy Peaberry's canine gang raised.

The six Talking Loaves continued to be relatively well behaved. They took pans, spoons and forks for makeshift drums and danced along to the music on the counter. Jennifer spent time dancing and clapping with them. *"I hope you get to be with your brother Millet soon!"* she relayed.

"Yes!" They called back to her over the roar.

When the music stopped, the dogs continued to dance as they moved out the door to the sled. It was snowing hard but their energy lit the air around them. Once the dogs were hitched to the sled, Jennifer, Llewellyn and Luna jumped in with the supplies. David yelled, "Hike!" as the team launched like a rocket; Zumulia, with the Talking Loaves gathered in her arms, Lily, Rose, Rainbow and Buster cheered them off.

The snow was not too deep; Peaberry and the team kept up a fast pace. Luna relayed intuitive commands from the leaders to David.

In the dark, with the glow from the dogs, the snow coming down in such large flakes, traveling through the snowy landscape by dog sled with the Vermont UN-Chained Gang was magical. *"Luna, it's as if I can still hear the dogs' wild music continue to play."*

"You hear the music because it's in their hearts," came Luna's voice in Jennifer's mind.

"I heard you! I heard you both!" yelled David. "I wish I could actually intuitively hear them too! But I still hear that music in my mind – Peaberry is a great fiddle player and those gals on piano and flute rock!"

"Good Earth word!" yelled Luna.

They traveled on for an hour until the team pulled the sled up to the front of Samuel's cabin. Tundra, Rampart, Umbra and Nicco were waiting for them on the porch. David set the snow hook on the sled as Jennifer jumped out to help unhitch the team. Amidst "Hails!" and "Well met!" the dogs danced around their friends. Finally Umbra showed David where to store the sled as the dogs entered the cabin.

Nicco and Tundra helped Jennifer get the wood cook stove lit so that everyone could have hot tea and the soup and snacks Zumulia had sent. After a good meal of carrot and zucchini muffins, cheese and soup they were ready to proceed. Jennifer and David tied glow weed to sticks so that the dogs could carry them in their mouths. The windup flashlight was mounted to Jennifer's rain hat for additional light in the underground tunnel. David and Jennifer helped Amos, Fuchsia and Flint into doggy backpacks and then donned their own. David had his knife, slingshot and bow; Bear and Fuchsia carried extra quivers of arrows attached to their packs along with drums and cymbals for Flint and Lucky. Peaberry's violin, in its case, was tied onto Flint's backpack along with the flutes for Lioness, Buttercup and Stormina. During the preparations Gretel kept coming to Jennifer, grinning widely at her, while baring her front teeth, "Eeeeeeee."

"Gretel, cut it out!" Luna said finally.

"I'm just smiling!" said Gretel.

"*I don't mind*," thought Jennifer.

"*See, I told you so, Luna*!" grinned Gretel again. With her long, greyhound, freckled muzzle like her father Peaberry, bulging blue eyes, and ears that went up halfway before flopping over, she was a goofy but loveable sight.

Gretel's mother, Lioness, came over. "Gretel, really! Jennifer may like you but people don't appreciate dogs grinning repeatedly into their faces… Jennifer, she really likes you and this is just her way of showing it."

Jennifer reached her hand out and patted the silky, short fur on Gretel's head. "*I understand, I don't really like talking much, either.*" Gretel grinned toothily again.

All black, shaggy Nicco stopped the banter. "Are we ready?" he boomed in his base voice.

"Ready!" said the dogs and David.

"Good. Follow Tundra and me," said Nicco. The dogs brought the group to a doorway that opened to a staircase leading to the basement. They wound through a series of hidden doors in the stones of the foundation and finally came to what looked like a solid wall.

"We must sing the hidden passage open," said Tundra. The dogs sat and focused on the wall. After a minute of silence they sang in a very high pitch. Jennifer sensed that they were using many notes that were not audible to humans. The wall started to vibrate - a portion in the center began to lighten in color until the stone became like soft clay. Finally it opened in the center, drawing back on each side. After they passed through the wall, it sealed itself and became solid.

Inside was a passage that stretched into darkness beyond Jennifer's flashlight and glow weed. The walls were rough hewn in the solid granite. "This is the Swinburg trail." Tundra explained. "No one knows who made it: The length that we have traveled is cut into solid bedrock. It seems as if the stone was melted, it is so smoothly hewn. It is part of the ancient system of tunnels and portals that run under much of Solaria."

Peaberry nodded. "The Court of the Wisdom Runners hopes the Servers of Light know how we can access the west through the old trails and passages. It is one of the reasons Contalia and Dohanos traveled through the Portal of Nordon to the conference."

Umbra and Rampart, carrying torches of glow weed, trotted on ahead to guide the way. David fitted an arrow into his bow as the group moved forward at a steady pace along the smooth stone floor of the passage.

"On our way through the first time, we found no traces of anyone having been here for the more than forty years that it has been closed," said Nicco.

"Did you see any open side passages?" asked Peaberry.

"Yes," said Tundra. "But we did not have time to explore."

"With the shadows about, and animals missing, we knew we would have to explore later. Also the Seers at Justin's Keep have old maps that might tell us where the trails and portals lead," said Nicco.

"I suspect we will find there are many hidden doors in these walls once we carefully examine them," said Luna.

"Agreed," said Tundra. "It is our guess there are several ways through to the west."

Jennifer nudged David. She wanted to tell him that it was the question that Millet, David and she had discussed at Justin's Keep but she did not want to interrupt the leaders' planning.

As the group walked they discussed what happened at the Portal of Nordon and possible ways of freeing the humans and canines trapped there. Nicco explained that the Ice Beings were in league with the shadows; they did not hold any energy for joy and humor, which had almost defeated them. Everyone listened and made suggestions. Jennifer tried to absorb as much as she could.

Finally reaching the passage to the portal of Nordon, Umbra and Rampart stopped so that the group could gather. "Onward?" asked Rampart. He had a white face and an all-black body.

"Let's hold for a minute," said all-black Nicco. "This portal may lead us directly into the midst of the Ice Beings or shadows gathered in the central cave. We have to have a plan for our arrival."

Tundra sat, her eyes, brown and blue, shining in the light of the glow weed. "David, Jennifer and Llewellyn - you are not Wisdom Runners or Seers. I want several dogs to ring you for your protection at all times."

"No singing directly if there are Ice Beings on all sides, as it will imprison us in ice like it did with Justin and the others," Nicco's rich, deep voice echoed through the passage.

Luna sat down next to Jennifer. "David, you can shoot triple arrows over the top of the heads of the dogs as we work. As Justin did, tip your arrows with glow weed."

"My understanding is that the dogs only used their energy and Solarian songs against the Ice Beings," said Peaberry.

"Yes," said Umbra. "The feeling that came from the Ice Beings was dense. The dogs were serious in their focus on fighting them – they were angry and desperate, which must be the key that the

Ice Beings used to freeze them. Justin's last direct order was to tell Tuvalla that the beings had no joy or humor – so this must be important!"

"Our canine Wisdom Runners are highly skilled and they got trapped. Contalia, Dohanos, Samuel and Lacino are renown, yet they were trapped. Justin Valor is a supreme adept - but he was trapped. Obviously, the Ice Beings, who come from a parallel reality, are beyond our usual skills," Peaberry frowned.

"That is why we feel the humor of Earth music may be the key to fighting the Ice Beings and freeing our comrades," said Rampart. "But, we don't know what the invisible force is that carried Tonka, Denali and Hunter out of the cave, chaining them there, in the first attack. When Justin and Samuel started to understand laughter would shrink the Ice Beings, the force hit both of them."

"What could it be?" asked Luna.

Jennifer's stomach clenched tight making it difficult to breathe. She reached out to stroke Luna's neck lightly with her fingertips.

Tundra shook her head. "We have talked about it with everyone at Justin's Keep. Tuvalla and the Seers had no idea. Tuvalla suggests that we take the dust on the floor of the cave and throw it into the air when we think it is around – it may let us know where it is and what it is."

Luna turned to Jennifer and David. "So, watch carefully. If at any time you see one of us being knocked, or things flying through the air, throw dust. If we can see a shape we may know where and how to counter it."

David and Jennifer agreed.

"But there are two things to remember. Justin knew they were losing and the only chance of not being killed was to have the dogs sing to imprison themselves in ice - he knew other Wisdom Runners would have a chance to save them later. So if we are losing, we must sing ourselves into the ice so that we have a chance to be freed later. Second, when Justin and Samuel laughed the Ice Beings shrank – so we MUST keep our humor," said Tundra.

"That's why we wanted you to bring the gold violin, your flutes, and drums. We feel that the music that you and Samuel have brought from the Earth has humor; the beat of the music will keep us going," said Umbra.

"We believe your golden violin will get through the ice to Samuel and our pack. They will directly experience our music, and that might raise the energy of joy in their minds in such a way that they are safely freed," said Nicco.

"It makes sense," said Luna.

Peaberry's eyes lit up, "The sound of my gold violin will get through to Samuel, through his gold tooth! He will know what we are doing, and he will imagine himself dancing, which should free him..."

"Exactly!" said Tundra, Umbra, Nicco and Rampart in unison.

"He was born on earth and knows the music. Freed, he should be able to help communicate directly with the other humans to help them free themselves," Nicco said.

"Okay. Then we start out with the Charlie Daniels tune about kicking the devil's butt," said Peaberry.

Nicco nodded his black head. "Yes. But if it works – then we switch to my special song. I want a chance to use MC Hammer on those Ice Beings!"

"Brilliant!" howl-cheered Peaberry and the Vermont pack in unison.

Surprised by their sudden exuberance, Jennifer had to hold back a giggle.

"Hey," said Rampart. "That's a cool word. Where did you get it?"

"It's Musher Jim's current favorite word," Llewellyn piped up in his high, yearling voice. "He got it from some of our British guests who were learning how to mush."

"We will have to adopt it," said Umbra. Tundra, Rampart and Nicco nodded their large heads in agreement.

"Brilliant!" Peaberry, Flint, Lioness, Amos, Fuchsia, Lucky, Bear, Llewellyn, Gretel, Stormina, Maple and Buttercup cheered.

Luna looked grave. "We have to realize this may not work; some or all of our comrades may be beyond saving. If Peaberry, Nicco, Tundra or I call a retreat then everyone is to run to the outside of the portal. We will take the sleds and return to Justin's Keep for reinforcements."

"Agreed!" said all the dogs.

"*But what can I do*?" asked Jennifer.

"Stay in the middle of the dogs we place you with. Hold Llewellyn's collar and hand arrows to David. Most important, no matter what you see, visualize the battle over, and all of us safe and back at Justin's Keep," said Luna. All the dogs nodded.

"Watch carefully and throw dust at any place where something invisible might be. If things look impossible, you and David take Llewellyn and run! Gretel, you go with them. Find your way to Justin's Keep."

"Okay, I understand," thought Jennifer. *"I don't like it, but I understand."*

"I don't like it either, but I will do my best if it comes to getting us safely back to the Keep," David said.

Staying close, the group moved down the passage leading to the left off the underground trail. Soon it opened into a small, round room with a domed ceiling. The rock was light pink, polished to a mirror-like finish. Jennifer saw the walls reflecting the group of Samuel's four large, shaggy dogs; Alaskan huskies in a variety of sizes and shapes; a white Siberian; a petite, fragile-looking girl who carried a backpack too large for her, wearing a rain hat over a mass of dark, curly hair; and a tall boy with long blond hair down his back to his hips, with a knife, slingshot and quiver of arrows, holding a drawn bow ready to shoot.

"Whoo-hoo! Look at us," said Amos.

"Ta-da-da-da! Charge!" laughed Flint as he sat down.

Gretel walked closer to the wall and bared her teeth to grin at her image, "Eeeeeeeeee," she said.

"I say, what a grand group we are!" commented Maple in his best, British gentleman's voice.

"The walls are rose quartz," said Nicco. "I wonder if it was a vein in the rock or if the makers of the tunnel lined it?"

"It feels like a vein," said Luna.

"Rose quartz vibrates in the energy of love. So if the makers actually used the rose quartz as a key to the portal, it calls for heart energy to activate it. Let's try it. We don't know where we might land in the Portal of Nordon or which way we will be facing. So let's ring Jennifer, Llewellyn and David now, Gretel be close on guard, before we begin to sing and visualize," said Tundra.

The dogs arranged themselves around the humans and yearling dog. Luna was at Jennifer's right side, Llewellyn between David and Jennifer. Jennifer thought about holding onto Luna's collar or taking David's hand, but she wanted to appear brave so she squeezed her toes tight and hoped for the best. Gretel crowded close, as did Amos and Fuchsia, their packs open so that the glow weed was near at hand and the extra quivers of arrows ready for David. Peaberry stood on his hind legs, gold violin at his chin; Stormina, Buttercup and Lioness had their flutes positioned. The group breathed together for a minute.

"Everyone set to go?" asked Luna.

"Mush!" they called in unison.

"Jennifer, David, Llewellyn - visualize us all in the Portal of Nordon right now!" called Nicco.

"Sing!" cried Tundra.

The group of dogs started singing. The air vibrated as rose-colored energy emitted from their chests and out into the room until it surrounded them. The pitch of the singing caused the chamber itself to vibrate. The pink, glimmering walls grew transparent as they produced a sound in harmony with the tones of the dogs – then they were in the main cave of the Portal of Nordon.

* * *

Chapter Eleven

One of the insidious qualities of Evil is that it drains the enjoyment out of life. It draws power from, revels in, and laughs at the fear, pain, and ruin that it causes; yet this is one of its main weaknesses. Real joy, love and humor from the heart will defeat darkness if those wielding the qualities are centered in the light of goodness.

Book of The Wisdom Runners

The cave was still lit from the energy that Lacino had raised. Peaberry, Luna, David, Jennifer, Nicco, Tundra and their canine group looked cautiously around at the weird theatre holding their frozen comrades. Across the cave, to the right, stood Dohanos like a statue in tableau with his dogs. Blocking the exit tunnel stood the ice enclosing Tonka, Denali and Hunter. Directly across from them, collapsed in a sitting position, blood running from his nose and smiling mouth, was Samuel, surrounded by singing, black and white dogs. To the left lay Lacino, staring out, dogs protecting him. Justin's group was close, to the left. The ice enclosing the dogs and humans was so clear that their friends were magnified: fur, eyes, features and expressions bigger than in life. In the main cave there was no evidence of shadows or Ice Beings.

"This is eerie," whispered Lucky. His brothers, Amos and Flint, nodded.

Jennifer shuddered.

"Try not to do that," said Luna. "We can't let the negative feelings get to us. It won't do anything to help our friends and it may attract the Ice Beings and shadows."

"Sorry!" said Lucky.

"Where is Contalia?" asked Luna.

"Down the tunnel to the left; near the actual portal into the parallel reality," answered Tundra.

Nicco cocked his large black head. "I suggest we get our hootenanny on. We need to be controlled wild – NEVER let our guard down – play our music and dance with courage!"

The dogs and humans took three deep breaths in unison. "One, two, three, four – hike!" cried Nicco.

Jennifer heard Peaberry's golden fiddle start the first bars of Charlie Daniels' song about the devil. The Vermont UN-Chained Gang formed a ring around Jennifer, David and Llewellyn, singing chorus. Lucky and Flint played drums and cymbals. Stormina, Buttercup and Lioness stood with their flutes. Nicco, Tundra, Rampart and Umbra rose up on their hind legs, warming up a doggie version of clog dancing in front of the group.

"Hey, Samuel, Justin, Dohanos, Contalia, Lacino and canine Wisdom Runners - this is for you!" bellowed Rampart.

The music from the dogs began echoing around the cave as they tested the acoustics. David fitted three arrows into his bow as Jennifer worked on tipping arrows with glow weed. Peaberry lowered his gold violin to his side, looking around the cave, filled with ice and spooky tableaus containing their friends. Nodding, he addressed the air overhead and the tunnels, "Hey Shadows! Hey Ice Beings! Hey you invisible son of a gun! My name is Peaberry, here with the Vermont Wisdom Runners! We're the UN-Chained Gang and we're unleashed on you!"

Peaberry placed the gold violin at his chin and began to wail bluegrass music on it. Jennifer was afraid this was not going to work but she joined with David as he stomped his feet in sync with Lucky and Flint on drums, and Samuel's four large shaggy dogs danced into the center of the room, sparks flying from their fur and stomping feet. The Vermont gang sang and played flute as Peaberry boomed his version of Charlie Daniels' "The Devil Went Down To Georgia":

> "Darkness you been up to your tricks again,
> You're pretty good, ole evil son…
> but you sit right down…
> while we show you how this is done!"

The cave started to glow as the music raised and Nicco, Tundra, Umbra and Rampart danced. When no shadows or Ice Beings appeared, Peaberry stepped forward to the center; the gold violin started to spark as he played. Stormina, Lioness and Buttercup on flutes stood just behind him. The group moved toward the reclining figures of Samuel and the dogs surrounding him, singing their rendition of Charlie Daniels' chorus:

> "Fire music in the cave – run, ice, run!
> Peaberry's brought the joy of the Vermont sun!
> Ice Beings meltin' like baking dough
> Shadows run from us – Go dogs, GO!"

As they danced, played and sang the gold violin began to radiate light, then shot a spark out that touched the clear ice enclosing Samuel and his canine companions. More playing and dancing brought more sparks until one pierced through to Samuel's gold tooth. The tooth began to glow with the same radiance as the violin.

The gang hooted and howled. Peaberry dipped down towards Samuel, "Come on, Samuel, son, the light of the Vermont sun is here. Get your brain movin,' you Earth-born, dancing fool!"

The dancing dogs sang:

"Fire music in the cave – melt, ice, melt!
Peaberry's brought the freedom – the light has dealt!"

The clear encasement around the tableau started to vibrate, then dissolve into mist. As the freed dogs and Samuel collapsed onto the cave floor, Luna and Fuchsia ran to them while the others continued to play, sing and dance; the two dogs sang white and pink healing light into the Wisdom Runners who shook themselves and started to rise. Samuel wiped the blood from his mouth and nose; seeing the wild dance party, his laughter echoed through the cave. After momentary coughing and shaking, the dogs with him rose to their feet, "Peaberry!" they yelled. "The Vermont UN-Chained Gang! You liberated us!"

Momentarily lowering his violin, Peaberry called out, "Hey Samuel, son! Glad you're back – get your feet movin'! And you furry fools – you too! Don't be wastin' this great music! Let's free Justin and his gang next!"

Jennifer watched as laughing and stretching, the unfrozen dogs started dancing on all fours with Nicco, Tundra, Rampart and Umbra, who continued to dance on their hind feet. All the doubt she felt melted with the music. *"It's working!"* she thought as she danced harder to keep up with them.

Samuel turned to David, still with bow and three arrows ready, ringed by members of the Vermont gang, and mouthed, "Harmonica?"

David laughed and nodded. He tossed him the harmonica from his pocket. Catching it in mid-air, Samuel stepped next to Peaberry. With the dancers, singers, flutes, drums and dogs pounding and stomping the beat, Samuel began to wail on the harmonica as they ringed the frozen tableau of Justin and his dogs.

The energy rose higher. "I can hear the dogs thinking in the ice! They know we are here!" shouted Umbra.

Samuel dropped the harmonica down and began to sing, "Justin's heart is full of the light of the sun, come on boy, you're a Wisdom Runner – RUN!" His grin turned into a full body laugh as his feet tapped away to the beat of tail drumming from Flint and Lucky; the trinkets and gold beads in the dozens of braids in his hair started to gleam with the same light as Peaberry's violin.

The gold violin sparked a beam of light towards Justin's group and another at Samuel's gold tooth; rays from both shot out, penetrated through the ice, causing it to vibrate. As the dogs danced faster, the ice transformed into mist, releasing Justin and the dogs surrounding him.

Luna and Fuchsia ran to the now moving dogs. Watching from the sidelines, Jennifer's heart was jumping with joy. She threw a large bag of cookies to help energize the recovering canines.

Samuel continued to dance as he reached for the coughing Justin, giving him a hand up. Justin started to roar and cough with laughter as his ears adjusted and he took in the hootenanny. "Peaberry, Samuel, gang! I used to think you guys were just up to crazy backwoods stuff when you played this music!"

Nicco danced nearer. "Did you hear us when you were still frozen?"

"We did!" shouted Fred, Sweetie and Angel as they started to dance. "We heard you and started dancing in our minds – then the ice started to melt into mist."

Justin rubbed his stomach where he had been hit before he was frozen. He picked up his bow and quiver before starting to dance with the group. "I had been in darkness, unconscious; then I heard you and saw you bring Samuel out. Then you were here, and we were free."

"What hit us before we got frozen?" asked Samuel.

"We have no idea what that invisible force was but we should be ready for it. I don't know if it has anything to do with the shadows and Ice Beings," said Justin. "By the way, have you seen them?"

"No," shouted Peaberry over the wailing on his gold violin. "But let's keep this party rolling! We have to get Lacino's group, then Denali, Hunter and Tonka before we start on Dohanos, Contalia and the dogs from your Keep who were with them."

The group danced, played and sang over to Lacino. Peaberry and Samuel bent low near where he lay in the ice. The violin and tooth glowed together, then sent a unified blast into the ice, which instantly melted into mist. The released dogs coughed as Luna and Fuchsia fussed over them and Justin fed them treats from another bag that Jennifer tossed towards them.

From the corner where Luna had ordered them to stay, Jennifer got down and hugged Llewellyn. *"It's going to be okay! It's going to be okay!"*

"Yes it is!" he answered happily in his high voice.

Across the cave Lacino tried to rise but could not. As the group sang and danced, Samuel and Justin bent to him. His eyes were glazed. "My left leg is broken. Prop me up against the wall and give me my bow and quiver of arrows so that I can cover you if anything shows up."

"Let us move you from the cave," Samuel thought intuitively, through the din of the music.

"No, don't move me," the Seer intuitively communicated. *"Keep the energy of joy and humor going. Try to get Dohanos and Contalia free – they have been in longer than we have; we need to get to the crystals and get them out of here."*

Samuel nodded and rose. Justin signaled to the Vermont gang, Jennifer and David to stay put. He motioned for ten of the dancing, singing dogs to guard either side of Lacino. Then Peaberry, Justin, Samuel and thirty dancing, singing canines moved to the pillars of ice holding Tonka, Denali and Hunter. They were soon free, up, and frenetically dancing with their companions.

Tonka stood on his hind legs, "YES! We knew Nicco and Tundra would get help! HAIL! And well met! Peaberry, Luna and the Vermont Earth UN-Chained Gang!" All the dogs howled once in unison before resuming the rescue effort.

Ringing around Dohanos' group, they raised the intensity of their singing, dancing and playing. At first nothing happened. Peaberry brought the gold violin closer, and Samuel shook his braids, which contained gold beads mixed in with the many-colored ones, as he grinned widely at Dohanos' blue eyes; the furry gals on flute sent silver rays into the ice with their instruments. The gold tooth and violin sparked, sending a spray of radiating beams into the ice. Mixing with the silver rays of the flutes they vaporized it. Peaberry winked as he drew back to let Luna and Fuchsia work on the dogs as Samuel and Justin helped Dohanos.

The dogs were soon on their feet, cheering Peaberry and dancing around with their long-missed comrades whom they hadn't seen for over a year since they had gone on the mission to the Servers of Light. After he finished coughing, graying, dark-haired Dohanos grabbed Samuel's braids. "*That's all I needed – your muggin' face grinnin' at me with that gold tooth of yours!*"

"*Glad to see you, too, man*!" laughed Samuel. Finding he was unhurt, Justin and Samuel helped Dohanos to his feet.

"*Where is Contalia*?" asked Dohanos. With the volume of the music, they were using intuitive communication.

"Still frozen, we think," thought Justin. *"Lacino's leg is broken, we tried to rescue you earlier but were frozen ourselves. Peaberry, Luna and the Vermont team came to our rescue. This fast bluegrass music seems to melt the frozen energy with its magic!"*

"*Where are the crystals?"* asked Samuel.

"Contalia and his dogs have them," thought Dohanos.

Dohanos picked up his bow. Justin motioned for fifteen dogs to guard the entrance tunnel that led to the trail and his Keep. Playing and dancing hard, the group moved past Lacino who saluted Dohanos with his bow and a wry smile.

The group worked their magic on the frozen tableau of Contalia and his dogs. They were soon free. Looking into Samuel's smiling face, Contalia thought, "*I have never felt more glad to see dreadlocks in all my life!*"

Samuel laughed, pulling him to his feet. *"When are you Solaria Wisdom Runners ever going to get it straight? These is ma' braids!"*

The only dog that did not get up was Franco. They tried to

revive him, but he was dead. "*We tried to save you earlier; Franco was attacked by the Ice Beings and shadows*," said Justin.

Contalia and Dohanos nodded and raised their salute to Franco; then, carrying his white, shaggy body, the group moved back to the main cave. Justin motioned for the music to stop.

"Good job, Peaberry!" said Contalia. "That violin, the flutes, drums, singing and your playing has saved us!" He wrapped Dohanos in a firm embrace. "The Vermont gang comes through! Is that David?" They looked over at David and Jennifer.

Peaberry nodded. "It's David, Zumulia's grandson. And Jennifer, the niece of our musher, Jim, in Vermont. And Llewellyn is my grandson, almost a year old."

"Well met!" Dohanos, Contalia and the dogs that had been frozen with them called loudly.

Jennifer followed David in a bow to them.

"We should get out of here. We can talk on the way. Lacino is hurt. Where are the crystals?" asked Justin.

Contalia produced a large bag from under his tunic. "I didn't gain this much weight on the mission!"

Out of the corner of her eye Jennifer saw movement. Pops and explosions came from the tunnel leading toward the next plane of existence. With all she could muster, she forced a scream to alert everyone to the seven-foot tall Ice Beings that were looming and moving towards them. Above them were shadows.

"*Crystals seem to be the magic word with these guys*," thought Justin to all. "Peaberry, shall we try again? No Solarian singing – let's stick to your bluegrass fiddling and lyrics."

"HALT!" yelled Nicco. The group looked at him. "Let's try my MC Hammer song now!"

Peaberry nodded. Justin, green eyes questioning, as well as some of the dogs from his Keep, looked at Samuel.

"Earth hip hop music – it's his favorite," explained Samuel. He turned to Nicco and Peaberry, "If it doesn't work we switch back to Southern bluegrass!"

Contalia and Dohanos raised their bows, fitted with triple arrows from the quivers David had tossed to them. "Anything that works," said Contalia.

"It's the humor – and joy. These beings seem to shrink and die when they are confronted with real fun and laughter," said Justin. "Laugh at them – it shrinks them. But watch for something invisible – we don't know what it is or where it might come from – but it's dangerous."

Peaberry put the violin to his chin, "One, two, three, four – hike!" He and the Vermont gang started playing and singing Nicco's version of MC Hammer's "Can't Touch This."

Black-furred, giant Nicco jumped towards the rear tunnel, standing on his hind feet; he moved with the grace and flexibility of an Earth human gymnast. As he danced hip hop style towards the Ice Beings, Tundra, Rampart, Umbra, Alex, Rock, Buck, Libby, Jose, Hannah, Topi, Thorn, Lawrence, Brazil, Coal, and Hermi danced joyfully behind him. Justin's dogs, formerly frozen with Dohanos and Contalia closely watched the steps and then joined in the lines of canines doing jumps and smooth moves in unison and individually.

Dancing back and forth in front of the shimmering, looming Ice Beings, looking up at them, in his base voice, Nicco boomed:

"Can't touch this…" Nicco turned and shook his furry black bottom and plumy tail at the Ice Beings.

"Can't touch this…" Nicco turned forward, did a quick two step and slid side to side and pointed at them. "Can't touch this…" Nicco jumped round and shook his bottom and tail again.

The dancing dogs behind the huge black dog, jumped, pranced and did combinations of steps in exaggerations of the hip hop dance moves that Samuel had taught them. As they danced, the shimmering eyes in the Ice Beings goggled, grew and started to bulge out of what seemed to be their heads. Peaberry stepped in and winked up at them as he played. Not believing their eyes, Contalia and Dohanos began laughing at the antics of the canine Wisdom

Runners. When Justin, Samuel and Lacino joined in, the Ice Beings started to shake like shimmering jelly.

With Peaberry and the Vermont gang's wild instrumental accompaniment, Nicco continued:

> "I told you Ice boys - Can't touch this…
> Yeah its how we livin' and you know…
> Look in my eyes – man – you can't touch this…
> Nicco time!"

The dogs danced and sang the chorus, "Ohhhhhh, Ohhhhhhh, Ohhhhhh!" as the humans laughed till they had tears in their eyes.

Jennifer loved it. She started jumping up and down and imitating the moves she had seen on MC Hammer's videos of the song. Llewellyn got on his toes and bounced along with her.

Samuel jumped in next to Nicco and danced, braids jiggling, beside him. The Ice Beings started shrinking.

"Ring the bell, school is back in! Darkness better learn a lesson! When we dance to this, you goin' get… MELTED!" rapped Nicco.

The Ice Beings shrank further. The dogs and humans danced on. David, Jennifer and the Vermont gang watched, stomped, played percussion and cheered.

Suddenly three Ice Beings turned black and jumped over their heads, slamming through the dogs protecting Lacino, pounding into his mid-section; then they shattered into pieces. Four more of the shrinking Ice Beings did the same, slamming into the wounded Seer.

Cocking his head Peaberry called, "Stop!" The dogs kept an eye on the Ice Beings, now a foot tall. Luna and Tundra ran to stand with the Vermont gang surrounding David, Jennifer and Llewellyn to protect them.

The cave was suddenly silent. Jennifer gasped when she saw Samuel bent over Lacino; blood gushed from his side - he was dying. "Get out, get the crystals and young ones out of here. Something is coming – I can sense it. Natab is controlling it – get out!" Lacino slumped over.

In the center of the cave, Elvis and Cash yelped as they were raised in the air, held by the scruffs of their necks. Both black dogs wiggled wildly, trying to loosen themselves. The dogs below growled, fur standing up on their necks and backs as they watched. Instinctively, Jennifer sank to a squat, gathering cave dust into her hands; she sprang up and threw it towards the air between the dangling dogs.

Seeing her, David did the same. They lobbed handfuls of dust at the large figure of a monstrous, cat-like creature emerging from the air. Seeing it, Justin, Samuel, Contalia and Dohanos fitted bows with triple arrows.

"Release them!" challenged Samuel to the silent, snarling figure as David and Jennifer continued to pelt it with dust.

Glaring at the men, it threw Cash and Elvis across the cave. The four men shot arrows directly into what would be the heart area of the apparition. Hissing, it backed up. Shaking itself, it started to disappear from view.

"More dust!" ordered Justin as he and the men shot the phantom monster again. Jennifer and David continued to pelt it. The men sent a third volley into it

"Peaberry, Nicco – suggestions?" Justin shouted. The Ice Beings started to grow behind them as shadows hovered at the ceiling level.

"Music does not effect it, from what I can tell," shouted Peaberry. "But these ice ghouls are going to be a problem, soon, if we don't start playing." Looking around they saw the Ice Beings had regained two feet of height.

"*Water*!" thought Jennifer. "*Cats hate water*!" She opened her canteen and flung the water up at the cat phantom. Hissing and snarling it started to shrink.

"Open the water containers!" yelled Luna.

David and Jennifer opened the spare water containers in their packs, as some of the dogs ran over to take huge mouthfuls of water.

Standing on hind legs they spat gushes of water up at the feline-like creature. Alarmed, it screamed and hissed, cowering against the wall.

"Hey, Natab!" growled Luna up at the creature. "If you raised this thing – I repeat to you – you are a disgrace to all cats! One day your sister, Tonga, Queen of the Hissing Cats, will bring you down if we don't do it first!" The dust began turning into mud on the cat phantom as the dogs continued to spray water all over it; glowering, Natab's face began to form in it.

"I'll get you! Sssssstupid dogsssss! I'll get David – you can't protect him! The cryssssstalsssss will be mine! Justin Valor, Peaberry, Luna – thissss is NOT over!" Natab snarled through the air.

"Keep spraying water and throwing dust!" yelled Justin. The four men raised their hands, sending light at the figure as the dogs spewed water at it. As the light met with the water on the cat phantom it screamed, exploded, then disappeared into the air.

"If Natab raised it there must be more entrance portals into this cave. The darkness that controls Natab and the shadows is in contact with these Ice Beings," yelled Justin as he picked his bow up again and turned to the Ice Beings. "When our energy hit the water on the phantom's surface it sent a jolt back at her; she won't be able to raise it again, at least not now."

"She doesn't want the crystals to enter Solaria – which must be why she teamed up with the Ice Beings," said Samuel. As they spoke the Ice Beings were back to seven feet tall. A few started to elevate towards the ceiling.

"I don't think those things have much intelligence," said Peaberry. "Humor and joy is poison to them."

Contalia nodded. "I wish Dohanos and I had known that while we fought them for months – they don't do well out in the open country but they kept us running. They became seriously dangerous when we got into the cave of this portal – the rock seems to energize them."

Suddenly the Ice Beings multiplied and started flying towards the ceiling, baring their long fangs.

"On guard!" yelled Justin. The Ice Beings attached themselves to the ceiling and began elongating down towards the group, and back again, as if they were each a large slinky toy; their movement was mesmerizing as they shimmered eerily.

"Music!" yelled Peaberry. The dogs launched back into the Charlie Daniels song about the devil and the gold violin and started dancing. Because the Ice Beings were no longer in a single group, Peaberry and the gang of canines were successful only in shrinking and killing those they could get nearest to with his golden violin, the flutes, and the dogs singing lyrics. Others, not near the instruments and singers, bounced threateningly at the humans.

Anchored to the rock of the cave ceiling, the Ice Beings bounced up and down trying to avoid the direct sound of Peaberry's gold violin as it shot out light; each time they were hit they turned black and crumbled into dust. A shimmering head came down towards Jennifer as David was turned, shooting three arrows into another, dipping Ice Being beside him. Welding her wide, toothy grin, Gretel rose up at its face, as it flashed its fangs at Jennifer, "Eeeeeeeeeeeeeeeee!" grinned Gretel.

If the shimmering Ice Being could have looked confused, it did. Gretel continued to sing a high, "Eeeeeeeeeeeeeeeee," as she waggled her head, from side to side, poking out her tongue and grinning wider. Peaberry played his golden fiddle and the gang sang:

> "Fire music in the cave – run, Ice, run!
> Peaberry's brought the joy of the Vermont sun!
> Ice Beings meltin' like baking dough
> Shadows run from us – Go dogs, Go!"

The Ice Being next to Gretel shook until its head popped off as its body turned black. "Ha!" said Gretel as she grinned at her mother, Lioness. She jumped out into the room at another upside-down Ice Being, grinned at it, and it too, turned black and popped apart.

David handed Jennifer his bow. "Jen, you shoot. I am going to switch to the slingshot." He took up a ball of glow weed and shot it directly into one of the Ice Beings who was threatening Justin from behind; the Ice Being turned black and broke apart.

Jennifer looked at the bow in her hands. *"I don't know if I can do this."* But David could not hear her as he focused on lobbing more balls of glow weed at the Ice Beings. She drew in her breath; her friends needed her.

Jennifer drew three arrows, aligned them in the string of the bow, took a breath, aimed and shot at an Ice Being near her. She missed as it pulled toward the ceiling. Taking another breath, she shot again and got it. "Good shot!" cheered Llewellyn.

"Keep going, Jen," said David as he shot repeated volleys of glow weed. Jennifer nodded and continued shooting, smiling a bit as more of her arrows hit their marks.

Contalia got separated from Justin and Samuel as he tried to defend Reglio and Snort from an Ice Being that descended behind them. As he shot the being, two descended from behind him, sinking their fangs into either side of his neck. When the shimmering ghouls let go of him, three shadows entered his body through the wounds. Dropping his bow, he sank to the ground on his knees, his face and hands turning black as the shadows took hold. They were sucking the life force from him and would soon have control of his body.

"Shoot me!" he screamed. "I don't want to become a dark force like Natab!"

Justin turned and saw what was happening. Jennifer stopped shooting and watched as Justin, with no hesitation, shot three arrows through Contalia's heart. The Wisdom Runner's blackened body slumped dead to the cave floor.

Jennifer screamed. Tears flooded from her eyes. Dropping the bow, she sunk to her knees as her mind shifted from Contalia to an image of her father lying dead on the floor. Her hands were wrapped around the gun as if she had just shot him. Had she?

"Jennifer!" wailed Llewellyn pressing close to her.

"Jennifer!" Her vision cleared. The battle raged around the cave but Luna's face was level with hers.

"Jennifer, steady yourself! Take a deep breath. Do not allow the dark forces to use your fear of your father's death against you to stir up doubt!"

Jennifer took another breath. Her friends were in trouble and needed her. *"I'm okay. I am okay."* She rose to her feet. Hearing the music, seeing her struggling friends, she felt new resolve as she picked up David's bow. Luna locked eyes with hers, then she turned and dashed back to help Peaberry's group.

In desperation, as the music increased, the Ice Beings turned black and flew at the humans. Two latched onto Justin's leg, as three attached themselves onto both of Dohanos' feet. Samuel stepped forward, launching arrows into Ice Beings as Peaberry's violin blazed golden light; the Ice Beings fell off, breaking into pieces before the shadows could enter.

"That's it!" cried Peaberry. "Demons, you ain't getting another one of us." Protecting Dohanos and Justin, the dogs danced, sang and raised energy until the cave shook. Ice Beings vibrated, shrank, turned black and disappeared; others streamed out through both exit tunnels with the shadows following, until the cave was empty.

The group checked both tunnels. "*Some went back to the parallel reality – unfortunately some have gone into Solaria*," thought Justin. He gritted his teeth and winced as Samuel, his arm around him, propped him up.

When they were sure that all was safe, Peaberry slowed and then stopped the bluegrass music. Handing his gold violin to Jennifer, he sat down, looking like a regular dog. She reached out to stroke his head.

"Roll call!" shouted Luna. Each dog and human called out in turn. Cash and Elvis did not answer. Dogs near them checked and confirmed they were gone.

Peaberry finished lapping water from a bowl Jennifer held for him. He stood and surveyed the room, shaking his head. "I guess that could have been worse."

Jennifer hugged Llewellyn as she looked around at the group. Dohanos could not rise; dogs ringed them, watching the cave ceiling and both exit tunnels for danger. David stood, slingshot at his side, staring around the cave. Luna was checking individuals for shock and wounds, speaking quietly to each. Most of the dogs were sitting, looking around warily. A number had gathered sadly near the bodies.

Justin sent Nicco with fifteen dogs to check the front of the tunnel and the sleds. Leaving the group to guard the sleds, Nicco returned. "All safe. There are four sleds that look to be in running order. It's a clear day - the dawn is just upon us."

"David, are you up to driving one of the sleds?" asked Samuel.

David nodded.

"Okay," said Justin. "I think, once on the sled, I can drive one; I'll support myself on the back handgrips. Dohanos should ride with David. Jennifer, Luna and Llewellyn with Samuel. Let's get the crystals and our fallen comrades out to the sleds, make teams and travel to the Keep.

Dohanos agreed. "The Keepers of Light instructed Contalia and me that as soon as possible one crystal is to be placed at Justin's Keep, four to the east, and one to Zumulia's. Once each crystal is in place, they hope to aid our Seers and Wisdom Runners to activate a grid of crystal energy to protect Solaria in the east, and to help open a path to the west for us to place the rest of the six."

Nicco cocked his big shaggy head. "Is that going to melt the darkness dividing us?"

Dohanos started coughing. Justin turned to Nicco and shook his head. "Later for this. Let's try to get home to the Keep."

Outside the cave, despite the pain he was in, Justin spent time to check on Jennifer, Llewellyn and David. "It's your first battle. I hope that it may be your last. But given the tide of darkness, and beings like Natab that serve it, that is not likely."

David nodded. "It's a lot different than hearing the stories and ballads, reading the tales and myths. I… well, I feel closer to my parents now. I understand more why they cared so much. Natab was lying; they were very brave."

Justin, Dohanos and Samuel looked at each other. "Your parents were some of the bravest that I ever fought with," said Samuel. "They cared about making a better world for all of us. You should be proud."

Justin gripped David's shoulder. "Your parents loved you so much that they gladly lost their lives protecting Solaria; they wanted a good world for you and all living beings."

"Jennifer, how are you?" asked Justin as the group of adult dogs and humans looked towards her.

She shook her head; she felt frozen and numb. "*I don't know*."

"Jen, no one can really understand fighting," said Samuel. "You handled yourself very bravely in there. I am thankful that you helped free us."

Justin walked over and looked deeply into her green eyes. "Jen, all evil and harm is insane, by its very nature. You can never understand it. We just have to do the best we can to stand for what our hearts and spirits tell us is the best course of action. As long as I live I will never like to fight – I do it when it becomes necessary because no other course of action is open."

Jennifer nodded as tears rolled down her cheeks. Llewellyn pressed against her leg. She reached down to touch his head.

"And how about you, Llewellyn?" asked Justin.

Leaning against Jennifer as she stroked his head, Llewellyn solemnly looked at the adults with his soft brown eyes. "I was afraid. My instincts told me to run at the Ice Beings and try to bite them, or to run as fast as I could out of the cave. But I was glad that Luna and the others brought me on this mission because I learned that with training, one day, I might be as effective in fighting evil and darkness as my grandfather, Peaberry, my mother Stormina and all of you."

Stormina nuzzled his ear.

"Wisdom in one so young. It's a good thing to be afraid – our fear teaches us not to envy those who follow the path of greed and evil. And, frankly, I always would rather run away!" laughed Samuel, the beads in his braids gently clicking together. "But I, too, learn by watching my comrades and am inspired to train harder – no matter how experienced in battle I am or how old I get."

"Luna, please try to talk with our young friends on the ride home. We will gather as a group when we are back at the Keep; for safety we should get started," said Justin, softly.

The tired dogs, Luna, David, Samuel and Justin put Dohanos into David's sled, respectfully loaded the bodies of their fallen comrades in a tow sled, packed weapons and supplies, and started on their way. Before leaving, the large group was able to communicate briefly with Tuvalla and Zumulia to let them know of their success, the crystals, and the news of those they had lost.

Chapter Twelve

". . . Death is given no power over love. Love is stronger. It creates something out of the destruction caused by death; it bears everything and overcomes everything. It is at work where the power of death is strongest, in war and persecuting, and homelessness, and hunger, and physical death itself. It is omnipresent and here and there, in the smallest and most hidden ways as in the greatest and most visible ones, it rescues life from death. It rescues each of us, for love is stronger than death."

Planet Earth Philosopher, Paul Tillich
as quoted in the
Book of The Wisdom Runners

Llewellyn and Jennifer sat on the window seat of their suite watching the activities outside. The snow-covered courtyard and fields behind the manse were busy with people, dogs and horses making a funeral pyre. Colorful banners stood on poles, waving brightly in the clear morning light as the sun was rising in a cloudless sky. The group sang as they worked.

"Are you surprised by their joy?" asked David. He was dressed in a bright red tunic.

Jennifer nodded up at him. Her arm around Llewellyn, she had been crying. *"Except for Lacino, I didn't really know them,"* she thought. *"My father has only been dead for a short time, but somehow I felt closer to these men and dogs than I did to him. I watched them die - I cried all night."*

Llewellyn nodded. "Brigitte gave her some herbal tinctures Tuvalla made, but she continued to cry." He gave her a quick lick of a kiss on her cheek.

"I don't understand why there is so much darkness to cause this... why did they have to die? Why did Justin and Dohanos get hurt? Why did your parents die?" Tears again flowed down Jennifer's cheeks. She took the handkerchief David pressed into her hand and dabbed her eyes.

"You have never been in a battle before," said David. "I have only had to fight shadows. I have heard the tales and songs, but that was my first major conflict."

"Tuvalla said that I needed to give myself time," explained Jennifer.

David looked out at the field. "Battles and fighting are traumatic. We all need time. Here in Solaria we are sad for the ones who leave us. But we celebrate the goodness in their hearts that they have brought to our lives; and the bravery they have lived in working for light and love."

Jennifer sighed deeply. *"I don't think that we are good at that on Earth. Many people stay sad all of their lives when someone they love has died."*

"We know that we are only apart from our loved ones for awhile. We will all be together, in the light," said David.

"*But how do you know*?" asked Jennifer.

"We just know. I feel the Creator; I know the Creator lives. It is only those that have chosen to do great harm, that we will not see because they will live their eternity in darkness... or until they learn that willful harm and hurting of others is not the way," said David.

"I don't know if I believe in God or the Creator," thought Jennifer. *"There is too much wrong in the world."*

"In Solaria we feel that the darkness in the world comes from humans and beings, like Natab, who choose personal power, love of harm, over goodness. This is not the Creator's choice; it is a personal choice that is against real love and truth," explained David. "On Earth, many people don't understand how they are making personal choices that cause the darkness to grow. Even small, selfish choices affect the whole of creation."

Jennifer kissed the top of Llewellyn's head. *"I don't know. I want to trust, I want to believe."* She looked out the window at the growing funeral pyre. *"My father was not good. Does that mean that I won't see him when I die? Or what about Toni: she may have killed my father; now she is in league with Natab. Does God – or the Creator – love them? And why were Contalia, Lacino, Elvis, Franco and Cash taken – they were working for light and love, to help others."*

David shook his head. "I don't know… I don't know how to answer you. This is something for Luna, Tuvalla, Justin, or Samuel to answer – they are wise. For now, why don't we go down for some breakfast?"

* * *

Jennifer, Llewellyn and David, holding Millet, stood with Kaarina and Brigitte for the procession carrying the bodies of the slain to the funeral pyre. Dogs, horses and humans wore bright colors and circlets of pine, braided with colorful ribbons on their heads. Humans playing flutes, drums and bagpipes led the group of dogs pulling the five sleds that carried their fallen comrades, two human and three canine; others followed or lined the path saying their goodbyes. At the pyre, humans took the litters from the sleds and carried them to the top.

Justin stood on crutches at the foot of the pyre. Tuvalla stood next to him with a few of the Seers. Samuel stood behind the wheelchair holding Dohanos. They raised their hands in salute as the bodies passed.

When the Seers carrying the five litters returned to the ground, Justin hobbled forward to face the assembled group of humans, dogs and horses. "Dearest friends, Wisdom Runners and Seers, we are gathered here to say farewell to the remains of our comrades. Because of the goodness in their hearts we know they now live in the light with our Creator. All five cared greatly for Solaria. Each one was an example, to all of us, in their dedication to bringing light and love here to dissolve the darkness. They died for Solaria while fighting by our sides."

Jennifer bowed her head.

"For our guests from Earth, Jennifer and Llewellyn, who valiantly fought with us, our fallen comrades would ask that I thank you for your contribution. They would also ask that I thank David for aiding Wisdom Runners and Seers in service to Solaria," said Justin. All turned towards them and nodded.

Justin continued. "Our lives here in Solaria have been enriched by knowing our wonderful companions. They had faith in our Creator. They had faith that dedication to truth and the wellbeing of all would translate into quality of life for generations to come, and a balance of order in all of creation. While they played, trained, studied, fought, mushed in dog teams and lived amongst us, they believed in all of their comrades: their belief, faith and support made us all better beings."

Justin dropped one of his crutches as he turned to face the top of the pyre. He raised his right hand. "Hail and well met! Be in peace and love – we will run together again in the light!"

Tuvalla and Samuel stepped forward with lit torches. "Contalia, Lacino, Cash, Elvis and Franco – Hail! – We will run together again in the light!" they said in unison and then bent to the wood pyre and lit it.

As the tall pile of wood went up in flames, the dogs sang in unison. The horses whinnied in continuous salutes as the humans stood with their arms raised. Against the backdrop of the mountain, the flames shot up into the clear blue morning sky. The group of friends and companions watched until late afternoon. Tears flowed from many eyes.

* * *

The large banquet hall was filled with laughter, mixed with sadness, as musicians and storytellers sang ballads and told tales of the many adventures and deeds of Contalia, Lacino, Cash, Presley and Franco. Millet had helped to make the delicious vegetable stews, fruit platters, egg dishes, pies, sweets and cakes that graced the tables; he beamed as everyone complimented him and told him how happy they were to have the Talking Loaves in Solaria again.

Jennifer had never seen such merriment in a group, especially one where they drank no alcohol and took no drugs. They genuinely loved each other and their fallen companions. They celebrated life as they smiled and cried.

Justin and Dohanos reclined on sofas near one of the massive stone fireplaces. Luna sat talking with them. When the number of well-wishers thinned, Justin beckoned Jennifer, Millet, Llewellyn and David to sit with them. "How are you four doing?" he asked.

"Thank you, fine," said David.

Jennifer nodded. Millet hugged her and gave her a kiss. "I'm glad to have my friends back, safely," he said.

In the firelight, Dohanos' blue eyes were in stark contrast to his dark, graying hair and weathered face. Tall, like Justin, the bulky muscles of his arms were as large as any wrestler that Jennifer had seen on TV. "You three fought bravely; you gave all of us, Peaberry, and the gang valuable support. Thank you."

Justin nodded. "Peaberry, Luna, Dohanos and I feel there would have been more casualties if you had not been there."

"Casualties." Jennifer thought. *"Before now I've only heard that word on the news or in the movies."*

Luna placed a paw on Jennifer's shoulder. Millet stroked her arm.

David looked squarely at the two wounded fighters. "You both have protected Solaria for many years. You were friends with my parents and fought side-by-side with them. It was an honor for me to finally be able to give you aid."

"Well said!" said Dohanos, as he raised his mug of hot, mulled cider and clinked it to David's mug. "Your parents would be well pleased with you. You are an honor to their memory."

"And now he will train with us, once Samuel returns from delivering four of the crystals to the east," said Justin.

Dohanos nodded. "It is time! And how is your fine, wise grandmother?"

"Concerned for your safety for the last year. She will be happy to know that you are safe," said David.

"I hope to see her soon," said Dohanos. *"And you, young woman from Earth, you fought very bravely. How do you like our Solaria?"* He intuitively communicated to Jennifer as he gazed steadily into her eyes.

"Thank you. I am glad that I was able to give you aid. I love Solaria," thought Jennifer.

"With bravery and bow shooting like that, maybe you will train to be a Wisdom Runner!" Dohanos looked at her thoughtfully.

"Isn't she a darlin'?" asked Peaberry as he came around the corner of the couch. His bulging blue eyes, freckles, pointy muzzle, and floppy, soft ears looked as goofy as ever, belying the great leader he was. "And my grandson, Llewellyn, and good friend, David, were invaluable!"

"EEEeeeeee! What about me?" beamed Gretel.

"And you, too, daughter!" Peaberry gave her a big lick as he settled on the thick rug next to her.

Luna stretched. "All of you were very brave."

"You haven't given me a chance to get that far!" laughed Dohanos. "I have thanked David; but indeed, Llewellyn, well done! You are a credit to your grandfather – you will do well if you study hard and try to emulate his bravery and steadfastness. And Gretel, you are zany and a tribute to your wild, crazy father!"

Llewellyn sat up straight, "Thank you, Dohanos!" He still had the sweetness and innocence of puppyhood about him, mixed with the gifts of a good heart, and strength of spirit that would make him a good Wisdom Runner in the future.

"And Peaberry, that was wild violin playing!" laughed Justin. "It was brilliant!"

All the dogs in the hall stopped their activities and shouted, "Brilliant!" Equines, canines and humans broke out laughing.

Dohanos and Justin looked at Peaberry with raised eyebrows. He laughed. "It is my musher Jim's favorite word of the month. Our Vermont gang taught it to Tundra, Umbra, Nicco and Rampart; now they have taught it to all the dogs."

"And you, Samuel, the Vermont pack and Samuel's dogs are going to have to teach all of us about Earth music," said Dohanos. "I have never seen such a powerful effect on shadows and Ice Beings in all of my life."

"Agreed," said Justin as he clinked his mug to Dohanos'.

Dohanos looked at Jennifer. "That idea of yours to throw water at the cat specter that Natab raised was very creative in the midst of the pressure of battle. And the dogs, taking your cue - spraying water at her specter – well, it was brilliant!"

"Brilliant!" bayed all the canine Wisdom Runners again as everyone broke into peels of laughter.

After visiting with the young ones, Justin grew serious. He called Samuel, the dogs, as well as Spelia and some of the horses. Tuvalla and Luna sat next to him. David, Millet, Llewellyn and Jennifer moved to the outside of the circle to listen in as the adults talked.

The group spent the rest of the evening planning the next morning's missions. Samuel and some of his dogs, with the aid of Justin's dogs, would go east to the Court of the Wisdom Runners with four of the crystals. One crystal would find its home in the Quartz Crystal Cave at Justin's Keep, while six would be kept in safekeeping to be delivered to the west when a way could be found through the veil of darkness. Peaberry, Luna and the Vermont pack would bring a crystal, along with Jennifer and David to Zumulia's Keep; some of Samuel's dogs would travel with them to protect them on their journey and remain to protect her Keep when Peaberry, Luna and the gang left to return with Jennifer to Vermont.

Tired, but not sleepy, Jennifer, David, Llewellyn and Millet went to their suite for a private visit – they knew that it might be a long time before they were all together again.

Chapter Thirteen

Often when we are working for the good of all, evil works to wear us down. Sometimes when we are battle weary, meeting it head-on strips us of our ability to know up from down, and left from right. Evil seeks to make us lose our heart connection with the goodness and light in eternity. Stripped of our reserves, with our back against the wall, we must call out to our Creator with trust and faith. Thus we pray for the ability to know when it is not weakness to stop our efforts and give our lives over to faith, letting the outcome be in our Creator's hands.

Book of The Wisdom Runners

In the dark of the morning, the teams gathered before the gates. Aides helped the teams into their harnesses, hitching them to their sleds. Peaberry and Lucky would lead, with Flint, Lioness, Buttercup, Fuchsia, Bear, Rampart and Maple from the Vermont Gang joining with Samuel's dogs, Fred, Sweetie, Thomas, and Sylvia running in pairs on the gang line pulling the sled to Zumulia's Keep. Tundra, Umbra, Nicco, Angel, Stormina and Gretel would run alongside to protect the team and the sled.

Going east with Samuel to take the four crystals to the Court of the Wisdom Runners were Alex in single lead, followed by pairs made up of Rock, Buck, Libby, Jose, Hannah, Topi, Thorn, Lawrence, Brazil, Coal, Hermi, Calli and Sookie. Daniel, Honey and Bunny sat in the sled with the supplies to guard the crystals. Justin's dogs - Betty, Cocoa, Taffy, Stanley, Price, Kenneth, Gloria, Robinson, Lance and Bandit would run guard.

After saluting Tuvalla, Luna, Llewellyn and Jennifer climbed into their sled with the packs of supplies and the crystal. David stepped to the sled as Samuel mounted the runners of his. The first set of massive gate doors opened, allowing Alex to lead Samuel's team into the tunnel through the Keep's massive fortress wall first, followed by Peaberry's team. When the inner doors closed behind them, the outer gates opened and they ran in earnest across the bridge of the moat to the long field beyond. Their teams were off.

They traveled for what felt like hours to Jennifer, but finally Samuel halted his team when the trail left the mountain foothills and entered the Plain of Vendona. Peaberry directed their team alongside. "Give our 'Hail' to our comrade Wisdom Runners and Seers in the east!"

"Go with love, light, valor and courage!" cheered each team to the other. Samuel saluted, pulled his snow hook, and waved as Alex led their team off for the east.

"Ready?" called Peaberry.

"Ready!" called the team.

"Hike!" called Peaberry as he took them onto the trail crossing the Plain of Vendona.

* * *

The team made excellent time; they stopped periodically so that Nicco, Tundra, Umbra or Rampart could switch into lead; and Angel, Stormina and Gretel could alternate with pulling team members. The kitchens of Justin Valor's Keep had supplied them with wonderful snacks and meals to keep their energy up. Often one of the dogs running guard would hop into the sled with

Jennifer, Llewellyn and Luna to tell stories intuitively and amuse the team as it ran - Luna translated audibly for David. They told true stories from their lives, jokes, and the myths and tales of the Wisdom Runners and Seers of Solaria; pack members added their own details as the storyteller continued the main thread of the tale.

One of the favorite subjects was about a dog musher known simply as "The Musher." They told of times when there were impossible battle odds and all seemed lost – with all resources gone – when Wisdom Runners only had prayer left to them, as they knew they would die. Some who had lived through the fighting, were saved by a team of huge dogs, seemingly made of white light, pulling a sled of light with a musher, radiant with light. No one knew who they were. They said that he and his dogs came from out of thin air, rescued teams of dogs and human Wisdom Runners; and then would vanish after healing the wounded and carrying them to safety.

"But why didn't he come to the Portal of Nordon to save Justin and the others? Why did we have to go?" asked Jennifer.

Piebald Tundra, with her face half black and half white with opposite color patches around each eye like a doggie rendition of the symbol for the Tao, paused a moment. "Well, Jen, that's a good question. We sense the Creator sends the Musher when the balance is tipped in the wrong direction towards evil. If Wisdom Runners through their own effort and work can bring a solution – then that is what we have to do. What you, Llewellyn, Peaberry, Luna and the rest of us did was creative and showed courage and faith in goodness and light."

Jennifer shook her head. *"But Contalia, Lacino, Elvis, Cash and Franco died!"*

"Death is not the worst thing, Jen," offered Luna. "Wisdom Runners live to sacrifice their lives, if that is what is necessary."

"But if the Creator - or God – or whatever, was good then why didn't he do something sooner? Why did he leave all of the Wisdom Runners frozen in the ice when they were fighting for the good? They were fighting for him!" Jennifer found herself crying again. She put her arms around Luna and buried her face in the fur of her neck.

Suddenly, as if waking from the bad dream of all they had gone through, she remembered Grace and wished she were in the sled with them.

Luna sighed. "There are many answers to your questions. And more questions after the answers begin to come…"

"You are asking, WHY? Why evil? Why did Contalia and the others die? Why did your father die? Why is your stepmother trying to harm people? Why did Toni hurt Grace and why can't Grace be with you right now? Why is there suffering in the world if our Creator is good?" said Tundra. "But 'WHY?' is a question that will drive you crazy."

"I don't understand," thought Jennifer as she wiped her eyes with a bandana she pulled from her pocket.

"Of course you don't," said Luna gently. "None of us do. At least not with our heads."

"Tundra is saying that any variation of the question, 'Why?' – when it is about life, death and evil - will drive you crazy because there are no answers that our minds can accept," said Luna. "We must learn to think with our hearts, not our heads, if we want answers."

Tundra nodded. "Jennifer – 'Why did your father, Contalia, or Lacino die?' - are questions that will not help. What will help is if you ask: What can I do about this to make it better for others? What do I need to learn so that I can turn this into a positive, learning situation to motivate me in my life?"

Luna shifted so Jennifer could hold her more tightly and allow Llewellyn close as well. "Also, what skills do I need to learn to help me make a difference so that this does not have to happen to others? When is it best for me to act? When is it best for me to develop my skills and bide my time? How do I better myself so that I can contribute to life, love and happiness for all of creation?"

Jennifer dabbed at her eyes. *"Can't we just ask The Musher to come to our aid?"*

"No, Jen," said Luna. "We ask our Creator for help and trust that it will come in a way that is best for all. Sometimes that means that we die or get injured in the effort. Sometimes it means that we are successful and live more days here to dance and celebrate. And sometimes it means that The Musher, an angel, a friend, or a stranger comes through with exactly the aid that we need. We know that ultimately, when we die, we will understand all that our minds weren't able to grasp here, in this life."

Tundra cocked her piebald head and nodded. "This is hard to absorb. Much will come to you if you focus on trusting and having faith in goodness, no matter what you see around you. It is bigger than but similar to visualizing your arrow hitting the target when you are shooting the bow."

A sneeze came from Jennifer's backpack. A hand popped out as the zipper was undone, followed by Millet's head with a purple cap that matched his purple, knit parka and candy-striped scarf.

"Millet, what are you doing here!" Luna's ears flicked with exasperation.

David started laughing so hard he could hardly stand on the runners of the fast-moving sled. Llewellyn joined in and gave Millet a quick lick kiss. Tundra's blue and brown eyes sparkled as she stifled a laugh. Jennifer bit her lip and reached out to take Millet in her arms.

"Stop laughing!" growled Luna. "You'll only encourage his naughtiness!"

Peaberry, out of harness and running a guard position, came to investigate. "Do we have a stowaway?" He blinked his bulging, bright, blue eyes. "Umbra, Nicco, team, bring the sled to a halt!" The team, David and guards slowed, then stopped the sled; all started laughing.

Gretel came over to add her grin and "Eeeeeeeeee," while Flint contributed his, "Ta-da-ta-da, Charge!" The dogs on the gang line fell over in the snow, rolling this way and that as they laughed and kicked their legs in the air, completely tangling their lines.

"Enough!" yelled Luna sharply, baring her teeth.

Tundra stood up and jumped from the sled. "Yes, actually this is quite enough! Look at the tangle you have all made! David, Jennifer, unhitch these silly canines so that they can have a good pee, and then a snack, while Peaberry, Luna, Nicco and I sort this out!"

The leaders decided that there was nothing to be done except press on towards Zumulia's. A repentant Millet explained that although he loved his apprenticeship at Justin's Keep, he did not like being separated from his friends and really wanted to see Zumulia and his brothers and sisters.

Finished with her exasperation, Luna suggested that when Samuel returned from the east they would transport the seven Talking Loaves to Justin's Keep as soon as possible, so they could be together and safe. A team, with Peaberry in lead, was hitched to the sled and the group took off again to finish crossing the Plain of Vendona.

* * *

The group reached the forest atop the bluff at the southern edge of the Plain of Vendona after dark. With so many dogs to trade places on the team pulling the sled, they decided to press on rather than spending the night in the small cave where Jennifer, David, Millet and Luna had stayed when they had started their journey. They stopped for a meal and rest and then started out again with Nicco in the lead.

Three hours in, they stopped again. The moon lit the clearing although it had to fight through the snow clouds that were gathering. "I don't like that," said Tundra as she sniffed the air.

"Neither do I, " said Peaberry. "Perhaps we should have stopped in the cave. All of us are tired."

Jennifer had been fighting sleep during the last hour. Her body ached from riding in the cramped sled.

Luna nodded. "The good thing is that we are two hours from Zumulia's if we keep going at this pace. We can rest, eat, sleep, and take shifts guarding once we get there." David and Jennifer passed out a snack and then helped with the harnessing and hitching.

Suddenly something crashed from the right of the trail. The dogs raised their hackles.

"David, bow and arrows right now! Jennifer – get my violin ready! Get the flutes for the gals," demanded Peaberry as he peered into the darkness of the forest.

Nicco came near. "Unhitch the dogs. Then I want Angel, Fred, Sweetie, Thomas and Sylvia to guard Jennifer, David, Millet and Llewellyn." Peaberry nodded. Another crash came from the forest.

Luna and Tundra sat next to each other, raising an orb of light that they sent into the air above them, fully lighting the clearing. "It has to be Natab," said Luna.

"Logical," said Tundra. "I sense her."

"Natab – are you so reckless that you are out there? Real cats have nine lives – not you!" taunted Luna.

Unhitched, the dogs formed outer circles around those ringing the young ones. "Here silly, silly, silly! Here silly, silly!" the front group crooned, punctuated with kissing noises.

In a rage Natab pounced into the edge of the clearing. Her gold eyes blazed in her oversized head; her tailless hindquarters hunched under her. Twelve cats landed behind her. "I believe you mean 'here, kiT-Ty, kiT-Ty. Here, kiT-Ty, kiT-Ty.' Your canine brainssss are sssso limited."

Luna cocked her head to the left, brown eyes shining. "Cats are smart, full of heart, intuitive, and brave, but you lost that when you chose to become a minion of darkness."

Peaberry winked at Natab. The rest of the pack laughed and called "Pssshhh, Pssshh, here silly, silly."

Natab caught in her breath, trying to control her rage. A few dogs took gulps of snow, holding it in their mouths till it melted and then sprayed the water onto Natab and her cats as they had her phantom image when fighting in the cave. She screamed and tried to pounce on Umbra, who danced away giggling, shaking his furry tail at her.

"How honorable issss thissss?" hissed Natab. "Thissss issss not behavior of Wissssdom Runnerssss!"

"No?" asked Luna. "What would you know of honor and Wisdom Runner behavior?"

Tundra, almost twice the size of Luna, nodded. "You gave up feline honor and our respect long ago, Natab. Your phantom attacked us at the Portal of Nordon. You attack children. You told David lies about his parents – you have no honor."

Seething, one of the cats behind Natab sprung; David caught him, mid-air, with an arrow between his eyes.

"Idiot boy!" screamed Natab. Her pride of angry feline creatures cowered behind her.

Jennifer and David guarded Millet, Llewellyn and the sled as Peaberry played a bluegrass tune on his fiddle. Stormina, Buttercup, and Lioness played their flutes and the rest of the dogs pranced, danced and sang funny ditties. Enraged, Natab and her pride turned and disappeared into the forest taking their slain friend with them.

The dogs regrouped. Peaberry shook his head. "I don't trust this. Especially since David killed another of her pride."

Nicco agreed. "Neither do I. Music works on Ice Beings and shadows, I am not sure if it is effective on Hissing Cats. What do you suggest?"

"Leave the instruments out, where they are easily accessible. And David's weapons. Jennifer and David, be ready to fight. We'll run beside the sled and keep our watch up," said Peaberry.

Jennifer and David helped to hitch the dogs chosen for the team. Cautiously, they got underway. They traveled an hour with no sign of Natab or shadows. They stopped for a snack, switched dogs, and started again.

Passing under a tree limb, a giant figure leapt, knocking David from the sled. Eleven Hissing Cats were on him before the team could stop the sled safely; the guards ran back to ring the cats.

"Jennifer, release the dogs from the sled gang line," ordered Luna. "Llewellyn, Millet, stay in the sled!"

When the team dogs were released, Luna told them to guard Jennifer, Llewellyn and Millet while she ran to the fray.

Jennifer started to run after her.

"Jennifer, stay!" Luna demanded over her shoulder.

After biting the prodigious hindquarters of the nearest Hissing Cats, causing them to run, the dogs faced those who had David surrounded; he was not moving – his clothing was torn where the Hissing Cats had mauled him.

"This cowardly ssssspawn of Zarcourt and Tumilia diesssss - here and now!" screamed Natab.

"YOU are NOT a cat! Playing is one thing, attacking children is only the realm of spineless, minion, puppets of darkness!" growled Luna.

"I can't wait to ssssee Zumulia's face!" grinned Natab, her yellow eyes flashing. "Her friend Sssssamuel's bessssst dogssss, her little, white doggie friend, fiddle-playing kook, and their Vermont doggie pack couldn't protect her grandssssson…"

"*NO!*" Jennifer stood just behind the group; she had David's bow drawn, aimed directly at Natab. Peaberry nodded, shifting slightly to make way for her.

"Luna is right! You aren't a cat! My cat, Fred, took care of me until my stepmother killed him! He was a real cat! YOU are not!" Jennifer stood straight. Her inner voice came loud in the Hissing Cat and canine heads.

Natab raised her paw, claws out. "Very brave, little Missssss Prissssssy! But Toni, your sssstepmother, will dessstroy you, if I don't do it firsssst. Firsssst we will kill your little doggie, Grace. But now your cowardly friend diessss!"

Jennifer's arrow pierced Natab through the shoulder. As it hit, she screamed and the dogs jumped on the Hissing Cats. Hissing, growling, barking and howling, the cat creatures and canines rolled through the snow, away from David's body. Jennifer shot two more cats, and the dogs tore the throats out of four more, before Natab went screaming through the woods with her pride. The dogs had only minor scratches since they had acted fast, shocking the Hissing Cats.

Luna and the dogs sent healing energy into David; he was bleeding from wounds all over his body. Tundra finally stopped them, "Move the sled back here; we'll get him into it."

Jennifer helped the dogs back the sled to where David lay. Coming to consciousness, he was able to lean on Nicco, Jennifer and Tundra to get into the sled. Jennifer tucked Llewellyn, Millet, and Tundra in with him; he was in horrible pain.

Peaberry moved close and spoke seriously with her. "Jennifer, you are going to have to drive the sled. Nicco and I will run next to you and communicate with Umbra and Tundra who will lead. Luna will stand on the sled with you, guiding you with braking – the team will get you through this."

Jennifer started to tremble; she shook her head. Luna looked at her, "Jen, stop it. You love David and you love all of us – we have to have your help with this sled. Breathe deeply, center yourself, and rise to the occasion. You can do this! NOW!"

Jennifer felt a shift inside herself. The same inner knowing that had guided her to pick up David's bow to save him, prompted her now. "*Yes, I can do this if you help me.*"

They hitched the pulling team and were off through the night. Breathing deeply, listening carefully, and trusting her canine mentors, Jennifer, with Luna standing on her back legs on the sled runners – forepaws on the back of the sled – mushed the sled towards Zumulia's.

* * *

An hour later, the sled pulled into the Keep. Jennifer and Zumulia helped the barely conscious David into the cabin. Peaberry, Buster and Maple pulled mattresses down from the second floor to make an infirmary bed in the middle of the great room where the others had cleared the furniture. Once David was on the bed, they arranged the couches and stuffed chairs around him in a circle. Lily, Rainbow, Stormina, Fuchsia, Rose, Buttercup, Lioness and Gretel jumped up on a couch together to croon healing melodies as Zumulia peeled off David's clothes to examine the wounds. Luna and Tundra sat quietly conferring with Zumulia as she worked.

The six Talking Loaves had grown to the same size as Millet. After hugging their brother they prepared food for the group. They swung on ropes Zumulia had hung over the stove from the rafters, to stir, smell and taste as they worked. They also boiled water on the stove for the compresses that were being applied to the wounds David had sustained from the teeth and claws of the Hissing Cats.

Eventually David was bandaged and resting comfortably; Zumulia had him sip herbal liquids to help with his pain. The dogs took turns singing healing songs. Zumulia gave Jennifer herbs for the trauma and instructed her to sit down and rest. As Jennifer ate a bowl of warm, spicy chili, Llewellyn jumped on the couch next to her and cuddled his compact body next to hers; she curled her arm around him, relaxing as she touched his soft fur.

Luna, Peaberry, Tundra and Zumulia sat near them to make plans. "Jennifer, I know that we would both like to stay, but you have seriously wounded Natab," said Luna.

Jennifer nodded, although she didn't know what that meant; she felt numb. She couldn't think of questions she should ask.

Zumulia sipped on a cup of chamomile and ginger tea. "The crystal is here now, so your mission is over. Nicco, Tundra, Umbra, Angel, Fred, Sweetie, Thomas, Sylvia and Rampart will stay with David and me. You must return to Vermont now. You must leave immediately."

"What? Why? But David . . ." thought Jennifer.

"We sense David will be fine," Luna soothed. "Zumulia and Samuel's dogs will sing to him. The Talking Loaves, with all the extra learning Millet has gotten at Justin's Keep, will help Zumulia make healing food and herbal medicines for him."

"Actually, Jennifer," said Tundra, "Your being here may place this Keep in more danger. It will take the Servers of the Light and Seers time to activate the crystal and its protective energy; until then Tundra, Nicco, Umbra, Angel, Fred, Sweetie, Thomas, Sylvia and I should be able to support David and help Zumulia keep danger at bay. Soon Samuel should be here with the rest of our pack."

Peaberry pushed into the conversation. "Jen, what she is saying is Natab will attack Zumulia's Keep if she knows you are here. You are the first who has ever actually wounded her. Natab serves darkness; she acts through her inflated image of herself, which means she will make stupid decisions, like attacking us in the forest."

Jennifer exhaled. She nodded.

"Luna and I are the pack leaders here, the alphas. That means you are under our care; but you also must obey us. Please get your things, help us into our harnesses, and say a quick goodbye because the storm is growing worse and we have to make it to the portal as soon as possible," said Peaberry, his blue eyes soft with caring.

"Do you want the gold violin and the silver flutes?" asked Zumulia.

Peaberry shook his head. "No, we can't get Jennifer back safely, and the violin and flutes. And we don't have time with this storm to dance and raise energy, nor can we, with David so wounded and the Hissing Cat poison in his body. Natab is wounded, we should not have to worry about her again tonight."

"But we have to go, now," said Luna.

Jennifer helped the dogs back into their harnesses, still wet from the journey from Justin's. With all of the focus on David, making food and herbal medicines, she had not realized that the storm had grown so strong. Zumulia helped her into her snow gear as she hugged Millet and his brothers and sisters.

"*I am going to miss you so much*!" she told Millet as she cuddled him one last time. Then she hugged Samuel's dogs who expressed their respect and love; the large, furry dogs told her that she was in their hearts, and they were wishing her peace and light for her life. She held David's hand for a moment as he lay sleeping.

The dogs said their goodbyes and went through the door out into the snowy night. While Umbra, Nicco, Tundra, Angel, Fred, Sweetie, Thomas, Sylvia and Rampart stayed inside with David and kept an eye on the Talking Loaves, Zumulia helped Jennifer hitch the Vermont gang to the sled. Peaberry took the lead position with Lucky beside him; the others quickly took their places in pairs behind them. The team was ready, despite being tired. Luna again stood on her hind feet on the runners, front paws on the back of the sled, with Jennifer on the runners behind her. Llewellyn jumped into the sled with Jennifer's pack and a bow and quiver of arrows that Zumulia gave them.

With Zumulia's blessing, they were off. The wind came from behind them, which helped their progress. The dogs moved quietly through the blowing snow, all business, with Peaberry giving an occasional intuitive command. Luna and Jennifer rode the runners of the sled as the team pulled them through the forest.

They came out into a large clearing where Peaberry called a rest. The snow had lessened to light flurries; the full moon was filtering light through breaks in the clouds. The dogs stood panting, scooping and melting snow in their muzzles to drink, as Jennifer checked their harnesses and lines for frays and tears. Luna followed beside her giving words of encouragement. Each dog smiled and praised Jennifer for her skill and courage; they took the treats she tossed to them. Peaberry was smiling the biggest grin of all; Jennifer saw where Gretel inherited her smile.

"You are doing well, darlin'," winked Peaberry. "We'll have you back to Vermont in less than fifteen minutes."

"Really?" came a hiss. "Don't bet on it!" Natab appeared directly in front of them, her yellow eyes lit from the evil within her; a bandage wrapped around her back, chest and damaged shoulder. Behind her were six Hissing Cats.

The dog pack started to bark furiously. "Haven't we seen enough of you for one night? It's not like we're datin', darlin'!" growled Peaberry. "Jennifer, unhook us right now. Natab is about to run out of lives."

Luna followed Jennifer down the line as she unhitched the dogs; she ordered Buster, Lioness, Buttercup, Fuchsia, Maple, Flint, Lucky and Bear to form the offense line while Gretel, Peaberry, Stormina, Amos, Lily, Rainbow, Rose and herself formed a ring around Jennifer and Llewellyn to sing and raise protection. Llewellyn hopped out of the sled to join them, bringing Jennifer the bow and quiver of arrows.

Standing in the middle of the circle, Jennifer fitted an arrow to her bow, shooting it over the heads of the two lines of dogs toward one of the Hissing Cats; it went wide, missing by over a foot. Taking a deep breath, she planted her feet and focused, seeing the arrow strike the cat nearest Natab. The arrow flew, hitting it between the eyes; Natab screamed as her cat crumbled to the ground. Thinking of David lying in the bed, near death, Jennifer sent another towards the chest of the cat on the other side of Natab, as the dogs sung a protective shield of light. The arrow struck home and the cat fell over.

Recovering from the surprise, Natab leapt through the light across the eight-foot distance to land on Maple. As he reached behind to bite her, Buster knocked her off and the three went tumbling through the snow. The four remaining Hissing Cats leapt at the frontline of dogs. Fur flew, barks, hisses and screams filled the air.

Peaberry kept the protective singing of the inner circle going. "Dogs, pull back," Luna ordered the pack members when the fighting seemed to be in a lull. The frontline backed away from the cats slowly. All had blood trickling or flowing from shoulders, ears, haunches, or paws. But the Hissing Cats were worse off - two more were dead.

"Who needs to exchange places?" asked Luna.

"No one!" called the frontline dogs. Buster and Maple stood defiantly staring at Natab. Flint, Lucky, Fuchsia, Lioness, Buttercup and Bear stood their ground, watching the three remaining cats, all of whom were in pain; especially Natab.

"Natab, this was a stupid move," called Luna. "How did you think that you and six of your Hissing Cats could defeat us?"

"Issss that what you think? That we're alone?" she hissed.

Jennifer let fly an arrow, which hit the cat directly behind Natab; struck between the eyes the cat was instantly dead. As Natab turned, hissing, Jennifer's next arrow hit the last cat on the side of his turned head; as he crumbled Natab screamed in defiance and disbelief.

Led by Buster and Maple, the dogs advanced on Natab with Lioness and Buttercup in fallback position. Wiggling her squat, powerful, tailless hindquarters, Natab sprung over them, landing in front of Luna and Peaberry. Natab rose, howling over Peaberry's head into Jennifer's face, "Your father'ssss evil issss in your blood! You are mine!"

With their fangs bared, Peaberry and Luna leapt at Natab's throat, rolling into a tumble with her in the snow. Buttercup, Lioness, Bear, Flint, Buster, Maple, Fuchsia and Lucky bit at any exposed cat part they could nip. Jennifer couldn't get a safe shot with her arrow. Over and over they went until Natab, using the claws on her powerful hind feet, caught each dog by the chest and hurled them away.

"I will be back later if you aren't finished sssssooner!" hissed Natab. She turned and ran off into the night.

The dogs gathered around Jennifer. Some were badly bleeding from wounds that the cats' fangs had inflicted. "*What do we do*?" asked Jennifer.

"Who can't run?" asked Peaberry.

Each dog, despite their wounds, answered they could. "Jennifer, hook us back up. We have fifteen minutes to the portal. We have to get you through, NOW!" said Peaberry as he limped towards the gang-line of the sled.

Jennifer looked for her mittens but couldn't find them. With Peaberry and Lucky in lead she started to hook the dogs up. Her hands ached; she could hardly move them after being in the cold so long. When she started to get onto the runners of the sled she saw that Luna was limping badly, the darkness of blood staining most of her white fur.

"Luna, get into the sled with Llewellyn!" Jennifer ordered.

Luna did not argue. She crawled into the sled with her nephew.

Jennifer bent to loosen the sled's snow hook. As she straightened to go she saw flashes and glimmers as the dogs on the line started to scream in pain. The Ice Beings and shadows were upon them.

Jumping off the sled she ran forward with Luna and Llewellyn behind her singing white and rose light of protection around her. The dogs on the line howled and writhed as she loosened them. As they got over the surprise they started to sing with Peaberry's lead. But it was too late, one by one they fell into the snow as the Ice Beings ripped into them with their fangs and the shadows sucked their life force.

As Peaberry fell at her feet, Jennifer turned and grabbed the singing Luna and Llewellyn to her. Taking a breath, she opened her heart and visualized light and love all around them in a protective shield that got brighter and brighter with each breath. She found herself praying, "*Creator – if you exist, please help us. Please help us.*" She spread the light over the whole of the team as she prayed.

The shadows and the Ice Beings started to back off and then rushed away with a whoosh, leaving behind them silence. Luna began to shake violently from the poison of Natab's fangs; her body began to go limp, then she slid from Jennifer's embrace onto Peaberry. Raising her head she said, "Jen, take Llewellyn, stay close to each other. Try to go to the portal; it's directly south of here. Put the protective light around you. Believe in yourself, that you can make it – just go! NOW!" Her white head collapsed into the snow.

Clutching Llewellyn in one arm, Jennifer reached out her hand and shook Luna, then Peaberry. "*Luna? Peaberry?*"

They lay still. "*Luna! Peaberry! Rose! Bear! Flint! Gretel! Rainbow! Lioness! Buster! Buttercup! Rainbow! Amos! Maple! Lily! Stormina! Fuchsia! Lucky! . . .*"

No voices and no intuitive communication answered her. Llewellyn pressed close to her and started to howl in his high, yearling voice. A scream ripped out of Jennifer's chest and throat.

Jennifer shook Luna and Peaberry harder and then bent to listen to each of their chests. They were not breathing. Jennifer's screams and howls from Llewellyn did nothing to revive them.

The air grew still. The snow had stopped and the sky cleared. In the light of the full moon the lifeless bodies of the dogs lay around the clearing amongst the bodies of the Hissing Cats. Jennifer wrapped both arms around Llewellyn and shook; this was worse than any nightmare she had ever had. Even worse than her father's death or the battle at the Portal of Nordon. "*NO! I can't let this happen! Why? WHY?*" There was no answer.

Jennifer took a deep breath. And then another. As she connected with her center she hugged Llewellyn tightly. "Please God, I don't know if you are there. But please God, help us! Help my friends! If you must take someone, then take me!" she said out loud. The first words she had spoken in months.

"Llewellyn, sing and visualize help coming! Please God help them! Please God, help us!" pleaded Jennifer as Llewellyn sang in his high voice.

Thunder sounded to the right of where she knelt with Llewellyn. Then the air appeared to tear vertically. A dog team emerged from the opening. Each dog was three times the size of the largest Solarian dog Jennifer had met, all white, glowing as if lit from within, with gold sparks of energy leaping from their fur, they ran through the air pulling a sled of light. The musher, dressed in white, shimmering clothing, set his sled's snow hook when the team landed on the ground near them. As he walked towards Jennifer and Llewellyn, they could not see his face hidden in the hood of his parka. He knelt down in the snow beside Jennifer, removing his mittens. His hands were both clear and white at the same time.

"Please, please help them! They are my friends!" she pleaded. Llewellyn nodded, sobbing.

When the musher of light touched Jennifer's shoulder peace

flooded through her. Then he placed his hand on Llewellyn's head, stopping his trembling.

Jennifer looked up towards him but could get no glimpse of his face. "Please, please help them! They are dead!" she said.

"They are not dead. It is not their time. Nor yours or Llewellyn's. They are just asleep. See?" His voice was soft and soothing. Moving his hands along Peaberry's body – the leader started to stir. Then he rubbed his hands over Luna and she too began to move.

"They will soon be up. First let's get you into the sled." He took his mittens and placed them on her hands, raw with the cold and snow. Then he gently lifted her, carrying her to the sled. Motioning for Llewellyn to get in beside Jennifer, he covered them with a soft blanket of white that smelled of sunlight, roses and lavender. Gathering Luna first, he placed her next to Jennifer in the sled. Then he picked up Peaberry, placing him on the other side of Llewellyn.

One by one he lovingly went to each dog, laying his hands on them - Rose, Fuchsia, Rainbow, Flint, Lucky, Lioness, Buttercup, Stormina, Gretel, Lily, Maple, Buster, Bear and Amos. As each stirred he gently carried them to the huge sled. Soon all the dogs lay with Jennifer, breathing easily, and holding up their heads; all of their wounds healed. She thought she heard Luna whispering in her ear to trust in goodness. Then the musher came and said, "Peace, all is well." He climbed onto the back of the sled and released his snow hook.

"Hike" he commanded. The great dogs of light soundlessly pulled the sled into the night sky. As the air whispered around them Jennifer closed her eyes.

Chapter Fourteen

Life really begins when you first become aware of yourself in relationship to the larger creation as a whole. As we wake it is hard not to cling to our first experiences of the brilliance and greater magic. We fear going back into the ordinary; we fear we will again be powerless and lethargic. The Wisdom Runner learns to walk with love, courageously, wherever the obligations on our path take us. If we follow the path that we are meant to walk, even when it calls us to the seemingly ordinary, we will find that in the end we have become the person we were meant to be. Thus we pray for courage to go on where we are called, no matter how mundane that might seem at times.

Book of the Wisdom Runners

Jennifer's body felt heavy, as if her arms and legs were made of lead. Lying on her back she tried to open her eyes and sit up. Memories raced in - she had to save the dogs. "Please help us! Please help us! Don't let the dogs die! Help my friends!" she screamed.

Gentle hands pushed against her shoulders, keeping her from rising. "Jennifer, you are safe! It's Aunt Sarah and Uncle Jim! We are right here," came her aunt's voice.

Heart racing, she struggled to get her eyes open and focused.

She was in the small bedroom, under the eaves of her aunt's cabin. Uncle Jim was on one side of the bed and her aunt on the other. Both looked concerned as they tried to restrain her gently.

"Jennifer, you are safe. We are right here!" soothed Sarah.

"Peaberry, Luna… the dogs! Help them… I'm so sorry, I'm so sorry!" Jennifer sobbed and shook. "Llewellyn! Luna! Peaberry! . . . help us! Help the dogs!"

"Sssssshh… Ssssssssh… it's okay. It's okay! Lay still," said Sarah.

"The dogs, the dogs! Help them!" cried Jennifer.

"Jen, listen to me," said Jim. "You are okay. The dogs are okay. You may have had a nasty fall so we don't want you to move just yet. But the dogs are okay."

Jennifer stopped struggling. The panic peaked, then faded a bit. "Peaberry, Luna, Natab and her cats, the light…" She started coughing, then started to choke. Her throat sealed tight.

Sarah gently pressed her shoulders until she sank back against the mound of pillows they had propped behind her. "Jennifer, hon, try to breathe. Try not to struggle. Everything is okay."

She looked from Jim to Sarah and wondered how she had gotten to Vermont. The dogs were dead, all was lost, she was sure of that. And where was Llewellyn? She tried to speak but no words would come.

"See, look here," said Jim as he patted his leg. Luna's white face appeared at the side of the bed. "We weren't allowing her on the bed until you woke because we were afraid she might jostle you. Luna is fine, aren't you?" He stroked the white dog, as Luna rested her head on the bed, her brown eyes watching Jennifer.

"Jen, look here," said her aunt. Peaberry stood on the other side of the bed, his startling blue eyes filled with concern. He moved his nose slowly towards Jennifer's until they were touching.

"Peaberry, be gentle," said Jim. Peaberry drew back slightly.

"Can you see the foot of the bed, Jen?" asked Sarah. Looking down she saw Rainbow, Lily, Gretel, Flint, Lucky, Rose, Bear, Buster, Amos, Lioness, Buttercup, Stormina, Maple and Fuchsia resting their heads on the quilt along the bottom of the bed. Llewellyn came around and rested his cute face next to Luna's, his plumy tail wagging. Jennifer reached out her fingers to touch Luna and Llewellyn.

"Jennifer, they are all here. We found you lying in the snow just outside the cabin door; they were lying close to you, covering you with their heads and bodies to keep you warm. Sarah and I picked you up and carried you into the cabin," said Jim. "We were late getting back from Burlington. Coming up the access road to the farm we drove into this freak snowstorm. Gary, Peter and Dale had been searching for the dogs after they broke out this morning. They were frantic when they couldn't find you, Luna, Peaberry and Llewellyn – when the snow came they panicked."

Suddenly Jennifer remembered the musher and dogs of light that had come when she lay sobbing over the bodies of Peaberry, Luna, and the others. She remembered the sense of peace as he assured her that they were only sleeping. He had placed his mittens on her cold hands and carried her to the sled with Llewellyn; then he woke each dog and put them in the sled till they were all together.

"Jennifer, we can't explain this, but somehow a snowstorm hit the farm. It's July! My four-wheel drive truck hardly made it to the drive; the snow got deeper the closer we got," said Jim.

"We joined the hunt for you. The crew had gotten out the snowmobiles and we searched everywhere. Sarah stayed in the barn with a walky-talky to communicate with us. We thought the dogs would come back to their home in the barn, rather than the cabin," said Jim.

"The guys kept checking in with me. Then I saw a huge light in the direction of the cabin. It flashed bright – and then it was gone. It took me five minutes to get through the deep snow. But there you and the dogs were..." Sarah gently squeezed Jennifer's arm. "I was so relieved."

"It was bizarre because we looked there several times," said Jim. "There were no tracks in or out... it was like the dogs flew you in from somewhere."

"Jen, the phone lines were down. The police and town snow equipment and vehicles are in storage for the summer so they were not able to get in. We got an emergency radio frequency and they put Dr. Carol on it. She said that since we had already moved you into the house and checked you over, finding nothing, we should keep you in bed and watch you," explained Uncle Jim. "In a few hours it will be light and we should be able to get out of here and get you to the hospital."

Sarah left for a few minutes to make warm milk and honey. Together the dogs, Uncle Jim and Aunt Sarah kept Jennifer company for the rest of the night. In spite of their first worries, they finally allowed Llewellyn and Luna to lie on either side of her.

* * *

As the sun came up over the eastern mountain ridge it brought a morning that was clear and bright; it promised a hot Vermont day. The temperature at the farm had returned to seventy degrees during the night and melted the snow off the trees, flowers and bushes. The snow on the ground was rapidly disappearing, allowing Peter, Gary and Dale to go home. Uncle Jim and Aunt Sarah drove Jennifer first to Dr. Carol and then down for a complete evaluation at the Dartmouth-Hitchcock Medical Center. A few days of tests allowed the doctors to release Jennifer with a clean bill of health. However, they advised that she be watched closely for several weeks.

Back at the farm, Jim and Sarah tried to be with Jennifer as much as possible. Sarah slept in a cot in the bedroom under the eaves, with her, as did Peaberry, Luna, Llewellyn and rotating members of the pack. Gary, Peter, Monty and Dale went out walking with her and the dogs, or sat on the porch, thrilling her with stories of dog mushing escapades from their racing days.

Jennifer found herself liking and trusting these gentle, dog-loving people. And she loved being with the dogs - but she missed speaking with Luna, Peaberry, Llewellyn and the pack. Her heart ached to know if David, Millet, Zumulia and the many others were okay. Had everyone in Solaria survived the night that she and the dogs were rescued? Who rescued them? Had Natab, the shadows, and the Ice Beings done horrible damage? These questions played over and over in her mind but no answers.

* * *

Two weeks after Jennifer was released from the hospital, her Uncle Jim and Aunt Sarah got a call from their lawyers in Burlington. Jennifer's stepmother had brought a suit with the Family court alleging that Jennifer was being intentionally neglected and abused; Toni claimed it was abuse that had landed Jennifer in the hospital. Over breakfast, her uncle and aunt assured her that the local chief of police was giving a deposition testifying to the freak storm and apparent accident: Monty, Gary, Peter and Dale were making formal statements, too.

"Listen, Jen, try not to worry. The statements and character references will put the judge in Los Angeles at ease. It is a formality. Our lawyers say they have word from the caseworker that the judge is willing to let you stay with us for the school year. They believe your stepmother is making a false accusation simply to cause trouble," said Jim.

Sarah took a sip of her coffee. "The courts move very slowly. Our lawyers feel it may be two years before an actual custody hearing will come up because your stepmother still has not been cleared of suspicion in your father's death. You will be fourteen. The court systems put a lot of weight on where you want to live when you are that old. But until that time… our lawyers expect legal trouble from her and many false accusations. But the bottom line is that you should not worry about this."

Jim cleared his throat and looked at Sarah. She nodded. "Jennifer, we think Toni has done this because while we were in Burlington on the day of your accident, we had our lawyers file a legal motion demanding that Grace be examined by a vet for possible mistreatment. We said that since Grace's actual ownership was in question, and Toni has a history of violence, we were concerned for her safety."

Jennifer felt her stomach clutch. Sarah placed her hand on hers. "Please try not to worry. Two vets examined her and felt that she was showing pain, which they thought was from a possible kick or fall."

Jennifer's tears started to flow. Luna got up and came close. *"Luna, I wish they could hear me."*

She looked into Sarah's eyes, then looked down as she stroked Luna's head.

"Jen, with the two reports a judge ordered that Grace be taken from Toni. He agreed to place her in a safe home, with a well-trusted corgi breeder in Los Angeles, until something is worked out so we can have her brought here."

Jennifer wiped her eyes. *"Grace, I wish you could hear me. Try to be brave!"* she thought.

Uncle Jim continued. "We talked to the woman who has her now. She seems very nice, caring and knowledgeable. She is part of a good group of people called the Corgi Nation. They are going to try to figure out who Grace's breeder is, so that we can have the original paperwork to find out who indeed owns her."

Sarah squeezed her hand. "Jen, the speech doctor who examined you at the hospital is also submitting a report that she feels you need Grace here to help you recover your ability to speak and more of your memory. We feel that given the circumstances of the police needing to question you to help find who is responsible for your father's death – Toni or someone else - the judge may agree."

Jennifer tried to breathe deep as she took a tissue from her pocket. She nodded her head, trying to let them know she was thankful.

Jim got up from the table and stretched. "Look, we have to go. My housekeeper, Mary, has come in to be here with you and the dogs until we all get back."

Jim eyed Luna. "Luna, I want you to please stay here while we are gone. No adventures!" He was serious but he was also playing "stern" with her. He turned to see if Jennifer was watching and then shook his finger as he stifled a laugh. "Do you understand, LUNA?" She turned her white head away from him as if she saw something interesting outside the window.

Uncle Jim and Aunt Sarah left with Monty, Dale, Gary and Peter. Mary stood with Jennifer and Luna watching the truck go down the long, tree-lined drive. When they disappeared from view, Mary suggested they sit at a picnic table where they could see the four dog yards. Peaberry was behind the closest fence watching them; Jennifer swore that he nodded and then winked at her with his bright-blue, right eye.

Suddenly there was pandemonium. The canine gang started barking, howling and singing at once. Around the corner of the barn the Lion Brothers came charging at Mary, Luna and Jennifer; they had dug out from the yearling pen. As Simba, Leonard, Aslan, Mufasa and Llewellyn ran by in an imitation of a cavalry stampede, Jennifer thought she heard Flint sound his, "Ta-da-da-da! Charge!" imitation of Uncle Jim's ditty, from the place he stood watching next to Peaberry.

Mary panicked, "You dogs, come back here!" The Lion Brothers made a wide arch and passed by again. This time Jennifer knew that Llewellyn was smiling directly at her. Mary gave chase, which seemed exactly what they wanted. With her grey hair twisting out of the bun that held it, she ran after them shouting, "You bad puppies! Come back here!"

Jennifer turned to see Luna scooting across the lawn in the direction of the pond. With her camera held by a strap around her neck, Jennifer ran after her. They quickly passed by the pond and into the woods beyond. Finding the old, rutted road they ran down the steep hill that led to the bridge. Luna disappeared into the underbrush as Jennifer slid down the path that led to the river. Catching up to Luna, the two stepped into the water and made their way to the tunnel under the bridge.

Emerging from the darkness of the tunnel Luna hopped out onto the sandbank, shook off the water and turned towards Jennifer. She rushed to her, falling to her knees, hugging the wet, white dog. "*Can you talk, can you talk?*"

"Of course I can," said Luna.

"I've missed you, I've missed you," Jennifer started to cry.

"Jen, I know. But we have been right by each other's side except for when they put you in the hospital – and even then the doctors and staff let me visit," soothed Luna.

"It's not the same," sobbed Jennifer. *"And what about David, Millet, Zumulia, and…"*

"Dry your eyes. We have to be quick because we don't have much time here," said Luna.

They followed the trail up its steep incline until it came out in the first field above the riverbed. In the distance stood David, with Millet in his arms. Samuel, beads and trinkets in his braided hair, waved as he held the handle of a small wagon filled with Millet's six brothers and sisters. Zumulia held her arms open, beckoning them. Surrounding the group were the pack of Samuel's black, white and black, and white dogs who jumped up, bounding to them as they approached. Jennifer ran until she could throw herself into Zumulia's outstretched arms.

"Jen, Jen, Jen, it is so good to see you again," said Zumulia softly. "I have to let you go as that camera hurts!" Jennifer had forgotten the camera around her neck in the dash off the farm.

"*Sorry,*" she thought.

"I missed you, we all did. We knew you all got safely back to Vermont, and that you were back from the hospital because Flint and Lucky brought us news," said Zumulia.

"*David?*" asked Jennifer. She tuned to look at him.

"I'm all healed! You were very courageous when you shot an arrow into Natab, killed two of her cats, and drove the sled to my grandmother's. Thank you," said David. "And Lucky and Flint told us all about how you killed more of the Hissing Cats – you are really brave and are learning to be an incredible shot with the bow."

"Thank you. I am so glad that you are okay," thought Jennifer.

"I think that the bards will be singing tales of this adventure," laughed Samuel. "We have much to be thankful for."

Jennifer looked at Nicco, Umbra, Tundra and the others. *"I could not have done my part by myself – the dogs are the ones to thank,"* thought Jennifer. *"And how are Tuvalla, Justin Valor, Dohanos, Kaarina, Brigitte, and all the Seers and Wisdom Runners at Justin's Keep?"*

"All safe," said Zumulia. "For now. Justin and Dohanos have healed well. The crystals you and the gang helped free from the Portal of Nordon have opened safe communication between our Keeps and the Courts of the Wisdom Runners and Seers in the east; the Keepers of the Ovens and Orchards are safe, as are the sixty-three other Talking Loaves. Our hope is that with the Servers of the Light will be able to work with the Seers and Wisdom Runners to help open passages to the West. In your time here you have demonstrated love, courage, and devotion, which are important keys to being a Wisdom Runner and Seer. They are also the keys to being a good person."

Jennifer gathered Millet into her arms and kissed him. His brothers and sisters were jumping up and down, begging to be held as well. She bent to them and kissed each in turn.

"*Now what will we be doing for Solaria*?" asked Jennifer. She was so glad to be back with her friends.

Samuel looked at Zumulia and then at Luna. "Why don't we take a few moments to sit under the tree, there?" The group of dogs, humans and Talking Loaves walked to the nearby maple tree and sat in its shade. Nicco and Tundra snuggled close on each side of Jennifer as the Talking Loaves and Millet cuddled on her lap.

Samuel smiled his wide grin, gold tooth glowing softly amidst the white of his teeth in his dark face. "We would like you to consider training as a Wisdom Runner and a Seer. But for now you must return to Vermont."

Zumulia continued, "You were born on Earth and still have ties there. You have certain things that you are meant to accomplish before you can come back here."

Jennifer looked at both of them and then to David who bit his lip and looked away. "*What things? I don't understand . . .*"

"Sometimes we don't understand what life has called us to do. Right now you need to continue the learning on Earth that you were meant to do there," said Samuel.

"Jennifer, our actions have brought some healing to Solaria and to the Earth. But we tipped the balance of what we can do right now. For this reason you have only this short time to visit with us and then you must go back for approximately a year of Earth time," Zumulia said quietly.

"But why? Can't Luna and I come through the portal to be here with you AND do whatever I am supposed to do on Earth?" asked Jennifer.

"Jen, there is little time. I know that it doesn't make sense. You are on a journey to find the special path of your life – for your heart, soul and spirit," said Samuel.

"For now you must go back to Earth. The portal will be closed to you," said Zumulia.

"But what if my stepmother gets the court to put me with another family, or send me to a private school in California, away from my aunt, uncle, Luna and the dogs in Vermont? How will I find you?" Tears started to flow down Jennifer's cheeks as she cuddled Millet and the Talking Loaves in her arms.

"Jennifer, we will always be watching for you. We cannot predict the future. Do the breathing exercises that you learned here, study well at school, keep your mind on good thoughts, and visualize love and healing for all. Trust if you need us we will find you. Continue to grow as a beacon of light," said Samuel.

"But what if there is trouble here and you need me?" asked Jennifer.

"You must have faith that we will find you," said Samuel. "Trust in goodness and truth winning out is one of the basics of the Wisdom Runner philosophy."

"Let's put that camera of yours to some good use," suggested Zumulia as she stood up. "You will have some photos to remind you that Solaria is real and you have many friends who love you."

Zumulia and Samuel led the group in posing for individual, small group, and large group photos. Jennifer had to smile at the clowning her dear friends managed. Afterwards they shared hugs. There were many murmurs of affection and encouragement from canines, humans and Talking Loaves.

Finally, Zumulia stood up. "Go, dear friends! Take our 'Hail' to Peaberry and the gang. Know that all of you are in our hearts."

"Okay, I will go. But first… who saved us? Who saved the dogs and me? There were dogs and a man that seemed like they were made of white light – who were they?" asked Jennifer.

Luna, Samuel and Zumulia looked at her. The dogs lifted their heads and sang joyfully. When they stopped, Samuel said, "Some would say it was the angels, come in the forms of dogs, and God himself; others that it was angels and the archangel, Raphael, the angel of the Wisdom Runners. We just say "The Musher" because we don't know who he is. He or others come when it is not our time to go on to the light. We don't ask questions, we just give our thanks."

He looked at her steadily, considering whether to explain further, then shook his head. "Now go, it is time. You are in our hearts!" said Samuel. Nicco, Tundra, Rampart, Alex, Rock, Buck, Libby, Jose, Hannah, Topi, Thorn, Lawrence, Brazil, Coal, Hermi, Angel, Fred, Sweetie, Thomas, Sylvia, Calli, Umbra, Sookie, Daniel, Honey and Bunny howled a cheer into the air. Millet tearfully hugged her.

David joined Jennifer on the path crossing the field. Nicco, Tundra and Luna trailed a short distance behind. "You have become a good friend. I will keep you in my thoughts." The breeze tugged gently at his long hair.

"I have never in my life had such good friends. Now I cannot believe that you and Solaria will be gone from my life . . ." thought Jennifer.

David handed her a slingshot. "Not gone - we are in your heart.

Take this home with you and practice. Remember what I taught you and when you next return we can have a contest!"

He stopped her for a moment. The small, green-eyed, raven-haired girl looked up into the blue eyes of the blond, longhaired youth. Suddenly her right arm shot up into the air in the sign of, "Yes!" He laughed, saluted and turned back towards the others. At the edge of the woods, Jennifer turned to see the group waving in the distance.

Nicco and Tundra stood on the top of the trail as Luna and Jennifer descended towards the river. "Hey, Jen!" called Nicco. She stopped and looked up at him; she knew she would miss his startling blue eyes in his massive, black, furry face. "Play some MC Hammer when you miss us! Next time you come to Solaria we'll teach you some dance moves!"

Piebald Tundra rolled her blue and brown eyes, "Classical music is much better for your maturing brain and school studies!" They both woofed, turned, and were gone.

Jennifer sobbed as she followed Luna. On the sand bar by the river's edge she fell on her knees shaking. "*I can't do this! I can't do this! I can't leave.*"

Luna turned and came to Jennifer. Jennifer threw her arms around her friend. "*Please, let's stay here*," she pleaded.

"Jen, there are times in life when we must do what is right whether we think we can or not. We may not understand why, but we do what we know is right. You did that in Solaria and now you can do this here and now. Someday you will look back at this day, and your time here, and you will understand that leaving now, to go on with your life on Earth, was necessary so that you can become who you are meant to be." Luna nuzzled Jennifer's cheek.

"But I'm leaving my friends, and I can't stand not being able to speak with you, Peaberry, Llewellyn and the other dogs. I need your advice. I need your guidance and wisdom. How am I supposed to grow up if I can't have you helping me?" sobbed Jennifer.

"Jen, remember this: whether I can speak out loud or not, and whether I understand you completely or not on Earth - I love you.

Don't ever forget that. I love you." Jennifer gripped her tighter, the tears splashing down her face. "Jen, talking or not, we dogs are always there for you."

"Come on now… you must be brave. We will have good times together no matter what, and you will have a good year," said Luna, starting to pull away. "I expect you to show courage, after all, you are a Wisdom Runner apprentice if you choose to be. Now, come on."

Luna walked into the water downstream. Jennifer wiped her eyes and cheeks with her sleeve and followed. By the time they were on the other side of the portal and up on the road her tears had almost stopped.

Just then the Lion Brothers came charging down the old, rutted road. Uncle Jim's housekeeper, Mary, pursued them on a four-wheeled ATV. The yearling dogs smiled from ear to ear as the woman drove maniacally after them, her grey hair blowing around her face like a banshee.

"You brats come back here! Oh, Jennifer, you caught Luna, get her back to the barn! Come back here, you hooligans!" They passed in a blur.

At the pond Jennifer and Luna found that Peaberry, Buster, Lioness, Rose, Rainbow, Lily, Flint, Lucky, Bear, Fuchsia, Buttercup, Gretel, Amos, Stormina and Maple had also escaped and were having a leisurely swim. Seeing Luna and Jennifer they left the water, shook and came to sit in front of Jennifer. She bent to them, trying to fight back the tears that wanted to flow again.

Peaberry pressed his nose against hers, then winked. When he did it again she knew she had not imagined it. Maple, gentlemanly and refined, lifted his white, socked paw and placed it on her arm. Although their voices were faint, she swore she heard them in her mind:

Rose, *"We are right here with you, cheer up!"*

Lily, *"We can still play and have fun!"*

Rainbow, *"I love you! Each time you hear me sing for you, remember that!"*

Maple, *"I say there, we do love you! Talking isn't everything!"*

Stormina, *"Luna and I will take you for lots of walks and we will sit with you when you are doing schoolwork."*

Fuchsia, *"We'll do lots of mushing here!"*

Buster, *"I'll hug with you anytime you want!"*

Gretel bared her teeth in a grin, *"I will help you practice smiling!"*

Bear, *"You can throw a ball with me."*

Peaberry, *"Darlin,' I will always love you! Make sure you get Jim to play our favorite Charlie Daniels tunes. We can still have a good time."* He winked his ice-blue eye again.

The rest sat quietly, blinking their eyes, and wagging their tails. Then, as a group, they placed their noses on her face as she reached her arms wide to them. After giving each wet dog a hug, Jennifer rose. With Luna by her side, and the pack surrounding, they walked up the hill to the barn to wait for the Lion Brothers to bring Mary home from their escapade.

* * *

The End of Book One

Luna Tales

Book One
The Wisdom Runners
Personages, Places, Terminology

Personages

On Earth:

Jennifer	Age 12. Has grown up in Los Angeles. Her birth mother died when she was nine months old.
Toni	Jennifer's stepmother. Age 52, she lives in Los Angeles.
Saul	Jennifer's father. He was murdered at the age of 49.
Popsi	Jennifer's paternal grandfather, age 91.
Jennifer's mother	We don't know her name or identity. Saul never told his siblings who she was. They were married in Mexico. Allegedly she became pregnant with Jennifer immediately, and died shortly after Jennifer was born.
Grace Corgi	Jennifer's Pembroke Welsh Corgi – her best friend.

In Vermont:

Luna	White ¾ Siberian husky. In Solaria she is a well-known Wisdom Runner.
Sarah	Jennifer's aunt, a retired professor of sociology. Age 56, she writes novels and lectures.
Jim	Jennifer's uncle. Age 54, he is an international champion sled dog racer who keeps a kennel of free-range, un-chained Alaskan husky sled dogs, The UN-Chained Gang.
Peter, Dale and Gary	Employees at Uncle Jim's sled dog center. They drive dog teams and teach the public about dog sledding, animal welfare, and preserving the environment.
Henriette and Lucy	ducks
Hawk and Eagle	chickens

Alaskan huskies in Vermont at the sled dog center:

Sled dogs in Vermont, they are Wisdom Runners in Solaria -

Luna, Peaberry, Flint, Lily, Lioness, Buttercup, Lucky, Fuchsia, Bear, Stormina, Maple, Gretel, Barney, Amos, Rose, Rainbow, Lily, Buster and the Lion Brother Pups - Leonard, Simba, Mufasa, Aslan, Llewellyn

In Solaria:

Solaria	A world on a plane of existence higher than the one where the planet Earth, and its universe, are located. There are many portals to Solaria from the Earth; one is in Vermont on Jim's farm and sled dog center.
Zumulia	A wise, older Seer running a Keep near a portal from Earth to Solaria. David's grandmother.

David	He is 14. He is Zumulia's grandson. His parents were both Wisdom Runners and Seers who died on a mission defending Solaria when he was six.
Tumilia	David's deceased mother. She was a wise Seer and Wisdom Runner.
Zarcourt	David's deceased father. He was a famous Wisdom Runner and Seer.
Millet	A young Talking Loaf. Talking Loaves are baked by the Keepers of The Ovens. They hold knowledge of how to grow, find, and prepare meals, herbal medicinals, and healing drinks.
Glacier	Luna's brother who left Earth to live with Samuel and his dog pack.
Samuel	Human Wisdom Runner who lives at the Lake of Sleoden. He was born on Earth, but now lives in Solaria.

Canine Wisdom Runners who live at the Lake of Sleoden with Samuel:

Nicco	A black dog, canine Wisdom Runner. He is a wise sled dog leader.
Tundra	A black and white dog, canine Wisdom Runner. She is a wise sled dog leader and healer.

Other canine Wisdom Runners who live with Samuel -

Rampart, Alex, Rock, Buck, Libby, Jose, Hannah, Topi, Thorn, Lawrence, Brazil, Coal, Hermi, Angel, Fred, Sweetie, Thomas, Sylvia, Calli, Umbra, Sookie, Daniel, Honey, Bunny

The Keep of Justin Valor

The Keep	This is one of the main centers of healing work in the land of Solaria. Behind its protective, gated walls lies a town that is home to canine, equine and human Seers and Wisdom Runners who are masters at healing and producing arts, crafts, sleds and weaponry in the many workshops of the Keep. They are renown in Solaria for their specialized work with gold, silver, gemstones, weaving, swords, tools, musical instruments, baked goods, herbal medicines and potions. There are many training grounds, including a year-round course for dog sledding. The mountain that shelters the Keep holds caves of dreaming, visioning, healing and protection.
Justin Valor	A Master Seer, Wisdom Runner, and adept. Many in Solaria say that he will be King of Solaria when King Saul dies.
Tuvalla Seer	Daughter of Justin Valor. A Master Seer and healer, she is in charge of The Cave of The Dreaming Children.
Lacino	Seer who is an aide for Justin Valor.
Kaarina	Seer working with Tuvalla Seer.
Brigitte	Seer working with Tuvalla Seer.
Donal and Michael	Seers working with Tuvalla Seer.

Equine Wisdom Runners at Justin Valor's Keep -

Sooka	An equine Wisdom Runner. She is a special friend to Justin Valor.
Rainia	Sooka's mother who has died. A Wisdom Runner.
Spelia	Sooka's father. He is on a mission to the west and has not returned because of the veil of darkness.

Canine Wisdom Runners of Justin Valor's Keep -

The dogs that went with Contalia and Dohanos to the conference of the Servers of Light:

Denali, Tonka, Nike, Jed, Kelsey, Ben, Hunter, William, Dollar, Lightfoot, Melody, Franco, Tunisia, Presley, Stanley, Moore, Charles, Chaucer, Vance, Reglio, Snort, Pike, Lulu, Nine

Canine Wisdom Runners currently at Justin Valor's Keep –

Betty, Cocoa, Elvis, Cash, Creflo, Taffy, Stanley, Price, Kenneth, Gloria, Robinson, Beth, Lance, Bandit

Court of the Wisdom Runners	The governing body of the Wisdom Runners. It convenes in the east in the city of Tacha.
Riana	She is a human Seer and Wisdom Runner, high up in the Court.
Teelee	A canine Wisdom Runner; Master of the court.
Contalia and Dohanos	Human Wisdom Runners and Seers. They left Solaria fourteen months ago, through the Portal of Nordon, to go to a conference in a parallel reality called by Servers of Light. They are high up in the court of the Wisdom Runners.
Natab	Female leader of a group of Hissing Cats that now serve the darkness.
Hissing Cats	Large, cat-like creatures. The band we meet in Book One have gone over to serve the darkness. Natab is their leader.
Goony Birds	Giant, very colorful birds that have great power of intuition, vision and healing. They are able to travel through many planes of existence. King Gifford is their wise leader; Prince Bartholomew is one of his sons.
King Gifford	King of the Goony Birds.

King Saul	Current, aging King of Solaria. His court meets in the capital city of Tacha, in the east. There are rumors that members of his court can no longer be trusted as they are corrupt.

Geography and Places

Lake of Sleoden	Near Zumulia's Keep where Samuel and his Wisdom Runner dogs live.
Zumulia's Keep	Located in Solaria near the portal that connects it to Vermont.
Cave at the Plain Vendona	Located in the cliffs of the southern edge of the Plain of Vendona. It is a safe place to send distance, intuitive communication.
Plain of Vendona	Huge plain, running east and west, south of the Nordana Mountain range. It is north of Zumulia's Keep.
Wisdom Cave Of Dreams	At Justin Valor's Keep. This is a cave that large groups can safely send intuitive, distance communication
Cave of the Dreaming Children	At Justin Valor's Keep. Tuvalla Seer is the Master Seer in charge of the healing and prayer work done in the cave by the Seers. Children who are abused, sick, traumatized and/or grieving the loss of loved ones - who do not have the support of loving adults and family - are prayed for by the Seers working in this healing cave.
Nordana Mountains of Verdona	A range of mountains north of the Plain Justin Valor's Keep is located in this range.
Portal of Nordon	Located in the far north of the Nordana Mountain range. It is a door to many higher planes of existence as well as parallel realities.
Swinburg Trail	An underground trail, originating under the Lake of Sleoden

Tacha	The name of the capital city and the province of Tacha. It lies far to the east, on the Plain of Vendona. King Saul has his court there and the Courts of the Wisdom Runners and Seers meet there.
Amethyst Cave	One of the healing caves accessed through Justin Valor's Keep.

Dictionary and Terminology

Hail	A formal greeting used by the Wisdom Runners and Seers in Solaria for members of their Orders.
Keep	A farm or town in Solaria that provides an outpost for members of the Order of Seers or the Order of Wisdom Runners
Glow Weed	Provides light without heat or fumes
Wisdom Runners	Highly trained dogs, horses and humans who dedicate their lives to peace, love, harmony, healing and balance in Solaria and beyond when the balance of order is threatened by trouble in Solaria and other parallel realities. Wisdom Runners go through years of specialized training to fight darkness and evil. All species are equal in the Order of the Wisdom Runners.
Seers	These dogs, horses and humans have special abilities in visioning, communicating at a distance, dreaming, healing, working with crystals, herbs, and plants. They train for many years and are dedicated to helping all beings find their individual gifts and become the best that they can be.
Servers of Light	They live in a parallel reality in a land of light and snow, on a higher plane of existence than Solaria is located in.

Alaskan huskies	A mixed northern breed of dog that is used primarily for dog sled racing. Dog mushers breed them according to their own preferences for size, coat length, and speed. They all have Siberian husky somewhere in their genetics, but are not standardized so they can range from 35 pounds to over 85 pounds. Their fur varies from long to quite short, like a greyhound's; they come in a multitude of colors and markings. Like their Siberian relatives, they can have blue or brown eyes, or one of each. Often used for sprint racing, they are also used in the Iditarod and other distance, endurance races.
Siberian husky	A strong, durable, northern breed of dog developed by the Siberian people that helped them live in a snowy climate. They are known for going on adventures by themselves if not watched carefully.
Alaskan Malamute	A large breed of dog that was developed by the Inuit and other natives of North America for their life in the rugged Arctic. The Malamute lived with their families, providing warmth and comfort; they also carried belongings, game, and made northern life possible for their human companions. They are bigger, with more massive heads, than the Siberian husky.
Solarian Malamute	The Solarian Malamute is a fantasy breed. The color patterns they have exist only in Solaria and are not the traditional color patterns of the Alaskan Malamute.

Common commands for a dog team:

Hike!:	Get moving ("Mush" is sometimes, but rarely used).
Kissing or tongue clicking sound:	Speed up, faster.
Gee!:	Turn to the right.
Haw!:	Turn to the left.
Easy!:	Slow down.
Whoa!:	Stop.
On By!:	Pass another team or other distraction.

Books are a long time coming. Each one is based on an accumulation of all the experiences of an author's life. It's a daunting task to try to thank everyone for all that they have done to support and contribute to bringing this work to birth. I can only try and hope that those that I have missed will forgive me!

A huge thank you to my wonderful story editor, Tanya Sousa. An incredible author in her own right, a school guidance counselor of many years, a lover of nature and animals – I could not have hoped for a better editor! She understands all of my autistic quirks and flights of imagination – helping me to ground areas of fantasy and fairy tale into words that allow a reader to see them too. She is the most patient soul! Please find and read her wonderful novel, The Starling God, and her many children's books!

And thank you to my line editor, Tova Bode Saxe! You bravely took on the line editing of an autistic and dyslexic – with humor! This book would not be in the world without you!

Karen Becker DVM – for your kind support of The Luna Tales, but more for being the wonderful doctor to animals that you are. You share the important information that we humans need to care for our loved family members. Integrative veterinarian medicine, good sense and natural breed and species specific care and diet are so important. I hope that many here will go to your website and subscribe to your excellent, free newsletter! Keep giving voice to our wonderful co-species – co-sentients!

Mikaela Jones – A Little Book Of Light – your constant smiles, good insights, humor, verve, love of animals, reading suggestions and your wonderful book! Thanks for being my friend! I urge all to go to Amazon and buy the Little Book of Light. It is the perfect inspiration and has a place on everyone's bedside table!

Barb Meyer – fellow Quaker! The humor, insights and inspiration that you share with the world is so very important. Thank you for helping with the journey and to Teg and Riley, too!

Derek Murphy – for your incredible cover design. You captured the flight from the false, up-side-down reality of Hollywood, to freedom in Vermont and Solaria, as well as Luna's indomitable spirit in helping children, teens and adults to find the light, goodness and joy within them. Thank you for being so patient.

Angela Robey of Angela Robey Fine Art and Silver Moon Ranch – thank you for your belief, good humor, great dialogue and the extraordinary painting of Luna's pond at Eden ETHICAL Dog Sledding. Your art work is so inspirational! And for the fine clean up line editing for the final edition! Also, Kevin Greif – for intelligent conversation and insight. And to both of you for being fellow travelers on this Asperger's Autism life journey. Special thanks to "Inca-dog" – gone too soon, Spock, a special feline, and the goats – Starla, Comet, Rocket, Bella, Bianca, and Rocket Man!!

Joyce Jones – my reader and friend! You have helped me work on environmental causes, read every word and change this book has gone through, have believed in the work my brother and the UN-Chained Gang do, and saved your pennies to come and visit several times. Thank you for your dash and wacky sense of humor, but most of all for your support and deep love of animals.

Grace and Vickie Ross – Grace thank you for agreeing to be a character in this book to be the comfort to Jennifer! And to Vickie for being a good friend on the road of life. Your humor, support and love of nature and your nature photography are so inspirational!

Tammy Perrott – for your wonderful support over the years to Musher Jim Blair and the UN-Chained Gang, Rainbow, and your canine family! And for all the work you do in foster and rescue for Pitties. You are a big-hearted gem!

J.J. Pumpernickel Adams and Midge – for the humor and support you have given to me, personally, the UN-Chained Gang, and so many in life and on Facebook. And the valiant effort of reading this while hiking the Appalachian Trail and for all that you do for all canines, especially the war and service dogs. And thank you to Grammy, too!

Val Thomas – for your belief in this book, but more, as my friend of decades, amazing and extraordinary in all that you have done and shared with so many humans and animals. Thank you for all of your support and your inspiration through the ups and downs of life. And of course – to Fred, Lance and the feathered friends gone on, Sidney and Bandit.

Brian Sullivan – for being such a steady influence and support to my sister, Hilary. And to my nephew and nieces, and your children. Stay the good people that you are and know that your mother/ grandmother, Hilary, loves you so much, and is proud of you!

R.G. Shnurr, Ph.D. – for your professional guidance and aid with being an adult living with autism.

Sandie Hartley, of Hartley Associations. Wonderful friend, inspiring and encouraging friend, with great insights for this book and life. Thank you for caring so much about animals, the planet and humanity! You are a gift to South Africa and the world!

Liz Maudlin – for your insight, heart to heart sharing, belief in this book and reading along! Your incredible photography, and the inspiration of your corgi pals, Fred and Empress Miss Lily, gone on, but always remembered; and now the wonderful Gus and Bruiser.

Deb Brandenburg – gone too soon! The good friendship, daily phone calls and check-ins, wisdom, trust, and support for The UN-Chained Gang, Musher Jim Blair, and I will always be a treasure in my heart. Barney Boots was one of my first FB friends and a daily dose of inspiration and laughter. Then the farmer, Min, with his piggle wiggles and steers that shared such great smiles. Your goodness lives in my heart!

Mabel Beachy Simpson – for your wonderful humor and understanding, and inspirational fortitude during very hard times. Thank you for being the favorite serving wench to Sir Thor of Bun Bun – "Bunny," Maxwell, and Matilda.

Michele Tripp and your BOYZ – Sunny, Charles, and Blue!!!!!

And now, your gal, Callie! You are one wise, tough lady, and my hero!!!

Sue Sternberg and Leslie Burgard DeFusco – incredible trainers, educators and good friends and believers in my brother, Musher Jim Blair, and The UN-Chained Gang!

Karen Stuck Mortensen – you are one strong, smart and intelligent woman who really understands the way of the world and what we need to do in our hearts.

Priscill Anne Alvik, and Bella – for caring, humor, silliness, and simply, being you!

Cheryl Janecky and Miss Parrot – your dedicated posting of the truth, spreading important information on a wide spectrum of topics and supporting the best for humans, animals and planet is inspiring!

Mim Kurman – wherever you are! Always in my heart!

Zen Walker – for being there during all the ups and downs of life from 2004 onward. Sending me fractals and encouragement, reading each chapter, loving it and encouraging me to be brave and keep going! A fellow Aspie (person with Asperger's Autism) – you have been the soul of Zen and the spirit of goodness. Thank you.

Genie and Jim MacKellar at the East Craftsbury Presbyterian Church – your early review of the book for being within Christian standards was so important. Thank you for your personal support and your belief in the work that my brother, Musher Jim Blair and the UN-Chained Gang at Eden Ethical Dog Sledding are doing. And thank you for your work with Guide Dogs – so important!

Brigitte Ledermann– for your belief and great support, great suggestions and Swiss precise line editing, wonderful meditations and conversations in your superb gardens and special retreat you so lovingly created. And thanks to Benny, Kiri, and Peter, too!

John and Doris Calder – for all your support, hospitality, Quaker goodness and being such a good friend to Charles Dickens. It is so good to know that Charles rests on your beautiful hill!!

Nancy McCharles and Annie – for your support and good nurturing!

Deb Kantor – friend, soul of goodness and a role model of how to travel through the rough seas of life. Kathy and Gary Duffy and their canine – good people, Maggie, Lacie and Abby – thank you for all your help and friendship. Carol and Dale Bray – for being patient friends, full of Christian charity and doing so much for community and the world – and your gardens! You are inspirations! Jackie and Allen Strait – for being you! And Gussie – without whose eggs Ralph and I would starve!!! John Stewart, Ph.D. – for who you are and your continued prayers.

My classmates from grade and high school – for fun, jokes, insights and support. Chou Chou Merrill (gone too soon, I miss your smiles!), Bob Caples, Paula Coykendall, Peter Lang, Anthony Dohanos, Laurie Hocomb Bullock, Susan Curtis Ifergan, Pat Saviano, Ana Pedersen Unum, Bill Sims, Fred Reynolds, Bobby Jackson, Peter Morris, Geoff Reed, Joanne Romano-Csonka, Jane Lavaty Cooke, Ian Ablitt, Mark Smollin, Prill Boyle, Eric Buchroeder, and the many others – you know who you are!!!!

Mary P Gai – for your support and goodness. You are a real hero in all that you do that few know.

Paul Vaast – thanks for the good humor and sharing Sadie!

Pat Filson Boyd – for your humor, patience, good sense, prayer and Christian goodness!

Don and Sue Torrey – Thank you for loving sled dogs and giving them such an incredible home. Sue – your boyfriend, Leonard the Champion Lead Dog, sends you a big hug and kiss!

David Rankin – for the good times, wackiness and your Scottish humor over the years! Let's raise a toast to Ian! And Ian's "little Sis," Anne McNamee-Oxley!

Carol Chandler – so many paths the same! Joanne Lewis West – wise fellow traveler on the path!

Chris Francese – brave friend! Keep going!

Ron Friedson for all you do. A special shout out to Sam

Friedson, now in Heaven. Eileen McManus Siegfried, thank-you for your friendship, and sending a toast to your wonderful father, Ed McManus; I will always thank him for his kindness to War Hand and I.

Nancy Hammet – for your light and wacky humor! You are a dancing Diva! We still need to do the book on Women Washing Dishes with Wolves!

Joan Lieberman – such Goodness in your heart! Keep walking your path! I will always remember your boy, Hendrix!

Carol Buckly of the Elephant Sanctuary and Elephant Aid International – https://www.facebook.com/elephantaidinternational/app/190322544333196/ – you are an inspiration and a true Wisdom Runner. And to Tara – for the many times you have niggled me during meditation. You are amazing!

Angel, Fred, Sweetie, Buttercup, Honey, Bunny, Daniel, Thomas, Sylvia, the finches, and the Keets – my feathered family that has brought so much to my life! AND you helped to bring King Gifford and his flock of Gooney Birds into being!

Carolyn Zoneilo and Stephen Morrissey – poets, inspiration and friends through some of the darkest of times. Thank you.

Adelita Chirino and Jim Cookman – for your priceless wacky humor, many fun times and great support.

Kaarina Towler – for your wonderful companionship, humor and special friendship. Despite the odds and the horrors, your life has given so much good to so many! And to Mr. Chase, the Irish Wolfhound, Blackie and Ginger – you are very special. I will always remember your kindness.

Annette Smith – you are one of the most inspirational, patient and caring people I know. You have stood with courage on the road of justice. You have protected Vermont and its people despite the corrupt interests that want to greedily dismantle all that Vermont has protected for generations. Vermonter of The Year!

Rob Pforzheimer – for your long term caring and bringing out the truth to so many. Shirley and Don Nelson – for your love of nature and enduring spirit in the face of lies, ruin and avarice. You are my heroes! Luke Snelling, Steve Wright, Robbin and Steve Clark, Kevin McGrath, Bonnie and Milo, Denise and Joan Liddy, Daphne and Keith Christiansen, Nancy and Del Warner, Jack Brooks, Tyler Mason and all for caring about and devoting years of your time and lives to Vermont, real ecology, and the Lowell Mountains.

Aliena Gerhardt – wonderful, passionate woman, warrior to help those animals and people who don't have a voice, and inspiring mother and lawyer, par excellence!! And what a great sense of humor!

Beth Bryant, MFT, Elizabeth Strazar M.A. and Tim Strazar – thanks for the support and caring, good walks, smiles and hours, meditations, meals, and of long hours of discussion!

Susan Brody, MSW, Eden Brody and Josef Brody – always in my heart! You have been such an inspiration on the path through the darkness into the light and the value of sharing the smiles and little things as we struggle against forces that would keep us down.

Barry and Janae Weinhold Ph.D. for all the grounded sharing, intelligent understanding of individuals and families and the sharing that you do in your books and workshops!

Gregg Furth, Ph.D. – my friend, Jungian Analyst, mentor, colleague. You shared with me the original German fairy tale, Frau Holle, that lived in my heart, mind and psyche for so many years, taking seed and helping to grow this book. Too soon gone from this earth, but living in my heart.

Thank-you to all of my mentors and teachers in Christianity, Jungian Analysis, mythology, fairy tales, comparative religions, psychology, sociology, community building, and history.

Selina Mochizuki – what a wonderful person you are! And your life journey is an inspiration! A great heart, soul, spirit!!! John and Jin are very fortunate!!!!

Stacy Crosby – can we clone you? You have been such a support to the UN-Chained Gang and all the many guests who come to Eden ETHICAL Dog Sledding – being dedicated and in for the long term!

Ingrid Bower and Heather D'Arcy for your long term support of Eden, love of your dogs and sense of humor!

Rodney Tinkum – for being the great guy you are and a dedicated, knowledgeable musher!

Leigh Sylvester – thank you for taking Fuscia into your family and being such a keen supporter of the UN-Chained Gang and Eden Ethical Dog Sledding!

Meghan White Lytton and Madeline – thank you for our new friendship and your special support of the vision and mission of The UN-Chained Gang and Eden. I will never forget doing dishes in the barn and seeing the two of you coming up the driveway! You are both inspirational!

Leslie Wright – COYOTE!! Thank you for being such a great friend to my brother over the decades. Thank you for your constant support and wisdom. You are the best! AND thank you for your inspirational sports writing and your non-profit – STRIDE: The Wright Foundation For Female Athletes – helping girls become leaders through sports http://www.stridefoundation.org/ and Facebook – https://www.facebook.com/Stride-The-Wright-Foundation-for-Female-Athletes-245464608229/. Our girls need this inspiration!

Sydney – thank you for all that you do especially with the boxes of Girl Scout cookies for our soldiers. Keep enjoying the outdoors, horses, and doing that archaeology research! And for your mom, Laurie Sincula, for being such a great support!

Geoff Reed – For your verve, being a fantastic dad to your daughters, a good husband, good man and support of autism and the truth about vaccines. Keep riding that Harley!

And for so many reasons – Vickie Neiduski, Tealia Rodigue, Anna-Marie Stewart, Buddy Jackie Bliss, Janice Powers Machalski, Bob Marotta, Paul Simpson, Linda Tisdale Baker, Kate and Kirby Ardissono, Shawn Murphey Agle, Tirana N Bill Chafin-Deal, Tracy Dorman, Miriam Nevelle, Tami Williams, Brenda and Mason Fellows, J Koda Rotwell, Lisa Woodward Brown, Phyllis Heisler, Lydia Glider Shelley, Pat Kerns Bivin, Mary Beth Stucky, Junior and Smoochies, Penny Gold, Deb Reid, Teri Smith, Sandi Tyler-Polsky, Terri New, Sue Strotheide (Jersey loves you!) Anna-Marie Stewart, Rosemary Janisch, Ritamarie Cavicchio and Master Owen, MaryLou Griswold, Alex Knight, Shelley Tucker, Urpo Klvimaki, Michele Kilbourne, Yasie Herron, Dan Grey Knox, Billie Stalh of Corgihouse, and all of my many wonderful dog and animal loving friends!

Judi Lundberg, Dawn Harviel, Soffie and Griffyn – supporters of so many and an inspiration in times of trouble.

Brenda Homer Fellows and Mason Fellows – thank you for naming The UN-Chained Gang at Eden Ethical Dog Sledding as your favorite international sports team! Thank you for the support and good humor, all you do for animals, and, of course, for allowing Mason's love-of-his-life, Grace Corgi, to appear in The Luna Tales.

Ron C. Starcher, Cocoa and Belle – for your good humor, "comportment" (said with French pronunciation!) and tireless work to raise money and recognition for canine causes!

Craig Thomas for the thrilling novels (find them on Amazon!), Carl Johnson (check out his art work!), Marsha Downs, and Peggy Burnett for being such good animal supporters!

Andrea Mikana-Pinkam and Mark Amaru Pinkham – for your wonderful sharing of ideas and photos of ancient ruins, your tours and Mark's books.

Keith Bryar – North American hero race musher an good friend. You lived life with passion and humor. Your friendship and support of Eden ETHICAL Dog sledding will be missed! Heaven has a great musher, now!

John Potash, Ed Opperman, Tom Fogelman, Tom Siebert, Tom Myer, Carey Yost, Teal Smith, William Ramsey, Marie Flick, Paula Bernoski. Jason Witherspoon, Tom Padgett, Karen Provenzano Folques, Marie E. LeBlanc, Liam Tucker, Lisa Kennedy for being the truth seekers that you are.

Arnaldo Lerma – for the great sharing, and being on the path.

Dave McGowan – gone too soon. Thank you for your kind

support and willingness to work together. (Author of Programmed to Kill and Weird Scenes Inside the Canyon.)

Craig McGowan – for sharing, kindness and support walking the path for truth!

Kelley Spearen and his trusty buddy, Kramer – thank-you for the inspiration and smiles!

In the Light, waiting at the Rainbow Bridge – Barney Boots, Fred Bumbles, Bear, Buster, Buttercup, Teddy, King the Cat, Fred The Red, Betsy, Arrow, Lassie, Maxine, Baby, Peaberry, Luna, Lioness, Rainbow, Storm, Stormina, Storm 2, Mud, Teddy, Jody, Thor, Buffy, Blueberry, Gus Sullivan, Kistle, Rusty, Charles Dickens, Chase, Spike, Buffy, Amos, Sandy, Licks, Flash, Beetle, Willy, Fusulli, Jessie, Abby, and so many more . . .

And of course – to my brother, Musher Jim Blair – you have been through so much of life's journey with me and all of our great canine and other "non-human" family members over the decades – all of the hard knocks. I am so proud of what you have brought forth with the dogs! And of course, The UN-Chained Gang – most fun loving pack of canines I have ever met!!! Jim, keep being the visionary that you are!

Acknowledgements

Editor – Tanya Sousa – Creating and connecting people with the idea that all living things deserve respect and kindness are the two most important threads running through author Tanya Sousa's life. "I love Einstein's quote, ...*if you judge a fish by how well it climbs a tree, it will live its whole life believing it is stupid,* ' she said, 'because that quote not only speaks to different forms of human intelligence, but different forms of intelligence overall. All living things are amazing — just differently gifted.'

Tanya's writing credits include the award-winning picture book, *Life is a Bowl of Cherry Pits* among others (find her work at www.RadiantHen.com) and an environmental fiction novel for young adults and adults, *The Starling God* (www.forestrypress.com). She also writes for magazines and anthologies. For more about Tanya and her work, visit her author page at: https://www.goodreads.com/author/show/6206702.Tanya_Sousa

Line Editor – Tova Bode Saxe currently lives with her husband and daughter in Bellingham, Washington. She grew up in Tel Aviv, Israel and spent many years in Vermont. She can be reached at succinctlyyours@gmail.com

Copy Editing – Angela Robey is a Fine Artist and co-founder of Silver Moon Ranch, an off-grid, free ranged goat dary in Witch Wells, Arizona. She can be reached at angelarrobey@gmail.com. View her artwork at http://angelarrobey.wixsite.com/robey-artworks

Cover Art and Book Design by Derek Murphy – a talented author, Ph.D. in Literature, wonderful marketer and incredible visionary who supports authors and and cover art that truly represents their books. He can be contacted at his website: http://

www.creativindiecovers.com/. Get his books on Amazon – you will love them!

Special thank-you to MC Hammer and Charlie Daniels for your wonderful, lively music that inspired the songs of the UN-Chained Gang in Vermont and Samuel's pack in Solaria. May generations of children, adults, animals and Canines be inspired by your spirit of love and joy! We encourage readers to go to your favorite music service to download the actual music that inspired Peaberry and the UN-Chained Gang for their Canine Music in Solaria: The Devil Went Down To Georgia by the Charlie Daniel's Band and Can't Touch This! by M C Hammer.

Musher Jim Blair and his pack of joyful dogs – The UN-Chained Gang - live in the mountain beauty of northern Vermont. Champion International sprint race sled dogs - they love sharing with children, teens and adults who come to visit from all over the world. The UN-Chained Gang are seven generations of pack/human raising of litters as wolves do- the pups are kept together for their lives, never sold. In addiction, dogs are rescued from race chaining kennels to join the UN-Chained Gang. Together they explore Canine Consciousness – and allow the true wisdom, sensibility, individuality and ability to make decisions on their own to emerge. The gang are studied by international experts. They believe that all sled dogs should be kept ethically, respected, live free, off chains, and have great opportunities for running, playing, cuddling with human, and have a comfortable, beloved retirement. Eden Ethical Dog Sledding's one hundred-and-forty acre Canine Consciousness Center, is set in the midst of five thousand acres of Vermont mountain exquisiteness. The center provides miles of specially built-for-dog-safety, groomed race-training trails, woods, ponds for swimming and meadows to run in – it is magical for dogs and humans in all four seasons of the year.

Learn about these great dogs and the Educational Year Round Adventure Opportunities they offer to guests from around the world, at their website: www.edendogsledding.com

Please support their work by liking them on Facebook, Eden Dog Sledding and the UN-Chained Gang: https://www.facebook.com/Eden-Dog-Sledding-and-the-Un-Chained-Gang-171237189604931/ -

Donations, sponsorship and adoption information for retired UN-Chained Gang members and to support the vision of ETHICAL dog sledding and The Canine Consciousness Project for sled dogs and all dogs can made through their website: www.edendogsledding.com

Biography

Deborah E. Blair, M.S., Ph.D. was raised by canines and other creatures. She loves nature and living in the wilds with her dogs. Born with Asperger's Autism, she has overcome years of abuse and challenges to become a lecturer, author, Quaker, meditation teacher and psychotherapist specializing in Carl Jung's work, dreams and journaling for over forty years. She loves helping individuals heal their personal story together with fairy-tales and mythology to support personal healing on their journey to finding their authenticity.

Thank you for your support of The Luna Tales – Book One – The Wisdom Runners. We need your help for this vision and venture! Please recommend this book to your friends, leave a short or long! review on Amazon and Goodreads. Please share the Amazon Link on your Facebook and Twitter. Ten percent of the profits are being donated directly to canine registered non-profit causes and autism causes and grants. A large portion of the remaining profits will go into the UN-Chained Gang's non-profit venture for education and the spread of the message of the Canine Consciousness and ethical treatment of all dogs and companion animals. We are also in the process starting two educational publication ventures: Healing Into Authenticity Press and The UN-Chained Gang Press.

Since you love dogs, animals, the planet and humanity, and want to help us spread the word, you can greatly aid us by giving The Luna Tale – Book One – The Wisdom Runners a good review on Amazon and Goodreads – Even ONE LINE – of support is great and will help us get our message out! Please put a link to Amazon on your Facebook and Twitter, encouraging buying The Luna Tales- for the adventure, the healing and sharing the message! It's a great gift for birthdays and holidays!

If you buy the paperback – please consider taking a photo with your dog (s), cats, horses, bunnies and any companion animal family member with the book cover, with a note giving us permission to use the photo(s) and a quick review for our website and support videos on YouTube- - and send it along to infothelunatales@gmail.com

Made in the USA
Middletown, DE
27 August 2020